T0006030

PRAISE FOR CHARLIE N. HOLMBERG

STAR MOTHER

"Readers will find entertainment and hope in this sweeping, mythic tale."

—*Publishers Weekly*

"In this stunning example of amazing worldbuilding, Holmberg (*Spellbreaker*) features incredible creatures, a love story, and twists no one could see coming. This beautiful novel will be enjoyed by fantasy and romance readers alike."

—*Library Journal*

"Gods and men mingle in this fantasy tale of celestial beings, battling gods, and time travel. Fans of Neil Gaiman's *Stardust* (2008) will appreciate the unique characters in this fantasy adventure."

—*Booklist*

THE SPELLBREAKER SERIES

"Romantic and electrifying . . . the fast-paced plot and fully realized world will have readers eager for the next installment. Fans of Victorian-influenced fantasy won't want to put this down."

—*Publishers Weekly*

"Those who enjoy gentle romance, cozy mysteries, or Victorian fantasy will love this first half of a duology. The cliff-hanger ending will keep readers breathless waiting for the second half."

—*Library Journal* (starred review)

"Powerful magic, indulgent Victoriana, and a slow-burn romance make this genre-bending romp utterly delightful."

—*Kirkus Reviews*

THE NUMINA SERIES

"[An] enthralling fantasy . . . The story is gripping from the start, with a surprising plot and a lush, beautifully realized setting. Holmberg knows just how to please fantasy fans."

—*Publishers Weekly*

"With scads of action, clear explanations of how supernatural elements function, and appealing characters with smart backstories, this first in a series will draw in fans of Cassandra Clare, Leigh Bardugo, or Brandon Sanderson."

—*Library Journal*

"Holmberg is a genius at world building; she provides just enough information to set the scene without overwhelming the reader. She also creates captivating characters worth rooting for and puts them in unique situations. Readers will be eager for the second installment in the Numina series."

—*Booklist*

THE PAPER MAGICIAN SERIES

"Charlie is a vibrant writer with an excellent voice and great world building. I thoroughly enjoyed *The Paper Magician*."

—Brandon Sanderson, author of *Mistborn* and *The Way of Kings*

"Harry Potter fans will likely enjoy this story for its glimpses of another structured magical world, and fans of Erin Morgenstern's *The Night Circus* will enjoy the whimsical romance element . . . So if you're looking for a story with some unique magic, romantic gestures, and the inherent darkness that accompanies power all steeped in a yet to be fully explored magical world, then this could be your next read."

—Amanda Lowery, *Thinking Out Loud*

THE WILL AND THE WILDS

"An immersive, dangerous fantasy world. Holmberg draws readers in with a fast-moving plot, rich details, and a surprisingly sweet human-monster romance. This is a lovely, memorable fairy tale."

—*Publishers Weekly*

"Holmberg ably builds her latest fantasy world, and her brisk narrative and the romance at its heart will please fans of her previous magical tales."

—*Booklist*

THE FIFTH DOLL

Winner of the 2017 Whitney Award for Speculative Fiction

"*The Fifth Doll* is told in a charming, folklore-ish voice that's reminiscent of a good old-fashioned tale spun in front of the fireplace on a cold winter night. I particularly enjoyed the contrast of the small-town village atmosphere—full of simple townspeople with simple dreams and worries—set against the complex and eerie backdrop of the village that's not what it seems. The fact that there are motivations and forces shaping the lives of the villagers on a daily basis that they're completely unaware of adds layers and textures to the story and makes it a very interesting read."

—*San Francisco Book Review*

HEIR

of

UNCERTAIN MAGIC

ALSO BY CHARLIE N. HOLMBERG

The Whimbrel House Series

Keeper of Enchanted Rooms

The Star Mother Series

Star Mother
Star Father

The Spellbreaker Series

Spellbreaker
Spellmaker

The Numina Series

Smoke and Summons
Myths and Mortals
Siege and Sacrifice

HEIR
of
UNCERTAIN MAGIC

Whimbrel House Book 2

CHARLIE N. HOLMBERG

This is a work of fiction. Names, characters, organizations, places, events, and incidents are either products of the author's imagination or are used fictitiously. Otherwise, any resemblance to actual persons, living or dead, is purely coincidental.

Text copyright © 2023 by Charlie N. Holmberg
All rights reserved.

No part of this book may be reproduced, or stored in a retrieval system, or transmitted in any form or by any means, electronic, mechanical, photocopying, recording, or otherwise, without express written permission of the publisher.

Published by 47North, Seattle

www.apub.com

Amazon, the Amazon logo, and 47North are trademarks of Amazon.com, Inc., or its affiliates.

ISBN-13: 9781662508691 (paperback)
ISBN-13: 9781662508684 (digital)

Cover design by Marina Drukman
Cover illustration by Christina Chung

Printed in the United States of America

To Brandon Sanderson.
Thank you for holding the torch
and lighting the way.

DOCTRINES OF MAGIC

Augury • Soothsaying, fortune-telling, divination, luck
1. Repercussion: forgetfulness
2. Associated mineral: amethyst

Psychometry • Mind reading, hallucination, empathy, intuition
3. Repercussion: dulling of senses
4. Associated mineral: azurite

Conjury • Creation, summoning of natural components
5. Repercussion: loss of equal worth to summoned object
6. Associated mineral: pyrite

Necromancy • Death/life magic, life force, disease/healing
7. Repercussion: nausea
8. Associated mineral: turquoise

Wardship • Shielding, protection, spell-turning
9. Repercussion: weakening of physical body
10. Associated mineral: tourmaline

Element • Manipulation of fire, water, earth, or air
11. Repercussion: fire, chill; water, dryness; earth, vertigo; air, shortness of breath
12. Associated mineral: clear quartz

Alteration • Shape-shifting, changing, metamorphosis

    13. Repercussion: temporary physical mutation

    14. Associated mineral: opal

Communion • Translation, communication with plants/animals

    15. Repercussion: muteness, tinnitus

    16. Associated mineral: selenite

Hysteria • Manipulation of emotions, pain

    17. Repercussion: physical pain, apathy

    18. Associated mineral: carnelian

Kinetic • Movement, force

    19. Repercussion: stiffness, lack of mobility

    20. Associated mineral: bloodstone

Chaocracy • Manipulation of chaos/order, destruction, restoration

    21. Repercussion: confusion

    22. Associated mineral: obsidian

Chapter 1

Merritt had just slipped back into a state of dozing when the voice of a mouse jolted him to alertness. *Hide hide. Hide. Hide hide. Hide. Food? Food? Hunt. Hunt. Hide.*

Groaning, he pushed the heels of his hands into his eyes. Every night. *Every night* since escaping Silas Hogwood's lair this had happened. Like that damnable man had cursed him. Like visiting the magicked haunt had jolted the ability he'd only had a trickle of previously. Merritt had lived thirty-one years of his life sleeping *just fine*, but the moment he formally met Silas Hogwood, the voices would not leave him be.

And *why was he so hot?*

Merritt ripped off his shirt and chucked it across the room, sighing as coolness prickled his skin.

Hide hide hide.

Wiiiiiiiiiiiiiiiind.

"Not you again," he croaked, scowling at the window. The gauzy curtains were drawn, but he could see the shadow of the red maple just outside, its boughs shifting gently in the breeze. That blasted tree pestered him more than anyone, Owein excluded.

He covered his ears, but of course, that didn't help. Communion spells weren't auditory—they went straight into his brain, and he hadn't yet found a way to shut them out. It wasn't a constant flow of plant and animal speech, thank the heavens, but it did increase at night. Perhaps because his guard was down. Or maybe everything on this blasted island was nocturnal.

Wiiiiiiind, the tree whispered.

"Yes, I know." Merritt whipped the blanket off, trudged to the window, and yanked back the curtains. The island was dark, save for the light of the moon and stars and the distant glow of a lighthouse. He couldn't see much of anything, but he could hear all of it.

Streeeeetch, wheezed the grass.

Wiiiiiiiiiiind, repeated the tree.

Coooooold, sang . . . a cricket? He wasn't sure on that one.

The voices spun and banged in his head, awakening a familiar headache that no tonic could dull. Merritt pressed his forehead to the cool glass of the window, trying to think about something else—his book, Hulda, the laundry, politics—but the voices pierced through, regardless.

For the love of heaven, shut up.

He pleaded. Prayed. He was so tired. Two and a half weeks of this, each night progressively worse than the last, and he was so, so tired. He banged his forehead against the glass. Once, twice, three times. Stopped counting and just banged, which worsened the headache, but if he could just shake the voices *loose,* maybe he could get a few hours of rest tonight. Just a few hours—

Bang. Bang. Bang.

"Merritt?"

The mental voices quieted as an auditory one pricked his ears. He pulled back from the window to see Hulda in the doorway, holding a candle, wrapped in a robe for modesty. Had he been so loud as to rouse her?

"Again?" she asked, sounding tired herself.

Merritt rubbed his eyes. *It won't stop,* he tried to say, but his voice didn't come. Muteness was a side effect of communion. An infuriating side effect.

He turned back to the window and punched the glass, hard enough to hurt his knuckles but not enough to break it.

He screamed a string of silent obscenities at the window and everything beyond it.

"Oh dear." Hulda pushed the door all the way open and stepped in. Paused when her candle illuminated him. "Oh dear."

Merritt met her eyes, which were trained on his chest. He looked down.

Right. Where had he thrown that shirt?

He couldn't apologize, so he just waved a hand and tromped to his bed, flinging the blankets aside, scouring until he found the thing hanging off his trunk. He shrugged it back on. Snatched a notebook off his bedside table and perched on the trunk, writing with a pencil. Hulda came closer to better see.

I guess we're even now.

She swatted him with her free hand. "At least your deplorable sense of humor is still intact."

A smile tugged on his lips, making him feel a little better. It just so happened that Merritt had—*by accident*—caught Hulda in her underthings on two occasions. Once during a private dance lesson she'd given to Beth, his maid, and again in that basement in Marshfield. Apparently dresses didn't lend well to sneaking through canal drains.

He hadn't minded in the slightest, but he did not tell Hulda that.

I'm going to cut down that tree, he wrote. He needn't explain; this was not the first midnight—or midday—conversation they'd had via this notebook because he couldn't speak. It took only a few spells for the island to rob him of his voice.

After setting down the pencil, he rubbed his eyes again.

"I'm sorry." Hulda lowered herself onto the trunk and grasped his shoulder. "I thought that draft would help."

He shook his head. The sleeping tincture she'd fed him before bed no longer worked. It only made his body feel heavy now.

Merritt flipped back a page and pointed at a dark passage written in capital letters from the night before. *I'M NOT TRYING TO USE IT.*

"I know." She rubbed that same shoulder. She rolled her lips together. "Merritt."

He shook his head. He knew what she was going to say.

"You *need* to go see him."

Exhaling slowly, Merritt ran a hand through his shoulder-length hair, half-knotted from tossing and turning through the night.

"He may very well be a communionist, too. Or at least know one," she pressed.

Nelson Sutcliffe, she meant. The man who was supposedly his biological father—an interesting fact Merritt had recently learned. A fun, jagged puzzle piece in the mess of his life. His secret parentage was the reason his father—Peter Fernsby, the man who had raised him—had hated him so much. Enough that he'd bribed Merritt's sweetheart to fake a pregnancy, all so he'd have a reason to disinherit Merritt and throw him out of the house.

But Nelson Sutcliffe was in Cattlecorn, Merritt's hometown. Merritt's parents were also in Cattlecorn. And he hadn't spoken to them—or any of his family—in thirteen years. Peter Fernsby had made sure of it.

Merritt was well aware that these new revelations needed to be confronted. That Sutcliffe and Peter needed to be confronted, too. He needed to—wanted to—take back the family that had been so unjustly ripped away from him. And yet the thought of stepping foot in that town made him sick to his stomach. Made his mind spin and stop working. He just . . . couldn't.

Wiiiiiind.

I know there's blasted wind! Merritt shouted without sound at the tree, then chucked the notebook at it. It thumped hard against the window and fell to the floor.

"Merritt." Hulda set down the candle and took his jaw in her hands, making him look at her. "Focus on me. Listen to my words. Try to shut the rest of it out."

Easier said than done.

The retort must have been in his expression, because Hulda added, "I know it's a monotonous exercise, but do try."

Merritt withheld a sigh and looked into Hulda's eyes, which were almost brown in the poor lighting. She recited a children's poem, and Merritt loosely followed it, more interested in the movement of her soft, full lips than the actual words. There was no way on God's verdurous earth Hulda would let him kiss her here and now. They weren't properly dressed, it was the middle of the night, and they were in Merritt's bedroom. She was far too prudent for that, which was truthfully for the better. But still. Right then, Merritt wanted nothing more than to be close to her. If he couldn't kiss her, he'd settle for laying his head on her breast, shutting his eyes, and maybe, *maybe*, falling asleep.

She finished the poem. Searched his face. "Any better?"

"Minutely," he wheezed.

She managed a small smile. "Let me make you some more tea. Maybe it'll help this time." There was doubt in her voice, but she was trying, and he appreciated her efforts. Taking up the candle, she stood, checking that the tie of her robe was secure. "And there is also the matter of—" She paused and looked over him, slouched on that trunk and rubbing his throat. "Never mind. We'll address it in the morning."

"Thanks," he said, but it came out rough and unintelligible. The sound of paws outside the door announced Owein, but Hulda slipped off and sent him back to bed. He'd spent the first few nights in Merritt's room, but his thoughts only added to the nighttime cacophony, so Hulda had moved him to the sitting room.

Twisting on the trunk, Merritt laid his head down on the mattress, sleep pulling his eyelids closed.

A moment later, the soft worrying of a mouse trickled into his mind.

"So I can only court you outside the walls of this house?"

Hulda rolled her eyes—Merritt wondered if she realized how often she did that, and how inconsistent it was with her otherwise meticulous and proper persona. She ran her hands over the surface of the dining room table before pulling them together. "It's not my intention to put *boundaries* on our . . . courtship," she said softly, like a young girl might. Like she still couldn't believe that nine days ago she'd returned Merritt's declaration and kissed him in the wilds of the island. Merritt tried to hide a smile, but he didn't do a good job of it. "I'm simply stating," Hulda went on, "that it's inappropriate within the confines of our roles as master of the house and housekeeper."

Merritt stifled a yawn—he *had* managed to get back to sleep last night, giving him a solid four hours of rest—and turned to the window, hoping the sunlight would keep him alert. A few snow flurries brushed by the dining room window, which had recently been repaired by a magic mutt with an absurd amount of chaocracy spells stitched to his spirit. It was midmorning, but the cloud-choked skies made it look much later—or perhaps much earlier. Winter was settling in on the East Coast, barely giving autumn much of a chance to show up to the party. Yet their little island still seemed apart from it all, its lingering leaves brighter shades of red and richer hues of yellow, the house somehow untouched by the weather despite its lack of mystical wizardry. Sometimes Merritt forgot it wasn't enchanted anymore—a little tidbit only those within its walls knew, plus one—and sometimes he suspected that maybe it still was.

Something clamored in the kitchen where Baptiste, their chef, was already preparing for lunch. Merritt wasn't sure where Beth had gone.

Likely making herself scarce. She had a knack for knowing when private conversations were underway, perhaps due to her gift of clairvoyance. It was odd to have a private conversation in what was technically a public room, but if Hulda was so concerned about Merritt courting her in the house, she certainly wasn't going to allow such a discussion in one of their bedrooms.

It was probably the lack of a shirt last night that had done it.

Something brushed his leg. Ah yes, Owein. Sometimes Merritt still forgot the house's former haunt had his own body again. Owein was a terrible eavesdropper. Understandable—when his spirit had possessed the house, he could watch and listen to anything he wanted. Now he had to actually make the effort to pad into whatever area exchanges were happening in. Still, he was rather good at it. Perhaps Merritt shouldn't have trimmed Owein's nails. Perhaps a bell and a collar were in order.

"As for *housekeeper*," Merritt emphasized, "you're not technically—"

"Yes, I know." Hulda knit her fingers together. She sat at the head of the table, just around its corner from Merritt, her back to the window, her hair swept away from her face less severely than it used to be, albeit with every pin and curl precisely placed. Like she'd been carved out of marble by Michelangelo himself. She wore her most rigid dress, the olive one with a collar high enough to choke and sleeves to the palms of her hands, and Merritt guessed that had been intentional as well. Setting boundaries would have proven much more difficult if that delectable collarbone of hers were showing. "I may not even bear that title anymore."

Her silver glasses had slipped down her nose. Reaching over, Merritt gingerly moved them back up. Her hazel eyes met his, and a lovely dusting of pink highlighted her cheeks.

Then she straightened, pulling from his reach.

Merritt sighed. "No word from BIKER?"

She shook her head. "Not since the resignation." She meant that of Myra Haigh, the head of the Boston Institute for the Keeping of

Enchanted Rooms. Myra, who had helped clean up the mess with Silas Hogwood . . . and who had started it in the first place. She'd resigned by letter only days after the incident in Marshfield, then vanished without an inkling of goodbye. Hulda had found out about it secondhand from Sadie Steverus, BIKER's secretary, and Merritt had heard it from Hulda. No one knew where Myra had gone, something that had obviously been troubling Hulda. It might not be so bad, perhaps, if it was simply an early retirement, but outside that dark, dilapidated house, away from the mess and the watchmen, Myra had, in harsh, hushed tones, been very clear about one thing.

Say nothing of this to anyone until I tie up the loose ends. It won't be long, but for the safety of us all, wait for my approval.

Said "approval" had never come, and Merritt had begun to worry it never would. Less skin off his back than Hulda's. Just yesterday the woman had clipped her fingernails short to keep herself from gnawing at them.

Hulda had been back to BIKER only once since Merritt's abduction, specifically to search for clues to Myra's whereabouts, but she'd come back empty-handed. The two women had been close before the Hogwood ordeal, making the nonattendance that much stranger.

"Then I suppose you're moving back to Bright Bay?" he asked. The Bright Bay Hotel was the front and headquarters for BIKER, with the institution's offices located in the back.

She frowned. "I think it's for the best. For now. But it's—"

I don't want Hulda to leave.

Merritt glanced between his legs, where the snout of a medium-sized mutt rested on the edge of his chair.

"Merritt?"

He glanced up, having missed what Hulda had said. "Sorry." He rubbed the back of his head. "I still can't manage two voices at once."

She blinked, then scooted her chair back and glanced beneath the table. Clicked her tongue in disapproval.

"He wants you to stay." Merritt shrugged, though in truth, *he* wanted Hulda to stay. He'd grown so used to her being around when he woke up, when he ate, when he worked . . . "But Boston isn't so far." Not with a magicked boat and kinetic tram to hasten the journey. It was a two-hour trip, give or take.

Her shoulders relaxed. "Yes, it's not far. And I, of course, will visit. I'm going to stop by Myra's home—see if there's anything of note there." She glanced around the modestly sized dining room, which had once been haunted with shadows and violently swinging doors. Now it was simple and quaint and . . . *home*, its walls a pale yellow, its trim newly stained cherry . . . Though how much like home would it feel without Hulda . . . ?

Perhaps he was being a little melodramatic.

"I could build you a house on the island," he offered, half-serious.

She raised an eyebrow. "In the winter? Single-handedly? There aren't enough trees here for a second cottage."

A smile pulled on his lips. "I'll do it entirely with wardship spells." Another recent revelation: Merritt could build invisible walls. Not that he had any sort of grasp on that unexpected bit of magical talent.

"That would hardly be private."

He let his face go lax, feigning confusion. "Why would you need privacy?"

She swatted his arm, and he chuckled. "You are a rake, Mr. Fernsby."

He caught her hand before she could withdraw it. "Surely that comment wasn't bad enough to warrant chastisement via my surname."

He could see her fighting a smile. "You are a rake, *Merritt*."

He placed a kiss atop her hand. "Let me escort you. I'll carry your bags. I need to see McFarland anyway." McFarland was his editor, also based in Boston. Merritt needed to turn in the ending of his book.

"I've only one bag," she countered, but her disposition softened all the same. Her eyes dropped to their still-entwined hands, and somberness crossed her features. "And what of Cattlecorn?" she asked.

His stomach sank. Perhaps it would be better to have Hulda out of the house so she could stop reminding him of his unwanted responsibilities. "What of it?"

"Merritt." She frowned. "You'll never gain control of your power if you don't ask for help. I don't know any communionists who can step in. And there's the matter of your family."

Pressing his lips together, Merritt released her hand and leaned back in his chair, balancing on its back legs. Hulda hated it when he did that, but she made no comment. "I did write a letter."

"To your mother?"

His gut churned sour. "To Sutcliffe." He'd tried again and again to write to his mother, whom he hadn't seen or spoken to in thirteen years—not since his father's machinations to disinherit him. But every time Merritt tried, he couldn't get past her name. He just . . . couldn't. He'd tried *Rose*, and he'd tried *Mother* and a slew of others, but regardless of the greeting, his brain would go blank or his lunch would threaten to crawl up his esophagus. He just *couldn't*, and he wasn't sure why.

For some reason writing to Sutcliffe, a man he knew by occupation and little else, was easier.

"That's good. You posted it?"

He ran a hand down his face. "Beth can post it." Or he'd just burn it and pretend he'd never learned the sharp truth of his past. Sometimes he wished he hadn't.

"You've not posted it? Isn't Fletcher coming this weekend to accompany you?"

"Post is quick," he offered.

Where is it? I'll give it to her. A tail whapped the floor.

"No."

"No?" Hulda asked.

Merritt lowered the chair onto all four legs. "No to Owein."

"What did he say?"

He waved his hand, exhaustion pulling on him.

Why not?

Rubbing his forehead, he mumbled, "Turn *off.*"

Hulda's lips pulled into a sympathetic frown. Owein whined beneath the table, sending a shard of guilt through Merritt's middle. Dogs couldn't talk, making Merritt the only outlet Owein had to be heard. Surely he couldn't fault the boy for speaking as much as he did. The "boy" who was technically a couple of centuries Merritt's senior . . .

"I'll see if I can find a tutor," Hulda suggested. "For the communion, and for the rest."

Communion, wardship, chaocracy. Those were the magics tied up in Merritt's blood. He'd love to get rid of the first. He'd still seen no sign of the last.

Merritt pulled his hands from his face. "How does one find a tutor? Magic is so diluted . . ."

She scoffed. "I do have *some* resources. In the meantime, reach out to Sutcliffe . . . and see what you can learn from your uncle."

Merritt glanced down at the dog. He kept forgetting he and Owein were technically related. How many "greats" was Owein again? Seven? Eight? "Owein doesn't have communion spells."

The table turned a bright shade of purple as the mutt showcased one of the spells he *did* have—alteration, or the magic of shape-shifting and metamorphosis. Because they shared a bloodline, Merritt's and Owein's magic should, theoretically, overlap. Wardship and communion came from elsewhere in the family tree, according to the records Hulda had pulled from the Genealogical Society for the Advancement of Magic. And while Merritt had no spells in the school of alteration, Silas Hogwood had been equipped with a spell of intuition, and he'd declared Merritt to possess chaocracy magic. Spells of order and disorder, which Owein, his umpteenth great-uncle, had used to make Whimbrel House a living hell before they reached a truce with one another. Something Owein's parents had passed down their line, though *if* Merritt had any of it, his magic wouldn't be nearly as powerful. Magic was a finite resource, after all, and there were too many nonmagical folk in his genealogy.

A headache was starting to pulse behind Merritt's forehead. Feeling Hulda's eyes on him, he said, "I'll go with Fletcher." His best friend also hailed from Cattlecorn. Having him tag along could make this . . . easier.

But Merritt still didn't want to go. He never said it aloud, but if penning a letter to his mother—and he made a living *as a writer*—made him sick, the thought of returning to New York made him positively miserable. He tried to mentally walk himself through it—packing a bag, buying a ticket, getting on the train and off the train, walking through town . . . but he could never finish the narrative, even just in thought. There was a thick, adamant wall there, too tall to climb and too wide to walk around.

And yet, inside it was a little boy who desperately missed his family. A little boy Merritt barely recognized, and—

"You look sick." Hulda rose from her chair and pressed her palm to his forehead.

"I'm fine. Just tired." He exhaled slowly and stood as well. Owein skittered out from beneath the table and darted into the reception hall after God knew what, his paws barely gaining purchase on the wooden floorboards. Merritt pasted on a smile. "Let's get your things. Plenty of time to get to Boston and back."

She studied his face, hazel irises darting right and left. "Not yet," she insisted. "Maybe you should get some rest."

He considered for half a second. "Maybe I should." Which he wouldn't—naps were slightly easier than sleeping at night, but if he stayed awake, he'd have more time with Hulda.

Besides, Merritt also knew no amount of rest would cure the ailment coiled in his belly like a snake, its fangs sunk in deep and slowly seeping venom. So he pushed it away, burying it beside the other half-rotted corpses he'd collected over the years. Poured on dirt and rocks and logs until the graves were hardly recognizable.

He was already starting to feel better.

Owein ran through thistle and goosefoot, stretching his legs. Everything was cold beneath his paws. It was so strange feeling cold again. Stranger even than having four legs, because he barely remembered what it was like to have two. Before this, he hadn't had legs in a very long time. Over two hundred years.

Time was a strange thing. He felt that now, too. When he'd been in the house, it'd been different. Everything had been different.

But Owein thought having a body was excellent. He'd forgotten how great it felt. Then again, the memories he still had of his human body were of being weak and sick and hot.

He might not have chosen the form of a dog, but it was infinitely better than being a house, most days. He hadn't adjusted to the cost of using his magic now—confusion and disfigurement—so he tried to use it less, but magic had been all he could do for so long, it felt strange *not* to use it. He tried to occupy his time with reading, which was boring but necessary, he guessed.

The wind whipped past his ears, pushing the taste of winter into his mouth. Muscles burned as he darted beneath the low branches of a half-bald tree. It was shaped a little like a balloon, and the urge to make it look more like a balloon rolled up his body, but he stopped himself. He didn't want his body to contort out here in the cold, and last time he'd taken on a big chaocracy project, he'd completely forgotten what he'd been doing halfway through it, thanks to the accompanying confusion. Frustrated, Owein barked at the tree instead.

And it *was* frustrating. For two centuries, Owein had *been* magic. That was why he was here, in this house, and his family was elsewhere, in heaven, or so Miss Taylor said. Since Owein hadn't wanted to die, his spirit had imprinted itself here.

He didn't remember dying. If he held very still and thought very hard, he could remember being sick. Remember heaviness settling in his chest—the chest of a person, not a dog. Almost remember the twitching of five fingers on human hands. But it had been so long, and it was hard to pull up memories of before.

He liked Miss Taylor. Beth. He called her Beth when she wasn't listening, which was always. She could sense his moods, thanks to *her* magic, but couldn't hear his words like Merritt did. Well, no one could really *hear* him. He didn't have a voice capable of forming human words. But no one had heard him before, either.

Didn't make it sit better.

Owein ran, chased a hare, leapt over a log, enjoying the newness of *now*, until his body started to ache and begged him to slow down.

He did, near the north coast of the small island—his home, and the only place he'd ever really known. He stood at the tip of a short cliff, the ocean about five feet down, lapping against dark rocks like it was trying to climb up and not doing so well with it. Lifting his head, he looked out into the bay, to land in the distance—

And his body seized up in a new way. His lungs shrunk, though he'd done no alteration magic. His body, warm from the exercise, sucked in the chill of the air. Owein retreated, a whine escaping his throat.

He didn't like it. The ocean and those unfamiliar spaces beyond. He shook hard but couldn't disperse the uneasy feeling. The fear creeping up like he'd stepped in an anthill. The shadows on the edge of his vision. He shook himself, and they went away.

The only time Owein had ever left his island was when that scary wizard had come for him. The man had put his hands on the walls of Whimbrel House and sucked Owein's soul right out of them. Shoved him into this body, and then hurt him. Owein didn't remember clearly the first time he'd died, but Silas's spells had felt . . . familiar. Not the pain shooting through his muscles as the wizard tried to wrench power from him, but the . . . He struggled to describe it. The *flashes*, the wavering, the darkness, had reminded him of *before*. Owein had writhed and cried and begged, but that man hadn't cared. If Merritt and Hulda hadn't intervened, Owein would have died. There'd have been no magic left to tether him anywhere.

Lying down in yellowing clover, Owein whined again and set his head on his front legs. No, he didn't like it out there. Portsmouth, after the rescue, had been exciting. Too exciting. It had been the only time he'd left the island, ever. There'd been so many people and *smells* and sounds and buildings he'd gotten overwhelmed before reaching the boat. Overwhelmed and terrified until he stepped foot on Blaugdone Island again. His safe space. His home.

Maybe . . . if Merritt or Hulda or Miss Taylor or Baptiste came with him, maybe he could visit the mainland again. Maybe.

Stepping away from the ocean, Owein jaunted to the house, never once looking back.

Chapter 2

Though Myra had often slept at BIKER during the week, she owned a weekend home on the north side of Boston—a small family home with a thatched roof, square windows, and a short picket fence in need of whitewashing. The gate wasn't latched, so Hulda pushed through easily, glancing over the yard and back to the road, wondering if anyone was watching her.

With only a trickle of hope, Hulda knocked on the door. Waited, listening for movement within. There was none. After testing the lock—it was indeed locked—she turned around and pulled the spare key from its hiding place inside the chute of a wooden wind chime hanging on the eave. She let herself in, locking the door behind her.

The front room was small and tidy; Hulda's hopes rose when she saw a teacup on the table—with augury, she could read the leaves and perhaps see where Myra darted off to. But upon inspection, the cup was empty of anything save dust, which did nothing to trigger her fledgling spell. Sighing, Hulda ventured into the kitchen, running her hand along the short counter, opening drawers and doors.

She ended in Myra's bedroom. The bed was made; Myra mustn't have been in a hurry to leave, despite the unlatched gate. The bedspread was a faded yellow, still cheery, and the curtains were drawn on the window. If there'd ever been a chest at the foot of it, it was gone. The side table, clear.

Hulda pulled out the drawer, finding an old Bible, a pencil, a couple of ticket stubs, and a handkerchief. Frowning, she closed the drawer and looked under Myra's pillows. Walked to the small set of shelves and perused the books. Nothing. A sigh pressed past her lips. "Where are you?" she asked, turning and scanning the room. "What have you done?"

Of course, Hulda knew what Myra had done. She'd helped Silas Hogwood slip from jail and used his repertoire of magic to enchant homes so that BIKER would flourish. She'd unleashed an insidious criminal on the world and on Hulda, and on the staff of Whimbrel House. But she'd come back to resolve the crisis. And she had managed it with aplomb—not a whisper of Silas Hogwood had touched the papers. No constable or reinforcer had come sniffing around Blaugdone Island. It was as if nothing had happened.

But Myra hadn't debriefed Hulda, either. Was the entire interaction with Mr. Hogwood to be kept secret? If so, why? Merritt had landed the killing blow, yes, but it had been in self-defense. There had been witnesses to the aftermath—local authorities. What had Myra told them? Did they realize what they'd stumbled upon?

What was Hulda supposed to *do*?

Releasing a shrill sound of frustration, Hulda sat on the edge of the mattress. Her spiraling thoughts were interrupted by the subtle crunch of paper.

Curious, Hulda repeated the maneuver, standing and then sitting in that same spot, and received an identical result. A cursory search revealed some letters wedged between the side table drawer and the bed. Hulda grabbed the slim stack and pulled it into the light.

It felt wrong to thumb through them, but if Myra could be located at any of these addresses . . . Hulda could spare the apology. One was of a business nature and two others personal, from friends, or so Hulda guessed. She would send telegrams to these places and ask after Myra.

Hulda frowned. If the letters could lead to Myra, she wouldn't have left them to be found. Unless she'd done it intentionally, knowing Hulda would come snooping. Then again, if Myra had wanted Hulda to find her, wouldn't she have left a communion stone or sent a windsource pigeon?

Sighing, Hulda plopped onto the edge of the bed. Gathered the letters together and tossed them onto the floor, trying to create a pattern to incite her augury. She repeated the action two more times, with little luck.

Well, at least she had addresses to write to. She really should be getting to BIKER; she'd yet to update Whimbrel House's file . . . though how would she accurately record that the place was no longer enchanted without mentioning the involvement of Silas Hogwood? Hulda frowned. She'd done nothing wrong, yet Myra had her feeling like a criminal.

She stood, but this time she heard a slight *thump* of the bedframe against . . . well, she wasn't sure. It didn't touch the side table. Peering between the table and bed, just past the letters, she spied a book that had toppled there, like it had been resting against the bedframe and was knocked asunder by Hulda's jouncing. Reaching down, she pulled it free.

"Oh," she said. She knew this book—she had gifted it to Myra last Christmas. It was a gray book with a green leather spine and corner protectors. The front read, *Miss Leslie's Directions for Cookery.* One of the many receipt books Hulda had read. She'd especially liked this one.

Myra had dog-eared a few pages. Flipping through, Hulda glanced at the recipes she'd marked. As she neared the last, she spied a piece of paper wedged inside, perhaps a scrap used as a bookmark. Still, Hulda pulled it out. It was small, folded, and—

It was a telegram. Curious, Hulda unfurled it and read the short message.

The receipt book fell from her lap.

Tell me where he is, or I will keep my promise.

Her fingers went cold. Was this . . . Was this a threat? Hulda flipped the telegram over, searching for another clue, but there was none. She carefully turned each page of the receipt book, but there was nothing else tucked within.

Was someone threatening Myra? Who, and why? And why hadn't she said anything? Why keep this telegram and not report it to the watchmen?

Because she's already on tricky ground. Hulda didn't know what bargain she'd made with the watchmen in Marshfield after Silas Hogwood perished, but . . .

Silas Hogwood. Hulda's eyes went to the time filed on the telegram. October 26.

The same day Myra resigned.

"Oh, Myra. What have you gotten yourself into?" She looked over the message again, this time shivering as her skin pebbled with internal cold. *Tell me where* he *is.*

Surely . . . Surely the sender of this telegram couldn't mean Silas Hogwood?

Hulda dropped onto the mattress again, fighting the nausea building in her stomach. "What did you do?" she whispered, as if the telegram could answer back. Hulda doubted Myra would have reported the message, and the sender must have felt confident its meaning would not be interpreted by the post office employee who'd typed it. But . . . had Myra left it here, in a book received from Hulda, because she wanted Hulda to find it? Or was it just coincidence?

It *had* to be coincidence. Silas Hogwood was dead. Hulda had watched the life flee his eyes and the breath leave his lungs. The message likely referred to someone else. A contractor for BIKER, perhaps? Or this was sent from a long-lost lover searching for a bastard child. Or perhaps a lost pet. But it was certainly sent to Myra, which made those assumptions ridiculous. Then again, perhaps her work with Silas Hogwood was not her only secret.

Hulda forced herself back to the present. "I'm being too dramatic." Yet uncertainty pricked her. She'd show it to Merritt, get his thoughts on the situation. Granted, Merritt's imagination was wilder than her own . . .

Reaching into her bag, Hulda ran her thumb over the communion stone there, the one paired to the stone in Merritt's possession. Withdrew and grabbed her pouch of dice instead. Strode to Myra's kitchen table, which was only large enough to seat two, and sat.

She shook the dice in her hand and scattered them over the table, letting her vision shift out of focus.

Nothing.

"Could you work *once* when I need you, and not when I'm performing parlor tricks?" Hulda set the telegram on the table and gathered the dice. Threw them again.

Clearing her throat, she stared hard at the dice. Attempted to cheat by arranging them in an actual pattern. She rolled them again, and again, and cursed all this magic nonsense and Merritt and Myra and the lot of it.

Shoving the dice into their pouch and into her bag, Hulda strode out the door and closed it quietly behind her, scanning the road for familiar faces. She had nothing to apologize for—Myra was her employer and her friend. Why wouldn't she try her hardest to search for her? Still, after locking the door, she kept the key on her person instead of returning it to the wind chime.

Focus on what you can *control,* she reminded herself.

Projecting a confidence she didn't feel, Hulda marched to BIKER.

⌒୨

The BIKER headquarters at the back of the Bright Bay Hotel felt empty.

Felt empty, Hulda specified, because they weren't technically empty. A few employees still lingered in the small offices and white hallways— Sadie Steverus, the receptionist, for one. She still sat behind her tall stained-wood desk, blonde hair pulled back simply, a new white blouse buttoned to the base of her neck. The librarian was likewise present, along with the custodian. Of course, headquarters was never really *full*. The location was more of a way station, where people stopped in, rested for a night in the spare rooms downstairs, and went off on their new assignments. But the halls were decidedly *less*. A few employees had taken off after Myra's resignation. And *Myra* wasn't here. If there was one thing Hulda had learned to count on in her life, it was Myra Haigh. Until now, Myra had been a reliable constant, always there even when she wasn't. She was a psychometrist, a mind reader specifically, and while Hulda knew the woman's powers could not breach long distances, her intuition certainly could.

And now Hulda felt like she'd been lamed, her crutch taken away. She tightened her fist around the folded telegram in her pocket. *Myra, are you safe?*

Was Hulda still upset with the woman? Indubitably. Myra had been the catalyst for Silas Hogwood's arrival to America, and while Hulda did believe she'd meant no harm, she was nonetheless partially culpable for the attacks on Hulda, Merritt, Owein, Mr. Babineaux, and Miss Taylor. Thank the heavens no one had gotten seriously hurt. Ultimately, Myra had tangled herself in her own webs of deceit. She'd recognized the error, and even cleaned up the mess afterward, only to disappear to God knew where.

Hulda very much wanted to know *where*. She'd been desperate to talk to Myra even before finding the vague and unsettling telegram. She wanted to set things straight. Ensure she was all right. Because, betrayal or no, Myra was Hulda's dearest friend. If she was in trouble . . . Hulda wanted to help. That, and Hulda feared BIKER would fall apart without her.

These thoughts plagued her as she entered her room, setting her trusted black bag on a chair but keeping the telegram on her person. Her trunk was still here—she'd never gotten around to shipping it to either her sister's place or Whimbrel House, and for the better. Propriety aside, she needed to be in Boston, if for no other reason than it was her best bet at finding Myra, or allowing Myra to find her.

Unsurprisingly, Hulda didn't sleep well that night. She gave it a good go but rose earlier than necessary to prepare for the day. She'd make an appointment for Merritt with the Genealogical Society for the Advancement of Magic this afternoon, to both review his pedigree and search for any possible magic tutors.

Magic tutors. It was still hard to grasp everything that had happened these last few weeks. The fact that Merritt had *magic*, and a good deal of it, being one. Hulda had known she was an augurist at a young age. She possessed only a single spell—the impuissant ability to see the future—and hadn't needed any training to hone it. To think a man could live to his thirties without ever suspecting there was magic in his blood. *To think!*

Despite the reality that Merritt still needed her help, Whimbrel House was no longer an enchanted house. Even if BIKER was intact, she and Miss Taylor technically *couldn't* work there anymore. That was, she couldn't as soon as she made the report about its lost enchantments. She supposed they could still work there outside of BIKER, but in truth, their magical skill would be wasted at Whimbrel House now. Then there was Merritt himself. *Merritt Fernsby.* Hulda blushed without having to think of anything more than that.

Sitting on her bed, she pulled out the telegram and read over it again, though it offered up no new insight. After that, she brought forth a different document—a few folded papers crinkled from travel and use. A letter, or perhaps a story, that Merritt had snuck into his manuscript just for her prior to sending it for her perusal. She'd reread the note every day since receiving it, like she needed to reassure herself it had really happened. That there was a man alive who actually cared for her *that way*. That the cycle of rejection and loneliness had actually stopped.

Her chest distended reading it. She nearly had it memorized. Letting out a sigh, she tucked the letter away and offered a silent prayer of thanks. Even with Myra gone, even with her career on the precipice, she was happy. Very happy.

After checking her hair once more in the mirror and grabbing her bag, Hulda headed up the stairs to Myra's office. She'd thumbed through it again last night, but the woman had cleaned out the space thoroughly, leaving no clues to her whereabouts. Still, Hulda might as well check one more time, while she had better light. Perhaps, if she was lucky, her own magic might kick in and reveal something useful.

Wouldn't it be something if Hulda could see the future on command . . .

She heard some shuffling as she neared the top floor. "Miss Steverus, do you know if Myra—"

She paused on the last step as strangers' faces turned to look at her. Three of them, plus Miss Steverus. All dressed finely, and it wasn't quite nine o'clock.

"Miss Larkin!" Miss Steverus darted around the desk, blonde bun bouncing. "Let me introduce you to LIKER's foreign team."

"LIKER?" Hulda repeated. The *London* Institute for the Keeping of Enchanted Rooms? The parent company to BIKER? What were they doing here? Even with kinetically aided transport, the trip across the Atlantic wasn't a comfortable one.

Miss Steverus bit the inside of her lip. "I didn't know they were coming, either."

"We did send a telegram," said a tall, severe-looking man with light hair and spectacles similar to Hulda's own, as was his sartorial aesthetic.

The telegram in her pocket felt heavy as a bag of coins, but of course, that was not the message they meant.

Hulda nodded. "Of course, you understand things have been in upheaval."

"Precisely why we are here," said a man who was very . . . square. Everything about him was square. His haircut, his face, his body, even his glasses. "We're here to perform an audit of sorts, and to reorganize BIKER back to efficiency." His British accent was both crisp and warm, which had Hulda thinking of peach cobbler.

She tried not to fish-mouth.

Miss Steverus gestured to the square man. "This is Mr. Calvin Walker, head of foreign affairs. And this is Mr. Alastair Baillie, corporate attorney." She indicated the lanky man who'd first addressed her. He looked to be of an age with Hulda. "Miss Megan Richards, secretary—"

Miss Richards, who had been studying something on the ceiling, turned around suddenly, eyes wide. They were dark, and her skin was a warm brown, speaking of Indian heritage. "Oh! Yes. That is, administrative assistant." She hurried over, and a piece of black hair fell from her elaborate hairstyle. She held out her hand, and Hulda shook it, impressed with the woman's grip. "Our accountant was unable to join us, so I'll be filling that role as well. Very nice to meet you, Miss Steverus."

Hulda smiled. "I'm Miss Larkin."

"Right! Miss Larkin." Miss Richards released her. "And this is Mr. Walker," she repeated, introducing the square man again.

Mr. Walker massaged his forehead. "Let Miss Steverus do the introductions, Miss Richards."

Miss Richards simply shrugged and hung back, peering over Miss Steverus's desk, suddenly interested in something else.

Mr. Walker refocused on Hulda. "Miss Steverus tells us you're BIKER's best employee."

Hulda snorted, then covered her mouth with her hand. Pushing past a flush, she said, "Miss Steverus is very complimentary. I hope your trip was untroubled."

"Easy as it could be, being thrown about the Atlantic in a kinetic barge," Mr. Baillie quipped. His enunciation was so sharp it nearly cut through the roundness of his accent. Straightening his narrow shoulders, he turned to Mr. Walker. "While the pleasantries are nice, we have work to do."

"And Miss Larkin is the first one we need to talk to." Mr. Walker raised an eyebrow as though not-so-subtly warning Mr. Baillie to mind his manners. He turned to Hulda. "You worked closely with Miss Haigh, yes?"

Mention of Myra sent her heart flipping. Maintaining a docile demeanor, Hulda nodded. "I did, when I wasn't assigned elsewhere." A knot formed in her stomach. What sort of audit did this man have in mind? "I'm afraid I don't know her whereabouts." *Please tell me you do.*

Mr. Walker frowned. "Unfortunate, as speaking with her directly would be . . . beneficial."

That was a negative, then.

"Hiding is a sign of guilt," Mr. Baillie said, and Hulda decided she didn't like him.

"Oh dear." Miss Steverus placed a hand on her breast. "Guilty of what?"

But Mr. Walker waved the question away. "Let us dig into this one grain at a time, shall we?" Stepping back, he gestured to Myra's office. "If you don't mind, Miss Larkin."

"Not at all." Straightening her back, Hulda entered the office and made herself comfortable in a chair. Mr. Walker and Mr. Baillie followed, the latter closing the door behind him. Mr. Walker took Myra's seat behind her empty desk, while his bespectacled friend tarried near the bookshelves.

"We have Miss Haigh's resignation letter," Mr. Walker said as he opened a briefcase and removed several folders. "But would you mind sharing your experience?"

Hulda blinked. "With her resignation?"

He nodded.

"I . . ." There was no mention of Marshfield, or Silas Hogwood, or a constable report. Myra must have been truly thorough, unless these visitors from LIKER were concealing the breadth of their knowledge. But if they'd truly only just arrived in the States, what could they possibly have learned? Squaring her shoulders, Hulda treaded carefully. She would speak only truth. Whether the omittance of other truths would be held against her . . . she'd mull over that later.

"I was not in Boston when it happened," she admitted. "I've been stationed at Whimbrel House—our newest acquisition. It's located in the Narragansett Bay, on Blaugdone Island, specifically."

Mr. Walker nodded. "I'll pull up that file as well. How are things there?"

Hulda considered the question for half a beat. "Temperate, thankfully. I heard about Myra—Miss Haigh's—resignation from Miss Steverus." She paused. "Might I . . . Would it be against decorum for me to read it?"

Mr. Walker glanced at Mr. Baillie, then pulled the handwritten notice out of the topmost folder. He passed it to Hulda. After adjusting her spectacles, Hulda read carefully, hoping to uncover another clue.

> *To whom it may concern,*
>
> *I, Myra Haigh, regretfully resign from my position as director of the Boston Institute for the Keeping of Enchanted Rooms. Significant family matters have pulled me away.*
>
> *Sincerely,*
> *M. Haigh*

The letter was insufficient. In addition to its brevity, it lacked a reasonable explanation for her defection. Myra didn't have any family in the States. Not close family. Hulda highly doubted that she'd suddenly sailed to Spain to reconnect with great-aunts or second cousins.

"Thank you." She passed the letter back.

Mr. Walker returned the letter to its folder. "Now, I understand you don't work directly with the overseeing of the company, but I must ask in case you *do* know something useful. We've sifted through BIKER's bank records and have found unaccounted-for funds."

Hulda blinked. She had not expected the statement. "Unaccounted? Funds?" Had Myra used BIKER funds to take care of the mess in Marshfield? Hulda's skin was growing warm beneath her dress. *I'm sorry, Myra. I'm not sure how long I can protect you.*

"That is," he went on, "funds siphoning to an unknown location once a month. We've tried the usual methods to trace them, but thus far to no avail." He sighed. "You don't by chance know where those funds were transferred?"

Her skin cooled as though a pail of water had been overturned above her head. "Once a month?" Not Marshfield, then. "For how long?"

"Years," he answered.

Hulda's lips parted. For a moment, she'd wondered whether Myra had been keeping Silas on payroll. But she'd only been working with the man for months, not years. Piecing together her thoughts, she asked, "Do you have an inkling of where the funds went?"

Mr. Walker frowned, obviously disappointed with Hulda's lack of knowledge—as was she. Myra had been keeping more secrets than she'd realized. "Unfortunately, no."

Hulda studied his features for a moment before her stomach performed a half twist. "You think Miss Haigh was embezzling?" *Surely not. Please no, Myra.*

Leaning back in his chair, he answered, "It's a possibility, but we have no actual evidence."

Hulda's stomach righted itself.

"The thing is, Miss Haigh didn't just resign. She disappeared."

Now it was Hulda's turn to frown. "So I've noticed. I'm afraid I haven't any idea where she is. I assume you've checked the obvious places? I certainly have."

"That we have, that we have. We'll check again, more thoroughly, now that we're here." Leaning forward, he drummed on his desk before fetching and opening another file. "And you're an augurist, Miss Larkin?"

Another unexpected turn. "I am."

He smiled. "Do you think you could read for me?"

She started. That was certainly not the question she'd expected. "I . . . I could try, Mr. Walker. But my abilities are temperamental at best." She reached into her bag and pulled out her dice pouch. Her precognition was tied to patterns, such as those seen in tea leaves, fallen sticks, or dice. Handing them over, she said, "You can try with these."

Suddenly gleeful, Mr. Walker took the pouch and poured the dice into his hand—seven in total. He kneaded them around a moment before saying, "Fascinating," and letting them spill to the desktop. "And you can just read it in those?"

Hulda leaned forward and glanced at the dice. She didn't actually do any mental work to find connections in patterns—her augury was a sort of sixth sense, and it kicked in automatically. Involuntarily. Or it didn't. "Technically, yes. But like I said, it's very temperamental—"

Her vision blurred as her magic kindled. Now *it works,* she thought with dismay. An image flashed by her eyes. It lasted only a heartbeat before dissipating.

Mr. Walker leaned closer. "Did you see something?"

She thought she heard Mr. Baillie cluck his tongue behind her, but wasn't sure.

Hulda blinked her vision clear and sat back. "Not anything of import, alas. But I would perhaps go sans mustard with your lunch today."

Mr. Walker stared at her for a moment before laughing. "Is that so?"

She knit her fingers together. "I just saw some dribbling from a sandwich onto that very suit. You were on the street and not in the office." In her experience, the future her augury showed would transpire, regardless of what she or anyone did to change it. It was as set as the past. She was willing to guess Mr. Walker would indeed get mustard on his sandwich, perhaps with the thought that he'd merely be careful. Alas, such was his choice. "I assume you'll be staying here long enough to become comfortable and have meals delivered?"

Mr. Walker nodded. "Hopefully not *too* comfortable, for while Boston has its charm, I'm eager to return home. Alastair, come over here and roll the dice!"

Hulda pressed her lips together, unsure her magic would be kind enough to repeat itself.

But Mr. Baillie merely drawled, "No, thank you. I'd rather choose my future as it comes to me."

Hulda peeked at him over her shoulder. He looked bored, yet there was a definite tension in his forehead. She couldn't fault him—many people didn't like to have their lives invaded by magic—one of many reasons so many were unconcerned about its preservation. There had been times in her life where Hulda had wished her augury would stay quiet. Nothing deflated hope quicker than a hopeless future.

The thought brought to mind Stanley Lidgett, the steward at Gorse End she'd once hoped to charm. Ultimately it was for the better that *that* hadn't panned out.

"Well." Mr. Walker collected his folders and tucked them together. "We will be performing an audit, as I mentioned, and seeing BIKER running smoothly again. We are looking for someone to replace Myra Haigh. Do you know a Mrs. Thornton?"

Hulda nodded. "I believe she's stationed in Denmark. She's been with BIKER for . . . two decades, I would guess."

"Yes, she's on our list, though the logistics of interviewing her are still in the air. And then there's Alastair."

Hulda stiffened and purposefully did not turn her head. "Y-Your lawyer?"

"Lawyer by trade, yes. He's very organized." He tipped his head toward Mr. Baillie. "I assure you BIKER would be in excellent hands with him."

Hulda tried to imagine the lanky, disagreeable man behind this desk, assigning her to jobs, reading her reports . . .

"And then our third candidate, of course."

Folding her hands in her lap, Hulda asked, "Third?"

Mr. Walker looked surprised. "But of course, Miss Larkin. I suppose Miss Steverus didn't have a chance to tell you that your name is up for the position as well."

Hulda found herself fish-mouthing again. Because despite being an augurist, she certainly hadn't seen *that* coming.

Chapter 3

The dog stared at the paper card and tilted his head to the side.

Merritt sighed. "Did you say something? Because I didn't hear it." His communion spell was a mess. Sometimes it went off on its own, and sometimes the signal got lost when he actually needed to use it. Or was it two communion spells? Were there separate spells for plants and animals? Or perhaps even a particular one for reeds and then another for, say, conifers?

Either way, it was utterly maddening. And yet not quite maddening enough to motivate him to seek help from the one person who should be able to give it. The letter he'd written to Nelson Sutcliffe still sat crinkled on the back-right corner of his desk.

O? The dog wagged its tail, and again Merritt wondered how much of the mutt had integrated itself with Owein, or if Owein simply embraced his identity as a terrier.

"Close. *Q.*" He set the card down and picked up another. "How about this?"

Owein's attention strayed to the office window. Its mullion was a wood so bright it looked almost yellow, which dropped down into a curving and curling apron Merritt doubted had been part of the original structure. Most likely it had been a fanciful change wrought by a certain boy wizard, especially given that this window did not match any of the others in the house. None of the windows matched, actually. It had taken Merritt a while to realize it, and yet he sort of enjoyed the eccentricity of the fact.

Merritt turned in his chair, the back of which pressed against his desk, to glance out the window, but there was nothing. Likely Owein had heard a whimbrel or something of the sort. Which was fine, so long as Merritt wasn't *also* hearing a whimbrel or something of the sort.

"This one?" Merritt tried again.

Owein's ears drooped. *This is boring.*

"Do you want to read or not?"

The terrier sighed in a very humanlike way. *Let's take a break and work on magic!*

Merritt cringed. "We've barely been at letters for ten minutes."

The dog whined.

Merritt set the cards aside and reached forward to scratch Owein's ears. Just like every other dog, possessed or not, Owein enjoyed this. Or perhaps he simply enjoyed being touched—a sensation he couldn't truly experience while stuck in the walls of this house. On the floor behind him was a large alphabet chart Hulda had made, which had gone mostly unused. The idea was that if Owein could learn to read, he would be able to spell out things he needed when Merritt wasn't around, or when Merritt preferred to keep his vocal abilities intact. "I can't communion every minute of every day. You need to learn to use that chart."

Truly, Owein fascinated him. Despite having a spirit some two hundred and twenty-something years old, Owein still behaved like a boy. He'd died at the age of twelve, and twelve was the age engraved into his heart. Perhaps his lack of maturity came from being alone for so long, away from the social and familial interactions that would have helped him grow up. Perhaps aging was a thing of the body and not the soul.

Merritt's hands slowed. A long breath passed through his nostrils. "Best to learn it quickly. And take care when you're running about the island. I don't know how close I have to be to hear you."

Owein pulled from Merritt's fingers and tilted his furry head to the side. *What do you mean?*

Unease scraped along Merritt's stomach. "Just take care."

Owein pushed his nose into Merritt's knee and huffed. Merritt sighed.

"You're not a house anymore, Owein." He ran his palm over his head. "Dogs . . . don't live as long as people do. So you have to decide what you want to do with the time you have left."

Owein pulled back, whined. Walked in a circle clockwise, then counterclockwise. *I didn't think of that.*

"Well." Merritt cleared his throat when his voice caught. Much more communion without a break would steal his voice entirely. Again. He'd be the one in need of the chart. "I don't know. This—your—body might only be a year old. Or it might be ten years, though you look rather spry. Perhaps three or four—"

Owein stepped to the chart and pawed the question mark in its lower corner.

Merritt held out his hands, palms up, unsure. "Dogs live about six, seven years . . . Perhaps a little longer, with good care."

His ears drooped.

"I don't mean to be the bearer of bad news." Merritt's voice softened, but this time it wasn't an effect of magic. "But I want you to understand you're mortal now. It's a trade. The immortality of being a house for the liberation of being a dog."

Owein looked out the window again, just for a few seconds. *I didn't choose this.*

Oh, how deeply those words echoed. *I didn't, either. None of it.* But he simply nodded. "Would you have, if given the chance?"

Owein thought about it only a moment. *Yes. I like feeling. I like being around you. Even when you're gone, it's less . . . lonely, like this. My heartbeat keeps me company.*

Merritt stilled at the answer. *Lonely.* Owein had been alone for a long time. Merritt recalled keenly the moodiness of Whimbrel House when he'd first moved in. The rats falling from the ceiling and the bathroom walls that had tried to skewer him—very much the acts of an adolescent acting out. And yet, Owein no longer seemed *bothered* by his decades of solitude.

Maybe he hides it, just like you do.

Merritt disregarded the errant thought. Elbows on his knees, hands clasped together, he asked, "How do you handle it so well?"

Owein's golden eyes met his, and the dog made a grumbled *Hmm?* sound.

"The darkness," he murmured, then shook himself. "That is . . . you were obviously upset, when Hulda and I found you. You seem rather chipper now. Like everything is all right."

Owein blinked. He took a moment to answer. Looked away. *Why should I be sad when so much is good?*

Merritt slouched. "Why, indeed." He could point out that Owein, a *human*, was trapped in the body of a dog. That his family was long dead. That he'd been hurt by a psychotic necromancer. That he was illiterate and couldn't speak to anyone but Merritt directly. But it seemed cruel to do so.

Why should I be sad when so much is good? Such a simple answer, and one Merritt wanted to cling to. Things *were* good. He was a home-owner. He had friends. He had Hulda. He had a new book coming out next year!

And he needed to go to Cattlecorn.

His stomach pinched, and he put a hand over it. He wasn't getting another ulcer, was he?

A knock on the door broke through his thoughts. The door was open, so he didn't need to invite Beth inside. She held a duster. "Mind if I tidy up?" she asked, her eyes instantly going to the dishes Merritt had left on his desk.

"Oh. Not at all." He swiveled around and collected the papers on the desk, which he'd accumulated in Boston after seeing Hulda to BIKER yesterday. Now that he was between projects, he figured he'd take up journalism again. Write a few articles to sell to local papers. So he'd gathered the contact information for the editors, along with pay rates and topics of interests.

But magic practice! Owein said.

"I need to head to Boston anyway," he replied, a decent response to both parties listening. Turning to Owein, he asked, "Do you want to come?"

To his surprise, the dog cowed. Shook his head no before saying, *I need to relieve myself.*

Merritt didn't need to translate, for Miss Taylor responded, "I know that look." Shoving the duster under her arm, she said, "I'll let you out, but go *on the grass* this time! I'll whap your backside if you track mud into the house again."

Owein whined and gallivanted into the hallway.

"Thank you." Merritt grabbed the carrier bag beside the desk. "I should be back before dark."

"I'll let Mr. Babineaux know." The maid offered him a smile. Picked up a mug and paused. "Do you want me to mail this letter?"

Merritt hesitated, his joints suddenly ninety years old. "I . . ."

She picked it up and turned it over. The address was already there. "You could take it on your way."

Owein poked his head back into the room, huffing his impatience.

"No." He spoke hard enough to garner a concerned look from Beth. "No, I won't . . . that is . . ." He ran a hand back through his hair. "Go ahead and send it. When you have a chance."

Owein whined.

Her gaze switched from him to the dog. The letter slipped into her apron pocket, and Merritt found himself oddly relieved not to have to look at it anymore. "I'm coming."

Owein shot into the hallway. Beth hurried after him, dishes in hand. Merritt followed, then stopped in the doorway. Turned to a pencil on his desk. Focused on it, squinted at it, scowled at it. He thought of it floating, or melting, or breaking—all the chaotic annoyances Owein had performed while enchanting these walls. But the pencil remained unchanged.

Letting out a long breath, Merritt pushed the strap of his bag higher on his shoulder and left to grab his coat.

Merritt wasn't sure if he should knock once he arrived at the unmarked entrance of BIKER headquarters. He supposed it was always better to knock than not to knock, so he rapped lightly and waited a full minute for an answer. Receiving none, he tested the knob—unlocked—and let himself in. He was somewhat familiar with the place, having given himself a small tour yesterday. He started toward the office. Seemed things were running again, judging by the voices coming from that direction.

Reaching the third floor, he spied Sadie Steverus—the secretary who had given him Hulda's sister's address after he'd gotten the splendid idea to woo her via manuscript—behind her desk, along with a black-haired woman, their heads pressed together as they looked over something behind the tall front shelf of the desk. To his left was a small sofa, upon which sat a man. A small side table that had once held a plant had been dragged in front of him, at least a dozen files scattered over it.

"I believe there's more office space that way." Merritt jutted his thumb to the right.

The man startled. "Oh! Hello." He bashfully glanced down the hallway. "You know, I'm sure there is. I don't know why I didn't think of that."

The black-haired woman, a few years Merritt's junior, jumped from her seat. "Hello!"

Simultaneously, she and Sadie asked, "May I help you?" The newcomer glanced apologetically at the BIKER secretary.

Merritt smiled at them. "Just here for Hulda Larkin."

Sadie nodded to the other woman, apparently giving her permission to take over. "She's right this way." She came around the desk, checking the clock as she went. "Goodness, they've been in there a long time!" She knocked on the door to what Merritt believed to be Myra Haigh's office and stuck her head in. "There's a guest here."

"Oh, we're well and finished," sounded a baritone voice from within, and seconds later a very robust man in his late forties exited, Hulda in his shadow, a skinny fellow right behind her.

The black-haired woman perked up suddenly, head swinging from Hulda to Merritt. "My apologies! You must be *Mr.* Larkin!"

Merritt laughed, altogether amused by the woman's enthusiasm, Sadie's blanching, and the bright shade of red swallowing Hulda's face. She blushed so easily. "Something like that."

Spine stiff as a brick wall, Hulda marched over to him. "This is Mr. Merritt Fernsby." Her mouth twisted. "My . . . associate."

Associate? Merritt glanced sideways at her. She didn't meet his eyes but stood so erect he thought her spine might snap, or she'd at least pull a few stitches in her shoulders. He glanced back to the newcomers. Who were they?

Not wanting to make Hulda uncomfortable—she'd explain later—he extended a hand to the first man. "Nice to meet you."

The robust man had a good grip. "Calvin Walker. These are my colleagues, Megan Richards and Alastair Baillie."

Hulda cleared her throat. "Mr. Walker is the head of foreign affairs with LIKER, the parent company of BIKER."

"LIKER?" Merritt repeated.

"London," she clarified.

He nodded. "All of you have truly terrible acronyms."

Hulda pinked a little more, but Mr. Walker grinned. "That we do."

Merritt put his hands in his pockets. "So . . . why is the London institute in Boston?"

The skinny man answered, "A matter not important to those *outside* the organizations," like he was tired and had better things to do than make new acquaintances.

Merritt eyed him. "But perhaps important to their clients?"

"Mr. Fernsby is the owner of Whimbrel House," Hulda quickly added. "BIKER's newest addition. Located in the Narragansett Bay."

She did not mention that the house was no longer magical, and Merritt chose not to disclose the information. Myra's wishes aside, Owein should have some semblance of privacy, so disclosing how Silas had sucked the boy's spirit right from the floorboards seemed in bad taste.

Before the silence grew too awkward, Merritt said, "I take it you're all magical in some sort of way."

Hulda dropped her head. Apparently the wrong question to ask, but surely there was no harm in it.

Mr. Walker seemed unfazed. "In a way, but I fear you'll be disappointed. I'm a conjurist, myself, though my bloodline is so diluted you would barely believe it."

Miss Richards chimed in. "And his magic is illegal."

Hulda perked up at that. "Truly?"

Mr. Walker chuckled. "Indeed. In both Britain and the States. I can turn small things into gold. But I shan't demonstrate."

Merritt whistled. "Impressive."

"Very small things," he added. "And, like Miss Larkin, Miss Richards is an augurist."

The black-haired woman folded her arms. "But my skill isn't nearly as neat as yours, Miss Larkin. I inherited luck, but it only works a little better than the average Jane. Wouldn't have thought twice about it if it didn't run in the family. But I am rather good at cribbage."

Merritt turned to Alastair. "And you?"

The man frowned. "I'm not a circus performer, Mr. Fernsby."

Mr. Walker clapped Alastair on the shoulder. "Hysterian, but like us, he has very little to show for it."

"Huh." Merritt didn't know what else to say. He'd never met a hysterian before—a wizard of the emotions, and of pain. It might have made him worry, were this, oh, the year 600 and magic were still somewhat potent.

He reached for Hulda's hand, only to have her withdraw and tuck it behind her back. He let his hand fall as naturally as it could to his side while his stomach dipped a little.

Hulda adjusted her glasses. "If there isn't anything else, Mr. Walker—"

"Not for now. But I'm sure something will arise by tomorrow." He nodded at Merritt. "Good to meet you, Mr. Fernsby. Alastair, attend me with the records, will you?"

The two took off down the hallway. Hulda headed straight for the stairs, so Merritt offered a quick wave to the others before following. She didn't speak again until they were outside.

"We should be careful with public displays." She folded her arms.

Merritt side-eyed her. "I'd hardly call it a public display. Besides, they were already assuming we were married."

Her cheeks pinked. "Regardless, BIKER is a place of business—"

"Then I'll hold Calvin's hand next time for a broader sense of normalcy."

She rolled her eyes. "Really, Merritt."

"Really, darling." He stopped at the edge of the sidewalk, took her hand, and pulled her knuckles to his lips. Met her eyes and held them until that flattering pink suffused her cheeks. Then he whispered, "Just let me enjoy you."

She opened her mouth but failed to say anything, and something about the fact made Merritt desperately want to kiss her—but he knew such a *public display* would sincerely embarrass her, so he restrained himself and headed in the direction of the kinetic tram station.

"What are the Brits doing here, anyway?" he asked.

"An audit," Hulda responded. "And to look into the oddity with Miss Haigh and Mr. Hogwood."

Merritt sobered. "I see."

"*We* did nothing wrong," she amended. "But I'm worried about Myra. But." She glanced around, then pulled Merritt off the road, toward a copse of oaks still holding on to most of their leaves. Turning her back to the road, she dug through her pocket and pulled out a folded telegram. "I found this at her home this morning," she whispered, handing it to him.

Merritt read the brief message. *Tell me where he is, or I will keep my promise.* His gut twisted like someone was making challah out of his intestines. Handing it back, he murmured, "Sounds like a threat."

"My thought as well. And the date is the same as her resignation." She folded the telegram as tightly as the paper would allow before pressing it into the depths of her pocket. "I'd rather not think this way, but I fear it may have something to do with Mr. Hogwood."

Merritt mulled on that. "Does he have living family? Who would want the body for burial?"

Hulda shook her head. "No, none. Not that I've ever researched, and believe me, I'm very familiar with Mr. Hogwood's genealogical line." She sighed. "That, and who could have known he'd died? And that Myra was involved? She's very efficient."

"With hiding bodies?"

Hulda bristled. "In general."

Merritt leaned against the closest tree. "Any idea who might have sent it?"

She shook her head.

"Someone tied to BIKER?"

"I highly doubt she would have involved anyone else from BIKER. Most of its employees are contractors. But LIKER certainly suspects something, even if it's just what they've evidenced from receipts and reports." She let out a long breath and turned toward the road, subtly signaling Merritt to follow. "I found addresses of recent letters as well; I'm going to write to them and see if I can find her whereabouts. The quickest way to solve this would be to talk to Myra directly."

Merritt nodded. "I wonder why she'd leave this on your shoulders."

"She couldn't have meant to. I know her. She . . ." Hulda drew in a deep breath. When Merritt offered his elbow, she took it. "She couldn't have meant to," she repeated. "She wouldn't have known about LIKER, surely. When I came to the office to investigate before, I didn't find any letter or telegram announcing their arrival; I believe it came after her disappearance. Oh, I don't know!" She pressed her fingers to her forehead. Merritt could only imagine the sort of headache that must be blooming there. "I don't know."

"Start with the addresses," he offered, trying to ground her. "One thing at a time."

"Yes, of course."

"Do you want to head to the post office?"

"No. No, I have an appointment for you at the Genealogical Society."

The Genealogical Society for the Advancement of Magic, she meant—a private organization with broad reach, seeking to track wizards and their genetic lines in hopes of creating magicked pairs in a futile attempt to slow the dilution of sorcery. Merritt scuffed the toe of his shoe as the conversation suddenly turned to him. "Already?"

A slight smile tugged on the corner of Hulda's mouth as she glanced at him. "I, too, am efficient." It faded. After a moment, she said, "There's the issue of replacing her."

Myra, she meant. Shrugging, Merritt offered, "They should just have you do it."

She hesitated. "Mr. Walker *did* name me a candidate."

Merritt paused his steps and met her eyes, trying to read her face. Her countenance still held to worry. "And what are your thoughts on that?"

"I . . ." She pushed her glasses up with her free hand, though they hadn't slipped so much as a millimeter. "I never considered it before. BIKER and Myra . . . they've always been coequal to me. I never thought of separating them." She paused, rolling her lips together, looking toward the lowering sun. "My entire path in life has always focused on my career. It's been the one thing I could control, for the most part." She glanced at her hand in the crook of his elbow; Merritt flexed, squeezing her fingers, earning the slightest smile in response. "So yes, I want it. Not only for myself, but if I'm appointed director, I'll have the ability to protect what Myra built. I would hate to see it go to someone else. Especially someone less . . . involved." She met his eyes. "So you understand why I must remain completely professional at BIKER. I need to portray myself as the most eligible person to take over."

He nodded. "I understand." Smirking, he added, "I'll be the best associate of your acquaintance."

She rolled her eyes.

They walked a few steps before Merritt realized something. "You wouldn't keep houses anymore. If you became director."

Her pace slowed. "I suppose not." She pressed close to him to allow another couple to pass by. "But I haven't gotten the position yet. It's between me, Mrs. Thornton, and Mr. Baillie."

He took a second to place the names. "Baillie. The hysterian?"

"The lawyer, yes." She let out an exasperated sigh. "I suppose I'll have to wait and see what happens. Put my best foot forward and be as embroiled as possible. Show my abilities, my skills, even if it means working long hours. In the meantime, LIKER is under the impression that Whimbrel House is still enchanted, domesticated, and under the care of its staff."

Not a hard ruse to keep up, if it came down to it. These long hours meant less time at Whimbrel House, but Merritt didn't point it out. No need to increase her stress. With luck, she'd get the appointment by the end of the week. True, Merritt had never met the infamous Mrs. Thornton, and he didn't really know Baillie, either, but Hulda seemed the obvious choice. She was available, she was actually a BIKER employee, and she was the most competent person Merritt had ever encountered.

They turned down the street for the Genealogical Society. Lowering his voice, Merritt asked, "And will you tell them about Myra?"

She pinched her lips together, considering. "I . . . don't think I will. Not yet. As far as I'm concerned, Myra's involvement with Mr. Hogwood, while hardly ethical, has come to its conclusion. It's completed and done. She's already given up her position as director in atonement. I . . . don't want to hurt her further. And I don't understand the rest of it." She touched her pocket. "I'm afraid to do anything that might have enduring consequences before I see the full picture."

"That's noble of you."

She glanced at him, concern imprinting her brow. "Is it?"

He nodded, and she relaxed a hair. In truth, Merritt didn't think Hulda Larkin *could* relax. God had made her out of steel and concrete and laced her together with thick whale-boned corsets. Something they would have to work on.

Releasing her hand, Merritt opened the door to the Genealogical Society. The clerk at the desk within perked up instantly and came forward to greet them. *Please have what I need,* Merritt said, half thought, half prayer. *Everything will be easier if you just give me what I need.*

"Mr. Gifford, good to see you," Hulda said, and Merritt repeated the name mentally three times to remember it.

"Miss Larkin. And you must be Mr. Fernsby?"

"Last I checked," Merritt replied, and the sudden thought came to him, *Or should I be "Mr. Sutcliffe"?*

The idea rankled him. He plastered over the discomfort and smiled.

Gifford glanced between the two of them, smile growing. "I hope you don't mind my saying so, but after reviewing your family lines, you really will have the most miraculous children, I'm sure of it."

Merritt barked a laugh while Hulda stuttered, "Y-You are too forward, Mr. Gifford. We are unwed."

At least she didn't claim Merritt as her *associate* again.

Gifford didn't seem the least bit chagrined. "My apologies. I have the full pedigrees you requested written up here." He guided them back to the desk. "And I took the liberty of penning yours as well, Miss Larkin. I've always liked framing and displaying them myself."

Leaning in close to Hulda, Merritt whispered, "This is just an awkward day for you all around, isn't it?"

Without looking at him, she said, "And I'm sure you're enjoying it."

"Most definitely."

Gifford handed each of them a crisp stack of papers. Merritt gawked. This man literally had the nicest handwriting he had ever seen. No wonder he framed his work.

"That's very kind of you, Mr. Gifford." Hulda retrieved a file folder out of that massive black bag of hers and carefully tucked the pedigree away, then held out her hand to take Merritt's as well. He passed it over. "What is the charge?"

"This one is free. You *are* our collaborator at BIKER."

Merritt murmured, "Something to mention to Walker." Another reason Hulda should get the position—she'd already established herself with local contacts.

He paused. If Hulda would be working long hours to prove herself worthy to assume Myra's position, what sort of hours would she work once she had it?

Rhode Island suddenly felt very far away.

Hulda smiled. "Thank you. But there is another matter I'd like to inquire about. Do you know of any magic tutors in the area? Ones that specialize in wardship, communion, or chaocracy?"

Gifford paused. "I . . . know where I can look it up." He glanced to Merritt. "I presume this is for you?"

Merritt rubbed the back of his neck. "Well, it's not for the dog."

Confusion weighed Gifford's brow, but he pressed on. "I can get the information for you, if you'd like. I'm sure at least one is in the Boston area."

Something about that made him uneasy. Was it just because he was unaccustomed to being a wizard?

Gifford stepped away for about a quarter hour and returned with a few cards in hand. "I have a wardist in the area who may be willing to work with someone."

"Communionists?" Merritt asked.

He shook his head. "Unless you're willing to travel to South Carolina."

Merritt's muscles sank down on his bones. "And roughly, what would tutoring cost?"

"Their fees have some range," the clerk confessed. "That is . . . if I might offer my services, I'm reasonable."

Hulda perked. "Your services?"

He nodded. "I've not a lick of magic myself, but I've researched it all my life. It's how I got the job here. I'm familiar with the methods of all eleven disciplines—studied at Oxford when I was a younger man." He glanced to Merritt. "That is, if you're not particular."

"Not at all." Anything to get this mess under control. Communion was truly all Merritt cared about, but it would probably do everyone around him good if he didn't accidentally put up invisible barriers or, say, melt the couch they were sitting on. "You're hired. My schedule is wide open."

Gifford grinned. "Excellent. Let me retrieve mine." He pulled open a drawer in the desk and fetched a ledger. Hulda touched the back of Merritt's arm and smiled at him—a smile he couldn't help but return.

Perhaps this wouldn't be too bad, after all.

⌒☺

While Hulda deemed it improper to live at Whimbrel House, given their romantic situation, Merritt invited her to dinner, and she accepted. The sun was setting, lighthouse keepers lighting their towers, as Merritt and Hulda took his little kinetic boat back to Blaugdone Island. It was a two-hour trip back to BIKER, but if it came down to the wire, Hulda could stay in her old room, or perhaps a boarding house on Rhode Island, if she was adamant about it. Merritt didn't mind escorting her back himself, but the issue of propriety of a man and woman alone in the dark might arise. Mayhap the entire household would have to accompany them.

The shades of orange, pink, and violet painting the sky made him forgive the cold wind whipping by them as they traveled. Perhaps if Merritt's novel somehow did remarkably well, he'd see to purchasing a covered craft.

He held Hulda's hand as she stepped off the boat, then wrapped her arm through his as they followed the well-worn path to the house, which was crusted with newly forming frost. The animal life had grown quiet around them, the vegetation shrinking down for winter, the trees a little more bare. But Whimbrel House glowed warmly, and Merritt smelled baked bread before reaching the house. As Owein had said, so much was good.

Beth must have seen them approaching, for she opened the door. "Good evening! You made good time. Baptiste just set out the roast."

"How wonderful." Hulda leaned in to him, and Merritt absorbed her warmth. "One of my favorites."

"One of Mr. Portendorfer's, too." Beth motioned them into the dining room.

Confused, Merritt asked, "Mr. Portendorfer?"

Entering the dining room, he saw his childhood friend sitting at the table, napkin already on his lap.

"Fletcher?" Merritt asked, and as his friend turned, Merritt's stomach sank.

Was it the third of November already?

"Criminy," he muttered. He'd forgotten he'd invited Fletcher to stay the night so they could set sail first thing in the morning.

Because Fletcher was escorting him to Cattlecorn.

It was time for Merritt to go home.

Chapter 4

Merritt's stomach shriveled to the size of a pea, making it impossible to put more than a bite of dinner into it. He tried to keep up with the conversation—how things were going with Fletcher's work as an accountant for a wholesaler, news about BIKER and Hulda's opportunity there, the turn of the weather, childhood anecdotes. Merritt thought he was doing a fine enough job of it, but both Fletcher and Hulda kept side-eyeing him and his still-full plate, which Baptiste, his chef, routinely frowned at.

Though Hulda was no longer working at Whimbrel House in any official capacity, she departed early to ready Fletcher's room, ignoring Merritt's insistence that they could manage. She was awfully stringent about her method of tucking sheets. Beth took the dishes to the kitchen and invited Baptiste to join her in a manner a little too obvious to be casual; she clearly intended to give Merritt and Fletcher a moment of privacy. And thus Merritt found himself alone with his best friend, who pulled up a chair beside him and stuck his elbows on the table.

"You're not sick, are you?" Fletcher asked.

Merritt ran a hand down his face. Rubbed his eyes. Mussed his hair. Considered saying yes and going straight to bed. "No."

"You didn't eat—"

"Let's postpone."

The men stared at one another for a couple of seconds before Fletcher repeated, "Postpone?"

Merritt shook his head before cradling it in his palms. "Just for a few weeks." His stomach squelched around what few morsels he'd stuffed into it. "I found a bloke who's willing to train me, so I don't need Sutcliffe after all—"

"But your family," Fletcher retorted, cutting him off.

Merritt dug a knuckle into his temple. "I know. I know, it's just . . . I can't . . . I'm not . . ."

"You need to confront this." Fletcher had the decency to keep his voice low. "Get it done. Your father has been a shadow over you all your life, and now you finally know why. We've talked about this."

Fletcher was the only person outside of Whimbrel House Merritt had confided in; the Portsmouth postmaster had likely grown weary from the number of letters passed between them.

Merritt just kept shaking his head.

"Might as well keep to our plans and go tomorrow," Fletcher pressed. "I came all the way down here."

Merritt sunk until his forehead hit the table. "I know. I'm sorry."

Fletcher sighed. "Don't be sorry, Merritt. I get it—"

"Do you?"

He hesitated. "Maybe not. I want to go with you. Support you. But I'm a working man. I can't just come at your beck and call."

"I know." Merritt's breath fogged, trapped in the space between the table and his arms. He forced his head up, and the dining room suddenly seemed too bright. "I know. I'll work it out. I just . . . I can't go. Not yet. Just started this nonsense with Gifford."

The excuse sounded hollow. His stomach tightened to a grain of sand. He winced.

Fletcher leaned back in his chair. "What a mess."

Merritt didn't respond.

"I should have brought some whiskey."

A small chuckle escaped Merritt's mouth. "Maybe. But I'm more in a bourbon mood." Though he hadn't had a drink in . . . he couldn't actually remember. He'd gone through such a perfectionist phase after moving out on his own, determined to prove his father wrong and also to ensure no one else had a reason to cast him away.

Straightening his spine, Merritt added, "Of course stay the night. But I might have to cross the bay if Hulda insists on heading out. I don't want her floating it alone."

Fletcher nodded. "If she'll wait until morning, I'll gladly escort her."

"Thank you." Merritt let out a long breath and traced the grain of the table, trying to sort through his thoughts, yet finding himself able to process only the pattern of the woodgrain. "Thank you."

～

Hulda exited the spare room to see Miss Taylor waiting for her, leaning up against a wall, absently petting the top of Owein's head. The dog noticed her first and whined, which brought up Miss Taylor's attention.

Miss Taylor addressed the dog first. "Bed time. Go on."

A low growl sounded in Owein's throat.

Miss Taylor planted fists on her hips. "Do you really want to try me, *little boy?*"

The growling cut off. Tail between his legs, Owein sulked downstairs. Hulda had set up a little bed in the corner of the living room before moving out, though he often came upstairs during the day and jumped on the foot of Merritt's bed, getting fur all over the duvet.

Miss Taylor glanced in the direction of the stairs. "Anything new on Miss Haigh?"

Hulda repressed a sigh. "I would tell you if I knew."

The maid shook her head. "If only I'd been there when all this happened. I could have sensed it. Maybe talked her down before she did anything rash."

"Who would blame you? You were recovering from injuries and on assignment, Beth." Hulda rarely used Miss Taylor's first name, but they were hardly in a formal setting. "And who knows if what she did *was* rash?"

Hulda still carried that telegram in her pocket. She'd stopped reading it. There wasn't anything more to study on the crinkled piece of paper.

Miss Taylor waited a beat before speaking. "Thought I should tell you. That is, I usually keep these things to myself, because it's none of my business what goes on with others. It's just . . . the magic has a mind of its own." She twirled her hand in the general direction of her head. Like Myra, Beth Taylor had talent in the school of psychometry, though her ability was weaker. Still, clairvoyance, even feeble clairvoyance, had definite uses.

Hulda paused, worry flickering like a lightning bug in her chest. "Merritt," she guessed.

The maid nodded.

The confirmation didn't surprise Hulda, but it weighed on her. "He was a little off at dinner."

"Not just at dinner, Miss Larkin." Miss Taylor's full lips tugged into a frown. "And not just the insomnia. I've sensed great trouble in him for a while now, even before the abduction. But yes, especially at dinner. The moment he saw Mr. Portendorfer . . . well, it felt like he'd slapped me with it."

Hulda pressed a hand to her stomach as though she might keep it from sinking. "Even before?"

She nodded.

Hulda leaned against the wall for support. "Everything that happened with Mr. Hogwood, Miss Mullan"—neither name she enjoyed saying, one being a murderer and the other Merritt's once-fiancée—"he seems to be handling it well enough."

Miss Taylor nodded. "Seems that way. But." She glanced over her shoulder again, as though needing to ensure herself the man of the house wasn't coming up the stairs. "That carefree attitude of his . . . it's a farce." She lowered her eyes as though ashamed. "There's something raw and hurting inside him. I try my best to cheer him up, but . . . I'm not sure what to do."

Hulda released a long, controlled breath. "I'm not sure, either." She glanced back to his bedroom, envisioning him there. Stuffing down feelings of uncertainty and inadequacy, worries that she wasn't enough for him, that he wasn't happy because of her, she milled about for reason and logic. "It's likely bad right now because of unfinished business. He needs to make amends back home."

Rolling her lips together, Miss Taylor tilted her head into a half nod.

Hulda pushed off the wall, standing straight. "Surely that will resolve something. This trip to Cattlecorn will be good for him." It had to be, else Hulda didn't know how to fix any of it. Fix this, fix BIKER, or fix this mess with Myra.

"I hope so," Miss Taylor murmured.

Hulda did not respond, for fear her doubts would leak into her tone and give her away completely.

Chapter 5

Merritt was not going to Cattlecorn.

He made the declaration after Hulda returned downstairs to announce Mr. Portendorfer's room was ready. She pushed away the urge to bite her nails—a nervous habit from childhood—and pasted on a smile for their guest. When that was done, she found Merritt retired to the sitting room upstairs, slumped in a wingback chair and staring out the window, though it was too dark to see anything beyond the glass. The sitting room was, in Hulda's opinion, the finest area of the house, which was probably why Merritt had retired to it now and why Owein, in his angry spiritual state, had guarded it so closely. It was matched well with colors of cinnamon, blush, and cream, unlike the garish green and burgundy of the living room downstairs. There was a bust of a laughing child beside the white-paneled fireplace, or at least there had been until Owein decided it was worth the side effects to change it once more. If Hulda recalled correctly, that bust's countenance had changed six times during her stay here. The worst had been the third iteration, which had included fangs, horns, and an oversized bowtie.

Worrying her hands, she entered, wondering how to broach the topic of Cattlecorn and Merritt's well-being, but Merritt spoke first.

"Stay the night, Hulda." His voice was low, soft. His eyes still watched the window. "You can bunk up with Beth if it makes you feel better."

The sight of him, the sound of him, eased into her like a mild tranquilizer, softening her backbone and shoulders. The night was dark and cold beyond the window. Dark enough that neither of them would be able to make out anything, save a distant lighthouse. "I suppose it is rather late."

"Yes, but I'll take you back to BIKER if you decide you'd prefer it."

She didn't respond immediately, instead taking a moment to study him. He had a good nose, not too large or small, and it widened slightly at the center of the bridge, adding character. His eyelashes were the same light brown as his hair, but when she got close enough, she could see how thick they were, how long. His hair looked more unkempt than usual, which meant he'd been running his fingers through it, something he did when he was troubled. His waistcoat hung over the settee—she didn't see his vest—leaving him in just his long-sleeved shirt, the collar of which was unbuttoned.

He glanced over, his blue eyes curious, tired, and deep, and Hulda chided herself for not seeing what Miss Taylor had. She shouldn't need clairvoyance to determine the man was bothered by his past, not just the life communing with him every night. She'd just been so absorbed with Myra and BIKER—

She crossed the room, grabbed a pink-upholstered armchair, and hauled it across the Indian rug so she could sit close and face him. "I'll go first thing in the morning. But why are you postponing Cattlecorn?"

Merritt grimaced, and she almost wished she hadn't asked. "Gifford, of course."

She frowned at him.

He sighed. "I have a few things to get in order first. Lost track of time."

Gifford was an excuse, and the remainder half truths at best. She debated pressing the issue, but he looked so exhausted. So worn down. "I can go with you, if you'd like. To Cattlecorn."

He raised an eyebrow, and the faintest, *genuine* smile touched his lips, sending a quiet thrill through her. "Traveling alone with a man to meet his family, eh?"

Hulda rolled her eyes. "We can, of course, include Mr. Portendorfer and even Miss Taylor. Not that anyone in Cattlecorn knows or cares who I am."

The smile lingered a moment before fading. "You've got this mess with BIKER."

"I'm sure the foreign affairs department can get along without me peeking over their shoulders." Though in truth, nerves built in her stomach like a swarm of gnats. How poorly would it reflect on her to take what would be excused as a sudden vacation when the institute was in such a poor state? "And Miss Steverus is capable," she added, though there was little gumption behind it.

"And if Myra responds? You wrote her all those letters in care of her friends."

She hesitated. "Well, we wouldn't be gone *too* long . . ." Though the idea filled her with discomfort.

He nodded, peeking out the window again. A silence—not an uncomfortable one—fell between them. The length of a few heartbeats before his gaze drifted back to her, watching long enough for Hulda to feel self-conscious.

She ran her tongue over her teeth, fearing something from dinner had gotten trapped there.

"You're beautiful," he said.

Her tongue died in her mouth. Heat filled her cheeks again—if she could have *one* wish, it would be to blush less! At least it made her match the draperies. She cleared her throat as quietly as she could manage. "A good attempt at changing the subject, but you'll have to do better."

He blinked. "Do better?"

She adjusted her glasses. "Something more believable, perhaps."

Wryness pinched the corners of his eyes. "Are you calling me a liar, Mrs. Larkin? Though I suppose it's *Miss*, now."

Hulda averted her eyes. "I said no such thing."

Merritt adjusted in his chair so his body faced hers. Leaning over, he planted his elbows on his knees. "I sense a challenge."

She gave him what she hoped was a withering look.

"You," he continued, unabashed, "are absolutely gorgeous when you flush."

Her heart thudded hard against her ribs at the forward statement. And, of course, her cheeks heated, earning her a mischievous grin from Merritt. She was so unaccustomed to compliments. At least, *these* kinds of compliments.

She swallowed to ready a retort, but Merritt pressed on.

"I've always wanted to run my fingers through your hair and see if it's as soft as it looks." He reached forward—Hulda had situated herself just close enough for him to do so—and plucked a single hairpin from her locks. Hulda froze, hot and cold at once, those gnats in her stomach multiplying a hundredfold, searching his face for . . . for *what*?

"When you're not monitoring yourself," he went on, "you have a very delightsome way of walking."

Her cheekbones were going to melt, her face was so hot. "M-Merritt—"

The expression on her face must have been something else, for Merritt chuckled and straightened. "I'm sorry, Hulda. You make it so easy."

She huffed because she didn't know what else to do. "Easy to tease?"

"Is it teasing if it's true?"

She squared her shoulders. "You are a poor judge—"

"I am an excellent judge of all things," he intercepted, hooking his foot around the leg of her chair and tugging her closer. He rose from his seat and put his hands on her armrests, his face hovering intimately close to hers. "And I'll not have you challenging that. Not under my roof."

He leaned forward and brushed his lips across hers, and in that heated moment, Hulda believed every word he'd said. The scents of ink, cloves, and petitgrain filled her senses, and a weak part of her—the part she had chained up and locked away because it hurt her otherwise—pulsed with jubilation and *want*.

Despite his forwardness, his lips were chaste—a good thing, since Hulda wasn't sure what she would have done if they were not. He pulled back and smiled at her.

"I'm going to see if Baptiste needs anything. Don't stay up too late." It was a joke, of course—Hulda kept pristine night hours. Still, as Merritt exited the room, not bothering to take his coat or vest with him, Hulda found herself comfortably rooted to her chair, so entranced by his words and his touch she could hardly remember the reason for approaching him in the first place.

Hulda passed the coin over to the postmaster's assistant after writing down a short and vague message to be delivered to Jamestown. Myra had a niece in Jamestown, so perhaps she was holing up there. Hulda could only hope. If Myra were to reply, she might not send word directly to BIKER. Perhaps to Whimbrel House. The next time Hulda saw Miss Taylor, she'd have to ask her to keep an eye out for it.

Stepping outside, Hulda pulled her navy mantle close and breathed in the crisp air. The sky was gray today, casting Boston in dreary light. She wondered if Myra was looking at the same skies, or if she'd traveled somewhere warm. Perhaps she *had* defected to Spain . . . With some sleuthing, Hulda might be able to find an address. But anything she might find at BIKER, the foreign affairs department would also find. Had Myra known LIKER would come? That they would look for her?

Had she actually been embezzling? Perhaps all this nonsense was tied to money schemes, and the telegram had not referred to Mr. Hogwood at all. But if not him, who?

Hulda considered this as she made her way back to BIKER. Perhaps Myra wouldn't answer anything so official as a letter or a telegram—something delivered by a person who could later identify her.

A windsource pigeon, maybe. They were expensive, but Hulda was getting antsy. What if Myra wasn't simply lying low, but was hurt? Sick? Sickness was what had gotten her into this conundrum in the first place—it had been her motivation for reaching out to an infamous necromancer for a cure. What if Mr. Hogwood's administrations hadn't been complete?

If nothing else, Hulda didn't want to leave their relationship on such a sour note. She hadn't spoken to Myra directly since berating her in her bedroom, seething that she would never forgive her if Merritt died. Then she'd stolen her horse.

The telegram weighed down her pocket, reminding Hulda that she wasn't the only one searching for Myra Haigh.

∽

Merritt wouldn't have realized he was dozing off if that damnable red maple outside the house hadn't woken him with *Faaaaallllllll.*

He tried very hard not to make his sleepiness obvious as James Gifford drawled on from a book of essays on magic. He'd finished the one on communion—which had only covered the various recorded spells under its umbrella and provided no insights into turning the magic *off*—and moved on to wardship, covering everything from the foundation of the magic to well-known users, spells, theories, and blah, blah, blah.

Even Owein had curled into a ball in the corner of Merritt's office, muzzle resting on his right leg. Merritt hadn't related the true nature of the dog to his teacher. For some reason, it felt safer to keep that private.

He pushed his thoughts toward Owein. *If I have to suffer through this, so do you.*

The dog didn't stir.

Merritt tried again. *Owein. Can you hear me?*

Nothing. He tried once more, this time letting instinct guide him. The thought seemed to push out from his forehead in a strange, slightly draining way. *I never should have signed up for this.*

Owein lifted his head. *Told you* I *could teach you.*

Merritt smirked. He'd never spoken *to* Owein using communion, only listened. Owein had no communion spells; he simply spoke "dog," or whatever the mental or silent version of "dog" was. All the translating came from Merritt's end. *You don't have communion spells.*

You don't need help with communion spells. He sniffed. *See? You're doing it just fine.*

If only that were true. Side effects tickled Merritt's throat, and he tried to clear it without interrupting Gifford. He wondered how much of the bookish drawl he'd missed. Would he be tested on it later? If so, he'd have to confess why he hadn't been paying attention. Then again, as long as the man got paid, did it really matter?

"Mr. Fernsby?"

He startled and turned toward Gifford. "Yes?"

"You said it ignited when you heard a story about your friend being in a dangerous situation, yes?"

It took Merritt a moment to piece together what the older man was asking. "Oh, yes." His wardship spell, which had sent Hulda on a wild-goose chase all over the house, searching for the source. For a time, she'd believed it to be the tourmaline beneath the foundation. In truth, Merritt had unwittingly activated the spell after Hulda had confided in him about Silas Hogwood. The magic had been enacted again while he was fighting the man, but Merritt didn't relate either story. He had no loyalties to Myra Haigh, but until Hulda was ready, not a chirp would escape him in regard to Silas Hogwood.

Gifford wrote something in a ledger that already had three pages of notes in it. "I wonder."

Stretching his back, Merritt asked, "Wonder what?"

"If it's tied to your protective instincts," he explained. "Seems that way, given these examples, and it's not uncommon for men. But you say there's been no evidence of chaocracy?"

"It's in the family line, but . . ." He shrugged. "I'm more concerned with the communion."

Gifford nodded. "It's not uncommon for magic to skip like that." He seemed not to hear the rest. "Magic subtracts with every generation unless it has other magic of the same discipline to add to, and sometimes it's finnicky still. In the same way two blue-eyed parents might have a green-eyed son."

"I'm aware." He stifled a yawn, not wanting to be rude. He was just so tired. "But I had someone tell me it was in there . . . somewhere."

"Oh? A psychometrist?"

Merritt blinked. "Something like that." He assumed it must have been a psychometry spell that had allowed Silas Hogwood to look into his blood and decipher the latent spells there.

He glanced to Owein. Perhaps not his blood so much as his spirit. Owein's blood and body were long gone, but his magic remained indefinitely tied to his soul. Thinking of it that way, Merritt felt retrospectively exposed. How much had Silas seen before he died?

Gifford scrawled another note. "There's an empathy spell in the school of psychometry that allows the reading of magic in others. Quite rare, actually. Who told you?"

That answered that question. Merritt glanced at Owein, who offered nothing. "A . . . fortune-teller on Market Street. In passing. Might have been loony—I shouldn't put too much stock in it."

"Huh." Gifford considered for a moment, then wrote another note. "Interesting. I wonder if the person was a recent immigrant; I can't think of any empaths of the sort registered in the state."

Owein laid his head back down. The floorboards near him began to ripple. Chaocracy, the manipulation of chaos. Or, when chaos was abundant, the manipulation of order.

Bad dog! Merritt shot.

I'm boooooored.

Then go outside!

It's coooold.

So help me, I will sell you to this man as a science experiment. How would you like that?

Merritt's right ear rang—another side effect of communion. He stuck a pinkie in it. Owein whined, and the floorboards settled before Gifford lifted his head.

"Excellent. We're making great progress."

Merritt leaned on his fist. "Are we?"

Gifford nodded. "Let me read you this most excellent essay on chaocracy . . . that is, unless you'd like me to leave it for you?"

Merritt straightened. Anything to make the torment end. "Yes, that would be best. But in your own studies, have you come across anything about controlling commu—"

A soft knock sounded on the door. Merritt paused. "Yes, Miss Taylor?"

Beth opened the door and stuck in her head. "Sorry to interrupt, but might I have leave for the rest of the day? I've been summoned to Boston."

Merritt stood. "BIKER?"

She nodded. "I assume LIKER wants to question me."

Merritt pressed his lips together. While Miss Taylor *had* witnessed Silas Hogwood's attack on Merritt, she hadn't had any interactions with Myra Haigh during that time . . . other than being assigned to Whimbrel House, and that had been handled by Hulda. "If they want to bother you so badly, they should come here."

Beth smiled. "I don't mind."

Sighing, Merritt pushed his hands into his pockets. "All right. Mr. Gifford, I don't suppose you would mind seeing my maid to the mainland safely? You can leave the essay here. And do bring me anything you can conjure up on communion, if you would."

Gifford closed his ledger. "Wouldn't that be a spell! A conjurist who could summon information." He chuckled. "But I would be delighted. In fact, I would love to learn more about you, Miss Taylor. Everything about the Boston Institute intrigues me."

Beth offered him a small curtsy. "I'll gather my things, then. Just in case it goes long."

The next morning, Merritt found himself pacing from the dining room, through the camber top entryway, into the reception hall, then into the living room, and back. Owein had taken to following him for a time, then got bored and lay by the beveled oak stairs with his head resting on the first step. Baptiste occasionally popped out of the kitchen, his hairy arms floured up to his elbows, and peered out the large dining room window.

Beth hadn't come home last night.

She'd mentioned the meeting might go long, but she hadn't taken much with her, and BIKER had windsource pigeons—birds enchanted to fly at near bullet speeds—did it not? Not so hard to send word. Merritt had even tried his selenite communion stone with Hulda, which she'd finally answered around eight, saying she was unaware Beth had come to Boston and would check up on her. There hadn't been a single update since. Merritt was likely overthinking things, but his stomach didn't feel good and his limbs had too much energy. Hence the pacing.

I should work on my articles, he said to himself. *I'm acting like an overprotective father.*

Not that he had any experience with such.

Sssssshhhhheeeeeee, the reeds whispered distantly. Merritt tripped on his feet and spun around.

"There she is." Baptiste's low and heavily accented voice pierced the quiet of the house. Merritt turned on his toe and hurried to the dining room window, where the Frenchman, even leaning against the glass, stood a full head taller than he.

Sure enough, a feminine figure was picking her way through the wilting reeds. The bright, autumnal sun reflected off the frost coating the island, making it hurt his eyes to look so far. When he squinted, he noticed a new boat at the dock before identifying the familiar silhouette.

"It's Hulda." He pushed his way to the front door and wrenched it open. Sans coat, he sprinted out to meet her. Worries crowded his head. Hulda wasn't really one to do a surprise visit, nor was she one to jog. Merritt met her halfway up the path, his breath clouding around his mouth.

"To what do I owe the pleasure?" he asked, but the attempt at mirth melted when Hulda met his eyes and he saw the strain around hers.

"Miss Taylor," she answered, breathless. "She's been transferred."

Chapter 6

Owein's tail thumped against the matted, curling grass as he watched Merritt and Hulda board their separate boats. He knew dogs wagged their tails when they were excited—he did it, too, out of an otherly sort of instinct—but this wagging was about nerves and the need for movement. He felt so cold and unsure. The wagging helped keep the darkness at bay, too. He didn't feel it or see it as much when he gave in to his dog side.

The dog hadn't been left alone in a house for decades on end.

The decision to leave for Boston had been made so quickly Owein had barely followed it. He'd heard harsh whispers, which had changed into sharp voices. At first, he'd thought Hulda and Merritt were fighting, but they weren't. Merritt was mad because of what she'd told him. Baptiste had . . . what was it Merritt called it? Brooded. He'd brooded darkly by the window, so darkly Owein could smell it, just like he could smell the traces of manure on Hulda's shoes and soap on Merritt's shirt cuffs. And suddenly Merritt had a bag on his shoulder and Hulda was leaving as quickly as she'd come, and the sun wasn't even at its peak yet, and *Beth was gone.*

That's what the others were doing—going to get Beth. Miss Taylor. But what if she didn't come back? Owein loved Beth. He remembered little pieces of his mother—not much, but pieces—and a lot of those pieces were in Beth. And she always tucked him in at night and snuck him morsels at mealtime and scratched behind his ears, which were somehow always itchy. Always opened the door when he had to use the bathroom, even if she chided him about tracking mud in afterward.

And suddenly she was gone, and now Merritt and Hulda were leaving, and *what if none of them came back?*

If they didn't come back, Owein would be alone again.

The darkness lurked. He wagged his tail harder.

He turned back to the house. Baptiste was still there. But if Beth and Hulda and Merritt didn't come home, wouldn't he leave, too? He wouldn't have a job anymore, right? Grown-ups always went where their jobs took them . . .

A soft whine came up Owein's throat. He refocused on the bay, watching the two boats get smaller and smaller. *Please come back. Please come back. Please come back.*

Please come back before I leave, too.

Because Merritt was right. Owein's years were numbered.

And all of it made him feel so alone.

◡◡

"Beth Taylor is *my* employee," Merritt said forcefully over the desk. Miss Megan Richards was perched where Miss Sadie Steverus ought to be. "*I* pay her wages. *I* house her. And no one here thought to notify me?"

He was dangerously close to yelling. The only thing that kept his vocal cords in check was Hulda's fingertips pressing into the inside of his elbow, not quite holding him back but promising to if he got ahead of himself.

Miss Richards, the Englishwoman with a luck penchant, fumbled with random paperwork on the desk. "Miss Taylor is an employee of BIKER—"

"She's a *contractor* for BIKER," Merritt snapped. "And *you are not BIKER.*"

The woman's lip quivered slightly, and guilt wove between his ribs.

Behind him, a male voice said, "Indeed, and yet BIKER is not anything until we reform it, Mr. Fernsby."

Merritt spun around to see the lawyer, Alastair Baillie, emerging from a room into the hallway.

"And?" Merritt asked, fire curling in his gut. "That's supposed to make my other points moot?"

Baillie fixed his pocket square. "There's a home in Canada that was built of magicked materials, and the value just skyrocketed. Now the previous owner wants it back from the individual he sold it to, and the issue has gone to court."

Merritt glowered. "I think we're having two different conversations."

Baillie removed his glasses and cleaned them with said pocket square. "We need a clairvoyant to help with the testimonies."

The nonchalance with which the Englishman delivered the information made Merritt's knuckles itch to connect with his nose. "A clairvoyant who is employed in the American housing market needs to be available to the Canadian court system?"

Baillie frowned. "Not that you would understand, Mr. Fernsby, but wizards of any type are rare and valuable. LIKER oversees BIKER, and BIKER oversees the entirety of North America, not merely the States. When special situations arise, it is our duty to find from the network the magical worker best suited to fulfill them. Miss Taylor went willingly."

"And decided not to send so much as a pigeon," Merritt countered. It wasn't like Beth to simply up and disappear without letting others know of her whereabouts.

Thiiiiiiirst, the plant in the corner whined. Merritt ignored it.

"Speaking of Whimbrel House—which is your abode, is it not?" As he strode near, Hulda inched closer to Merritt's side. "I can't find the file on it."

"Oh." Hulda reached into her bag. "That is, I have it. I meant to replace it."

And mark that the house is no longer enchanted, Merritt thought. She hadn't, yet. Her way of buying time. Not surprising. He wished he could speak to her mind the way he did to Owein's, but human-to-human mental communication fell under psychometry, not communion.

Hulda handed Baillie the file, which he tucked under his arm. "You do have the legal right to protest, of course," Baillie went on, face slack like it'd been sculpted by a bored artist, "but it cannot be formally done until BIKER is reorganized. Might I suggest you stay out of the way so that our work might be finished sooner rather than later?"

If Merritt had hackles, they would have risen at the statement. And this guy was a candidate for Myra's replacement? If Baillie took the job, Merritt would thank the Lord that Whimbrel House was now an ordinary home and he'd have no reason to ever interact with the man again.

Though he still might, with Hulda being employed here. Unless he could convince her to switch jobs or leave the field altogether, but he highly doubted she'd be keen on either idea.

"Seventy years," Merritt muttered.

Baillie raised an eyebrow. "Pardon?"

Merritt folded his arms. "Seventy years since the United States became a sovereign nation, with its own rules and laws. Remind me, again, which American university you got your degree from?"

Baillie offered a closed-lip smile that barely tilted his lips enough to be called one and pressed past Merritt, heading in the direction of the library, if Merritt remembered correctly. Drawing in a deep breath, Merritt turned for the stairs. Paused and glanced back to Miss Richards. "Water that damn plant." He jerked a thumb toward the fern and took the stairs down, Hulda close behind him. She didn't speak until they reached the main floor.

"You need to control yourself," she murmured. "People don't respond well to vitriol."

Merritt turned to her. "I wasn't using vitriol. I was being *clear*." He shook his head, then rubbed his temples. "Are you not *angry?*"

"I am." The cords in her neck looked ready to snap. "Of course I am. But I have to handle everything carefully for the sake of the position."

Merritt sighed. "Walker wasn't even around."

"*Mr.* Walker doesn't live in a bubble. Both Miss Richards and Mr. Baillie report to him." She pressed a knuckle into her chin, thought for a moment, then dropped her arms. "It's just . . . I saw Beth as she was leaving. She *did* go willingly." That much she'd explained earlier. "But she seemed confused."

Merritt rubbed his eyes. He was so tired. Worry over Beth had only added to the nightly discourse that kept him awake. "I would have been, too. She came here expecting she might be gone overnight, not forever."

"Not forever. But . . ." Hulda clicked her tongue. "I don't know how to say it. *Very* confused." Huffing, she put her hands on her hips.

Merritt hesitated. "Like chaocracy confused?"

Hulda scoffed. "No. It's . . . hard to explain. She seemed focused, but as though she had a headache or perhaps an attack of vertigo, although she *did* walk straight. Couldn't spare a moment to chat, even though it's most unlike her to be brusque . . . See what I mean? I can't properly express it. If I were Myra, I could just *show* you what I meant. Replay it. Or if she were here, she could do it for me."

"No such luck." He kept his voice low, so as not to be overheard. "If Myra were here, Beth would be, too."

"Myra would have sent Beth away as well, if the case were truly urgent. Perhaps she was just eager to get to her assignment."

"Maybe. I can't help but think the whole thing seems suspicious." He forced his shoulders to relax. "No news?"

Hulda shook her head. "Unfortunately, no, but I've sent out a few more missives. It might take several days to reap anything from them."

Merritt wiped his hand down his face. "Thanks for alerting me. I should really invest in a telegraph, or another communion stone. Or a pigeon. Though I think the former would last longer." He paused. "And I wouldn't have to feed it."

A corner of her mouth ticked up, which allayed some of Merritt's simmering frustration. "Notwithstanding, I believe you owe Baptiste a cow."

He chuckled. "That was if my second novel does well, not if I finished it. Perhaps for Christmas." He moved toward the exit. When she did not join him, he stopped. Tried to push the frustration aside, or at least ignore it for the time being. "Hulda, let's go out."

She blinked. "I have some assignments from Mr. Walker—"

"Tonight, then." He cupped her shoulders. Cattlecorn aside, Beth aside, he still had Hulda. *He still had Hulda.* "We can't control LIKER and we can't control Beth, but . . . let's do something fun." An idea sprung to mind. "We passed an ice pond on the way here." It wasn't quite cold enough for a pond to freeze over, but the water was shallow and enchanted by a Canadian elementist, or so he'd heard.

Hulda tensed. "I haven't skated in a very long time . . . and it's hardly appropriate."

"Appropriate! It's fine—people are loosening up, you know. Or let's go . . . buy soup or something." He shrugged. "After work. I have some errands to run in Boston, anyway." Especially now that he didn't have an employee taking care of the grocery list. "I'll wait for you."

She searched his eyes, and the lip tilt climbed higher. He could see the shift in her countenance when she decided to give in. "All right. I'll meet you here at five."

A little bit of the tension in his chest untwined. Merritt picked up her hand and kissed her second knuckle. "Five it is."

∾

Hulda, having decided to be brave, agreed to the ice-skating when Merritt returned for her. They had never really done anything pertaining to routine courtship, unless one considered fighting for one's life in a dank basement routine courtship. No man had ever bothered to court her before. She'd never been asked to a dance, or to dinner, or even on a carriage ride. And thus the idea of ice-skating seemed very romantic, even if Hulda was wildly out of practice.

However, once they arrived at the large, she dared say *pharaonic*, pond already crowded with several dozen people—none were Myra, for she'd gotten into the habit of checking whenever she was out—and Hulda strapped on the skates Merritt had collected for her, she realized the horrible mistake she had made.

She was going to make a buffoon of herself.

Merritt grasped her elbows as she stood. "Easy. Just walk normally."

His warmth somehow seeped through her coat, chasing away some of the November chill. The sun had set, and twilight was half-faded away, but tall lamps around the pond—all enchanted by a German conjurist—had been lit, casting flickering halos over cobblestones and skaters alike. They stood at the edge of one such halo, and the glimmer made a few of Merritt's hairs look blond. If he was going to protest the social normative and wear his tresses long, he should really tie them at the nape of his neck and pretend to be a proper gentleman, and yet Hulda had grown quite accustomed to the carefree way they sat on his shoulders, just a little too long to dust them.

"One does not walk normally in these devices," she countered. She was ready to plead her case, to declare herself unfit for the activity and beg they do soup instead, when she glanced over Merritt's shoulder to the other skaters. Several of them were couples, gliding closely together, leaning inward to converse. Holding hands.

Heaven knew she wanted that. She'd wanted that all her life.

Steeling herself, she pushed one foot in front of another, hiding her trepidation, and let Merritt step onto the pond first. He certainly had his balance down. But that was for the better, wasn't it? It would be far worse to skate with someone equally as clumsy as herself.

Her first step on the ice held, but her second slipped. She teetered hard to the right before Merritt looped an arm around her waist to keep her upright. But the relief at not falling right on her bottom was quickly replaced by the acknowledgment of their bodies pressed together. Even the waltz wasn't so close!

Her face heated, which she supposed was a good thing, given the cold. There were eyes about, and her mind invented several more pairs glaring right at her. "Perhaps this isn't the best idea." Especially at a mixed-sex rink.

He grinned—he genuinely grinned, and Hulda recalled what Beth had said the other day about his state of mind. Perhaps it wasn't so bad as they feared. "No one is watching us. Why would they? Everyone is too concerned with which direction their own toes are pointing."

She supposed he had a point. Biting her bottom lip, Hulda allowed Merritt to pull her onto the pond. She clamped her hands on to his forearm.

He laughed. "I don't want to patronize you, but would you like some tips?"

She nodded, too focused to speak.

"Worry about your center, not your limbs." He put his arms around her again and patted her corset, which did indeed make her *very* aware of her center. "Bend your knees. Don't push your feet straight forward. Angle out a little. Like a *V*."

He pushed forward, holding her tightly. She watched his feet and copied them, slipping several times. Thank goodness the sun was down enough to hide the burn of embarrassment. But Merritt moved slowly, and he didn't move his less-than-appropriate arm from her waist until she got her balance under control. Once that was set, he linked their arms together, offering a little more support than a simple handhold would.

"You're a natural," he said after half an hour of slow laps around the pond.

She snorted. "I am skilled at many things, but very few of them are physical."

"Perhaps we'll try dancing next time."

A bubble of happiness filled her chest. She glanced up at him for a second before wobbling and turning her gaze back to the ice. "I would like that."

They skated for another half an hour. A wayward child nearly toppled both of them, but it was an overall enjoyable experience, nonetheless. Though, as Hulda removed her skates after, she feared her ankles would be quite sore come morning.

Merritt laced his fingers with hers as he walked her back to the Bright Bay Hotel, sticking her hand in his coat pocket for extra warmth. She wanted to lean on his shoulder as they strolled, but perhaps that would be too forward of her, and what if Mr. Walker had worked late and came out as they neared BIKER? Hulda could imagine the conversation. *Miss Larkin? Did you not say Mr. Fernsby was a client of BIKER? It isn't appropriate to be so familiar with him—*

Her eyes scanned the street ahead of them, looking for familiar faces, ready to disengage should she spot one. "Do you need help finding someone else?"

It took a beat for him to catch her meaning. "To replace Beth? No. I'm sure Baptiste and I can clean up after ourselves." He sighed. "I do hope she's all right, though. I suppose it might be better for her to move on, with the enchantments gone."

"The enchantments are still there, just in a different form. A form I do believe Miss Taylor is fond of. Regardless, she has a good head on her shoulders. I conjecture she'll be just fine." They reached the entrance, and she stepped back to let Merritt open the back door of the building, pulling her hand from his warm grip at the same time. Once inside, her coat felt too warm, while her nose was half-frozen. "I'm sure it's not her first instance of sudden transferring. We've all dealt with it."

"Even you?" he asked as they walked toward her room.

Hulda scanned the hallways and listened to the stairs. Saw and heard nothing. It seemed the hotel was empty, or at the very least, her LIKER colleagues had turned in for the night. The men would be on another floor, and Miss Richards seemed like someone who preferred to go out. That gave Hulda some confidence in their privacy. "Yes, rather recently, in fact. I'd just come home from a long stint in Canada myself, only to be assigned to some wayward place in the middle of Narragansett Bay. The owner was quite dreadful."

Merritt chuckled, but she didn't miss how he muffled a yawn. "I've met him and must agree."

They reached her room. The hallway was poorly lit, though the seventh hour had only just chimed. Hulda turned toward him; he ran his palms down her arms.

"How many of these rooms are being used?" he asked.

"Very few." And a good thing, or she would have needed to say goodbye to him at the back door.

"I enjoyed this," he murmured.

The bubble expanded, and she felt like a young girl again. "I did, too."

Leaning close so their foreheads brushed, he said, "I miss you."

Her pulse quickened. She couldn't imagine any man, let alone this man, saying such words sincerely. Not to her. Yet here they were, and a silly sliver of herself wondered if this was all a strange ruse. Like Merritt might erupt with laughter at any moment, and someone—Mr. Portendorfer, perhaps—might burst from one of the quiet rooms and say, *We got you good, Miss Larkin!*

Fortunately, neither incident happened.

"We've managed to see each other," she tried.

"I suppose." He tilted his head and pressed his lips to hers, sending her pulse galloping like a racing horse let through its starting gate. His lips were soft and warm, or at least warmer than hers, and little spikes of excitement lanced up her jaw and down her neck. His hand came behind her head, cradling it, like he wanted to kiss more of her, and Hulda wasn't precisely sure how to let him—or if they even should. That is, they'd only declared themselves to one another not quite two weeks ago. Was there a rule to such a thing? And this *was* a place of work, even if the offices were all on the top floor . . .

She didn't have long to fuss over it, for Merritt's lips moved from hers to her jaw, and those spikes intensified. She felt as though she'd skated miles around that pond.

He kissed below her ear.

"Merritt." She was alarmed at how breathy her voice sounded. At how titillating his administrations to her were becoming.

"Hm?" He pressed his lips to her neck, and her body jumped to life, sending her thoughts into very indecent places cloaked in shadow. That was the only reason she could fathom for why the next words slipped from her mouth.

"I'm not going to sleep with you."

Merritt froze. The hand on the back of her head went lax. He raised his head to meet her eyes. "What?"

Heart hammering, she scrambled, "That is, I know you have . . . I mean to say—"

"I never asked you to." He pulled away, and regret painted the inside of Hulda's everything. The light was so dim, but was that hurt or anger in his blue eyes? Perhaps it was both.

She swallowed. "I didn't mean it like that."

A single dry chuckle came up his throat. "How else could you have meant it, Hulda?"

Her mind scrambled for an answer. *It's just that I'm a virgin and I know you're not, but I know I shouldn't have brought it up and I'm digging into that hurt and why did I say that—*

He ran his hand back through his hair. "I'm not some coital maniac. I didn't take you out to get under your skirts."

Her cheeks blazed. "I-I know that, but—"

"But what?" He took another step back, distancing himself from her. Her bones seemed to shrink inside her body. "I'm sorry. I shouldn't have said it."

He looked away. "Even if you hadn't said it, you would have thought it."

A rush of cold cooled her skin. "No—"

"I should go." He adjusted his coat.

She wrung her gloves over her hands. "A-All right." Her thoughts struggled to order themselves. "P-Perhaps I could stop by this weekend, and—"

"Don't bother."

His voice was so soft, not sharp at all, but it sliced through her, nonetheless. Without looking at her, he added, "I need to go to New York, anyway. Might as well pack now."

"Right." She spoke a little too loudly in an attempt to keep rising emotion from her voice. "Right. With Mr. Portendorfer." Had they arranged to leave again already?

He glanced at her, and she wished for a candle to better read his expression. "Good night, Hulda."

He strode away without further ado. Hulda watched him go, listened for the opening and closing of the door before pushing her way into her room and pressing a fist into the popped bubble in her chest, blinking away tears of shame.

༄

The coach rattled as it pulled close to town. No kinetic trams ran through the small town Merritt had grown up in. His elbow hurt from being propped up against the narrow windowsill on the far end of the cab, but he didn't move it. There were no curtains for privacy, so he just stared at the passing scenery. Had been staring at it this whole time, even though he was tired. He'd never been good at sleeping in carriages. On the bright side, the thing moved fast enough that—thus far—none of the wildlife had tried to talk to him. Not that it mattered if he went mute. He'd hardly spoken a word since boarding.

The coach had filled along its route, then emptied again, save for one other soul—an older woman in a posh violet dress who sat as far away from him and Fletcher as she could possibly get. Fletcher, across from him, had remained relatively quiet. He lived in Boston, so Merritt had saved the postage and marched straight to his friend's home after the ordeal with Hulda, spewing his readiness to get away. Fletcher was an agreeable sort, but he'd insisted they at least wait until after working hours the following day to leave.

Merritt had met Fletcher in Boston before sunset the next afternoon, desperate to be away and yet wishing he'd never made the promise to go.

Right now, Fletcher was resting his eyes. Not sleeping. Fletcher's mouth did a weird thing when he slept, regardless of whether it was prostrate on a bed or upright on a hard, jolting bench. At the moment, his mouth looked perfectly normal.

Merritt was sick with thinking. Thinking about Ebba, thinking about Myra, thinking about Sutcliffe and his mother and his father and Cattlecorn. About Hulda. Despite his silent pleas, his mind had fixated on the tangled mess, stretching it out and braiding it into knots, and there was little inside the cramped vehicle that could distract him from it.

Hulda's words still chafed, though a good night's rest had helped. How could she think so little of his character? *I'm not going to sleep with you.* Might as well have castrated him right there.

Of course, it wasn't her fault those simple words had affected him so. Maybe Hulda had only meant to warn him . . . but warn him from *what?* All Merritt wanted was to love her, and to show her he loved her because he knew she doubted herself. He could see it in her eyes and the twist of her mouth, in her stance. Hear it in her carefully curated words and unsure tone.

Hulda made him happy, and he'd like to think he made her happy, but God help him, while he knew that instant in that hotel hallway was less than a blip in the scrolls of the universe, it had cut deep. Lucifer's hell, he'd made a mistake—a monumental one—but it had been only *one time.* The pain of everything tied to that day had more than scared him away from the sporting district during his long bachelorhood, and he'd never gotten close enough to another woman to even have the opportunity.

He sighed, and his breath left a film on the window. Maybe after he slept on it again, he'd be able to internalize Hulda's apology, which had seemed genuine, because this was a stupid thing to wallow over. All of it was stupid. *He* was stupid.

And he would rather be anywhere right then than that coach, because it took a fork in the road and there was Cattlecorn, just as he remembered it, and heaven help him, he was going to vomit on his shoes.

"Merritt."

He glanced at Fletcher.

His friend leaned forward and knit his dark hands together. "You're far away."

Finally pulling his sore elbow from the window, Merritt rubbed his eyes. "Wish I were."

"Do you want to stop by my house first? Mom will be happy to see you."

But Merritt shook his head. The sooner he got this over with, the better. "I'll get off by the school and meet you tonight." The constable's office was near there, and Nelson Sutcliffe should be in by now—Fletcher had said the man was still constable, or at least he had been on Fletcher's last visit home. Beth *had* sent that letter, as she'd been instructed, before Merritt could change his mind about it. For better or for worse. After speaking with his biological father, he'd swing by his . . . his old house, and . . .

That line of thinking thickened into a ridge, and he couldn't push his thoughts beyond it.

Leaning forward, Fletcher clapped him on the shoulder. "I'll wait up for you, all right? You have someplace to go. Don't forget that."

Merritt nodded, though in truth, he didn't really hear the promise.

The coach drove away, and Merritt's mouth dried to cracking. He could hear the sound of distant children at the school, but otherwise the area was quiet. Shoving his hands into his pockets, he walked with wooden legs, his knees hinges in need of oil. He blinked, and half the road was gone behind him. He didn't remember walking so far.

This would be tricky—Sutcliffe's office was attached to his house, and Merritt hadn't said precisely *when* he would be coming . . . or had he? He'd drafted four different letters to Nelson Sutcliffe, and now he couldn't recall which one Beth had mailed and which he'd fed to the fire. Regardless, he hadn't set off for Cattlecorn when he had originally intended, so the point was moot.

Think of sleep, he told himself. *Get answers, get sleep.*

He didn't know the constable well. He recalled running into him at the post office once as a youth, and the man had tipped his hat and then chided him for recklessness. He remembered the Barleys' wagon breaking a wheel near the mercantile and Sutcliffe helping move it to the side of the road . . . All in all, Merritt would never have guessed the man was his sire . . . but then again, maybe he wasn't, and all these records and such were wrong.

Cuuuuuurrrrrrl, the grass at the side of the road whined.

Merritt arrived at the house. Sure enough, the west door was labeled *CONSTABLE*. He stood and stared at it for a long time, until he heard someone on horseback coming up the road. Not wishing to be seen unnecessarily, he knocked and opened the door.

The space inside was cramped but adequate, with a desk that appeared to have been made by a novice carpenter. There were narrow shelves behind it that again made Merritt think of the post office, and then a table scattered with a few knickknacks. A door opposite him led into the rest of the house.

Nelson Sutcliffe, notably older now, glanced up from behind the table. He had dark hair—Merritt's was light, like his mother's—and a more prominent jaw than Merritt. But the harder Merritt looked, the more similarities he saw. The set of Sutcliffe's eyes, though not the color, and his nose . . . their noses were exactly the same. Maybe he was imagining it—

"Can I help you?" Nelson Sutcliffe set a paper aside and stood. "Hope there isn't trouble in . . ." He paused, looking Merritt over. His forehead creased, but his lips tilted just a little. "Merritt Fernsby. You sure have grown."

Merritt's fingertips, embedded in his pockets once more, pressed into his thighs. "Did you get my letter?"

That smile broadened slightly, but the rest of the man fell. "I did, I did." He came around the desk. "Come, let's go inside."

Merritt eyed the other door. "Your family—"

"Wife is shopping, and the kids are grown," he said.

Merritt froze. Why hadn't he thought of that? *Kids.* He had half siblings. *Family.* Mind racing, he tried to recall the Sutcliffe children. Their names, what they looked like . . .

He numbly followed the constable into the house, through a tidy kitchen, and into a modest sitting room. Sutcliffe sat down on the end of a yellow sofa. Merritt hovered near the door.

Sutcliffe chuckled. "I'm not going to eat you."

He lowered himself into the farthest chair, displacing a cat when he did so. *Hate,* it spat. *Hate.*

Merritt stared after the feline, wondering if he should apologize, but the cat continued on its way, disappearing down the hall. "Your children," he managed.

The smile returned. "All boys. Newton, Thaddeus, Hiram."

The names were familiar. One of them had been in his year at school. Merritt could recall where the boy had sat—behind him and to the left—but had it been Newton or Thad?

"No portraits in here, but . . ."

"But I can't talk to them, anyway, right?" Merritt's voice wasn't bitter, just . . . dead.

Sutcliffe leaned his elbows on his knees. "They don't know. Mary doesn't know, either."

So Merritt couldn't even approach them. Say, *We're brothers,* and cobble together a part of his family he hadn't known he'd lost.

Sutcliffe broke the silence. "I'm surprised you sorted it out. How—"

"Were you ever going to tell me?" Merritt spoke around a growing lump in his throat.

The smile fell. "No." A deep breath. "Rose"—Merritt's mother—"asked for my silence. I respected her wish to let Peter raise you as his own . . . I hoped he would accept you."

"You didn't fool him," was all Merritt could say. While Merritt's father—stepfather?—had never outright beaten him, he'd been dissatisfied with Merritt from the start. Merritt had always figured it was because he was a son and his father preferred daughters. Like that somehow made sense.

Peter Fernsby had always been kind to his sisters.

"Didn't think I did." Sutcliffe made a fist under his chin. "Peter never liked me. Wasn't meant to be."

Merritt scoffed. Silence returned for several seconds. His stomach was lead and his bones were glass. "Care to tell me what happened with Anita?" Seeing Sutcliffe's blank expression, he added, "My grandmother?"

"Oh. Yes. That house out in the bay." He nodded. "It's been in my line for ages. No one ever did anything about it. It was out of the way and"—he chuckled—"*haunted*."

An image of Whimbrel House came to Merritt's mind unbidden. The yellow-hued structure sat in late-morning sunlight, which accentuated its even blue shingles and bright, mismatched windows. Wild grasses and flowers surrounded its foundation, and the white railing stretching across its porch guarded its four-paneled cherrywood door. In truth, despite all that led to his receiving it, that house had been and was a blessing in his life. It was his safe haven. It had led him to Hulda or, rather, led Hulda to him. It had opened his eyes to magic and given him a place to think and recover and simply *be*.

"But I wanted to contribute somehow," Sutcliffe was saying. "I was . . . I still had a responsibility toward you. Thought if nothing else, the land had to be worth something. Rose didn't want it tied to her, so I gave it to her mother. Nice woman."

"She's dead," Merritt quipped.

"Ah." Sutcliffe adjusted on the sofa. "We used the guise of gambling, like I lost it in a game of cards, you know? To hide it from your father."

Merritt stared at the old carpet under his feet, tracing patterns in its worn threads.

"How is it?" Sutcliffe asked.

"Good. It's . . . good." He should thank him, but his tongue wouldn't form the words. Merritt rubbed his hands together, trying to warm cold fingers. "How?" he managed. He knew he should be asking about the magic, but there was so much more he wanted to know. So many scabs picked that needed balm.

"How what?"

"How did you and my mother . . ." He avoided eye contact. "How did it even *happen*?"

Sutcliffe grinned. "Well, when a man and a woman—"

"Don't patronize me."

The grin faded. "You're right; I shouldn't. Guess I haven't thought too hard on how this affects you." He adjusted again. "That is, I heard about your father—"

"Disowning me because I was a bastard?" *Now* the bitterness leaked out.

The constable splayed his hands as though in surrender. "I'm sorry, Merritt. Had I known it would lead to a child—"

"So you'd have preferred it if I'd never been born."

Sutcliffe's eyebrows drew together. "Don't put words in my mouth." But his expression relaxed. "It was a mistake. *You* are not a mistake, but Rose and I . . . She was a witness to a robbery at the bank. Just a small thing, but I looked into it and talked to her a bit. We both grew up here. Went to school together. I'd always liked her but never had the nerve to—" He waved a hand. "But that doesn't matter. One thing led to another, which led to you." He sighed. "It was only the one time."

Only the one time wasn't an excuse. Merritt knew from experience.

Another deep breath. "So," Sutcliffe went on, "how'd you figure it out? She say something?"

Merritt met the man's eyes. "I haven't spoken to my mother in thirteen years."

Sutcliffe didn't respond.

Leaning back in the chair, Merritt said, "My . . . housekeeper . . . figured it out through the Genealogical Society's records. There were some instances of wardship in the house, and—"

"Wardship?" The man perked up. "You got it?" The smile returned. "The magic?"

"Apparently." Merritt couldn't share the man's excitement. He didn't even think he could stand, heavy as he felt. "Perhaps if my father had been more present in my life, I would have known sooner." Merritt wondered how many times he'd have to wipe the smile off Sutcliffe's face before it stayed off.

"That's incredible, though," the man pressed. "Skipped me."

Merritt's hopes dribbled into puddles on the floor. "All of it?"

Sutcliffe nodded, and the hopes iced over. *So much for getting help from him.*

"I'm . . . I'm honestly surprised it showed up in you." Perhaps to fill the silence, Sutcliffe continued, "There was a break in the family line a while back . . . one side joined some sort of magic cult to build on what they had, and the other joined the Quakers." He chuckled. "They hate magic. I'm actually from the former, but the magic never took in me. My father, though, he could talk to plants." He shrugged.

Merritt straightened. "Communion spells?"

Sutcliffe nodded.

"Is there a way I could talk to him . . . ask him a few questions about how he manages it?"

Sutcliffe frowned. "Unfortunately, he went the same way as your grandmother. Passed away nearly ten years ago, now."

The man might as well have punched him in the gut. It took Merritt a moment to regain his breath. Licking his teeth, he tried to get moisture in his mouth. He didn't want to ask for a drink.

"Your sons?" he tried.

"Newton has a sliver of wardship—can make small walls. Most useful for windows, but he's got such a weak constitution it's not worth it for him. Last time he caught pneumonia . . ." He looked past Merritt, face sagging, lost in thought.

"Are there other relations living who have communion? Someone I could ask . . ." His studies with Gifford could go only so far if, indeed, he'd learn anything. Oddly embarrassed, he added, "The magic is new to me. I'd like some pointers, if nothing else."

"Yes . . . a couple. Here." Sutcliffe stood and exited the room, returning less than a minute later with a piece of paper. He handed it to Merritt. Two names were scrawled on it, with addresses. One was in Maine, and the other in Delaware.

"Communionists?" Merritt asked.

"Wardists, both of them."

If Merritt were made of glass, a slim crack would have climbed up him at that comment, ankle to knee. He needed the wardship help, too, but . . . but he was *so tired*. He just wanted to turn it off. He needed some semblance of peace, even for just *one night*—

"But," Sutcliffe lingered, "say I just recommended them . . . if you would. That is . . . I don't want Mary hearing about this. You're what, thirty, thirty-one now? It's been a long time, but for her it would be a new wound . . . you understand."

Merritt ground out an "I understand." Poison churned in his gut as he processed Sutcliffe's underlying meaning. *You have an entire family out there, but do be careful what you say to them, or they'll know my secret.*

What would his half brothers think—what would these people on this paper *think*—if they knew who Merritt was? If they knew he *existed?*

"I wanted you, boy." Sutcliffe's voice was nearly a whisper. "Couldn't have you, but I wanted you." He rubbed the back of his neck and paced toward the sofa but didn't sit. "I'm sorry. For my part in all this trouble. If I could make it right, I would."

"Would you, though?" Merritt asked, barely audible to himself, but the way Sutcliffe stiffened, he knew the constable had heard it. "Would you reach out to my mother? My father? Would you tell my *brothers* who I am? Would you make *that* right?"

Sutcliffe stood there, utterly crestfallen, without an answer.

And that was how Merritt left him.

Chapter 7

Owein was bored again.

Before, when he was a house, he'd make mischief when he got bored. Find new ways to use his spells to entertain himself, especially if he had a resident. He enjoyed finding ways to rile people or create puzzles for them to solve. When there was no one—when it was dark and lonely, which was often the case—he'd resort to startling doves on his eaves or playing with ants on the porch.

But he couldn't do that now. Not if he didn't want to feel sick. He loved having a body and wouldn't trade it for anything, but it also reacted poorly to spells. Contorted when he used alteration, which hurt, and his mind went cuckoo when he used any of his four chaocracy spells. What was the point of having spells when they came with such burdens?

Baptiste had gone into town, Merritt had left for New York, and Hulda and Beth didn't live here anymore. *What if they don't come back?*

Owein whined and tried to occupy himself. He sniffed around Merritt's room, then the office. He'd spent the morning staring at letters on the mat Hulda had made for him, practicing the sounds of the ones he recognized. Later, with nothing better to do, he headed into the library. Couldn't read anything in there, not yet, but some of the books had pictures. Not that he could reach most of them.

He sniffed around the spines, stopping when he found an interesting scent, and pulled a few off the shelves. He could hear Beth's voice in the back of his head, scolding him, warning him not to slobber or leave teeth marks, but she wasn't here. Maybe if he damaged a few spines, she'd somehow sense it and come back. He'd rather be scolded by Beth than be unscolded and alone.

At the end of the first wall of shelves, he pulled out a cracked leather book that smelled oily and old. A paper fell out next to it. Blank, but Owein had noticed some shadows on the other side as it fell. Abandoning the book, he sniffed the paper, pawed at it, then licked its edge until it turned over.

Owein's breath caught as the image became clear. A small painted portrait. He stepped over to see it right-side up.

It wasn't in color—or maybe it was, and his dog eyes couldn't tell—but it was so familiar to him. The set of the eyes, the breadth of the cheekbones, the bow of the lips. He knew that face. Where did he know that face?

It took several seconds before his mind whispered, *Mother.*

A new whine came up his throat, weaker and higher pitched than the last. Owein's ribs felt like they were closing in. He walked a circle around the portrait and returned to his starting point. Tail whapped the floor a few times before he lay down, muzzle on his paws, nose inches from the little painting.

Mother was never coming home. None of his family were.

Merritt is family, he reminded himself.

He lay by the portrait for several minutes before padding to the window and pressing his paws to the sill so he could look out over the island and wait for his family to come home.

❧

Hulda was miserable, and it was not due to the necessity of working on a Saturday.

She'd been unhappy since Merritt left Thursday night. Truthfully, if there was a way to pluck her brain from her skull and deposit it elsewhere for safekeeping, she'd do it. She'd analyzed and reanalyzed every single moment of that exchange, to the point where her mind was beginning to fester with insanity. What if she messed things up? What if Merritt wouldn't see her anymore after this? What if she never got another chance?

She didn't know how to handle . . . this. This kind of mistake, this kind of hurt, this kind of *relationship*. It was so new and different. She had no experience to guide her. Her résumé was greatly lacking, practically a blank paper with her name scrawled at the top and nothing more.

Part of her feared she'd *meant* to push Merritt away. She was a master of that—shoving aside any thought of love so she could manage life without disappointment. So she could achieve that which she could control. Now she had love, or at least she hoped she still had it, and she didn't know how to turn those safety measures off.

So yes, the anxiety over Merritt was bothering her. And yet . . . that didn't explain the entirety of the *weight* crushing her today. Certainly Merritt's lack of response to the messages she'd left him via their linked communion stones added to her disquiet, but he wasn't necessarily avoiding her. He may not have brought his stone with him to Cattlecorn. Miss Taylor was gone, and Baptiste seldom had reason to go upstairs. More likely than not, her messages hadn't been heard by anyone. Even so, the concern refused to be quelled.

Part of her unease had to do with the questions she had on Miss Taylor's unceremonious departure. There was that strange look of ravelment on her face, the memory of which formed an incessant itch between Hulda's shoulder blades. And then, of course, Myra. She'd received only one reply to her search via telegram, only to discover a dead end.

Another portion of her disquiet related to the files LIKER's foreign affairs department had started digging into—every case Myra had overseen and approved, as opposed to those redirected from London. If Myra had done anything untoward outside her dealings with Mr. Hogwood, it would be in those files. Hulda highly doubted Myra had mishandled her work . . . but Whimbrel House was included in those accounts, and if LIKER discovered the house wasn't enchanted anymore, Hulda would have to explain. She'd have a tough time doing so without implicating Myra, or herself. While Hulda had not been involved with Mr. Hogwood's doings, she had withheld information, and that in itself was damning.

She wondered if she should come clean.

Not yet. Give Myra time.

How much time was up for debate. Perhaps Hulda should institute a deadline for herself. At the very least, a deadline for reporting the magic had faded at Whimbrel House . . . not that it was presently receiving any services, with Beth's transfer. And with herself occupied in Boston, she might not need to be conclusive about it. At worst, Merritt could formally refuse BIKER services and keep Owein's secrets to himself.

Hulda sighed, thinking of Merritt.

Yet none of those thoughts and worries, even the ones about Merritt, could explain the utter despair winding through her body, so potent that she almost lost all equanimity and burst into tears while looking up a simple record.

And yet, she felt so much better the moment she stepped outside. That was the strangest thing of all, because this was the *second* time today the pattern had repeated itself, and it was not yet noon.

Had work become so hardscrabble that simply shifting away from it relieved her gloom? She was still worried, of course, about all those things. Wondering when Merritt would come home and how she would explain herself. Curious as to why she couldn't find Miss Taylor's new address. Sick over Myra and the difficulties she might be facing. But those things seemed manageable, standing outside the Bright Bay Hotel. Perhaps it was the sunshine, or the crisp autumn air. Either way, it was incredibly bizarre.

She mulled over it as she ventured toward the recorder's office, which was close enough to BIKER that she needn't hire a ride. If nothing else, she could use the exercise. She considered Merritt's timeline.

He may be home as early as tomorrow, if things were dicey. But if everything went well, he might stay the week, or longer.

God let it go well for him, she prayed in her heart. *He needs this.* Even if it meant she'd be left deliberating over her discomfort that much longer.

Their exchange bothered her, but there was nothing to be done for it at that moment, so she forced herself to focus on Myra. She could get things rolling for LIKER and then visit Myra's abode this afternoon. See what she could find. Yes, she'd do that.

Since it was Saturday, Hulda couldn't speak to any staff at the recorder's office herself, so she slipped the record request through the slot in their locked door and turned back for BIKER. When she reached the building, that insubstantial dread built in her stomach again, like she'd eaten bad eggs. She steeled herself with a deep breath. The sooner she finished the work Mr. Walker had assigned to her, the better. She was just . . . not herself today.

After slipping inside, she took the stairs up and nodded to Miss Richards at the desk—Miss Steverus was at home—and went down the hallway to the records room, where she'd set up her work on a spare table with a gimpy leg. So far, so good—her mind seemed to be under control. Just a couple more files to research before she handed her work over to Mr. Walker.

She'd been reading for only five minutes when a sinking feeling started in her middle and tugged on her shoulders. Hulda straightened her back as though she could relieve it physically and tried to focus, but the subtle sensation grew like a snowball rolling down a hill, collecting ice as it descended. Her thoughts turned heavy. Her heart hurt. It became increasingly hard to read, and she *didn't know why*—

"Miss Larkin."

She started and looked up at Mr. Baillie standing in the doorway.

"Am I interrupting?" he asked.

Hulda blinked, ensuring her eyes remained dry, and tried to ignore the melancholy taking root in her bones. "Not at all. How can I help you?" She managed to keep her feelings from her voice, at least.

He stepped in, leaving the door ajar. "I was curious. What are you thinking of the position? Of director, I mean."

Her eyes were starting to burn. "Oh, I . . . I haven't considered it too closely," she lied. Baillie, after all, was a candidate for the same position. "Not with all this work going on. Who knows? Perhaps Miss Haigh will return."

Mr. Baillie sniffed—the closest thing to a laugh she'd witnessed from him. "I highly doubt that." He studied her. "It's just that . . . you don't seem happy here."

A pang, like a slender dart, pierced her heart. Hulda suddenly wanted very much to be alone. She cleared a thickening throat. "I disagree, but thank you for your concerns." She cleared it again. "I assure you I am most content in my position. Concerned, yes, but I have been with BIKER well over a decade, and with reason."

He nodded, though his expression was slack. "Do you have children?"

The question took her aback. She expected to blush, but . . . the growing heaviness within her put a lid on any heat. Her fingers were growing cold. "I . . . No. Why do you ask?"

Why did she feel a sob forming in her chest?

"But don't you want them?" he pressed. "Forgive my intrusion. It's just . . . the director position is a very time-consuming appointment. Far more than that of a mere housekeeper."

Was that an insult? She was more than a housekeeper, after all. Her primary function was in diagnosing a house's enchantments and overseeing staff assignments. Her muscles felt so tight, but she wasn't angry. She was just *morose*. And then Merritt came to mind, and another dart pierced right where the first had, and she shuddered.

"If you do decide to step down . . ." Mr. Baillie shrugged. "That is, if Mr. Walker assigns me to the task, I assure you I will see your position elevated."

Why are you telling me this? She didn't voice it, because there was a veritable frog in her throat, and she wondered why Mr. Baillie thought to discuss the situation with her at all. He wasn't the friendly sort.

And then anxiety, not sadness, flared to life inside her, raising gooseflesh on her skin, sending shivers up her limbs and down her sides. The shelves of records were looming in on her. She was so high up. Were the windows secure? Was—

Hulda stood up abruptly, knocking the small table back. A few papers fell to the floor. The sensations abated slightly, and she glowered at Mr. Baillie.

He raised an eyebrow. "Are you all right?"

"Fine," she snapped, and held on to that flicker of anger as she marched past him and into the hallway, feeling a little more herself with every step until, suddenly, all the heaviness and sorrow and *fear* evaporated like it had never been, and Hulda *knew*. She *knew* what he had done.

She barged into Myra's office—Mr. Walker's office—without knocking, startling the man from perusing a ledger.

"Miss Larkin!" He jolted. "What is it?"

It took monumental effort to quietly shut the door when she very much wanted to slam it. "I am afraid to say I believe Mr. Baillie is enchanting me."

Mr. Walker blinked. "He isn't married, but I don't think—"

"Mr. Walker!" She stomped a foot. "I did not say I am enchanted *with* him. I say that he is a hysterian who has been using his magic on me for the last two days!"

It was the only thing that made sense. The sudden changes in emotion, the relief when she left the building he was stationed in . . . Her feelings were being warped and expanded by spells!

Mr. Walker's face went slack; then his mouth formed an *O*. "Would you like to sit down?"

She strode closer to the desk, but did not sit.

"I appreciate you bringing your concern to me," he said carefully, and Hulda could already feel where he was going with this, "but while Mr. Baillie *is*, technically, a hysterian, he's a very poor one. Quite clumsy with it, to an embarrassing degree—which is why he pursued law instead of psychology or the like. Believe me, if he were trying to rile you, you would know. That, and Mr. Baillie is a professional I've worked with for years. I assure you he's trustworthy."

"But I *do* know," Hulda protested. "That's why I'm here." A thought struck her. "Did he perchance interact with Miss Taylor before her reassignment?"

Mr. Walker blinked. "I . . . He was in the office, I believe, but I'm the one who gave her the assignment." Rubbing his chin, he went on. "To ease your mind, I believe Alastair's only spell is one of, well, silliness. Have you, uh, been feeling silly, Miss Larkin?"

Hulda removed her glasses and rubbed between her eyes. "No. Quite the opposite." She shoved her glasses back on. "Of course you have more experience than I do." She tried to keep calm, which was proving far easier now than earlier. "But I've had . . . feelings . . . that have been highly amplified while in his presence. Nonsensical emotions without root—"

"Without root?" he repeated softly.

Hulda paused. *Merritt. Myra. Miss Taylor. BIKER.* Were they without root? No, they weren't. Indeed, she had a lot on her plate. Heaping mounds on her plate. It was just . . . Hulda had never struggled this much to deal with those things.

Perhaps it was different, with her heart so heavily involved. Hulda had always been someone who led with her mind.

She began to doubt herself, and where there was even a tendril of doubt, there could be no certainty. And what proof did she have, other than her own suspicion?

"Perhaps not," she admitted.

Leaning back in his chair, Mr. Walker stretched his arms. "Never hesitate to bring a problem to me, Miss Larkin. We'll get this mess sorted out soon enough. But go home. Take a break. Relax a little. We'll do well enough without you until Monday."

She shook her head. It would not reflect well on her if she went home while another director candidate worked on.

But Mr. Walker closed his ledger and stretched. "I might go home, too. We're hitting a wall today. No use in pointless work."

That eased her concern . . . except that Hulda's "home" was currently inside this very building, on the first floor. She would still be in the same building as Alastair Baillie.

She chewed on her lip.

"Thank you," she said. "I think I will."

She left the office door ajar, and when she returned to the records room for her things, she was relieved to see Mr. Baillie had left. She put her heavy black bag on her shoulder and took the stairs outside, sucking in cool air like it was medicine.

Walking down the street, she pulled out a fist-sized piece of gray selenite—her communion stone. Pressed her thumb into the tiny rune on its surface.

"Merritt," she murmured, ensuring no one was close enough to her to overhear. "Merritt, I'd like to talk to you. Let me know when you've returned. Please."

She walked and waited. Didn't expect an answer, and yet when none came, disappointment flooded her chest.

Sighing, she slipped the stone back into her bag. Turned at the next intersection. Could she find refuge at Whimbrel House while Merritt was away? Perhaps she could set up at Myra's house and search for more clues, though she knew in her heart that was a lost cause. Besides, it might not reflect well on her, should anyone from LIKER find out.

Go home. Take a break.

Home.

She *could* visit family. Her sister wasn't far, just over in Cambridge. Hulda didn't like showing up without proper invitation, but Danielle never seemed to mind.

So for the second time in three weeks, Hulda departed for her sister's.

This was it. This was where Merritt would turn to get to his parents' house. There would be an old yellow barn at the end of the road, and Annie Bells would have her little shelf of tarts outside her door with a bucket to deposit coins if you wanted to have one. He wouldn't get that far, though. His was the fourth house from the end of the lane. Hip-high fences made from twisted tree branches encircling it, and a plum tree stood in the front yard.

This was where Merritt would turn. And yet, he couldn't move his feet. He couldn't even stand in the intersection and glance down that way, because what if someone saw him? Recognized him? Said something to . . .

He rubbed his eyes. The chill had seeped into his bones. His heart was beating too fast. His palms were sweaty, itchy. His clothes were too loose and too tight, and his stomach was inside out, and the trees were *ssshhhing* in his head—

A hand clapped his shoulder, making him jump. Turning, he felt an uncoiling of relief when he saw Fletcher's familiar face.

"How long have you been standing here?" his friend asked, soft and low.

Merritt paused. Checked his pocket watch. But he hadn't checked it when he got here, so he still didn't know. A while. The sun was setting. The sky was orange. He was cold.

Fletcher said, "Do you want me to come with you?"

"No." It was more a breath than an answer.

This was where Merritt would turn, to go home.

But he couldn't.

Chapter 8

Danielle was indeed surprised to see Hulda again, and so soon, as Hulda had stayed with her briefly just over two weeks prior, only to leave as abruptly as she had arrived. Normally, Hulda would be embarrassed by such inappropriate behavior, especially as a guest in another's home, but when it came to family, propriety suspended itself, and any potential slights were usually forgiven by the following morning, if they had caused any offense in the first place.

Danielle had a small staff, thanks to her husband's success as a lawyer, and her cook had prepared a most excellent dinner of quail and pudding. Not wanting to postpone the meal or put out the Tanner family with her problems, Hulda kept her concerns to herself and dined. Stuffed and tired from travel, she determined to wait until morning to burden her sister with her grievances, but Danielle was not known for patience, and thus her sister summoned her to the parlor the moment the children were put to bed.

The parlor was small yet quaint, well furnished and more intimate than cozy, lit with nearly two dozen candles for their sudden tête-à-tête. A marble-topped table sat in its center with two green-upholstered chairs with cabriole legs on either side of it, and two more on either side of the window, whose heavy maroon drapes were pulled aside to reveal lace curtains underneath. The walls were papered with a clean design of tiny navy flowers in parallel rows, and the carpet gave the illusion of individual forest-green tiles. The fire in the small fireplace was lit and cracking, and when Hulda arrived, tea was set out on the table, Danielle stirring her cup with a small silver spoon.

Danielle did not care for tea, so Hulda knew immediately the setup was intended for her.

"I hope you're ready to let out your secrets," Danielle said as soon as Hulda sat down. She wore a dress with a pleated bodice and flower-shaped collar, possibly of her own design, that was such a vivid pink it seemed to clash with the room.

Hulda sighed, then stalled with one, two, then three sips of tea. "I suppose there's no way around it."

"None at all." Danielle raised an expectant eyebrow.

Hulda stared at her cup. "In truth, I came here to do that very thing, though it seemed an easier exercise than I'm finding it." She chewed on her lip. Glanced at the door, but it was secure, and Hulda did not think her nephews would dare sneak about. "That is, there's a man—"

"A *man*?" Danielle leaned forward with a grin. "You haven't brought up a *man* in some time! Who is he?"

Hulda turned her cup on her saucer. "His name is Merritt Fernsby, and he's an author who lives in the Narragansett Bay."

Danielle sat up straighter. "Does this have anything to do with your very sudden departure two Sundays past?"

Hulda fidgeted in her seat. "Perhaps."

She clapped her hand loud enough to startle. "Delightful. Narragansett Bay—so Rhode Island? And how do you know him?"

Ignoring her sister's delight, Hulda focused on facts. "His house was—is—enchanted, so I met him through BIKER."

"I see. And is he aware you've a fondness for him?"

Hulda's cheeks warmed. "He is well aware. I . . . That is . . ." She took her hands from her cup for fear she'd spill tea, and instead weaved her fingers together in her lap. "That is, it is a mutual affection, enough so that I thought it best to move out lest rumors begin—"

Danielle shrieked, and Hulda nearly lost her seat.

"*What?*" Her sister, who'd always been prone to dramatics, slid from her chair and knelt in her heavy skirts, grabbing Hulda's knees. "You mean you've a real beau? Hulda, *this is astounding!*"

Hulda pinched her lips together, forbidding a smile, and cleared her throat. "Yes, well, it is an exciting venture. I'm very new to all this, and I'm trying to mete out affections appropriate to the timetable . . ."

Danielle was staring at her blankly.

"What?" Hulda asked.

"You're not like this with him, are you?" She rose and planted herself back in her chair.

Hulda blinked. "What do you mean?"

Her sister rolled her eyes. "Reserved and stiff, you ninny."

Hulda straightened. "I am not, thank you."

"But," Danielle pressed, "did you come all this way to see me absolutely melt at this fabulous news, or is there something else?"

Averting her eyes to her sleeves, Hulda picked at their simple trim. "Well, I've made something of a fool of myself, and *no*"—she could feel her sister's eager-rabbit-eyed stare without even looking up—"I will not tell you the details, because it is personal to him. Suffice to say, I recently misspoke about something of sensitive nature and am unsure how to proceed."

"Have you magicked any of it?"

Hulda frowned. Danielle hadn't inherited any of the family's weak augury and, even after so many years, did not quite understand how it worked. "Nothing solid, no."

Danielle let out a long breath. "Have you tried asking *him* how to proceed?"

Hulda's fingers wove tighter together. "He is away at the moment."

When Danielle didn't respond immediately, Hulda glanced up to find her sister studying her hard enough to form two lines between her brows. Hulda sipped her tea, waiting for the scrutiny to end.

After a minute, Danielle said, "You have this thing you do, especially when things change or become uncomfortable."

Hulda shook her head. "I handle change quite well. You know I move frequently, visit numerous households—"

"Don't interrupt." She pointed a manicured finger at Hulda's nose. "It's a little hard to describe. It's this sort of stoicism you adopted in your early twenties. When it gets severe, you're more of a statue than a person."

Hulda wilted.

"Not in a bad way . . . not entirely," she amended. "But . . . well, you've always had an old soul, but the older you get, the more, I don't know, *afraid* you become of being human. Your emotions are in a cage stiffer than that corset." She poked Hulda's middle. "If they were horticulture, they would die from lack of sunlight."

Hulda frowned. "I believe I'm following your metaphor." She forced herself to relax. Sipped her tea, held the cup in her lap. "I understand what you mean. Admittedly, I'm not sure how to change it."

Danielle looked her in the eye. "Do you love him?"

Every muscle from shoulder to knee tightened. "It's a little early to be calculating—"

Danielle swatted Hulda's shoulder. "Stop it. *Do you love him?*"

Hulda chewed on her bottom lip. Stared into her tea. "I do."

"Then *show* him!" She swung her arms out, nearly knocking over a vase of day-old flowers. "Break one of those bars, Hul. Let in the sunshine. Humans are emotional creatures, even you. You've got to crack the shell on the egg and let him see the soft flesh underneath."

Hulda returned her cup to her saucer. "If you must be poetic, you should stick to one form of imagery. Else it becomes confusing."

Danielle chuckled. "Are you confused?"

She took a moment to think on it. "No."

Reaching over, Danielle took her hand and squeezed it. "If this Mr. Fernsby fell in love with you, that means he loves who you are, bars and shell and all." She smiled. "That says a lot for his character. I think it's romantic."

"You think everything is romantic." She sighed.

"What?"

A shrug. "I feel a little silly getting advice from my *younger* sister."

"Alas, you do not have an older one," she quipped. "Now, let's talk about reciprocation when he returns from this trip. One step at a time. I want to hear all about him so I might enlighten you with my wealth of relationship knowledge and stellar advice."

So Hulda told her the whole of it, leaving out Silas, and by the time she turned in, she felt a little less heavy.

By the time dinner was served, Merritt managed to stitch a smile back on his face and boil down his errant thoughts to a simmer. He'd mentally retraced his steps through town and felt fairly certain he hadn't seen anyone who might recognize him. That is, he saw plenty of people, many of whom *he* recognized, but they either didn't notice him or didn't look his way twice. Which made him wonder how different he looked. Had he not written ahead, would Nelson Sutcliffe have been able to name him? His own son? But it wasn't worth dwelling on.

He'd embraced Ruth, Fletcher's mother, upon arriving, which had both helped and hurt. Fletcher's father was still at work, and his two siblings were out of the house—Amos was in Manhattan finishing a butchering apprenticeship, and Keri was dining with her fiancé's family.

"But she'll be right back here tomorrow, mark me." Ruth finally sat down after seeing the others served.

Merritt pierced a piece of gravy-smothered chicken with his fork but didn't lift it to his lips. "I heard she was engaged."

"About time, too. Real nice boy." Ruth nodded. "Father's a wainwright, but Jon wants to be a pharmacist."

"Interesting." His stomach was small and hard as steel, but Merritt pushed the chicken into his mouth and chewed, anyway. He didn't want to be rude. A distant part of him knew the food was good; he just had no appetite.

"Truth be told, I thought she'd be getting a ring from you for a while there." Ruth laughed.

Merritt chuckled, the sound growing more barbed with every vocalization.

The Portendorfers had taken him in after his father cast him out and Ebba left. Keri had been kind to him, and they'd tried it for a week or two until she straight-out told him she couldn't handle his brokenness. And rightfully so. He'd used her as a human crutch.

The chicken turned oily in his belly. Better for all of them that she wasn't there.

Thankfully, Fletcher took over for him, chatting about his job and the upcoming holidays—easy topics Merritt could comment on without much effort. No mention of murderers or magic. Fletcher was the only person Merritt had told about the Hogwood mess, and he wasn't keen on sharing with anyone else, even the woman who had been like a mother to him after his own was stripped away.

Still, it was a relief when the meal was over. Merritt helped with the dishes to give his hands something to do, then lingered by the door, sure he was going to vomit everything he'd stuffed down his gullet. He reached for the knob twice, but his body was kind enough to hold on to its meal, and the flora and fauna of the evening seemed fit to leave him in momentary peace.

And so Merritt took to staring out the window, though there wasn't much to see. Just a few lights in windows or hanging by doors. Freeman,

Fletcher's father, came home and greeted him before going in to eat. The draft from the glass was cold. Merritt leaned his forehead against it, and it fogged up from the heat of his skin.

And he thought about . . . nothing.

He must have been there awhile, because when Fletcher approached him, Merritt had completely forgotten where he was.

"Sutcliffe have much to say?" Fletcher asked.

Merritt kept his gaze fixed on a candle in the house across the way. "Enough."

A few seconds slipped by. "Maybe tomorrow we can—"

"I don't want to talk about it," he whispered.

Fletcher sighed. "You need to talk about it."

"I don't."

"That's your problem." He kept his voice low, so as not to be overheard by his parents. They had their own conversation going, which provided a buzz of background noise. "You never want to talk about it. Not when you got here with little more than the clothes on your back, not after you moved, and not now."

Merritt didn't answer.

"This is the *whole reason* we came here."

"It's *my* problem, Fletcher." He folded his arms against the cold but didn't move away from the draft. "I'll deal with it my way."

"Your way is not dealing with it at all."

Merritt clenched his jaw.

"Don't you want to feel *better*?" Fletcher pressed.

Cuuuuurrrrl, grass whispered through the walls. It faded almost as quickly as it had come.

Merritt focused on that candle. It felt like it was lit inside his own gut, slowly melting away his insides, burning them. "What kind of a question is that?"

"One you need to answer. Merritt." Fletcher moved to put a hand on Merritt's shoulder, but it bounced off a hard, invisible wall.

Merritt pulled his eyes from the glass. Wardship. When had he erected that?

Fletcher blinked and ran his palm over the unseen shield. "Not that I didn't believe you," he said carefully, "but . . . this is the first time . . ."

First time he'd seen Merritt do magic, he meant.

Swallowing against a tight throat, Merritt attempted to will the shield away. *Protective instincts, huh? What am I protecting here, Gifford?*

Reaching out, he pushed on the wall. It held. A trickle of despair coursed down his throat. "I don't know how to take it down," he rasped.

Fletcher chewed on his lip and followed the wall out about four feet, where it ended. "Try relaxing."

If only it were that easy. But Merritt forced deep breaths into his chest. Shook out his shoulders. Thought about a candy store and the flavors of all its different wares.

He knew the moment the wardship spell vanished because Fletcher stumbled. Must have been leaning against it.

Merritt expelled a shaky breath and searched the darkness outside for that candle. Someone had blown it out.

"We can try again tomorrow," Fletcher offered.

Shaking his head, Merritt said, "No. Thank you, Fletcher, for everything. For coming with me. But I need to leave."

His friend frowned. "Mom is expecting you tomorrow. Keri's coming."

But Merritt shook his head. "I can't stay here." He sucked in another breath, but it had little effect on his fraying nerves. "I can't see them yet. There's a morning coach heading out before the church bells ring. You should stay. Spend time with your family. But I can't—"

His throat squeezed shut. He couldn't finish the sentence without emotion leaking into it.

The two men stood before the dark window for another minute before Fletcher murmured, "You've been holding it in for thirteen years. Let it go."

Merritt's throat squeezed even tighter.

"Even if the worst happens," Fletcher went on, "you know we're your family, too, right?"

Merritt shifted away, his throat so tight he could barely breathe. He blinked rapidly to banish tears.

The most frustrating part was that he wasn't entirely sure why he was crying.

Chapter 9

After going to church with Danielle and spending the day traveling by carriage, kinetic tram, and boat to Blaugdone Island, Hulda found herself doing something she always insisted was not in her job title: cooking for a client. Then again, she was not presently housekeeper at Whimbrel House, and Merritt was much more than a client, so in the end, it was simply her putting her receipt books to good use to make a gesture to a man she deeply cared for.

Hulda left the oven door open to keep the meat pie warm without burning it. She'd managed to bully Baptiste out of the kitchen for the second time that day—she'd made a late lunch, too, just in case Merritt came home early. He hadn't. So she'd cooked dinner, his favorite, in hopes he'd return tonight. If he didn't, she'd be back for dinner tomorrow.

Setting the table, she felt strange about not leaving a place for Miss Taylor. With both her and Merritt gone, the house was rather quiet, minus Owein loudly chewing on a bone in the corner of the kitchen. She imagined that, having gone centuries without enjoying food, he loved every morsel he could get. She'd spent the day reviewing the alphabet chart with him so he could communicate with people other than Merritt. He was doing decently well with his literacy—she'd instructed him for nearly an hour that afternoon, until he got so fed up with her he'd hidden under Merritt's bed.

Owein's head popped up, one ear lifted. He dropped the bone and ran to the front door before Hulda even heard footsteps, pressing his nose to the seam and sniffing loudly. When it opened, Hulda's pulse set to hammering.

"Hey, old boy," Merritt said softly as Owein stood on his hind legs, his front paws propped on Merritt's thighs. It was hard to believe there was a boy in there when he acted so much like a dog, but then again, perhaps Silas Hogwood hadn't removed the dog's spirit before shoving Owein into the same body. Perhaps he couldn't—there were different necromantic spells for humans and animals. Merritt rubbed Owein's ears and scratched under his chin.

Hulda dared to step to the edge of the dining room, though she didn't make herself known. She'd worn her yellow dress today, the one that the dressmaker had fumbled by giving it a round collar. Although she didn't care for the cut, Merritt seemed to like this one, and she figured it might help her return to his good graces.

She clasped oddly clammy hands in front of her and waited silently, trying to sort out what to say and feeling silly about all of it, when Owein finally jumped down and Merritt lifted his head. He paused when he saw her.

Goodness, he looked so *tired*. Had the travel been hard? Had the visit not gone well?

She cleared her throat. "I thought I'd make dinner," she tried, which had not been on her list of first things to say. "It's meat pie, your favorite. I just need to fetch it out of the oven."

Merritt took a couple of steps forward and glanced into the dining room, where three places were set—two for them and one for Baptiste, though Hulda had a feeling he'd eat privately tonight. She'd lit a few extra candles for better light. Brought them herself so as not to waste his.

When he didn't respond, she licked her lips and asked, "It *is* still your favorite, isn't it?"

His Adam's apple bobbed as he swallowed. He crossed the room to her, moving on legs that belonged to an old man, and plopped his forehead on her shoulder.

"Thank you," he whispered.

Something about the words, about the weariness to his voice, made her eyes sting. She wrapped her arms around him. "It was no trouble." She leaned her cheek against his head. "Do you want to eat . . . ?"

"In a moment." His arms loosely encircled her. He didn't lift his head. "In just . . . a moment."

Hulda nodded. Squeezed a little tighter.

They stayed like that for a long time.

"He seemed . . . fine," Merritt explained after dinner. He and Hulda sat in the living room on the faded maroon sofa across from the faded emerald settee—Hulda still disliked the color scheme of the space, but she hardly had the right to update it now. Though, if Owein was willing, perhaps he could simply *change* a few things for her. Not the wainscoting—that was quite ornate if a tad bizarre, and it gave the space character. She'd have to speak with him later, though until he mastered his spelling, she wouldn't understand his replies.

Merritt sat at the end of the sofa, elbows on his knees, staring at the patterns in the carpet. He was talking about Nelson Sutcliffe, his biological father. "Just fine," he continued.

"At least he's in good health," Hulda commented. If she scooted a little closer, she could rub his back . . . but was that too intimate a gesture?

"Not just in good health. He was just *fine*." Merritt straightened, removing the opportunity. "Like, *Oh, here he is, my son whom I haven't seen in thirteen years, and oh yes, I did have an affair with your mother, ta-ta, isn't that unfortunate. Be a good lad and don't tell anyone.*"

Hulda slouched. "I see. Was he so patronizing?"

"Not patronizing." Merritt shook his head, causing locks of half-wavy hair to fall over his shoulders. He pushed them back again. "Not really. Just . . . I don't know. If it were me, I think I'd be more . . . invested. But I suppose he disconnected himself from the situation a long time ago. Either way, there are no communionists to help me."

She nodded, though he didn't seem to notice. "At least there's the house."

A sigh. "At least there's the house." He leaned back and stared up at the ceiling, which had once opened up to drop cobweb nooses and dead rats on them. "I think I'd trade it in for someone who cares."

A little worm niggled in Hulda's belly. She thought again of what Miss Taylor had said to her but sought optimism. "We wouldn't have met, if not for that."

A small tipping of his lips. "True." The almost smile faded. "And I never did go home."

She paused. "Isn't Mr. Sutcliffe in Cattlecorn?"

"I went to Cattlecorn," he amended, "but I didn't go home." His elbows returned to his knees. "I didn't see my mother. My sisters . . . though they'll have moved out by now."

He looked so sullen. Hulda tried, "How old are your sisters?"

He thought for a moment. "Scarlet would be thirty-three, Beatrice twenty-seven." Pressing the heels of his hands into his eyes, he added, "Misery me, I don't even know if they're married. Scarlet was seeing a fellow . . . but I don't know."

He reached for his collar, and Hulda noticed he was wearing that worn striped scarf of his. The one his sister—Scarlet?—had made him. The one that had gotten him trapped in that hole in the kitchen shortly after they'd met.

She reached for him. Hesitated. She didn't have anything like this in her life . . . Her parents were sensible people with good heads on their shoulders, affectionate enough while being firm with discipline. She'd always been close with her sister; the longest they'd been apart was just over a year, when she was stationed at Gorse End, Hogwood's former estate, and couldn't get home for the holidays. Her upbringing was quite normal, magic aside. Quintessentially normal. Never a source of conflict.

"I'm sure they're . . . doing well for themselves," she tried.

Merritt dropped his hands. "Yes, I'm sure." He stood, stretched his back. "I might turn in early. Traveling was tiring." Managing a weak smile, he said, "Good night, Hulda."

Hulda stiffened. He was leaving. She wanted so badly to support him, but he was leaving, and his tone had changed from solicitous to tired . . . Had she said the wrong things? She was trying to find the bright side, but perhaps that wasn't what he wanted. But how was she to know what he wanted? She couldn't begin to empathize with the situation. It was all so over her head—

He was moving toward the reception hall. *Show him,* Danielle had said. *Crack the shell on the egg.*

But how did she do it? How did she stop being a statue?

He was nearly gone. Her breathing quickened as her mind tumbled, searching for something, *anything*—

"I picked the stitches on my sister's dress!" she bellowed. Heat flushed from her hairline to her breasts.

Merritt paused in the entryway. Turned. "What?"

She worked her mouth for a moment, trying to sort through her thoughts. "I . . . that is, when I was in my teen years . . . I was so hurt that Danielle was invited to a local dance and I wasn't, especially because she'd been asked by a boy my age whom I fancied . . . that is, I was jealous, and I picked the stitches on the back of her dress, and I wasn't there, but the bodice popped open halfway through the night, and Danielle ran home, bawling. I felt horrible afterward, but I never told a soul. Not her, nor my parents and friends."

He stared at her, lines etched in his forehead, for several heartbeats. "Hulda . . . why are you telling me this?"

She took in a deep breath. "I . . . I'm trying to be vulnerable. I know I struggle with it." Averting her eyes, she clicked her nails together. "Danielle pointed out to me that I have these walls of stoicism—she referred to them more poetically—and while I know I can't empathize with you, I can *sympathize*, and I don't mean to be an iron rod in a dress, it's just how I've always dealt with these things. But I don't want you to have to deal with them alone. I'm . . . I'm learning how to bend."

She glanced up. A subtle smile had formed on his lips, bolstering her courage.

"Thank you," he said, gentle and sincere. He pressed a palm into the side of the entryway and leaned on it. "I appreciate it. And I wouldn't say you're an iron rod . . ."

"Just a statue," she suggested.

He shrugged. "A statue made of softer clay than you realize, I think."

Her flush receded. "I can work with that. And . . ." *Click, click, click* went her nails. "I would appreciate it if you could tell me . . . how you wish for us to proceed with this . . . that is, what you would like me to do. I want to support you, Merritt."

His stance relaxed. After pushing off the wall, he crossed back to her and offered a hand, which she took. He pulled her off the couch and embraced her.

"You are," he murmured. "I notice the effort. I appreciate it. I'm . . . honestly not sure what else there is to do. Unless you want to move back in."

She rested her head on his shoulder. "I don't think that's wise. Not with this audit. And what I *have* said of Whimbrel House, it's not in need of a magically inclined housekeeper."

He sighed. "I know."

She drew her hand down his back. He didn't pull away. This was acceptable, then. Up and down a few times, before pulling away. A few of Owein's hairs clung to his sleeve; she reached to pull them free, but before making contact, her vision shifted, augury flooding her senses.

There he was, in front of her, wearing his navy coat, unbound hair flying behind him—running. He was running. *They* were running. Through . . . it looked like Boston, but Hulda couldn't pinpoint where—

And the vision dissipated, just like that. She refocused on the hairs but couldn't conjure it up again.

"What did you see?" Merritt asked.

Hulda blinked. "I'm sorry, what?"

His lip pinched to one side. "Surely you're not forgetting already."

Forgetting—ah, yes, it was coming back to her. It really wasn't fair, having forgetfulness as a side effect of augury, when she couldn't control the use of her power. In truth, the fugue was as wily as the magic itself, coming and going as it pleased. Though she supposed that had been a particularly intense vision—

She paused. "How did you know—?"

He shrugged. "You get this sort of vacant look on your face when it happens."

She wondered what sort of vacancy took over her features and how strange it might appear. "I saw us running. Through Boston."

"Running?" he repeated, stepping back, pulling the rest of his warmth with him. "Us? When?"

She shook her head. "I don't know. I didn't get a good enough look." She frowned. "Not too far distant, I think."

He smiled. "I was thinking of taking you to a play. Perhaps we'll be late for it."

She rolled her eyes. "Then we'd best leave early."

"I'll look into tickets tomorrow." He clasped her hand and squeezed it.

She squeezed back. "Go get some rest, Merritt Fernsby. You need it."

He glanced out the window to the navy night beyond. "Let me make sure you get back to the mainland first," he said. "I'll grab my coat."

"One more thing, Merritt. Well, two."

He turned to her.

She related what had happened at BIKER with Baillie and the way she suspected he'd manipulated her emotions in an attempt to convince her to drop her play for the director's position.

"He claims he doesn't have that ability?" Merritt asked, suspicion lacing the comment.

She nodded. "*Claims*, yes." Doubt crept in. "Mr. Walker confirmed that the only hysteria spell Mr. Baillie possesses is one of puerility."

"Come again?"

"Silliness," she amended.

His lips twisted as he mulled over it for a moment. Hulda, by habit, slipped her hand into her pocket and thumbed Myra's telegram. She kept it on her person. For what reason, she couldn't adequately say. She'd memorized the short message, and yet felt the need to keep proof of its existence close . . . and perhaps out of sight of anyone else.

"The thing is," Merritt spoke carefully, his words hesitant, "and don't be offended by this—"

Hulda's back straightened. "What?"

"It's just . . . *why* would Alastair Baillie want to be the director of BIKER so badly?"

Hulda stared at him a couple of seconds. Did he really need to ask? "BIKER is a valuable and necessary institution. It oversees all enchanted residences in North America—"

"But," he pressed, "there aren't that many, right? That's why Myra hired Silas to enchant new ones, yes?"

Hulda paused. "I . . . well, yes. But there is still prestige in the position, and we often take up European work. LIKER can't oversee everything."

"Of course. It's just . . . lawyers make nice money. I imagine one working for LIKER would have a lot of pennies in his pocket. And isn't LIKER more financially robust than BIKER?"

She didn't like to admit it, but she nodded.

"And Baillie is English," he offered. "Why leave all of it behind and move to the States, just to oversee a smaller company?"

Hulda turned the telegram over in her hands. "Perhaps it isn't about money."

Mr. Walker's voice sounded in her memory. *You don't by chance know where those funds were transferred?*

She bit her lip. Pinched the telegram in her fingers and pulled it out of her pocket. "I wonder," she said as she unfolded it, "if this isn't about Mr. Hogwood, but about the missing funds."

"As good a theory as any," Merritt tried. "You think Baillie sent it?"

"I'm sure I could come up with a story for anyone sending it. *If* it's about BIKER's missing funds, then it *could* be from LIKER. Perhaps someone hired a private detective with a heavy hand." She considered. "Or it could even be from someone within BIKER."

"LIKER has been searching through all the files, have they not?" Merritt asked.

She nodded. "Myself included. I don't understand how none of us have found a clue yet. But the financial statements seem sound. There's money missing." She ran her thumb over the inked words on the telegram. "I *need* to find Myra. I need to ask her. But I have no idea where else to look." She could travel to the addresses from the letters herself, she supposed, if she didn't hear back.

Except . . . she knew Myra. And if Myra didn't want to be found, she never would be.

⌒⊚

Merritt reloaded his rifled musket with practiced ease before lifting it to his shoulder and shooting at a hanging piece of the poor birch he'd chosen as his target. The tree was dying, anyway. If its appearance hadn't been enough of a clue, he would have known from its silence—it was the only tree on the island that didn't talk to him. It was situated away from the house, so any errant bullets wouldn't hurt anyone. Not that he'd had any errant bullets yet. After all, this had been Merritt's mode of *dealing*, as Fletcher had put it, for years.

His shoulder was getting sore. He reloaded, anyway. Almost out of ammunition. *Damn.* And Beth wasn't around to order in more for him. Shocking, how easily he'd become accustomed to having help. He used to do everything himself without qualm. Granted, he'd also lived in a city and not on an island in the middle of nowhere, but still. Hopefully LIKER would figure things out soon so he could *formally complain* about them abducting his maid.

He thought he still had some rounds under his bed for his Deringer. Two more bullets blew a dying branch off the east side of the tree.

Can't even tell them who I am. Merritt had gone over Sutcliffe's contact list after Owein's lesson that morning—though Merritt really should get on the articles Gifford had left him—and even though four days had passed since his meeting with his actual father, the list of names still rankled. What the hell was he supposed to say? *Nelson Sutcliffe said I should contact you about magic. For no reason at all. Except I just so happen to have the exact same spells you do. Also his nose. But don't tell his wife.*

He lowered the rifle. His fingers were getting cold. His nose was starting to run. But the sun was bright, and his breath didn't cloud in the wintry air. Hearing footsteps marching toward him, he turned to see his chef picking through the sleepy reeds.

Sleeeeeeeeeep, they whispered. That's how Merritt knew. He envied them their rest.

Baptiste had a box of bullets under his arm.

"Bless you." Merritt accepted the box and reloaded.

Baptiste's dark eyes took in the battered tree. "Is expensive hobby. You should shoot deer instead."

Merritt lifted the rifle to his shoulder. "Aren't we a little tired of venison?"

Wood chunks sprayed as the bullet hit.

"Never tired of venison." Baptiste folded his arms. Merritt noticed he wasn't wearing a coat. "Venison is *versatile*." He used the French enunciation of the last word.

Merritt shot again. Pulled out new bullets. "I don't suppose you want a turn."

A single, dry chuckle escaped the Frenchman's lips. "No. I don't use guns, anymore."

"Anymore?" He snapped the muzzle back into place and aimed.

"Is why I left France. No one would hire felon."

Merritt shot his first errant bullet and turned to Baptiste. "Pardon?"

He shrugged. "You never asked."

Merritt took a moment to process this, hearing a *You do everything without me!* complaint in the distance before catching the brush of Owein's dark tail in the distance. "Were you incarcerated?"

Baptiste nodded.

"How long?"

"Only two years."

"Only two years," he repeated, and laughed. "Well, that's something, then, isn't it?" He unloaded the rifle on the birch, sighed, and decided to save the rest of his ammunition. "We'll wait to tell Hulda about that one."

Owein reached them, panting. *I want to try!*

"You have to grow thumbs first."

A small whine sounded in the dog's throat. The ground in front of him began to quake and reassemble itself, taking the form of a pistol . . . before crumbling around the edges as Owein shook his head and whined again.

"Save it for when it's worth it, kid." Merritt stuck the muzzle of his gun into the earth. Owein still hadn't adapted to the side effects of magic, and he *hated* them. Merritt didn't need communion to know that.

Don't go into town.

Merritt quirked an eyebrow. "And why not?"

Owein pawed the reeds. *Because I get bored.*

"Baptiste can throw you a stick."

The chef tilted his head.

The dog whined. *I want Beth back.*

Merritt sighed. "I'm working on it, believe me." A familiar itch tickled his throat.

Don't go.

Stepping over to Owein, Merritt set the gun aside and rubbed his cold, floppy ears. "I can't just not go into town." He cleared his throat, shaking off his own side effects. He considered a moment. "You could come with me, if you'd like."

Owein pulled back and whined. Surprising—Merritt had been sure that tail would be wagging happily. *No.*

"Why not?"

The dog didn't answer. For the better, Merritt supposed. If he used this spell for much longer, he'd lose his voice.

Today Merritt had to visit Gifford at the Genealogical Society for another lecture on magic, one that would hopefully be more helpful than the last. Then he was swinging by BIKER so he could take Hulda to dinner. He hadn't seen her since Sunday. He'd thought to come earlier in the week and make sure everything was all right, after what Hulda had shared with him about Baillie, but she'd insisted Sadie Steverus would be close by, and it would reflect poorly on her if she had too many social calls at the office. That, and the man supposedly had no power beyond the ability to incite feelings of silliness in others. Perhaps he should have run a children's puppet theater instead of going into law.

Regardless, Merritt was greatly disliking this new arrangement of theirs.

"Which reminds me." He turned to Baptiste. "I'll be out this evening as well."

Baptiste dropped his arms from their knot across his chest. "Who am I supposed to cook for, hm? Who? Not Miss Larkin, not Miss Taylor, now not you."

He can cook for me.

"Owein says you can cook for him," Merritt related.

Baptiste threw his hands in the air and stalked back to the house.

Unless it's venison, Owein added, making Merritt's throat itching a little worse. *I'm tired of venison.*

⌒୨

"Miss Steverus."

Sadie Steverus looked up from her desk; Miss Richards was running an errand, leaving the BIKER secretary free. "Yes? Oh, Miss Larkin, you don't look well."

Hulda didn't *feel* well, either. In fact, all week she'd been suffering from those same waves of sorrow, displeasure, even anger. They came and went, and they were more confusing than ever. Not only had Hulda resolved one of the more stressful issues in her life—she and Merritt were back to normal, if not better than before—but it wasn't even *that* time of month for her. Chewing on the inside of her cheek, Hulda glanced down either hallway for the dozenth time, ensuring no one was nearby.

"Do you know," she whispered, "if hysterians can cast spells from a distance? Or how long their magic might last?"

Miss Steverus blinked. "You mean Mr. Baillie?"

Hulda motioned with her hand to urge Miss Steverus into silence. "N-Not Mr. Baillie," she lied, "but I suppose I could ask him. He just . . . seems not to care for the discussion."

Miss Steverus nodded. "He's embarrassed about it."

That gave Hulda pause. "What makes you say that?"

The secretary glanced toward Mr. Walker's closed door, which made Hulda feel a pulse of longing for Myra. She'd received another response to one of her missives, but the writer hadn't seen Myra in two full years. "Monday, Mr. Walker was bothered by something, and he asked Mr. Baillie to cheer him up, and it was just a mess. He has such little command over the ability, I'm not sure. I do believe"—she leaned closer—"that most hysterians can't *give* you a new emotion, they can only manipulate the ones you already have. At least, those are the common spells in the pool."

Hulda pressed her lips together. She didn't *already have* the tormenting sensations that had plagued her this last week . . . or did she? She was worried about Myra, not to mention frustrated that she couldn't find her. Those feelings might have been manipulated to greater depths. In truth, hysteria, the ninth school of magic, was the one she knew the least about. She'd never tended a hysterical house before—buildings tended to lack emotions.

"As for the distance issue." Miss Steverus tapped a pencil against her lips. "I could look it up after hours."

"Don't bother yourself, I can do the same." It was nearly five o'clock, besides. She'd arranged to meet Merritt outside. Perhaps Gifford would know—

"Miss Larkin."

Her heart flipped as she turned around to spy Mr. Baillie approaching, and she immediately feared he'd overheard something. But she'd been so quiet . . . surely not. "Yes?"

"I'd like to discuss Whimbrel House with you." He gestured toward the small office he'd taken over. "If you wouldn't mind."

Hulda glanced out the window at the fading sun. They'd need lanterns soon enough, though BIKER was stocked with many elemental ones. "Might it wait until morning?" She was eager to spend time with Merritt, and not just because of Danielle's advice.

Mr. Baillie frowned. "I will be brief."

Tucking away her nerves, Hulda nodded and followed his lead. Miss Steverus offered a smile. The gesture pleased her, and she latched on to that satisfaction. If she was cheerful, she couldn't be depressed by a hysterian, right? That was, presuming his spells were more than he let on, which was total assumption on her part. Then again, both Mr. Walker and Miss Steverus believed him harmless. And Mr. Walker, at least, should know what the man was capable of.

But as Mr. Baillie closed the office door behind him, Hulda also recalled the side effects of hysteria: physical pain and apathy. While she hadn't detected any signs of pain in the lawyer who was now pulling a chair across from the one she was to sit in, he was certainly one of the most apathetic persons of her acquaintance. But that didn't mean he was bespelling her—

"Sit, please." He indicated the chair.

Hulda gathered her skirts and sat in the chair, putting about three paces between herself and Mr. Baillie. Pushing forward confidence, she asked, "What would you like to know?"

Mr. Baillie opened a familiar folder. "Whimbrel House was your last assignment?"

"Indeed, up until Miss Haigh's resignation."

"Why are you no longer stationed there?"

A flicker of trepidation entered her heart. She ignored it. "Because BIKER is . . . askew, for a lack of a better word. Miss Haigh and I had been discussing my removal from the premises."

"Why?"

That flicker turned into a cold screw of unease drilling into her chest . . . but she was speaking the truth. Nothing about Whimbrel House itself would indict Myra. Or her. She'd gone over her story several times, both alone and with Merritt.

Was this fear she felt hers, or . . .

She studied Mr. Baillie's face, searching for a tell. But he merely looked at the file in his lap. When she didn't respond, he glanced at her over the rim of his glasses.

"Because Mr. Fernsby had an adequate staff and was capable of overseeing the house himself."

He wrote something down. "Not because you are having an affair with him?"

The screw sharpened into a knife. Redness pricked Hulda's cheeks, but she straightened her back, trying to conquer it. *How does he know?* She supposed he may have seen Merritt reach for her hand when they met . . . or perhaps Miss Taylor had said something? Either way, it was known, and denying it would do no good. And why should she? She hadn't broken any rules. "You overstep your bounds, Mr. Baillie."

"In this case"—he lifted his pen—"it is my job to do so."

Hulda swallowed. Her pulse was beating too fast. "*Affair* is a poor term to use. It suggests one of us is married and also that we've had sexual encounters. Neither is true. And, I will state for the record, we were not involved until *after* I left my post."

Mr. Baillie penned something else. *Calm down,* Hulda told herself, but if anything, her emotions were heightening. Surely this wasn't all in her head!

"What does this have to do with Miss Haigh?" she pressed. Strain was entering her voice. Hulda prided herself on staying professional and collected at all times—like Danielle had said, she'd mastered it. Something was wrong. She felt it in her gut.

"What is your personal relationship with Myra Haigh?"

Her hands closed into fists. "If you wish for me to repeat myself, she has been my employer for several years, and yes, I consider her a friend."

"Do you know her location?"

It was getting hard to breathe. Why could she not breathe? "I've already stated to the entire department that I do not." A headache was blooming at the base of her skull. She swallowed. "Why are you doing this?"

"It's my job to—"

"Not the questioning. Why are you using magic on me?"

He glanced up. "You're mistaken, Miss Larkin."

She shook her head. "I am not. I am . . . I shouldn't feel this way." She was too hot under her dress. Panicked and frustrated . . . No, not frustrated. Angry. She was angry. Frenetic. So frenetic her eyes were moistening.

Mr. Baillie lowered his file. "If you can't control yourself, we can postpone until morning."

Hulda stood. Too quickly, for her head spun. "I can *control* myself just fine," she ground out as her nerves unraveled. "Stop this at once, or I'll report you!"

Closing the folder, Mr. Baillie set it on his desk and calmly rose to his feet. "Miss Larkin, I'm afraid you've become quite hysterical."

Her breathing was coming hard, like she'd run here from the port. Her skin was flushed. The knife in her heart twisted, fire stoked, and she began crying. She covered her face, humiliated, only to be slammed with a wall of mortification—

And through her closed fingers, she thought she saw the corner of Mr. Baillie's lip tick upward.

"Stop!" she shouted. She hadn't meant to shout, but she couldn't control . . . she couldn't make it stop . . . she couldn't—

The slightest breeze whisked past her. Something hit the wall.

And suddenly the knife pulled clean from her chest, and while she emotionally bled, the feelings dissipated, leaving dusty traces in their wake. Pulling her hands down, Hulda gasped.

Merritt was there. Merritt was there, and he had Baillie shoved up against the closest office wall. The lawyer's glasses were askew, but his face was as unreadable as a bronze bust's.

"What. The *hell*. Are you doing?" Merritt growled.

Mr. Baillie tried to straighten, but Merritt shoved him against the wall again. Mr. Baillie was the taller man, but he was thin, lightweight. "Unhand me, Mr. Fernsby."

"Answer the question and maybe I will."

"I am merely asking Miss Larkin about Whimbrel House."

"And leaving her blubbering in the office?" he snapped. "We could hear her from the reception room!"

Humiliation churned in her gut, but at least *that* sensation felt natural. Removing her glasses and wiping her eyes, she said, "Merritt, let him go."

Mr. Baillie added, "I suggest you do as she says if you don't want legal repercussions."

Merritt visibly seethed. "Says the hysterian unwinding a colleague in his office."

"You are mistaken," Mr. Baillie said plainly.

For a moment Hulda thought she saw a flash of red from the corner of her eye, but when she glanced over, there was nothing there. The door, however, had been left wide open.

"Merritt," Hulda warned.

Merritt winced. "You're doing it to me right now, aren't you?"

The question confused Hulda, until she realized, by the frown on the lawyer's lips, that he meant the hysteria. Mr. Baillie was trying to bespell Merritt!

That smirk . . . that uptick of his mouth as Hulda sobbed . . . If Mr. Baillie wasn't using magic on her, he was a lunatic.

But this . . . this was not going to help either of them in the long run.

Merritt pressed harder; Hulda ran up and put a hand on his shoulder. "Merritt."

"If you're innocent," Merritt growled, "why aren't you calling for help?"

Mr. Baillie's eyebrow twitched. "I'm not afraid of you, Mr. Fernsby."

"You should be," he snapped. "And if you're trying to make me fear you, you should know I am nothing but *angry* right now."

It was only a flash, and Hulda wasn't sure either man noticed it, but for half a heartbeat, Mr. Baillie *did* look scared.

And he should. Right now, Merritt was the personification of a feral dog.

"Merritt." Her voice was steady, even as her chest constricted like an overused chimney. "Let him go."

It took a moment, but Merritt backed off. Removed his fingers one at a time. But when he stepped away, Mr. Baillie remained pressed to the wall.

A wardship spell was holding him there.

Merritt said nothing more, only scowled at the man and put a hand on Hulda's back. Getting hold of herself—running through a mental checklist of her appearance—Hulda let him guide her from the room. As they reached the reception desk, Miss Steverus stood, but Hulda preempted any commentary by saying, "Please see Mr. Baillie removed from the wall."

And then they left.

Chapter 10

Despite the length of the trip, they returned to Whimbrel House instead of going out—Merritt certainly wasn't in the mood to sit out in public, and if he wasn't feeling up to it, Hulda certainly wouldn't be. She was quiet on the kinetic tram and kept her face turned toward the window, likely so other passengers wouldn't see the pink around her eyes. By the time they reached the little enchanted skiff at the port—the smallest boat docked there—Merritt had more or less gotten a hold of his own blundering emotions. The boat's kinetic spell had propelled them out a short ways before Hulda finally spoke.

"You should not have done that."

Merritt glanced over, the wind blowing his hair from his face. "Come again?"

She sat rigid-backed again, as if becoming the "iron bar" she'd described herself as would protect her from feeling whatever it was she didn't want to feel. Still, she looked at him earnestly, all those feelings glimmering in her hazel eyes. "I *have* to keep things professional, Merritt! I have to put on a good face—"

"That was already out the window when I arrived," he countered.

She folded her arms as the wind ruffled her collar. "Violence certainly wasn't the answer."

Merritt snorted and looked out over the bay. The boat seemed to be taking an awfully long time to cross the water. "You're welcome."

He saw her slouch—a good sign—from the corner of his eye. "I'm not angry with you," she said. Paused. "No, I am angry with you. But I'm also grateful for your intervention. And I don't know how to manage any of this." She flung her hands up in the air. "If Mr. Walker finds out . . ."

He turned back to her, pulling his hands from the edge of the boat—the wintry air was beginning to sting them. "If Mr. Walker finds out, then Baillie will have to show his hand." Then, under his breath, he mumbled, "Silliness my ass."

Hulda shook her head. "I don't share your confidence. Women are so easily labeled as hysterical."

Now Merritt slumped. "I don't know, Hulda. I'm sorry. I was already frustrated when I got there—same old reasons." He waved a hand, as if doing so could dismiss them. "Sadie said you'd be out in a minute, and then I heard you—" Her face paled, or he thought it did—the twilight made it hard to tell. So he added, "You weren't *loud*, but you're . . . you . . . and I just picked up on it. I was so *angry*, Hulda. When I walked in and saw his smug countenance while you looked like you were falling to pieces . . ." His voice drifted off. He cleared it. "I was angry. And then I was *furious*. The longer I held him against that wall, the more furious I became. It had to be him. He was doing something to me."

She nodded. "I believe he was. As for myself, I wouldn't have . . . behaved . . . in such a manner otherwise."

Merritt returned his hands to his pockets. "No, you wouldn't have. Not much rattles you."

She smiled at the compliment. Merritt hunkered down against the cold. He was so tired of feeling this way. He was always angry nowadays. It made his head pound and his stomach hurt. At least this, right now, was a different flavor of angry.

"I'm worried," Hulda said after a minute, as they passed the light of a lighthouse and Blaugdone Island came into view, "that I'll be disqualified from the director position, if not let go from BIKER entirely. I hate to think of what that might mean for me . . . and for Myra."

Frowning, Merritt scooted forward as much as the little boat would let him and reached for Hulda's hand. She'd been smart enough to wear gloves. "That won't happen."

They neared the coast, forcing Merritt to reach over to the kinetic seal and slow the craft down.

"They might transfer me," she said.

Merritt hesitated, the possibility reverberating through him like someone had used his bones for a bell. He guided the boat toward the sandy place where he always docked it. If Hulda was transferred, they'd be separated. And she could be sent anywhere—the West, Canada, Britain . . . Would he even be able to follow her if that happened? Would Owein? Baptiste?

He shook off the question as best he could. "We'll worry about that if and when it happens. You're the best candidate for the position. And if what happened tonight is marked against your character, the LIKER lot are utter morons."

He stepped out, helped Hulda do the same, then hauled the craft up the bank enough that the sea wouldn't reclaim it. They took the worn path to the house, where Owein greeted them excitedly, his tail whipping about hard enough to be a weapon. Baptiste was sipping coffee in the dining room. Merritt led the way to the smaller breakfast room, where he and Hulda doffed their coats, though Merritt kept on the colorful scarf his sister had made him. Habit.

To his surprise, Baptiste brought out a cured-meat board, plates, mugs of cider, and some cheese, setting everything down silently. "Bless you," Merritt said. Neither of them had eaten, and he'd told Baptiste not to prepare anything.

The chef nodded and left them to their privacy. Whatever the man had done in France to earn two years' jail time . . . Merritt mentally exonerated him.

"The next question is"—he forked a piece of salted duck—"how much trouble am I in?"

Hulda considered for a moment, sipping on cider. A thin piece of hair had come down from its pin and fallen across her temple. It curled at the end. Rather becoming, he thought. She answered, "American magic laws are rather lax. It's not illegal to use magic, but it is illegal to use magic to do illegal things."

"Is it illegal to stick someone to the wall with a wardship spell?" While he didn't want to damage Hulda's reputation, he *was* pleased with that—because it must have been humiliating to the lawyer, and also because he'd done it *on purpose.* Maybe Gifford's lessons were paying off after all.

"Assault is." She frowned.

"It was defense," he countered. Chewed. "He's fine."

"He is, but . . . I don't know. It's up to him whether he wants to press charges."

"If he does, then we press them back."

She chewed and swallowed a bit of cracker and cheese before answering. "I've reported him once, but Mr. Walker—everyone there—seems to believe him incapable of such exertions. *If* he's the responsible party, he's somehow convinced his colleagues he doesn't have the ability to wield his magic in such a way. But I will file another complaint. Threaten to take it to the courts. Perhaps it will be enough to stay his hand."

He stared at some olives. "Perhaps you shouldn't work there."

She shrugged. "It's my job. I could take a brief leave, but . . ." She wound her fingers together. Unwound them.

"But you still want the director position."

She nodded. "I would *despise* seeing BIKER in the hands of Alastair Baillie."

Merritt stabbed an olive. "This is a joke. All of it."

Rolling her lips together, Hulda pushed her plate away and met his eyes. "Let's talk about something else. How was Mr. Gifford?"

Merritt leaned back in his chair. He knew Hulda hated that, but it was comfortable. "Good enough. He had me try an array of chaocracy tests, and I failed every single one." He shrugged. "The genes skipped Sutcliffe entirely, and according to him, none of his other biological children have them . . . unless they're like me and unable to tap into them. More likely, the chaocracy genes skipped me, too. Magic adds on magic, right? The only magic markers on my mother's side of the family were back in the 1300s, according to the records."

Tapping her nails on the table, Hulda said, "And you're sure Mr. Hogwood said you had it?"

"Yes, but how *sane* was the guy, really?" He glanced over, looking for Owein, but the terrier was elsewhere. He whined whenever Silas Hogwood's name came up, and for good reason. "Maybe he just sensed it in the house."

She held her mug of hot cider in her hands but didn't drink it. "Perhaps."

"Perhaps. Perhaps, perhaps." Merritt looked over the cured-meat board, but nothing on it was currently appetizing. "Maybe there's a journalism opportunity in all of this. Not about the genetics of magic . . . there are so many scholarly works on *that* subject that Gifford will never stop reading them to me. But something else."

"I would advise against detailing what happened with Silas Hogwood."

He considered a moment. "I wonder what was in the police report, if one was even made."

"I'm not sure what influence Myra used . . . No one at LIKER has mentioned it, so she might have erased the record entirely. But she can't erase memories. I don't know." She took a sip of cider. Swallowed. "I wish I could talk to her."

"I know." He reached over and placed his hand over hers, and was rewarded with a small smile. "It will work out, one way or another. God willing."

"Will it?"

"That or we move west." Which made him wonder how dire things would have to get for Hulda to choose him over BIKER. Would she choose him here, now, if he asked?

He studied her face. The strong line of her jaw, her high cheekbones, hazel eyes with long lashes, bold nose.

He listened for Baptiste but didn't hear him.

"You know." He ran his thumb over her knuckle, feeling . . . daring. "You've never *really* let me kiss you."

That got her attention. Her spine went ramrod straight, and her cheeks took on a pretty hue, warmed by the candlelight. "Pardon?"

"Pardon what?"

Her gaze shifted between his eyes. "Pardon, I'm not sure what you mean." And her lips parted ever so slightly, looking warm and soft and perfect.

He scooted closer to her. Gazed at her. Took up that slightly curled tendril of hair and wrapped it around his finger.

She leaned forward, and that was all the invitation he needed.

He had always been so careful with Hulda. Knowing she was inexperienced with romance and men, he started carefully. Pressed his lips to hers, soft and sure. Twirled that lock of hair around his finger. Then he tilted his head and pressed a little firmer, and she reciprocated. When her lips parted for air, he took her bottom one between his. Expected her to start, but she didn't, which encouraged him. Releasing that lock of hair, his hand came around the back of her head, pulling her closer, claiming her, working his lips across hers. She was a quick learner, and hesitated only a second when he ran his tongue across the entrance to her mouth.

God knew it had been a long time since he'd kissed a woman like this. The heat of it coursed down him like a warm shower. The smell of the sea mingled with scents of rosewater and rosemary, like she was an exotic, delicious meal ready to eat. Needless to say, it was a good thing Merritt was sitting down.

Her hands found his shoulders, and she let him in. He tasted cider as he explored her softly, and when her tongue met his, a burst of magic zipped through his chest, and he knew he should pull away soon or *really* get into trouble.

But Merritt took his time, slowing down little by little. He played with her mouth and stifled a groan at how wonderful she felt, and when he finally broke the kiss, her flushed skin and hard breathing felt like some kind of trophy.

She licked her lips, and he resisted kissing her again.

To his surprise, she said, "I don't even know your middle name."

Merritt laughed, and all the troubles of the day dissipated under the force of it. "It's Jacob."

She mouthed, *Jacob*. He wanted to taste the name as she said it.

"And yours?" he asked instead, a little huskier than intended.

"I don't have one," she admitted.

Her maiden name could become a middle name, but Merritt didn't voice that. Instead he kissed her again, this time chastely. And while it might have been his imagination, he thought he saw a line of disappointment between her brows at the brevity of it.

Had they been deeper in conversation, Merritt might have missed the knock on the front door. A firm knock, deliberate. His chest soared for an instant at the thought that it might be Beth returned from her bizarre assignment, but Beth wouldn't knock . . . or might she think it necessary, after having been away?

He glanced at Hulda, whose ear was tilted toward the sound. "Mr. Portendorfer?" she suggested.

Shaking his head, Merritt rose from his seat; Hulda did the same. They slipped through the kitchen and into the reception hall. Baptiste had beaten them to the door. On the porch stood a middle-aged stranger, thin framed but well dressed, with a thick peppered mustache. When he saw them, he removed the bowler hat from atop his head and nodded.

"My apologies for interrupting at the dinner hour," he said, his accent thickly British. "I was told I might find Miss Hulda Larkin here."

Merritt straightened as Hulda answered, "I am she . . . Might I ask what you need?"

The man nodded. "Simply put, Miss Larkin, I'm here to speak with you concerning Silas Hogwood."

Chapter 11

Hulda's breath stuck somewhere between her larynx and the back of her tongue, and it took earnest effort to get it moving again.

"I beg your pardon?" She credited herself on the steadiness of her voice.

"Just a few questions." He glanced to Baptiste, hesitated, then looked at Merritt. "If I may."

Merritt nodded. Hulda felt his hesitance in his stance, in his aura, but he didn't show it. To herself, she broiled. *Why couldn't I have foreseen this?*

What was she supposed to do?

Owein trotted out curiously, tail wagging. Merritt put out an open hand, staying him. A soft whimper escaped the dog, but he sat.

"Your name?" Merritt asked. Bless him, Hulda had completely forgotten about exchanging pleasantries.

The stranger nodded, sticking his hat under his arm. "You may call me Dwight Adey. Is there a room you would prefer?"

Hulda managed to assert, "The sitting room," at the same time Merritt gestured to his right and said, "The living room is fine."

Mr. Adey smiled like a patient father might. To Hulda, he replied, "The sitting room will do nicely. Again, my apologies on the intrusion, but I will be brief. And, if you'll excuse the impropriety, I would like to speak to Miss Larkin alone."

While Hulda's gut loosened, Merritt bristled. He said, "For a stranger, you are asking a lot."

"I am, I am," Mr. Adey agreed. "But I assure you, I've only a few questions."

About Silas Hogwood, Hulda filled in, and hoped she didn't look pale. "Of course," she replied, ignoring Merritt's hard gaze. *I did nothing wrong. I did nothing wrong.* Still, she'd have to play this carefully. "I did work for the man. This way."

She gestured to the stairs. Mr. Adey nodded his thanks and followed.

Both Merritt and Baptiste took the stairs after them, quiet as hounds on the hunt.

Hulda allowed Mr. Adey to step into the sitting room first—which thankfully was still in order—and passed an unsure look to Merritt in the hallway. She left the door slightly ajar. Any proper British woman would do as much, so Mr. Adey shouldn't comment on it . . . and he didn't. He made himself comfortable on a chair, and knowing Merritt and Baptiste were very likely eavesdropping, Hulda took a seat on the settee, setting a good ten feet between her and the stranger.

She cleared her throat. "Forgive me—this is unexpected. Are you"—she swallowed, trying to keep her calm—"with LIKER?"

"Oh, no." He set his hat aside, but kept his coat on. "I work for the royal family. I'm a detective."

Hulda would not have been able to hide her shock at the easy confession even if her augury *had* sent her a clue. "I . . . I don't understand. It's been some time since I worked for Mr. Hogwood—"

"I sought you out because of the letters you sent the warden of Lancaster Castle."

Hulda paused for a beat, then let out a careful breath. "Lancaster Castle . . . yes. That was"—she mentally counted—"roughly six weeks ago."

She relaxed a hair. If Mr. Adey was set at Lancaster Castle, then he was behind on the timeline. He might not know anything about Myra or what happened in Marshfield.

He nodded. "Yes, you wrote concerning Mr. Silas's well-being." He pulled from his vest pocket a letter, which Hulda swiftly recognized as *her* letter: the very one she'd sent across the sea.

Just be honest. Hulda steadied herself. "Yes. I . . . Well, it may sound strange, but I could have sworn I saw him in Portsmouth. I was involved in his arrest some ten years ago—"

"I am aware," he said, not unkindly.

"—and it startled me. I'd worried he'd been released." She swallowed. "The warden told me he'd passed away."

All true.

"Hmm." He sounded disappointed as he returned the letter to his pocket. "That is what the warden told me as well. You've nothing else to add?"

Instead of answering, Hulda asked, "Do you believe him to be alive, Mr. Adey?"

"It is my duty to confirm that very thing. I do not believe he died in prison, Miss Larkin. Indeed, I have substantial evidence to prove he did not." He pulled out a pad of paper and a pencil. "Portsmouth, you say? About what date?"

Though her mouth went dry, she answered, "Mid-September. I'm afraid it might take me a moment to recall the exact day."

He wrote. "About where?"

Hulda paused, pulling up that fateful day. "I believe . . . Cromwell and King Charles?"

He scribbled away. "And do you, Miss Larkin, believe it was Silas Hogwood whom you saw?"

Her body heated at the inquiry, and she prayed it would stay away from her face. *Merritt is at the door. It's all right. No one is accusing you of anything.* Still, she answered carefully. "The warden indicated he was deceased. I dismissed it." Or at least, she had tried to.

Oh, Myra, what am I supposed to say? I can't do this much longer!

"And now"—Mr. Adey looked up from his paper—"that I have told you he may be alive?"

She swallowed. "If that is true, then he may very well be in Portsmouth."

"And why would he be in Portsmouth, Hulda?"

That question was too forward, and Hulda didn't mask her frustration. "Are you not the detective, Mr. Adey?"

Again, that paternal smile crossed his face. Thankfully, he put his writing implements away. "Indeed I am."

"If *I* may ask a question."

He nodded.

She hesitated but a moment. "Does the Crown intend to hunt down Mr. Hogwood and, well, put an end to him?" If so, she and Merritt had done them a favor.

Mr. Adey stroked his mustache. "No."

Her lips parted at the simple answer.

"Between you and me, Miss Larkin"—he leaned forward, elbows on his knees—"the Crown is the Crown in part because it is formed by a family of the highest magical influence. Silas Hogwood is also of considerable magical influence."

It took Hulda a few seconds to grasp his meaning, and her stomach clenched with nausea. "You mean to capture Mr. Hogwood—that is, *if* he is living—and marry him into the royal family? *Mr. Adey!* That man is a murderer of the highest degree!"

The detective wasn't the least put out by her chastisement. "I said nothing of marriage, Miss Larkin."

She was so stunned she didn't know how to answer.

Picking up his hat, Mr. Adey continued, "You see why this is a private investigation. It would not look good in the public eye to see the gears behind the clock's face, if you understand my meaning."

Hulda floundered. Mr. Adey placed his hat atop his head and stood. Hulda bolted to her feet as well, desperate to learn what she could before this strange man left. "H-Has he already . . . fathered . . . children?"

Giving her a pointed look, Mr. Adey said, "That is not for either of us to know. Indeed, I've said too much." He reached into a new pocket and pulled out a card. "If you see anything else, hear of anything, no matter how small, please send it my way. I can see you rewarded if you do."

Hulda's gaze locked on to the paper, but her feet were rooted to the carpet—something she might have blamed on Owein, were he still tied to the house. And so Mr. Adey crossed to her. She took the paper, numb.

He started for the door.

"Mr. Adey." Hulda whirled toward him. "Why are you telling me any of this?"

He smiled yet again. "Let's be honest with each other—you won't tell a soul. And if you did, who in their right mind would believe you?"

The walls around them flashed blue just then. Chuckling, Mr. Adey tapped a knuckle on the wall. "Enchanted houses. They are quaint, aren't they?" He tipped his hat to her. "I'll see myself out."

He opened the door. Merritt and Baptiste had made themselves scarce—only Owein sat in the hallway, his tail staying oddly still as the detective made his way out. Hulda passed a silent thank-you to him—the simple alteration spell would maintain the ruse that the house remained magical—and followed Mr. Adey as far as the stairs. Merritt waited at the bottom of them, his shirt sleeves rolled up to his elbows, a grim look on his face.

"Good night, Mr. Fernsby," the detective said, catching Hulda off guard. She didn't recall Merritt introducing himself.

Baptiste showed the stranger to the door, and then through it. Likely the cook would follow Mr. Adey all the way to his boat and make it look like a courtesy rather than suspicion.

Hulda descended the steps on quiet feet. "I don't think we need to worry about him. Did you hear?"

Merritt's gaze remained locked on the front door. "Most of it. But tell me anyway."

She did, and while she believed Mr. Adey had already stepped out of their story, the stress of the meeting never left Merritt's shoulders.

∽

Gifford arrived bright and early the following morning to torment Merritt with more essays on magic. One of which had been written in the 1400s. He wore a suit that looked like it had come from the same era, though it was in good repair, and his hair was oil slicked to one side.

"How lovely," Merritt said as he invited Gifford into the living room. A change of scenery was needed, so he thought, though the burgundy drapes and forest-green wallpaper wasn't exactly a cheery combination. Perhaps something more peaches and cream was in order, but he knew Hulda had plans for the space. He stifled a yawn before lowering into an armchair, though in truth, he was grateful for Gifford's arrival. Not only from the hope they might discover something useful to him, but because he wanted a distraction from the detective sniffing at Hulda's skirts. "But are they about communion?" He dared to hope.

"Oh yes." Gifford poised himself on the sofa and opened his briefcase. "I've highlighted what I've determined to be the most pertinent, and I'll leave the rest with you for your personal study."

Merritt nodded. "I appreciate it." He *had* read the previous essays and articles, and while he knew a lot more about his abilities in a theoretical sense, he was no better equipped to wield them than he'd been before.

"This one"—Gifford pulled out the copy of the ancient paper—"hypothesizes there exists a spell that not only permits a person to speak to insects, but allows the *controlling* of them as well. Isn't that fascinating?"

Merritt tried to imagine what he might do with an army of beetles, or perhaps butterflies. "I suppose . . . Was it ever proven?"

"Not by scholars, no." He thumbed through the pages. "Quite disappointing, really. If only there were magic that would let us travel through time! How incredible it would be to go back to the fifteenth century and see magic in higher potency. What we might learn!"

Merritt smirked. "Wouldn't learn much if the plague got you."

"Ah, but I would be a century too late for that." He set down that essay and picked up the other. "At least, for the big one. But . . ." He shuffled a paper, and Merritt could see he'd underlined so many passages with yellow pencil it would be quicker to read what he *hadn't* selected than what he had. "The theory of personal entanglement for magic comes up again in this one."

Merritt leaned forward. "Remind me what that is?"

"The idea that an ability is directly connected with something of one's person, usually the intangible."

Merritt processed this. "Such as when you suggested my wardship was tied to my 'protective instincts.'"

Gifford beamed. "Yes! Precisely." He went on to read an incredibly verbose passage about it, of which Merritt managed to follow about seventy percent. If the scholar had been paid per word, the way Merritt was for his newspaper articles, he'd be a millionaire.

"So"—Gifford's shift in tone signaled an end to his reading—"we might just need to find what your communion is tied to. I think his reasoning that it's a pertinent connection is spot on. Wardship, protective instincts. They fit together like a puzzle. Communion may be related to speech, or communication, or . . ." He scratched his temple. "Well, we'll think on that one. And chaocracy could be tied to cleanliness, perhaps, or even anger."

Merritt snorted.

"Pardon?"

"Not anger," he answered, glancing toward the window. A few fallen leaves stirred outside. As if sensing his attention, something—it felt like a hare—whispered, *Listen. Still. Listen.* "I'd be an expert at chaocracy if that were the case."

"Oh dear." Setting down the papers, Gifford turned bodily toward him. "I hope it's nothing serious."

Merritt pasted on a smile. "Oh, no. Just some family business. You know how frustrating that can be."

"Ah, yes." He reached into his briefcase and pulled out a thermometer. "I was thinking, however, that it might be interesting to take some vitals, both of you at rest and casting a spell . . . if you can, of course. Are you willing?"

Merritt sighed. "Of course." Sitting up, he straightened his vest. "Whatever you need."

☙

Hulda arrived at the Genealogical Society for the Advancement of Magic at approximately a quarter after eight the morning after Mr. Adey's visit. Normally the society didn't open to the public until nine, but admittedly, Hulda was used to special treatment. Unfortunately, the ones who usually gave it to her were not present, unaware of her last-minute decision to do some professional snooping before she made her appearance in the BIKER office. The spare time had her fretting in front of the office over the incident with Mr. Baillie and then pulling out Mr. Adey's card, glancing over two addresses upon it, which she'd already memorized: one was in New York, another in London proper. She'd lost sleep mulling over the detective's unexpected visit, but had come to the conclusion he posed no real threat to her. At worst, he would miraculously track Silas Hogwood back to Blaugdone Island and to Marshfield, only to learn he'd attempted the murder of three persons and lost his life in the process. Hulda couldn't be penalized for withholding what she knew—she was an American citizen, and the English government had no power over her. Even had her path never crossed with that of Mr. Hogwood, Hulda doubted even the best detective would be able to track his final whereabouts in the States. Not without Myra Haigh's help.

He might be another fellow who ends up looking for you, Myra.

There were many of them now. Herself, the writer of the mysterious telegram, Mr. Adey. Did Myra know about the last? Doubtful. Should Hulda hire a detective of her own to track down the missing woman?

She was mulling over the idea when a society bookkeeper arrived, spotted her, and unlocked the doors to the building.

"Anything I can help you with today, Miss Larkin?" she asked, stepping back to hold the door for Hulda.

Hulda nodded her thanks. "Just a light would be helpful. I'm happy to peruse on my own. I'm sure you've better things to do than tend to me."

The woman nodded, fetched her a lantern, and walked her to the door that opened onto the stone steps leading down to the basement, where most of the records were stored. Then she left her to it. Hulda released a relieved breath about halfway down; she had worried over what excuses to use if the woman had insisted on accompanying her. She didn't want any chance of her inquisition getting back to BIKER.

Because, in truth, she was not here to dig up information on a client or the owners of an enchanted house. She was here in the hope she might uncover something on Mr. Alastair Baillie. Because not knowing was driving her a wee bit mad.

Hulda knew the Genealogical Society almost as well as she did BIKER, so she found the aisle and shelf she needed quickly. Found some Baileys and some Baillies, but not even a sifting brought up any records of Alastair. She wasn't surprised, only disappointed—Alastair was an English citizen and had never lived in America, and it would appear none of his close relatives had done so, either.

Twisting her lips, Hulda shoved the Bailey and Baillie boxes back where they belonged, picked up her skirt, and trudged back upstairs, where the morning light streaming through the windows hurt her eyes. Mr. Gifford's reception desk was empty; Hulda blew out her lantern, set it aside, and helped herself to a pen and parchment. Scrawled a written request for genealogical records to a contact in Britain, leaving off the reason for why she needed them. With luck, her name and association with BIKER would be enough. At the end, she did say, *Please write directly to me.* Last thing she needed was Mr. Baillie or Mr. Walker opening up her questionable post.

After folding up the letter, she stuffed it in her black bag and checked the time. She had enough left to run to the post office before getting to work. And when she got to work, she was going to check the stock of wards to see if Myra had left her anything to protect one against hysteria.

If Mr. Baillie *was* indeed more masterful in hysteria than he claimed, the very least Hulda could do was ward her bedroom walls.

⌒

"You want to *hire* him?"

Hulda stood on the opposite side of Mr. Walker's desk, completely flummoxed. She'd come in to file another formal complaint against Mr. Baillie, who had been conveniently absent when she arrived, but the conversation had immediately gotten away from her.

"You didn't mention he was a wardist." Mr. Walker gestured to the chair in front of him, and Hulda hesitantly sat. "We always have a place for people with talent."

She worked her mouth until Mr. Walker chuckled. She snapped it closed and organized her thoughts. Here she was ready with a defense and explanation about yesterday's horrendous events, and . . . for all the twisting and turning she'd done in bed last night, *this* was not one of the reactions she had prepared for. "I . . . will inform him of the offer."

"What is he doing now?"

"He's an author."

"Really? Anything I'd know?"

"*A Pauper in the Making* is published. It's something of a crime adventure."

"Interesting!" He wrote down the title.

"But, Mr. Walker, I need to discuss Mr. Baillie with you."

He nodded. "I'm not surprised."

Her pulse danced beneath her wrists. She squared her shoulders to fight embarrassment. "Oh?"

"You and Myra Haigh were close; it's understandable that you'd be upset about the investigation and the audit. I'm happy to approve a holiday for you."

Her gut shifted. "Is that what Mr. Baillie told you? That I was upset over Miss Haigh?"

He tilted his head. "Is that not the case?"

"He *used magic* on me, Mr. Walker." She did not yell, but one might call the force behind the words excessive. "He riled up my emotions until I could barely think straight!"

He frowned. "Mr. Baillie is—"

"A weak hysterian. So you've said." She clutched her armrests. "And I insist you are mistaken. Ask Miss Steverus if you need validation of my character, Mr. Walker. I am not some simpering, afflicted woman. Mr. Baillie has targeted me, I believe because you've selected me as a possible replacement for the director position here."

Mr. Walker's frown deepened, but he didn't outright dismiss her, which she supposed could be taken as a victory.

"Thus Mr. Fernsby's . . . reaction," she added.

Opening a drawer, Mr. Walker retrieved a thin ledger and opened it. Flipped a few pages. Dipped his pen. "I will look into it. In the meantime, it might be better for you and Mr. Baillie to work in, let's say, *individualized* spaces."

The extent of Mr. Baillie's ability still unknown, Hulda wasn't sure how distant they'd need to be for her to avoid his spells. Still, relief breathed out of her. She was being taken seriously. "Thank you, Mr. Walker."

"Make my offer to Mr. Fernsby. He's welcome to drop by and discuss."

She nodded. "Of course."

She discussed a few more matters of business with Mr. Walker before taking her handy black bag with her out of his office. He'd requested the next set of files for years 1840 through 1841, but as Hulda turned down the hallway toward the records room, she collided into the last person she wanted to see.

Mr. Baillie.

He too had files in his arms, and they flew into the air when they collided, floating to the floor like fat snowflakes.

"Pardon." Hulda adjusted her glasses as he adjusted his. She didn't make eye contact with him, but she was a decent person, so she crouched and helped him pick up the papers, glancing over them quickly to see if they were anything of interest. They were not.

However, the pattern of the mess flashed in her mind, and suddenly she saw Mr. Baillie, posture shrunken, hair mussed, his face shiny with perspiration. Backing away, like he was in some sort of trouble. His face was as serene as usual, but fear glimmered in his eyes. He was looking at something—

The background blurred. She tried to focus on it—

She blinked, and the vision faded. Yet another premonition too brief to make sense. If only she had a few more drops of augury running through her veins!

"If you would." Mr. Baillie held out his hand, waiting for the papers Hulda still clutched. She'd completely forgotten she held them, but the amnesiac side effect of the spell quickly faded.

Shaking herself, Hulda passed him the papers, but Mr. Baillie stayed put, blocking her path.

"An inquiry for you, Miss Larkin"—his voice was flat and apathetic, as it always was, and he forewent any sort of apology for the crash or thank-you for her aid—"concerning the man who came here yesterday evening."

Flustered, Hulda asked, "You'll need to be more specific."

"He said his name was Dwight Adey. His business concerned you."

A zip of lightning shot from the nape of her neck to her ankles. Squaring her shoulders, she said, "I spoke with him. Thank you for your concern." She moved to sidestep him, but Mr. Baillie didn't budge, and she certainly wasn't going to compress their bodies together in order to pass.

"What did he need of you?"

Her eyes narrowed. "It was of a private matter."

"If you would oblige me," the lawyer pressed.

Why on earth did the man care about Mr. Adey? Perhaps, were it, say, Miss Steverus asking, she *would* oblige. But she detested this man and owed him nothing.

"The situation does not require that I oblige you. If you'll kindly shift your person to the side so I might pass."

Footsteps behind her drew her attention; just Miss Richards walking by, offering a friendly wave. Whether it was surrender or fear of a witness that made the lawyer stand down, Hulda would never know. But he moved and took off down the hallway, his stride even and unbothered.

Hulda watched him go, put out by his request, unnerved by his association with Mr. Adey. But above all else, she was curious. The unexpected vision of him stuck to her mind like a sandbur.

Was Mr. Baillie in some sort of trouble? Or rather, was he going to be?

She excogitated the idea as she went on her way, finding no solace in the possibility.

⁓

"I'm not interested."

Hulda and Merritt sat in a modish soup-and-sandwich shop not far from the docks, at a table wide enough for public decency near one of several slat windows letting in sunlight. The air smelled of bread and beer. The place operated off an elementally enchanted oven, created by a renowned Dutch elementist in the late seventeen hundreds. The wizard was now deceased, but the magic still held strong, pumping heat through the brick building and keeping the draft from the windows at bay.

Merritt, who had spoken, stirred his spoon through his clam chowder, waiting for it to cool, blinking sleep from his eyes. He'd come to Boston for lunch, both to make any necessary apologies and to hear what had happened with Mr. Walker. Hulda had relayed the whole of her morning's experience to him, ending with Mr. Walker's job offer.

"I didn't think you would be." Her chowder was untouched. She pulled her roll apart to butter it. Something about the soup shop reminded her of England—the brickwork, perhaps, or the low ceiling. Perhaps it was merely the dreariness beyond the windows, like it might rain any moment. England was beautiful, yes, but it certainly rained frequently.

Merritt set down his spoon. "This doesn't make sense."

"Hm?" It was all she could manage with food in her mouth.

He propped his elbow on the small table and leaned his head against his fist. "As you said, I assaulted the man. Why not report me?"

She swallowed. "I think he did."

"Did he? Did you ask what he said?"

She retraced the conversation with Mr. Walker. "No, I didn't."

"Baillie doesn't seem the forgiving type. So why not prosecute? Why not get revenge?"

Perhaps we've misjudged him, Hulda thought. And yet . . . after what happened in that office, Hulda was positive she hadn't. But that vision she'd had—the one of Mr. Baillie perspiring, retreating, and scared— nagged at her.

She related it to Merritt, who frowned. "Who was he retreating from?"

She shrugged. "I haven't a clue. Augury delights in being vague. At least, mine does."

Shaking his head, Merritt stirred his soup again. "None of this sits right with me."

Hulda watched the shifting of his expression as she blew on a spoonful of soup, giving him a moment to work out whatever was in his head. She wished she had Myra's ability to read thoughts. What was he thinking right then?

Sighing, he sat up. Ate a spoonful. At least his appetite had returned. She'd noticed he wasn't eating well—at least not during the meals she'd shared with him. She tried to keep an eye on his waistline to see if he'd lost anything there, but it was hard to tell under vests and coats and improperly tucked shirts. Perhaps she'd ask Baptiste. She would have preferred Miss Taylor, but she wasn't an option at the moment.

The change in appetite didn't have anything to do with her, did it? The thought made nerves spark in her stomach.

Don't be foolish, she chided herself. *Not after he kissed you like that.*

Her cheeks warmed.

"Maybe if he brings Beth back, I'll consider," Merritt finally said. He met her eyes; his looked like the sea did right now, cool and blue with hints of gray. Unsettled. "You haven't heard anything?"

She shook her head. "Unfortunately, no. I tried finding a file related to where she's been sent, but without luck."

"Probably Baillie as well."

"He's a cad, certainly, though I'm not sure what benefit he would have, personally, to steal your maid." She took another mouthful of soup. "If something was amiss, Miss Taylor would have had the opportunity to write us by now and explain. Perhaps she was just feeling out of sorts that afternoon."

Merritt rubbed his eyes. "I suppose that makes sense."

Pressing her lips together, Hulda reached across the table and gently grasped his forearm. "We'll sort it out. I'll check again."

He pulled his hand away and laid it over hers, his countenance softening. "I appreciate your efforts."

She smiled at him.

"What are your plans for Christmas? I meant to ask you."

The question surprised her and sent a flurry through her torso. *Christmas.* If he was asking, he intended to still have her around at Christmas. The thought was thrilling, though she tried not to react like a fool-headed girl. "I honestly haven't thought of it."

"Do you usually see your sister?"

"Or my parents."

He glanced away, considering, and the saddest realization struck her. Did Merritt usually spend Christmas alone?

He had Fletcher, of course. He'd stayed with the Portendorfers during his excursion to Cattlecorn. But did he go there on Christmas? Or did he stay away so as not to intrude, or because he couldn't bear to be so close to his own family, yet so far away, on the holiday? That seemed like a Merritt thing to do. If he stayed away from Cattlecorn, how did he spend his holidays? What had he done in his little apartment in New York when the Christmas bells rang?

"I do think," she amended, "it might be nice to spend it at Whimbrel House."

A ghost of a smile crinkled the corners of his eyes. "You don't have to do that."

"You're correct." She squeezed his hand before pulling away. "I don't *have* to do anything. I'm a free woman, Mr. Fernsby." She took up her spoon. "I can only imagine what horrors two bachelors—three, if you count Owein—have been visiting upon that poor house, and Christmas celebrations can only make it worse. If nothing else, you should be supervised."

He chuckled. "Why do you think I'm trying so hard to retrieve Beth?"

She bit down on a smile and pulled off another piece of roll. "The real problem is how to get a fir across the bay and to the island. I've no desire to decorate a weeping cherry."

Nodding, he said, "I'll see what I can do."

$$\sim\!\!\mathcal{9}$$

Thanks to the speed of kinetically powered ships, Hulda received her response concerning Mr. Baillie's genealogy two days after requesting it. She saw the letter atop a stack Miss Steverus had collected that morning, and quickly swiped it before Miss Richards returned from her tea. Surely, despite Hulda being the addressee, the LIKER secretary would have opened it. She seemed to enjoy being in the know.

Hulda did not open the envelope until she was safely tucked away in her room downstairs, which she'd warded with a linen spell-turning ward containing tourmaline right at the door, something that ensured the room was her safe haven from the cloud of conflicting emotions she often felt upstairs. She'd been tempted to ward the window as well, but it wasn't good for the body to be around too many wards, so she'd determined to play it safe.

Hulda tore the top of the envelope in a neat line and retrieved the letter inside.

> *Miss Larkin,*
>
> *It dismays me to say I cannot fulfill your request without the proper paperwork; you know how it goes. If you send me form 26A, I should be able to dig up the information you need, but privacy laws bind my hands otherwise.*

But I didn't want to send you only written disappointment, so I made a stop at the local paper archive and did a little digging. It's probably not what BIKER wants, but alas.

Alastair Baillie is thirty-seven years old and was born in Leeds. Couldn't find any public information on his parents. He studied at Oxford and graduated in 1831. He currently works for the London Institute for the Keeping of Enchanted Rooms (did you know that?), though he's done court work. His most notable work was with the will and probate of Silas Hogwood, as well as his defense for Hogwood versus the Crown in 1836.

Hulda nearly dropped the letter. She reread that last sentence. "Silas Hogwood?" she whispered. Her lungs struggled to take in air as two separate dilemmas overlapped. This was entirely unexpected.

Alastair Baillie was Mr. Hogwood's estate lawyer . . . and his attorney.

It doesn't matter. Silas Hogwood is dead. Merritt had crushed in the back of his skull with a crowbar. Hulda had watched him take his last breath. And while Silas was a necromancer, among other things, no necromancer could resurrect his own corpse.

Swallowing, she continued reading.

Thought that was interesting, so I looked into it a little more (it was no trouble). Apparently Silas Hogwood passed away recently—surprised it wasn't bigger news, considering his trial being widely publicized.

Mr. Baillie also worked on that case with the food poisoning at the royal ball back in '37, which is interesting. Right before LIKER hired him, I think, but I couldn't find specifics in the periodicals.

Happy to send you a transcription of the articles if you like. If it's simply the family line that holds interest

for you, forgive an old man his musings and ship over (or
telegram) 26A.
   Sincerely,
   Marcus Duggat

Hulda slunk into a chair and read the letter again from the beginning, suddenly no longer interested in Mr. Baillie's bloodline—she
wouldn't be able to get a form to order them legally, besides. Finished,
she set the letter down, then rubbed gooseflesh popping up beneath her
sleeves. Even in death, Mr. Hogwood haunted her. Still, he *was* dead,
for real this time, so why did this revelation bother her so keenly? Of
course he would need a lawyer over his estate and hearing. Why not a
lawyer with a sharp enough reputation to work for LIKER?

She wondered, again, at Baillie's question regarding Mr. Adey.
Hulda highly doubted the detective had revealed his true purpose for
his inquiry; he'd wanted to speak to Hulda alone, without even Merritt
in the room. Even so, she could not help wondering whether Mr. Baillie
knew that the other man was searching for Silas. Was Mr. Baillie still
connected to Silas Hogwood, or had their relationship terminated after
his incarceration and falsified death at Lancaster Castle?

Hulda exhaled a breath, which mussed a loose strand of hair that
hung against her forehead. Reaching up, she smoothed it back and
tucked it beneath a pin before digging into her bag for her communion
stone. Pressing the rune, she murmured, "I'd like to talk to you as soon
as you're able. In person." She needed to share the information, and
with Myra gone, Merritt was her closest confidant. Though how much
she could trust Myra were she present was uncertain.

Forcing herself to stand, Hulda steeled herself and reached for the
door, pausing just before she touched the knob. *Better to know than
not to know,* she thought, and crossed to the small desk in the corner.
She scrawled out a quick note, unconcerned for her penmanship, to
Alice Pearshold, one of the maids who had worked under her at Gorse

End. Although Alice wasn't associated with either enchanted household society, the two women had kept in loose touch since Mr. Hogwood's arrest. Acting like she'd only just heard the news of Mr. Hogwood's demise, Hulda asked Miss Pearshold if she knew anything further about the court case or the dealings of the estate. She signed her name at the bottom of the letter, then added, *Please send your response to Whimbrel House*, and scrawled the address for its Portsmouth mailbox.

She absolutely would not let any curious secretaries or wayward hysterians get their hands on that letter.

Owein knew how to use a door. It wasn't easy, without thumbs and real fingers, but he knew how to do it. Still, Merritt had said he'd cut a swinging entrance in the back door for him soon, with hinges on the top, because otherwise either the doors got scuffed with Owein's attempts at opening them or everyone had to take turns letting him out to poop or run or chase mice. He could do it himself, but everyone had gotten mad at him when he'd warped the back door—it still didn't fit in the frame just right, even though he'd fixed it—and he hated the side effects of alteration spells even more than those of chaocracy. He never knew *how* his body would mutate, or how long it would last, or how painful it might be. So he waited for Merritt to cut him a door.

When the others were gone, Baptiste left the back door cracked open, just as it was now. Owein pushed into the house with his nose, then used the top of his head to close the door. He shook off frost and water from his coat, then stood by the stoked oven for a count of ten to warm up. Checked on Baptiste, but he was sleeping. Baptiste stayed up even later than Merritt did and napped in the afternoon a lot. Owein let him be. Baptiste got *mad* when he was woken up, and now that Owein was no longer a house, he wasn't immune to other people's ill tempers.

Owein sniffed around the kitchen. Everything *smelled*. Good, bad, and in between. And everything left traces of smells, like snails left traces of snot. He could find things by smell faster than any other way, except maybe sound. He snuffed around, finding a few morsels and crumbs around the oven and the edges of the cabinets, since Merritt and Baptiste didn't sweep as thoroughly as Beth did. Then he used his back leg to scratch behind his ear—he still thought that was funny, though he couldn't really do it any other way—and scampered into the breakfast room for more morsels. He found a hard piece of dried meat and ate it up. He wanted to savor it, but the dog side of him scarfed it right down.

He didn't know how the dog side worked, but he didn't mind it. He was just happy to have a body. To be alive.

He thought of that dark, dank basement where Silas Hogwood had pinned him to a bench—

Shaking, refusing the memory, Owein was making his way into the dining room when he heard the front door snick shut. Very quietly. Was Merritt also trying not to wake Baptiste? But Baptiste was four rooms away and snoring, and if his own snores didn't wake him up, the front door wouldn't, either.

Owein padded into the reception hall and saw the backside of a man in a light-brown suit. Kind of a mousy brown, or the brown of the inside of a cattail after he'd chewed it up. He didn't know this man. Not by sight, and not by smell. He smelled like hickory, paper, and sweat.

The man turned and spied him, looking a little surprised. "Of course there's a dog," he said. His voice was a little funny, but in a good way. Like it was full of big bubbles. He stepped back and patted his trouser pockets, then his coat pockets. Pulled out a morsel of something and tossed it Owein's way.

Owein bolted after it. It was something meaty, but he'd lapped it up before he could identify what. Chewed it with his back teeth and swallowed. Yum.

The man was heading upstairs.

Owein tilted his head. Where was Merritt?

Approaching the door, Owein broke the order of the wood, resulting in it melting enough for him to stick his head through. He scanned the island. No sign of anyone else, except—

Whimbrel!

He darted forward to chase it, then planted his paws.

Wait, no. Man. Follow the man. Maybe?

After retreating into the house, Owein returned the door to normal and shook from head to tail, dispelling the foggy feeling inching into his brain. The man was already upstairs, but Owein could smell him. He tromped up after, sniffing. He'd gone to the left, into Beth's room.

Owein barked at him. *What are you doing?* he tried to say. *Who are you?*

But the man couldn't hear him the way Merritt could. He opened a couple of drawers, frowned, and returned to the hallway. Owein barked again.

"Shush." The man's tone grated. The dog side of him cowed, but Owein also *shushed* it and followed the stranger, sniffing. What was in that bag he was carrying?

The man went to the room at the end of the hall—the sitting room. Beth had never let Owein on the furniture, but he'd been sitting on it a lot lately. Waiting in the doorway, he watched the man snoop around, then pull a potato—no, a rock—from his bag and slip it into the edge of the unlit fireplace.

Owein's ears raised. He trotted over. The man tried to kick him, but Owein was too fast. The man hurried back into the hallway, and Owein went to the rock, smelling it. It smelled like a rock and a little bit like the man. There was a letter on it, but not one of the letters he knew. A magical symbol of some sort? Hulda had hung stuff with magical symbols all over him when he'd been a house, but none like this.

Owein got a weird feeling in his stomach, and he didn't think it was from the treat. Who was this man? Why was he here without the others? And why had he entered so cautiously, making the front door snick?

Owein followed him. Found him in the library, replacing a book. Was there another rock behind there?

He should tell Merritt, but Merritt wasn't home.

Oh well.

Owein sat in the doorway and barked at the man. The man frowned and grumbled, "Mutt."

So Owein made the floorboards expand and swallow his left foot.

The man stumbled, dropping his bag. It made a *thud* because it was full of rocks, and one of them fell out. The man jerked his leg, trying to get it free, but Owein had already shrunk the planks and stopped his spell. The floor was hard again, and Owein's body was trying to grow a second tail in retaliation for the magic.

"What on earth?" The man knelt and scratched at the floorboards. Owein trotted over and made the man's suit jacket bright orange, just because he could. It made his toes itch, but it was such a little spell he didn't mutate.

The man went wide eyed behind his glasses as Owein jogged to the window on the far wall. It wasn't as easy as a dog, but he bared his teeth and made the walls shift inward, blocking out the window so the man couldn't escape that way, if he managed to break free. That made his shoulder blades sharpen, but the mutation would go away soon enough.

"What are you?" The man flailed harder now. "Release me!"

No, Owein said, not that the man could hear. He bolted for the door, feeling the stranger's fingertips graze his fur as he passed, like he was trying to grab him. Owein didn't like that.

He went out into the hallway and closed the door with his mouth, leaving spit on the knob. Then he melted a little hole into the wood so he could watch the man.

Sitting like a good dog, Owein guarded the library and waited for Merritt to come home.

Chapter 12

Merritt found himself playing with his pocket watch outside the kinetic tram station in Boston, opening and closing its cover, pinching his skin in its hinges, winding it slowly, one tick at a time. He'd just turned in two articles to a local paper, one opinion piece on static wages in the working class and another on his lessons with Mr. Gifford and the dreadful essays the man loved leaving him with after each appointment. There *were* some interesting tidbits in those essays, and Merritt thought he might as well put them into modern words. He worried the bibliography of his citations might make the piece too long to publish, but he'd submitted it anyway.

He glanced up from his watch at just the right moment, for he spied Hulda through the bustling Monday crowd, coming his way, her strides longer than a woman of her height should be capable of, that familiar black bag slung over her shoulder. He straightened and smiled, then reached into his own satchel as she approached.

"How was work?" he asked.

She wiped perspiration from her forehead. It was cool outside, but nothing a brisk walk couldn't thwart. "Rather congenial, actually. A certain colleague of mine was absent most of the day."

"Most excellent." He pulled a letter free and handed it to her. "You know, you needn't send your mail to my box just for an excuse to see me."

Instead of laughing, Hulda snatched the gray envelope from his hands and tore it open.

Merritt leaned closer. "Something important?"

"It's from Miss Pearshold." She pulled the letter free and turned her back to passersby.

Merritt waited while her eyes shifted back and forth. When she didn't share, he asked, "Who is . . . ?"

"The maid"—she read further—"from Gorse End."

Merritt stiffened. "You told me about Silas's connection to Baillie. You failed to mention following up with your past coworkers."

Her eyes lifted from the paper, her focus far off.

He stepped closer to her, almost touching. "What does it say?"

Her hazel gaze focused on him. "Not a lot," she murmured. "She says she believes the estate is still run by Stanley Lidgett, and she hasn't heard anything about Silas Hogwood's death or a change in ownership."

"This Lidgett fellow is his steward?" Merritt asked.

She nodded. "He was there, when they arrested him. Mr. Hogwood, I mean. Yet the only person he seemed disgusted with was me." Her cheeks pinked slightly.

"I don't suppose you want to write to him," he tried.

She folded the letter. "No, I do not. I highly doubt he would respond, regardless." She nodded to the tram; Merritt offered her his arm and escorted her aboard. Despite fiddling with his pocket watch, he hadn't noticed the time. They were the last to board, and the tram took off only a minute afterward.

Hulda was deep in thought, so Merritt let her think as the vehicle rushed them into Portsmouth. By the time they stepped off, she said, "I don't know what else to do about it. It's likely nothing. And yet, when I thought that before, it proved an erroneous presumption."

"Hmm." He offered his arm again as they strode toward the docks. "Have you ever fallen down the well?"

She glanced at him. "Do many survive falling down a well?"

"I mean in research," he amended. "Sometimes I go to the library to look up something for a story or an article, and while searching, I find some other nugget of information I hadn't before considered, so I start researching that instead, which may lead me to a quite interesting fact that has nothing to do with my work. So then I read articles and books and the like on that, until I've spent all my time learning about something that isn't actually useful to me in the long run."

She studied his face. "Your point being?"

"Besides the fact that I know an awful lot about the mounding habits of gophers"—he smiled—"my point is that it may be better to focus on the immediate problem on hand."

She sighed. "Mr. Baillie." Paused. "Myra."

Nodding, he added, "Silas Hogwood is dead." He hesitated as a strange swirling sensation coursed through his gut. Quieter, he added, "I know that better than anyone."

She beat the letter against her palm. "And it *does* seem unlikely that the steward of Gorse End would ask the head of BIKER for the dead body of his decade-previous master, especially five months after his recorded death. If the message is about Silas at all. Who knows how many secrets Myra was keeping."

She reached for his hand and squeezed it, though when they strode past a sailor, she released it.

They slipped into his inherited rickety boat—which might be due for repair sometime soon—and sailed their way to Blaugdone. The sun had not yet set, so the lighthouses were still dark. The water was calm, and they made good time, pulling ashore in less than twenty minutes. Merritt stepped out first, then offered a hand to Hulda. With no witnesses around, she clasped it with a smile, then pinched her lips as her underskirt caught on something by her bench.

"I'll get it." Merritt bent over the boat and tugged the fabric off a wide splinter, Hulda keeping her balance with a hand on his shoulder. He then clasped his hands around her waist and lifted her from the boat, eliciting a delightful shriek in response. He did not comment on the pinkening of her cheeks, and she did not chide him, so he merely offered his arm and escorted her to the house.

"Do you find all those layers necessary?" Not only were they catching on old boat benches, but she'd taken up a handful of them to keep them out of the reeds, for the worn path still wasn't wide enough to accommodate two people walking side by side.

"They do well in the cold," she said.

"So do trousers."

She frowned at him. "I'll be sure to inform the local ton of your brilliant observation. Women will be donning breeches by June."

He smiled. "And men, corsets."

"Why on God's good earth would a man wear a corset?"

Merritt shrugged. "I suppose for the same reason a woman wears one."

She considered that a second before saying, "That's nonsense."

"My point exactly. I—"

Hhhhhhheeeeeeeeeee, the wind whispered. No, not the wind, the reeds. He stopped in his tracks, a shiver coursing up his spine like someone had traced it with an icicle.

Hulda's hand touched his shoulder blade. "Merritt?"

Owein barked from the house, and Merritt's stomach tightened.

"Hurry" was all he said before grabbing her hand and taking off toward the house. Owein's barking didn't stop, only grew louder. Had he seen him coming? Too many things whirled through his mind for him to make sense of any one of them.

He released Hulda's hand at the porch and flew into the house. "Owein?"

Owein barked from upstairs. Merritt took the steps two at a time and found his chef and the terrier standing outside the library.

I caught a man! Owein shouted.

Baptiste wore a dark expression. "There is a stranger in the house. Owein has locked him in."

"Stranger?" Should he get his gun?

"Who?" Hulda asked.

Baptiste shrugged.

Merritt lurched for the doorknob—Owein had done something to the door, in addition to carving a little peephole in it, because it stuck, but it gave way when Merritt forced his shoulder into it.

The first thing he noticed was the darkness—the window was gone. Owein pushed between his legs, and the far walls split, the glass windows and evening sunlight reemerging.

And sure enough, there was a disheveled man off center in the room, his foot and ankle swallowed by the floorboards. He wore a garish orange suit coat and held a bag of something on his lap. He didn't even bother looking up when Merritt entered.

Hulda gasped. "Mr. Baillie?"

Merritt had recognized him instantly, but something about hearing his name, in Hulda's voice, no less, filled him with rage. Like Baillie's name was a lit match. Now another fire burned inside him, choking smoke seeping into his limbs. His fingers twitched. Fine hairs on the back of his neck stood on end. His vision tinted red.

"What the hell are you doing in my house." It was a question, or it should have been, but it sounded more like a threat.

Mr. Baillie's shoulders hunched. "I can explain."

Baptiste pushed through. "He was planting these."

He held something out to Merritt, but Merritt's bones were steel joists, so Hulda took it instead. "Communion stones?" A pause. "You . . . You intended to *spy* on us?"

The fire grew hotter.

"Release me, and I'll explain," Baillie said, and it was the first time Merritt had ever heard a lick of emotion in the lawyer's voice. Weariness, and . . . fear?

Several stiff seconds passed before Owein padded forward and shifted the floorboards.

Mr. Baillie rubbed his ankle, which had a red ring around it, adjusted his socks and trousers, and stood.

Hulda grabbed Merritt's arm around the bicep. Could she sense he wanted to pummel the man?

"He'll not be happy after this." Baillie didn't meet their eyes.

Hulda took the bait. "Who's he?"

"Mr. Walker." The man pushed up his glasses and looked at her, then Merritt. Sighed. "I'm far enough now, and enough time has passed, that his hold on me is wearing thin. He'll wonder why I'm missing. Why I haven't reported back."

"Explain." Merritt's voice didn't sound like his own. It was too low, too heavy.

Baillie rubbed his hands together. "Mr. Walker is not a conjurist; that's only what he tells people. He feigns his ability to create gold because he won't be required to prove it."

"I don't understand." Hulda's grip on Merritt's arm loosened.

"He's a psychometrist, Miss Larkin." He moved his bag to his shoulder. "An adept one. Not like Miss Haigh—as far as I know, he cannot read thoughts. But he can control them."

Hulda gasped. A niggle of doubt pressed into Merritt's mind. Faded, resurfaced. He tried to make sense of it.

Mr. Walker, a psychometrist? *Controlling* Mr. Baillie? Was it Walker, then, who'd pushed Baillie to torment Hulda, or had that been his own doing? Was that why Mr. Walker hadn't taken Hulda's accusations more seriously?

Baillie took what appeared to be a steadying breath. "He's had me under his thumb for years. He sits back and schemes and lets others carry out his missives." He considered a moment. "I don't think he's manipulated Miss Richards."

Merritt considered this, prodding it for holes, sick to his stomach from the effort. "And for some reason, Walker wants you to plant communion stones in my house."

Hulda's fingers tightened on his arm.

But Baillie nodded. His face was impassive, as always, but there was strain around his eyes. A little more inflection to his voice than usual. "It's been hard to glean his intentions, but sometimes he lets his guard down, or makes an offhanded comment that lends me a clue. BIKER is not in need of an audit, only a director. But word reached Walker about Silas Hogwood's arrival to America, and that Miss Haigh was somehow connected to it. And Miss Haigh was also connected to *you*." He gestured to Hulda.

Hulda's grip tightened nearly enough to hurt. Merritt put his hand over hers, trying to ignore the simmering beneath his skin. Trying to hide the reaction before Baillie could spy it.

He knew. Somehow, he knew. Part of it, at least.

"He's obsessed with Silas Hogwood," Baillie continued, and doubt twisted in Merritt's mind again. "He's praised him, in private. Hogwood, that is." Baillie swallowed. "I think he wants to emulate him. *That's* what he's trying to track down. Hogwood's methods, his notes, his magic. And Miss Taylor . . ."

The fire in Merritt's gut cooled to embers at Beth's name. "What of her?"

"She's a clairvoyant, of course." Baillie adjusted his glasses. "If he ever came across her, she would know exactly what he was doing. That's why *I* sent her away, not he . . . but you weren't there. Of course you wouldn't know that." He shook his head, rubbed his eyes. "And he's *always* using magic in one way or another, even if it's just to prevent us from seeking help. So he removed her. He sent me here, to do . . . this."

He gestured to his bag with a look of disgust.

Merritt clung to doubt. "But he would have side effects from such constant use of magic."

"Dulling of the senses," Hulda murmured.

"Easy enough to hide," Baillie said.

Releasing Merritt, Hulda shook her head. "I can't believe it. All this time, Mr. Walker has been . . ." She rubbed warmth into her arms.

"This is the LIKER man, yes?" Baptiste asked. His expression had softened.

Hulda nodded.

But Merritt stared hard at Baillie. The Brit met his eyes. Neither blinked.

"If I disappear after this," Baillie spoke quietly, "you'll know why."

"If his hold has loosened," Merritt ground out, "then you should run."

Baillie shook his head. "It's not so simple."

Merritt wondered at that. Why on earth not? If Merritt had been mentally enslaved by a wizard, he'd run at the first lick of freedom. The wonder of it coiled and thickened . . . but was that him? Baillie was a hysterian. He'd witnessed that firsthand. Though Baillie's manipulation of his emotions in the BIKER office had felt more intrusive. This was more . . . subtle. Natural or artificial?

Merritt cursed inwardly. If only his wardship allowed him to make walls that kept out magic rather than things, he'd be able to tell.

"We have to do something about it." Hulda turned toward him. "Merritt—"

"How quickly did you sympathize with him?" Merritt asked, gaze glued to Baillie.

Hulda pulled back. "What?"

"He's a hysterian, Hulda."

She bit her bottom lip, considering.

Baillie shrunk. "My touch is . . . not subtle, and only works on occasion. I can demonstrate—"

"No," Merritt growled, and the embers reignited. "You will *get the hell out of my house.*"

Baillie's mouth worked over a few silent half words before spilling, "O-Of course. I understand." He started for the exit.

"Drop the bag."

He hesitated. Baptiste took a step forward and folded his thick arms over his barrel chest. One glance at him and Baillie set the bag down, leaving the communion stones in a heap on the floor. Merritt didn't move aside, so Baillie had to awkwardly push past him to reach the hallway.

"Follow him," Merritt said to no one in particular. Baptiste and Owein both heeded the order.

Merritt stood there for a long time, blood getting hotter, pressing and pulsing against his skin. Hulda seemed torn between staying with him and following the retreating Baillie. She started, "Do you really think—"

But when Merritt moved toward the bag, her words caught. Crouching, he opened it. Seven more communion stones inside. Eight chunks of pale selenite, including the one Hulda held. Maybe more— he'd have to ask Owein. These stones were expensive. How could Baillie afford so many? Had they really been funded by Walker, and therefore LIKER?

Who, or what, was he supposed to believe?

Whimbrel House was his safe haven. His space away from the world. His light in the dark.

Could he not have peace even in his *own home*?

Exhaling, he half expected flames to come out of his nostrils. He heard the front door shut. Palming one of the communion stones, he strode toward the window and watched Baillie retreat nearly at a run, Owein nipping at his heels, Baptiste striding behind. He hadn't even noticed another boat. Where had the man docked?

His hand tightened around the selenite. He could almost feel it melting under his writing calluses. But when he looked down, it was just a stone.

And he envied it.

He'd been a stone. As close to a stone as he could get, and he'd been happy—most of the time. Then everything had been upturned. And no matter how hard he tried, he couldn't organize the mess back into any kind of order.

He wished he'd never seen Ebba's name on that poster.

Wished he'd never sought her out.

Wished he'd never spoken to Sutcliffe.

Wished Hogwood had kept his damn mouth shut about his magic.

He wished he'd never gotten this house.

But that wasn't quite right. Without the house, there wouldn't be Hulda, and Owein would still be an angry spirit, and Baptiste might be on the streets—

His lungs tightened. Fluttery, clammy sensations lapped over his skin. He couldn't breathe. What was wrong with him?

"Merritt?" Hulda's voice sounded far away, like she stood on the roof and called down through the ceiling.

His pulse beat too fast, too erratic. His heart was in his skull, pounding, pounding, *pounding*. The room was slowly spinning; he was about to snap at Owein to knock it off, but Owein wasn't in the walls anymore. He wasn't even inside the house.

Merritt struggled to breathe. His stomach turned, threatening to upend its contents.

"Merritt!" Fingers touched his shoulder, burning into him like pokers left too long in the hearth. He jerked away from them. Dropped the rock. The *thud* of its landing echoed in his ears.

Everything was closing in on him. The walls, the books, his clothes, his *skin*. He had to get out. He needed *out*.

He didn't remember moving, but suddenly he was in the hallway, bolting like the house was alive again, like the shadows were chasing him, like the walls had grown spikes and sought to crush him. Panic surged up his throat. He was sure the front door would stick, that it wouldn't let him out—

He wrenched it open. A million voices filled his ears, like every blade of grass and dying leaf rushed to speak to him at once, whispering in a language he didn't understand, hushing each other, climbing over one another, and Merritt couldn't run fast enough. He couldn't breathe. He couldn't think. He couldn't do anything.

Trapped. He was trapped, and his bones were the bars of his prison.

The fire grew and grew, pushing back the November chill. He ran until the smoke choked him, until his legs ached, until he couldn't take another step.

Merritt collapsed, falling to his knees.

And the whole island exploded.

Chapter 13

He lay in the midst of a strange world.

He didn't know where it was or what it was called. He couldn't remember his name. It was all so . . . confusing.

He lay back, looking into the sky. It was snowing, but the snow was violet and tumbled from the heavens like down feathers. The trees were upside down. The ground had shifted into sharp, uneven steps. Plants were uprooted and lying on their sides, but a few of them danced. He blinked, trying to understand, but they continued to dance. Wilted reeds moved on legs made of twisted roots and hopped around, spinning and dipping and teetering. Everything else was so quiet. No bird call, no rabbit thumps. Just silence under the lazy lavender snow.

Merritt lay there, watching everything, for a long time. Trying to puzzle it out, but his brain was like . . . like what? There was a simile that would describe it, he just couldn't narrow in on it. Something sweet. Sugar? Cookies . . .

Oh, molasses. His brain was like molasses.

The cold slowly seeped in, pressing between the fibers of his clothing. It was getting darker, which made the snow take on a more plumlike hue. His breath clouded in uneven spheres above his lips before whisking away. A few of the reeds grew tired and stopped dancing, toppling over to rest.

He felt like he had to do something. Go somewhere, talk to someone . . . but it was so cold. His fingertips were starting to throb.

Slowly he sat up. Globs of mud fell from his back. The purple snow turned a dirty white.

There was a dog in front of him.

"Hello." His voice sounded rough, scratchy. "Who are you?"

The dog stared at him, then whined like it was trying to say something.

Merritt blinked. "Are you lost?"

The dog barked at him. Hesitated. Whined again, then took off.

Merritt rubbed his fingers together. Cold. Tired. Maybe he'd lie down and sleep awhile. Maybe he'd remember where he was—who he was—when he woke up.

A sound pierced the quiet: the shifting of fabric. Someone knelt beside him and brushed hair from his forehead. "Merritt."

He glanced over at her. At her hazel eyes and pretty hair. Stared at her for a few seconds before saying, "I know you."

"Yes, you do." Her voice was soft and delicate, like a mother's.

Something about the comparison hurt, like a barb just behind his navel.

She stroked his hair. "You're confused. Let's get you inside before you catch a chill."

"It's cold," he said.

"Very cold," she agreed.

"Confused?" he asked.

She nodded. "It's a side effect of chaocracy." She glanced up at the upside-down trees. All the dancers had gone to bed. The snow—was it snow?—had settled around him, more like puffs of fur than crystals of ice. "And you used a lot of it."

Some distant part of him knew that was wrong. *He* couldn't have done that. He didn't know how.

Quick padding sounded behind him. He turned. The dog from before was approaching with something in his mouth. Merritt knew that dog. He had a name. It was . . . house. It was like a house. It was . . . *Owein.*

The dog dropped a large piece of paper on the ground. It was wrinkled and dirty and had bite marks in it. Hand-drawn letters of the alphabet covered it. The dog pawed one. *F.* Then another. *A. M. I. L.*

It looked up at Hulda and whined.

"*Y,*" she said, and pointed.

The dog pressed its muddy paw to *Y.*

Merritt blinked. The dog pushed its nose into his forearm.

Family. Family?

It hurt to think. His head was radiating with something unpleasant. *Owein.* Family. His great-great- . . . uncle.

The world blurred, but when Merritt blinked, it cleared. Something hot ran down his cheek.

He had family.

That stabbing sensation behind his navel dulled a little.

The woman—Hulda—took his hands and pressed them to either side of her neck. Her skin was warm. "It's my turn to take care of you," she whispered, and pressed cool lips to his forehead. Grasping his elbows, she helped him stand. "Let's get you home."

℘

With Baptiste's help, Hulda had gotten Merritt into bed. By the time she'd boiled water on the stove, made him a cup of tea, and brought it to his bedroom, he'd returned to himself.

He sat upright, his vest removed and his sleeves rolled up, his attention on the dark window. Candlelight flickered across his features, distorting them, but when Hulda set her candle beside his, his solemn expression settled.

He didn't appear to notice her until she pushed the cup at him. "Oh," he managed. "Thank you."

She searched for a chair to pull up and, when she didn't find one, sat on the edge of the bed. "I hate to say it," she treaded carefully, "but Silas Hogwood was right."

"Hm." The teacup warped the sound. He sipped and winced. "Goodness, Hulda. There's a *lot* of sugar in this."

She shrugged. "Sugar makes sad things better." She often indulged when she was sad. She'd eaten scads of candy the night Merritt had taken off to Manchester, looking for Ebba Mullan.

He considered that and took another sip. "I can't fault you there." He watched the liquid swirl in the cup, and though Hulda had many questions, she kept them at the back of her tongue. Now was not the time to burden him. Not so soon after recovering from the most extreme backlash of chaotic confusion she'd ever witnessed. Not so soon after erupting in the first place. How much had he been carrying, how many fuses had he struggled to put out, to make such an *explosion*? It was no wonder he'd struggled with chaotic spells. They'd been buried beneath everything else.

"I'm sorry . . . about that."

Hulda didn't need to ask for clarification. It was fortunate Blaugdone Island was small and had no other human inhabitants, though several of the nonhuman ones had suffered. Still, the weak apology dug into her heart like a corkscrew into a bottle of wine. "Don't apologize, Merritt." Lowering her gaze, she picked at the duvet. "I know you've been dealing with a lot, and I haven't been around to help you—"

"Hardly your job to—"

"And it isn't a path you chose," she pressed on, meeting his eyes. She managed a smile. "Gifford will be so excited."

Merritt ran a hand down his face. Glanced at the window. "I . . . *I* did that." He tensed. "The house—"

"Is fine," she finished. "You only hit the edge of it, and Owein has already repaired it. However, the trees and . . . Well, we'll have some spare firewood this winter and rabbit stew for dinner."

His lip quirked at that, but the near smile didn't last. He watched the tea. She watched him watch the tea.

"Sutcliffe wants it all to stay under wraps," he said. He'd mentioned as much before. "I really should reach out to the people he mentioned on that list." He gestured to his night table, where the list was pinned down by two empty mugs, which only reminded Hulda of Miss Taylor's absence, which in turn reminded her of *why* she was gone. "But I can't even tell them who I am. I have an entire undiscovered family tree out there, and I can't tell them who I am. Well." A dry chuckle escaped him. "I suppose I *could*. I don't owe Sutcliffe anything. But that might ostracize me further."

Hulda had tried to imagine, multiple times, what she would do in Merritt's position. She couldn't quite wrap her head around it, and she hated how useless that made her feel. She couldn't just read a primer on managing broken families and secret affairs and give him a tidbit of advice that would make it all better. She couldn't do much of anything right now.

"It must be hard," she tried.

He cleared his throat. Drank tea. "You're right. I didn't ask for this. For any of it." He peered back toward the window, and Hulda knew he was lumping Sutcliffe's magic in with his family problems. "But how many of us do? Ask for our problems, I mean." He winced.

"Too hot?" she asked.

He shook his head. "Even now, they're talking to me." His voice was barely above a whisper. "There's a spider waiting for a morsel in here somewhere. And that red maple keeps reminding me it's nearly winter."

She rolled her lips together. Best talk to him as much as she could before he lost his voice again. "You're suffering for the choices of your parents. And your father." The one who had raised him, she meant, but Merritt seemed to understand.

"He never wanted me," he whispered.

Her throat grew thick. "But didn't your mother? Your sisters?"

Merritt reached up to his neck, feeling for the scarf he often wore. When he didn't find it, he tensed, gaze darting around the room until landing on the dresser, where Hulda had laid it out to dry. He relaxed visibly. "Yes. I think so," he said, near voiceless, but from communion or emotion, she wasn't sure. "They always were good to me. I didn't really—"

His words cut short. He cleared his throat again. "I never got to say goodbye to them. I wrote, in the beginning. Letters. A few a week, then once a week, once a month . . . I never received a single response." He ran his thumbs up the length of the teacup. "I'd always hoped that was my father's doing, and not theirs."

"How could it be theirs?" She took one of his hands from the teacup and curled her fingers around it. "Merritt, do you realize how amicable you are?"

He chuckled. "I know a housekeeper who would have disagreed with that sentiment not too long ago."

"Amicable and tidy are not synonymous." At least his hands had warmed up. She should probably get a bath drawn for him. "You are a *good person*, Merritt. You are nothing short of delightful."

His face fell. Panic rose as Hulda reviewed her words for possible misinterpretations. Her expression must have been fraught, because Merritt said, weak as a fish on land, "She used to call me that."

Hulda glanced to his collar. "Your sister?"

"Ebba."

That woman's name still riled her, but she held on to an insouciant expression.

"Delightful," he added, and she could hear tears in his voice. They weren't in his eyes—he did such a remarkable job of putting on that mask Hulda would envy him for it, if it weren't so disheartening.

He shook his head but kept his hand in hers. "I loved her, and she used me."

Hulda had nothing to say except "I know."

He finished the tea and set it on the side table with the other cups, then leaned back against the headboard. "I'm too afraid to go back home. To face them."

She squeezed his hand.

"I'm a coward."

"You are not."

He shook his head. He didn't believe her.

She scrambled for something to say. Some sort of bandage for the situation. A joke, perhaps? Some inspirational poem or lyric? If only there *were* a primer—

A primer . . .

"What if," she tried, "this were a story?"

He eyed her.

"One of your stories. Which it is, but I mean like *The Path of Rubies*." Which was the title of his latest book. "What would your hero do if you had to write his ending?"

Merritt rolled his lips together. "I'm not sure. I don't like knowing the ending."

"Then perhaps you could write it."

"Easier said than—"

"I mean actually *write* it," she amended. "On a piece of paper. You can write about what might happen, how you might react . . . just for yourself, not for anyone else to read it. It might help if you get your thoughts out of your head and onto something solid. Something that you could burn or feed to Owein."

That tick of a smile returned. "That's not the worst idea."

"Of course it's not." She sat up straighter. "I'm a professional."

The small smile held, and it warmed her through. His hand squeezed hers; she squeezed back. Then he stiffened and held very still for a long moment. Not even his chest moved with breath.

"Merritt?" she whispered.

He shook his head, a wondering expression pulling up his mouth and widening his eyes. "It's . . . gone."

"What is?"

"Their voices." His words were underlined by a weak laugh. "Just like that . . . they stopped. The spider, the tree . . ."

Hulda's chest warmed. "Maybe," she said softly, carefully, "they've stopped talking because you finally started listening to yourself."

His eyes met hers, that wondering look making him appear younger. Leaning forward, she kissed his forehead. "In that case, I suggest you sleep. It's long overdue."

Merritt released a long, cleansing breath and sank back into his pillow.

He was asleep in less than a minute.

ᠺ

Hulda had thought Merritt would rest through the night, but he was up three hours later, when the sky was black but the hour not too late. It worked well for her, as she would not be traversing the bay tonight. The Bright Bay Hotel and BIKER were the last places she wanted to be right now. Regardless, the candlelight under the door gave him away. Hulda knocked to announce herself, and then stepped in quietly.

"How are you feeling?"

"Good," he breathed. "Better." He rubbed his eyes, then dragged his hands down his face. "Better."

"Good."

"The spider caught something."

She paused. "Oh, Merritt, I thought it was over. I'm so—"

"No." He shook his head, a smile lifting his mouth. "No, this time I listened for it."

She sank into the chair by the bed. "Perhaps you don't need a tutor at all. You're a natural."

He snorted. "I'm sure when I get a good look at the outdoors tomorrow, I'll beg to differ."

She bit her bottom lip.

Merritt sighed. "There is the matter with Baillie and Walker."

Hulda had not forgotten about the lawyer's startling confession. "The stones—"

"We got them all," she said. "Mr. Babineaux threw them into the ocean."

Merritt relaxed. "You seemed to believe him. Baillie, that is."

She nodded. "That is . . . perhaps his story would not seem so feasible to me had I not divined for him when we collided in the hallway at BIKER. He was *afraid*, Merritt." She shook her head. "But Mr. Walker . . ."

"He seems like a good man."

She frowned. "So did Silas Hogwood."

That gave Merritt pause. "Have you seen anything? *Could* you see anything, in the future, that might give us a hint as to how to proceed?"

She deflated. "I can certainly try, but you know my abilities aren't dependable." She considered a moment. "I could see myself in his shoes. And yes, I felt sympathetic toward him. Then again, I don't know how much of that sympathy was mine and how much might have been his doing. Still, it's my understanding that hysterians—today's hysterians— can only work with existing emotions." She shrugged. "Everyone says he's weak in his magic, himself included, and it could be true. Certainly most of us are weak these days. And yet the way he made me feel at BIKER says otherwise. Even if Mr. Walker was forcing him to do it, the magic is still there."

Merritt frowned. "Is it possible Mr. Walker could have enough of a hold on him to have forced him to break into Whimbrel House? The distance is considerable."

She shook her head. "You've caught me in nescience. I don't know." She bunched a fistful of her skirt in her hand. "Myra would know."

"No luck there."

"No luck there," she repeated.

"Where did he sail? When he left."

Hulda shifted. "North, back to Boston."

Merritt's jaw clenched for a moment. "If Mr. Walker is truly controlling him, why did he go back?"

They sat there, considering, for several seconds.

"If it's luck we need," he tried, "perhaps we could enlist Miss Richards."

Hulda shook her head. "I'm not sure if sharing with her is the best course of action. Miss Richards is with LIKER. She has no loyalty toward us. And if Mr. Baillie is correct in regard to Mr. Walker, then she might be under his spell, too." An idea wriggled to the front of her mind, making her perk up. "But there *is* Miss Steverus."

"Sadie?" Merritt asked.

She did not comment on his lackadaisical use of an acquaintance's first name. "Miss Steverus studied magic in geology—she's the one who turned me on to the theory that the wardship magic in Whimbrel House might be from tourmaline."

"Which proved incorrect."

She waved away the comment. "Regardless . . . I believe azurite is the stone connected to psychometry. Perhaps there's a way to utilize it to test if Mr. Walker is, indeed, as Baillie claimed. I'll check with Miss Steverus, but I'll need to be discreet."

He rubbed his chin. "In the meantime, we let Baillie go."

Her stomach tightened. "It doesn't seem right, does it? Perhaps we should file a report with the watchmen. Or the local government. And yet"—her insides shriveled—"how could he possibly know about Mr. Hogwood? And to indicate Myra . . . I dare say he's more informed than Mr. Adey."

"I haven't a clue." He rubbed his eyes. "We have to move forward with what information we have."

"The options do seem rather limited, don't they?" Hulda slouched down. "Especially with Miss Taylor in Canada. Mr. Baillie may truly be a victim. There's no sure way to know unless we confront Mr. Walker. But I think it prudent to hold off on any confrontation until we know more." She looked out the dark window, as though she could see across states to the Massachusetts coast. "And perhaps fall down the well a little farther. If Mr. Baillie spoke in earnest about Mr. Walker, then Mr. Baillie won't admit his failure here. He'd be condemning himself along with us. If he was speaking falsely, well, he can take comfort in believing he's fooled us."

She felt Merritt's eyes on the side of her face. Met them. He still looked tired, but . . . better. Certainly better.

"What are you thinking, Miss Larkin?"

Rubbing her hands together, she said, "We never saw what Myra did in that basement. I doubt there's much left to see . . . but I want to see it. I've wondered, perhaps, if that's where she's hiding. It worked for Mr. Hogwood . . ."

"Tomorrow?"

"No." She smoothed her skirts. "No, but soon. I don't want to slip away too quickly and alert Mr. Baillie or Mr. Walker. I'll look into the azurite first."

He nodded before punching his thigh. "I just can't believe that toad of a man is a victim in all of this."

Careful with her words, she said, "But if he is . . . he didn't choose it, either."

Merritt stilled. "Didn't choose it."

She flushed. "I'm sorry. I shouldn't have—"

He waved away her apology. "Don't apologize, Hulda. You should be a storyteller, the way you brought that around." He eyed her, a spot of mischief glimmering in his tired eyes. "Might I assume you're staying the night?"

She folded her arms and lifted her nose. "Don't tell anyone. I have a sparkling reputation to uphold."

"Says the woman who's already shared my bed once."

Mortification stripped her insides like turpentine. "That was not my doing, it was Owein's! And I was technically still in *my* bed—"

Merritt beamed at her. *This man!* But if teasing her brightened his mood this much, she would let him torment her until the end of her days.

"Rogue," she spat, standing and swiping the errant cups from his side table. "I'll ask Baptiste to make you a light breakfast; I'm not entirely sure how much this all took out of you."

"You don't work here anymore," he quipped. "You can't tell him to do anything."

"I chose my verb deliberately, *Mr. Fernsby.*" She strode to the door, glancing down at the cups as she went.

And in the tea leaves, she saw a pattern.

The room changed; it was the same room, but she was elsewhere in it, her back pressed to the mattress, Merritt's hair against her cheek, the sensation of his mouth on her neck, and—

And—

Hulda dropped the cups. Two of the three shattered against the floorboards.

"Hulda!" Merritt leapt from the bed and rushed to her. "Are you all right?"

She blinked, but the vision was plastered behind her eyelids. She was most definitely unrobed, and so was he, and his hand was on her—

Dear Lord, what had she just seen? But that was a stupid question. She knew *exactly* what she had seen!

Merritt grabbed her shoulders. "Hulda! Are you hurt?"

Was that her future? But of course it was—she possessed no magic outside of foresight! And they were . . . they were . . .

She blinked and saw his concern-crinkled eyes hovering in front of hers, which only made her face heat to an unbearable temperature. "I-I-I already forgot!" she lied. There was no forgetful side effect for *this* nugget of future. "That is, I-I'm fine, just clumsy." *Lie, lie, lie.* "I thought I saw a mouse."

"A mouse?" Merritt released her and spun, scanning the floor.

Gravity pulled the heat from her face into her body until it crackled like an egg on a frying pan. Hulda crouched and scooped up the broken ceramic, earning her a minute cut, but it was worth it to pick up and *leave*, because her skin was ripening like a tomato and she had to get out—

Had she been wearing a ring? She hadn't seen her hands in the vision. She'd seen Merritt's, but it was the wrong hand! And it was on her . . . on her . . .

"I don't see a mouse," Merritt said. "Or hear one . . ."

"I think Owein is calling." Her voice sounded strangled. "Be right back!"

And she fled, heart wampishing and mind reeling, gooseflesh covering every inch of her.

Still, as mortified as she was, she had to admit that she was equal parts embarrassed and delighted.

Chapter 14

Hulda waited outside a local bookshop early the next morning, swallowing a yawn from her less-than-adequate sleep the night before. In truth, she wished she hadn't had to leave Whimbrel House at all, and not only because BIKER was confusing and she was unsure what to do about Mr. Baillie, or how to act around him and Mr. Walker in light of these new unproved revelations. What she *couldn't* do was run—she couldn't abandon BIKER and all she and Myra had dedicated their lives to. But all her studies, experience, and memorized receipt books hadn't prepared her for all this perturbation.

Crossing the island this morning, the air cold and smelling of winter, a huge swath of trees and plants uprooted, revealing dirt and puddles beneath, had sobered her. She wanted to stay by Merritt's side. She wanted to help him navigate this. She wanted *him*.

But work and justice were unkind taskmasters. And thus she waited outside the bookshop until—

There.

"Miss Steverus!" she called as she stepped out into the road, catching sight of the BIKER secretary arriving for work. The woman wore a high-waisted skirt and a clean white blouse. She turned and scanned the area for who had called her until her eyes landed on Hulda. Her nose was red from the morning chill.

"Miss Larkin, how are you?"

Hulda caught up to her quickly. Miss Steverus moved to continue walking to BIKER, but when Hulda held her ground, she paused. "Quite well, thank you. I actually wanted your thoughts on something."

She blinked. "Oh?"

"Your study with stones and magic—"

She smiled. "Ah, yes! How is that tourmaline?"

That was right. Neither Hulda nor Myra had ever caught Miss Steverus up on the second source of magic of Whimbrel House, though she was well equipped to guess, thanks to Merritt's use of wardship at the office. "It's quite docile," she answered truthfully. Then, to cover her tracks, she added, "But I was speaking to Mr. Fernsby the other day, and we were debating over the stone for augury."

"Amethyst?" she asked.

Hulda snapped her fingers. "See? I was correct. It's the simplest to remember."

The secretary chuckled. "I suppose it would be, for an augurist."

"Mr. Fernsby claimed it was azurite."

"Ah, I can see how he'd be confused." She adjusted a small purse on her shoulder. "Augury and psychometry are closely related."

That confirmed azurite as the psychometrist's stone, then. "One can't merely store mind reading or the like in a stone, though. What would such a stone do, anyway?"

"Not mind reading, no. But hallucinations, yes. Though I'm not sure such a thing could be procured. It's illegal here and in England, and truthfully, I've not yet heard of anyone in the States who can perform that spell adequately enough to entrap and sell it."

"Thank goodness for that!" Hulda chuckled awkwardly, but Miss Steverus didn't seem to notice, only smiled. Hulda gestured toward BIKER, and they began walking to the hotel. "Does it react any other way?"

She considered. "A good, pure stone will change in the presence of psychometry. Usually darken, so a paler stone is best. Amethyst would also work, if you want to try it. An amethyst pendant might look well with your complexion."

Hulda touched her neck. "You think so?" She was genuinely curious.

"Oh, yes. It might be interesting to test how it reacts to you." She grasped the door in the back of the Bright Bay Hotel and held it open. "After you."

Hulda nodded her thanks and headed in. She'd get started on her files right away, then at lunch venture into the city to a tiny magical supply shop she frequented on behalf of BIKER. If they didn't have the azurite she needed, surely they could point her in the right direction.

The azurite was set.

She'd purchased very small crystals of it and placed them in strategic locations around the office, even managing to sneak one behind a book in Mr. Walker's office. She'd tucked another into Miss Steverus's pencil jar, one in the stairwell, and one in each room on the third floor. Two in the area where Baillie often worked. He had, indeed, returned to Boston, though Hulda had seen only glimpses of him. Either Walker had him hard at work or he was avoiding her.

Walker. What Merritt said had, well, merit. Mr. Baillie had insisted he was able to speak freely because the bond between he and Mr. Walker had weakened over time and distance. Why, then, would he return to his tormentor's sphere of influence? It seemed suspicious to say the least, and yet Hulda knew that many hard situations were inherently complex in nature. By all means, would it not be easier for her to run away? To write off Myra, or forfeit her knowledge of Silas Hogwood? Granted . . . if Mr. Baillie had been truthful, then Mr. Walker was one of the last people she should confide in. Indeed, she kept some azurite on her own person. She'd jump in the bay before she let any psychometry spells—feigned or real—control her.

Hulda had also purchased a clean ledger and documented the shape, weight, color, and placement of each stone. In truth, the work was very similar to what she might do for the testing of an enchanted house. It was just that most enchanted houses were very forthcoming about being magicked, and thus didn't require such a scientific approach.

On her last page of notes, she detailed a single carnelian crystal, which had been notably more expensive than the azurite. Carnelian was the stone associated with hysteria. While the azurite would stay in her pocket, the carnelian piece hung from a thin cord around her neck, long enough that she could tuck it into her bodice. If Mr. Baillie was going to play spell games with her, she wanted to know—and have proof if she needed it.

In fact, when she did pass him in the hall toward the end of the day, she subtly pulled out the cord to let the carnelian show. He said nothing of it, nor did he speak to her at all. He only pressed the side of his index finger to his lips, signaling secrecy.

Oh, I'm very interested in your secrets, Mr. Baillie, Hulda thought as she slid into the records room. *And I intend to uncover every last one of them.*

Merritt had never really gotten a good look at the place of his temporary captivity. The only time he'd been to Marshfield was on his involuntary adventure with Silas. In truth, there wasn't a lot to see—at least, not in the area he and Hulda had ridden through. BIKER owned a small stable, but for this unsanctioned trip, Hulda had taken Myra's personal horse, which, while stabled on BIKER property, belonged solely to her.

She'd left it behind when she disappeared, leaving another jagged puzzle piece to her disappearance that didn't quite fit with the rest.

Merritt hadn't realized how run down Silas's house—if it was even his—was. The roof was partly caved in, several windows were broken, and the wood paneling was splintering if not missing entirely. The place was made of a dark, aged wood, making it look positively foreboding.

"Right out of a storybook," Merritt commented before pulling up the reins. He'd walked the last mile, having relearned that God had not built his buttocks for Western saddles. He helped Hulda down, then found a tree surrounded by some patches of grass the beast could snack on for a bit. Merritt didn't intend to stay long.

After securing a knot, he closed his eyes and listened. He still hadn't mastered this, but he was certainly getting better at it. He felt Hulda's cold fingertips touch his elbow in question, and he'd nearly given up when the grass ahead of him whispered, *Sleeeeeeeeeeep.*

He opened his eyes. "I don't think anything excitable is here."

Hulda nodded, her gaze dragging to the two-story structure. "I have a feeling it's abandoned." She eyed the canal. "Let's try the front door."

Merritt smirked as they headed that way. "Remind me again how you made it down there last time?"

She swatted his arm with the back of her hand. "There was a wardship spell surrounding the place. I had little option."

Letting the joke slide, Merritt walked with his hand outstretched, but it never connected with any spell. The magic was well and truly gone from this place.

The porch creaked precariously underfoot. The front door was askew, likely kicked in by the watchmen who'd come to rescue them. A chunk of the door had splintered off and stayed secured to the frame where the handle had been. Hulda retrieved her enchanted lantern and lit it; the sun was still up, but inside, the walls loomed dark.

The place didn't look lived in—no clothes, no furniture, no signs of life. In truth, it looked very much the way Merritt had expected to find Whimbrel House when his grandmother's lawyer bequeathed it to him. The interior was almost as weathered as the exterior. The staircase was missing two consecutive steps, and everything smelled of mold and mice.

Hulda wordlessly handed him the lantern, then retrieved her dowsing rods. She walked the length of the room with care, testing each step before shifting weight onto the forward foot. The rods never reacted. She shook her head—no magic here.

"Hulda." Merritt spoke just above a whisper. They were alone—there was no reason to believe they couldn't chat normally—and yet there was an intensity in the air, perhaps created only by memory, and it felt dangerous to disturb it. "Can't powerful wizards inhabit houses postmortem?"

Hulda froze. "They . . . can." She swallowed. "Those dolls should have been destroyed, but"—she shook herself—"Mr. Hogwood was naturally very powerful."

More powerful than Owein, who'd inhabited his dwelling for centuries. They exchanged a long look. Gooseflesh rose on Merritt's arms.

"My dowsing rods detect nothing here." There was a slight rasp in her voice. Still, she dug into her bag and pulled out a single ward—it seemed to be all she had with her. "Stay close."

Evidence indicated Silas had only occupied the basement, accessed by a stone stairway that connected to the main room. Merritt led the way down on stiff legs, the smell of mold intensifying with each step. It wasn't hard to determine why—there was about an inch of standing water on the floor. From the pipes, rainwater, or Silas, they would probably never know.

A rat skittered off to the right. Merritt listened for it, but either his communion didn't want to cooperate or the rat had nothing to say.

They waited at the bottom of the stairs for several seconds, listening. Outside of the rat, there was only a steady dripping a ways off.

Merritt glanced back to Hulda, who checked her dowsing rods. "Still nothing," she said, and encouraged him onward with a nod.

He stepped into the grimy water and wondered if he'd be able to wear his shoes again after this. A strange, sad pang for Beth radiated through his chest. The upkeep—or lack thereof—of his things always made him think of her, of how well she'd taken care of all of them without making it seem like work . . . and of the lack of answers he had for her departure. Owein, too, missed her terribly.

"Not all deceased wizards inhabit their residences," Hulda murmured. "Enchanted dwellings would be far more common. And I don't think Mr. Hogwood would want to haunt something so rundown and isolated. Be trapped inside it for Lord knows how long." She took a deep breath. "I came in that way." Changing the subject, she pointed to a room that opened to the hallway. "The pipe led into there."

"Naturally or magically?"

She shook her head. "I don't know."

Merritt shivered. "This place is going to give me nightmares." He strode forward carefully, listening, holding the light high. Without Silas's lights, it was dark as pitch outside the reach of the lantern.

They came into the large room where the fight had happened. When they entered, the light fell onto a skewed, warped door made of iron bars. The shrunken people Silas had siphoned magic from had once been tucked behind those bars. There was no trace of them now. Not there, nor on the cobbled floor, nor on the broken shelves. The bench was still there—the one Owein had been tied to—and no one had cleaned up the shattered glass.

"Watch your step." He pointed to the glass.

Hulda slipped by him, staying in the ring of light, and looked around. Her hands were tight around the dowsing rods, skin stretched over her knuckles. She walked the length of the room once before saying, "There was magic here, but not anymore. Which we already knew."

Merritt nodded. "I wonder what they did with the dolls."

Hulda shuddered. "I'm not sure I want to know." She turned slowly, taking in the space. It wasn't as large as Merritt remembered it being. "I doubt anyone has been here since that night. Myra is . . . thorough."

Merritt walked in a little farther, the light highlighting burn marks from Silas's fire spell. "What exactly did she do here?"

"What indeed, Myra." Hulda touched one of the marks and frowned. "I admit . . . I'd hoped maybe this had been her hideaway. It's nonsensical, but nothing else reasonable has panned out."

"I've a feeling Miss Haigh is too classy for dungeons."

Hulda's lip ticked upward, but not enough to form a smile. She started down the next hallway, and Merritt followed, coming up on the cramped room where he'd been bound. A shiver like the legs of a dozen beetles crept up his backbone. They came around the corner, back to the stairs. And that was that.

"Do wizard spirits sleep?" Merritt whispered.

She shook her head. "Why would they need to?" She took several seconds to think. "I'm positive he isn't here, Merritt. Perhaps Myra made sure of that, too. She would have exorcised him, surely."

He heard the rat again. Reached out to it. *What happened here? Hide. Hide. Smell? Search.*

Merritt rolled his lips together. Hulda reached over and took the light, then retraced their steps back to that main room. He followed her, his steps squelching all the way.

Light. Light.

A new voice. A moth? No, it felt like . . . a spider, although not quite like the one in his room. *What happened here?* He pressed. *What did you see?*

Human. Humans. Light.

He pressed back. *The human in black. The one with magic. He died here.* He tried to imagine the scene—Silas crumpled on the floor, Hulda's crowbar in his hand. *What happened after?*

Humans. Humans.

"I wonder," Hulda said, "what they did with him."

With whom? Merritt tried to say, but found his voice gone. He cleared his throat, garnering Hulda's attention. "Silas?" he rasped.

She nodded. "I wouldn't mind seeing his grave. Just for closure."

"Is death not closure enough?" He sounded like a frog.

"Not with him," Hulda answered, and retreated back into the hallway, taking the light with her. "Not with him."

The edge of the lantern's glow glimmered off something that caught Merritt's eye.

"Hulda." He moved toward a large stone near the ruined iron grate. "Hulda, come back this way."

The circle of light shifted as she stepped toward him, until it fell across a smooth stone a foot and a half across, egg shaped. In the shadows, it had looked like another gray rock, which the basement was full of. But the light revealed half of its body was pale and translucent; the half they would have seen only in reversing their path. That's what had caught the light.

Crouching by the rock, Merritt ran his hand over it until he found a large rune engraved on it, confirming his suspicion. "Communion stone," he murmured.

Hulda gasped and knelt beside him, setting down the lantern. "My goodness, it's the largest I've ever seen!" She hesitantly touched it. "Where could they have found such a prodigious chunk of selenite?"

"I wonder if he made it himself," Merritt offered. He touched the rune—which was the size of his hand—on the side—

"Don't—" Hulda warned.

"How else will we know?" Merritt asked.

Hulda held her breath, her body still as the selenite chunk in front of them. Merritt kept his hand on the rune.

He hummed a note of disappointment. "Perhaps he hadn't made its pair yet. Or it was destroyed."

Hulda shook her head. Opened her mouth to speak—

"Master?" came a male voice from the stone, slightly garbled. "Master Hogwood? Is that you?"

Merritt froze as though he, too, were made of the crystal. Hulda's eyes rounded to the size of matzo balls.

"Devil's blaze, Silas! We've not heard from you for—"

Hulda's hand whipped out and pulled Merritt's fingers from the rune, breaking the spell. The stone fell quiet.

His heart thundered like he'd been running. He looked at Hulda. "What? Too dangerous to ask questions?"

Hulda, pale as selenite, shook her head. "I-I know that voice. I know who's on the other end of the stone."

Turning his hand around, he clasped hers. "Who?"

She swallowed. "Mr. Lidgett. Stanley Lidgett, the man who is . . . was . . . Mr. Hogwood's steward.

"He knew Silas was here."

Chapter 15

November 18, 1846, Marshfield, Massachusetts

Hulda paced across the wet, stony floor, suddenly unaffected by the chill in the dungeon-like basement of Silas's abandoned hideaway. She chewed on the knuckle of her right hand, thinking.

"His steward?" Merritt asked, standing but remaining stationary. "Are you sure?"

She nodded. "I worked with him. I'm sure."

He worried his lip. "It's been ten years—"

"I know his voice!" she snapped, then paused, taking a deep breath to settle herself. Offering Merritt an apologetic look, she said, "I know his voice. I . . ." Her flush drove the chill back even further. "I fancied him, once upon a time. I know his voice."

"Oh." The surprise on Merritt's face morphed into something bordering mischievous. "Did you, now?"

She would not give him the opportunity to tease. Not now. Not after this new revelation. "It must be why the stone is so large." Her boots clacked as she returned to it, but she didn't dare touch it again. "It has to carry across the Atlantic. Unless Mr. Lidgett is in the States, which I doubt." She gnawed on her knuckle again, caught herself, and tore her hand from her mouth.

Merritt touched her elbow. Gently, like she was a wild animal. "Tell me what you're thinking."

After drawing in another steadying breath, Hulda explained, "I'd wondered, after the arrest, if Mr. Lidgett knew of Silas's . . . actions. Mr. Hogwood kept only a skeleton staff, and he interacted with his steward more than anyone else. Understandable—Mr. Lidgett was responsible for the upkeep of the estate. But still." She flexed her fingers. "What if Mr. Lidgett is still working for him but doesn't know he's dead?"

"Right. Right." Merritt's grip tightened. "Let's slow down. Mr. Lidgett would be working, possibly, at Gorse End, for the new owner?"

Hulda paused. "Miss Pearshold said there is no new owner. Mr. Hogwood had no children"—the thought brought Mr. Adey to mind—"no family that I know of. His immediate family was dead." Her gaze drifted to the shelves where those horrible dolls had been stored.

"But the estate should have gone to someone, correct?" Merritt asked. "I'm not entirely familiar with British law, but isn't a man's property forfeited if he's indefinitely imprisoned and has no heirs?"

"Supposedly?" Hulda wasn't sure herself. "If I've learned anything from my visit with the detective, it's that wizards are not always treated as the common man. Neither is the peerage. For all we know, Silas was having"—she blushed—". . . conjugal visits."

"Or using a cup," Merritt offered.

Hulda met his eyes, unsure of his meaning . . . and then it clicked, and her jaw dropped. "Really, Merritt!"

He shrugged. "Makes sense."

"Regardless," she pressed, "Silas must have appointed some sort of heir, or perhaps . . ." She hesitated, following the train of thought.

Merritt gave her only a few seconds to do so. "Perhaps what?"

She shook her head. "I don't know. If the Crown wanted Silas Hogwood alive, perhaps they struck a deal with him. Shortened his sentence, gave him special treatment, threatened him . . ."

"How much can you threaten a man already in jail?"

Hulda turned away, resuming her pacing. "Gorse End was very important to Mr. Hogwood. What if the Crown seized it and hung it over his head somehow? Perhaps he was told they'd refrain from selling it if he did as they asked . . ."

Merritt glanced at the communion stone. After a minute, he asked, "Can an aristocrat will his estate to someone who isn't family?"

Hulda's steps slowed. "I'm afraid I also am not well versed in British law. But someone of Mr. Hogwood's stature surely had influence over such things."

"I'm thinking about what we talked about before. With BIKER."

Now she stopped pacing altogether. "BIKER?"

He nodded. "How—and I know you disagree with me on this—BIKER doesn't seem *worth* the trouble for Baillie or whomever to go to such efforts to secure it."

She nodded, her mind a giant knot. "Yes, we did . . ." The knot loosened. "Mr. Baillie being Mr. Hogwood's estate lawyer."

Merritt nodded. "Mr. Baillie who seems far too interested in you and BIKER. And that stone connects to this Lidgett fellow, who seems to have been a very, *very* loyal servant."

She stared at him for a beat. "Do you think Mr. Lidgett was the heir to the estate?"

Merritt threw up his hands, unsure. "Possibly? Partial heir? What better way to ensure the loyalty of a staff member than to promise him payment? And Silas wouldn't have been able to pay him in a traditional way from prison."

Hulda considered this. "*If* Mr. Lidgett was in Mr. Hogwood's will, he would have been paid out when the prison recorded Mr. Hogwood's death in June."

"Unless the estate *was* seized by the Crown," Merritt added. "Mr. Adey proves they're involved. It makes sense."

She glanced to the stone, then surveyed the dark, menacing room. "If Mr. Baillie is attached to the inheritance, then he might be waiting to be paid as well. He was *very* curious about Mr. Adey."

"Because if Mr. Adey finds Silas's body, then proof of his death would activate his will. Because if Mr. Adey is asking, then the English government lends no weight to his initial death certificate." Merritt dug his hands into his pockets. "It's a decent theory, I think."

Hulda nodded. "Yes, it is. But only a theory."

"We could ask the stone."

"Perhaps it's best not to. Not until." Groaning, she permitted a curse past her lips. "Damn it, Myra."

He offered her a sympathetic smile. "We can't wait on her forever."

"No, we can't." Hulda snatched the handle of the lantern, making the light sway across the water-riddled stone walls. "I need answers."

Merritt stepped close, stilling the lantern with one finger. "Is there anyone else you can write to?"

"Who will answer me? No. And any more inquiries on my part will only bring Mr. Adey's focus back to me."

"We did nothing wrong, Hulda."

"Perhaps not." Her heart sank. "But our silence says otherwise." Grip on the lantern tightening, she added, "I should have spoken up from the beginning. Myra . . ." Emotion leaked into her voice. "I fear she's abandoned us."

He took both her shoulders in his hands and waited until she met his eyes. "This is her mess, not ours. It will pass. We'll figure out our end of things soon enough. You'll take over BIKER, if Walker has any sense to him, and we'll move on from this." His thumbs rubbed her sleeves. "Silas died in a British jail in June."

Hulda nodded, only somewhat comforted. "I need to know he's really gone," she whispered.

Merritt pulled her into an embrace. "Then I'll prove it. I promise."

Chapter 16

The journey back to Boston stretched long and tense. After returning Hulda safely to the Bright Bay Hotel, Merritt stayed at a small inn on the south end of Boston before heading back to Marshfield in the morning. A few inquiries led him to the home of the constable, who was away.

"Do you know where I might find him?" Merritt asked a petite blonde woman with frizzy hair. He presumed her to be the man's wife.

"He usually walks about the city in the morning," she explained, the slightest Irish lilt to her voice. "Takes the horse down Main and then up the little path between the book collector and the Bennets' home—that is, it's a little lodge with pink stone." She adjusted her shawl, then self-consciously touched her hair. "In case anyone needs him. He might check up on the volunteers."

"His watchmen?"

She nodded. "And then he comes down Webster. I think if you take that route backward—around the town counterclockwise—you'll run into him. We've a painted gelding he takes out, and he wears the blue jacket and hat, even though it's big on him." She blushed. "Haven't had a moment to unpick the stitches and fit it better to him."

Merritt nodded. "Thank you for your help." As he was about to step off the narrow stone porch, however, what the woman had said niggled at him. "Haven't had a chance to tailor his coat?"

She nodded. "Just with the littles." As if on cue, a baby cried from within the house. "We're still getting settled."

"Settled."

She nodded. When Merritt held her gaze, she added, "Only been here a fortnight."

Chest tightening, Merritt said, "Only a fortnight? Ma'am, was he not in office on October 15?" That was the night it happened—the abduction, the fight, the death.

She blinked. "Oh, no. That was Constable Harold. He retired and moved to North Carolina. Quite suddenly, they tell me. We were in Duxbury before, and my brother heard about it—so we came over to fill the spot."

Merritt knew he was gaping at the woman, perhaps making her feel uncomfortable, but he couldn't help it. His mind was slow to digest the information. *The man is called in to take care of Silas Hogwood, then suddenly retires and moves several states away?*

Myra, is this your doing?

He caught himself marveling at the reach of the woman's influence and had to shake himself back to the present. "Um, do you know where in North Carolina he might have gone?" Merritt tried. Could he manage a trip so far south?

The woman shook her head. "Afraid not."

Dead end. Merritt massaged his hands. "Thank you for your time . . . That is, do you know the names of the volunteers? Any who would have been volunteering in October?"

"October? Um." She closed her eyes. "Oh, Mr. Wade. Spencer Wade. He works at the sawmill, just there." She stepped out of the house, ignoring the wailing babe within, and pointed down the road. "You can't miss it. Might have seen it on your way in."

He had. "Thank you."

She nodded, then stepped inside, seeming relieved to end their strange conversation.

Merritt stepped back onto the street, mulling about the information. *Would it have hurt to give us a rundown of what you did, Myra?* A wagon passed by, so Merritt hopped onto the back of it to the sawmill, the driver unaware until he hopped off and got a skeptical glance. Inside the sawmill, he asked after Spencer Wade, and a boy sorting tools pointed to a man who looked to be in his late forties working on a log. Merritt came close enough to be seen, but waited patiently until the bloke stepped away from his work.

"Who are you?" Wade asked before Merritt could get a word out, brushing callused hands together to remove sawdust.

"Adam Smith." Merritt extended his hand, and the man shook it. Best not to involve his true self unless absolutely necessary. "I have a few questions regarding an incident that happened about a month ago."

Wade looked him over, brows bent to nearly touching. "You Canadian?"

That gave Merritt pause. "Not the last time I checked."

Wade shrugged. "Figured only a Canadian would wear his hair like that."

"Ah, well." Merritt pulled his hair behind him, as though he could hide it. "My barber died a couple years ago, and I never got over it."

"Hmm. I got work to do, so what do you want?"

"There was an incident late at night at an abandoned house near the shore—"

"Huh?"

Forbearingly, Merritt repeated, "The abandoned house north of here, by the shore. Adjacent to the canal?"

Wade squinted at him like he were some sort of specter for several seconds before his eyes lit up. "Oh! Right, right. About a month ago."

"Yes. Were you there? When it happened?"

"Yeah, I was." He ran a hand back through his hair, absently shaking more bits of sawdust from it. "Least, I remember Harold rounding us up and riding out. The house . . . it's a bit . . ." He chuckled. "Not gonna lie, I got drunk as a peahen in heat that night. It's a blur."

Merritt's lips parted, both at the news and at the strange metaphor. "You came out in the middle of the night to a crime scene and then decided to have a drink?"

"I think?" He glanced back at his station, perhaps wondering if he'd get snipped at for leaving it. "I remember the house. Some bloke had died in there. Nice woman took me out . . . er, don't tell my wife that."

Merritt's shoulders fell. "Was she Spanish, by chance?"

Wade only shrugged. "She got me the nice stuff. Works real well. Don't really recall."

"Try, please." Merritt's patience was thinning.

Wade folded his arms and leaned onto one leg. "Me and some guy from . . . Plymouth, maybe? . . . kept watch outside in case any nosy folk came by." He snickered. "Heard there was some woman inside in nothing more than her drawers."

A flicker of heat coursed up Merritt's torso. It was one thing for *him* to tease Hulda about that, but he apparently did *not* like it when another did, especially another man. However, he was distracted by the sudden rattling of a toolbox on a nearby bench, and Merritt forced himself to calm down, just in case it was his doing. He hadn't been able to replicate any chaocratic spells since Baillie's intrusion, but Gifford had theorized they were tied to Merritt's temper.

He refocused on the situation at hand. "So you didn't go inside?"

"Not till after, no. Charlie did. Must've been a real mess—he wasn't the same after that. Why are you asking?"

"I work for a paper," he said, which wasn't entirely false. "What folk from Plymouth?"

"Damned if I can remember." Wade ran a hand down his face.

Letting out a tight breath, Merritt asked, "Can I talk to Charlie, then?"

But Wade shook his head. "He ain't here no more. Left around the same time Harold did. Acting real strange. Sorry, that's all I got."

"You said someone died. Do you know who?"

Wade shrugged.

"Okay." Merritt put his hands out and motioned, like he were talking to a child. "If a body is found in Marshfield, what do they do with it?"

Now Wade looked at him like *he* was the slow one. "Put it in the cemetery."

"But if the man isn't from Marshfield? If he needs to be identified . . . or can't be?" Unlikely anyone around here would lay claim to Silas. None of the locals would have recognized him.

"Go to the coroner, I guess."

Merritt nodded. "And where can I find him?"

There wasn't a coroner in Marshfield, apparently, but there was one in Plymouth. After receiving some quick instructions, Merritt thanked the man and stepped out of the sawmill.

When he hopped on a wagon headed toward Plymouth, he asked for permission first.

⁓

Hulda struggled more than ever to focus on her work, and she didn't feel the slightest pull of a hysterian's magic.

Stanley Lidgett. Why else would he have a communion stone connecting him to Silas Hogwood if he wasn't part of it? He could not feign ignorance anymore. Not after Silas's arrest and conviction.

Shuddering, Hulda pulled her cardinal shawl closer around her as she trudged back to BIKER, having just made another trip to the Genealogical Society for the Advancement of Magic at Mr. Walker's request. Her mind wound down an unnecessary road, imagining what might have been had Mr. Lidgett returned her affections all those years ago, only for her to discover he was an accomplice to murder . . . or, at the very least, far too forgiving of homicidal malefactors. What if she'd married the man?

Let it go. She had enough anxieties to sort through without adding morbid fantasies atop them. Slipping her hand into her bag, she pushed past the file she'd collected for Walker—a record of the past owners of an enchanted abode in Connecticut Myra had overseen three years ago—to the communion stone connected to Merritt. There was no point in it. He couldn't leave a message for her to listen to later, and she'd strictly forbidden herself from checking on him during the day for fear of greater distraction. He'd been just fine when he'd arrived in Marshfield this morning. He'd reach out to her when he had information.

Jerking her hand free, Hulda forced her thoughts to the world around her. She nodded as she stepped around a young woman pulling a wagon of eggs and one caged chicken, then dodged a pile of horse dung in the road. The day was overcast, creating a chill that nipped at her nose and ears. Her strides were quick and long, in part to keep her warm, and in part because she was past due to record any changes in her carefully placed azurite.

"Hulda?" she heard. Turning, she studied the street but spied no one waving to her. When a voice called, "Hulda, are you there?" again, she realized it was coming from her bag. Retrieving her selenite communion stone, she pressed the rune on it and asked, "Merritt?" Then continued walking.

"I'm relatively sure our man is dead."

Her stomach tightened as if trying to hold her heart in place. "You found him?"

"I . . . believe so. I can't be sure. It's strange, Hulda. Are you in a private place?"

She looked about her. Not private, no, but noisy enough not to be overheard. "Speak carefully," she replied.

"The constable at the time up and left. Very suddenly. Out of state. Another watchman apparently vanished, and the one I spoke to said a woman got him drunk as a sailor, so his memory of the night is blurry."

"A woman," Hulda repeated, careful.

"Our woman, I'm sure," Merritt's voice crackled through the enchantment. "But there was record of a dead body, and another record of a body being delivered to the Plymouth coroner October 17. It was cremated."

Hulda's stride slowed. "Cremated? Are you sure?"

"That's all I have. No name, no identification. No one claimed him, so they cremated him." A pause. "I don't know who else it would be."

Hulda mulled over this long enough for Merritt to repeat her name.

"I'm here," she murmured, turning the corner and seeing the Bright Bay Hotel down the street. "Did they preserve the ashes?"

"I . . . don't know. I can ask. I'm not too far out."

"The records—"

"Didn't say. He let me see them. There's nothing else there that I haven't told you."

Hulda hummed deep in her throat. "Perhaps—"

Another woman, tightly bundled in winter clothes, bumped into her just then, shoulders colliding hard enough that Hulda nearly dropped the stone. Stumbling, she righted herself, then glared after the woman, who hadn't so much as offered an apology. She continued on her way, a little hunched over. Probably old, but with a strong walk, nonetheless. Shaking it off, Hulda said, "Well, that's the end of that well." She would take comfort in it. She had to. Silas was dead, and Mr. Lidgett was none of her concern.

"Seems to be."

"I'm nearly to BIKER," she added. "I'd rather not discuss any more while I'm there. Do travel safe, Merritt."

"Anything for you, darling."

Hulda rolled her eyes, but her lips curled into a smile, regardless.

No more sound emitted from the stone, so she slipped it back into her bag and stepped into BIKER's headquarters.

∽

Owein pressed his right front paw onto the letter *E*, then looked up at Baptiste.

The two were in Merritt's office, Hulda's mud-spotted letterboard spread out on the floor. The large Frenchman had taken up residence in Merritt's chair and folded his burly arms across his chest. A simple nod told Owein he was correct.

He lifted his paw a fraction, then set it down on the *E* once more.

"*A,*" Baptiste corrected.

Why would there be an *A* in *tea*? Shaking his head. Owein lifted and replanted his paw on the *E*.

Baptiste leaned forward. "Is spelled *T-E-A*. Tea."

Owein pawed the *E*.

The chef grunted. "Why would it be spelled *T-E-E*? That is nonsense."

Because that's what it sounds like, Owein wanted to say, but Baptiste couldn't hear him, so Owein continued to paw at the *E*, the paper threatening to tear beneath his nails.

"Stop. *Stop.*" Baptiste nudged him off with the tip of his boot. "Try, uh." Baptiste rotated his wrist, trying to think of a simple enough word. "Leg. Do *leg.*"

Owein looked at the letterboard, sounding out the first letter in his mind.

Legs skittering over the floor, infested but alone.

The thought pushed into his mind like a nightmare, dark and thick. Owein shook his whole body like he was wet, and it faded away.

"Owein. *Leg.*"

Lifting a paw, Owein touched down on *L*, then *E*, and then *E* again, followed by *V*.

"Leev?" Baptiste asked. "No, it's . . . oh, leave. You want to be done?"

Owein shook his head. Started over. *U-L-E-E-V*, he spelled, then whined.

It took Baptiste a beat to understand, which probably meant Owein had spelled it wrong. Baptiste clasped his large hands together and leaned his elbows on his knees. "No, I am not leaving. I do not plan to." He paused. "I am not a strong swimmer."

Owein huffed at the poor joke.

He felt a tendril of that worry, that darkness, simmering in the back of his skull.

It was getting worse, somehow. Owein had woken during two nightmares this last week. Nightmares he could barely explain, let alone spell. Visions of being cold and dark and twisted and lonely. He didn't know how to tell Baptiste. And Merritt . . . Merritt always smelled sad or angry, and when he didn't, he was off somewhere with Hulda, doing whatever they did across the bay. Owein didn't want to make everything worse. He didn't want to make Merritt sick again, like he'd been when he broke the island.

So Owein focused on his letters, spelling out *L-E-J*, which Baptiste corrected with a *G*.

As for the rest . . . he'd just have to wait for it to go away. He'd get better.

Eventually.

⟡

Hulda was exhausted as she pushed open the door to her room on the second floor of BIKER headquarters, checking the ward as she went.

Today was an absolute mess. Her mind had been elsewhere, meanwhile Mr. Walker had directed her and Miss Richards to comb through financial records all day. Mr. Walker was a wolf on the hunt, determined to figure out where the missing funds had gone . . . or, perhaps, to keep the women distracted while he dealt with other enchantments, if Mr. Baillie was to be believed. Between assignments, Hulda had snuck to her carefully placed azurite crystals and recorded their changes. She thought the one in the records room looked a little different, but she'd gone three hours later than she would have liked, and it could have been a trick of the lighting. She didn't have an opportunity to bring it closer to the window, because Mr. Baillie had walked in just then, acknowledging her with nothing beyond an apathetic glance.

Hulda sighed. What was truth, and what was lie?

Attempting to rehash it now made a painful headache spring between her eyes. After tossing her black bag onto her bed—it landed on its side and spilled half its contents—she sat on the mattress, massaging the sore spot. What she wouldn't give for some lemon drops and a nice book right now. She was in the mood for fiction, oddly enough. She missed the days of sneaking into Merritt's office to read his latest work. She missed Whimbrel House. She missed Mr. Babineaux and Owein and Miss Taylor. And she missed Merritt.

She still got to see him, yes, but it wasn't quite the same. Her head hurt, and her heart hurt, and she wished she could just fall asleep and snooze through all of tomorrow, but alas, at this rate, Mr. Walker would have her working through Saturday again. She would do it, for BIKER.

What if he never intended to give her BIKER, regardless of her work?

Groaning, Hulda pulled her hands away and arched her back, stretching it out. Reached over and shoved things back into her bag— ledgers, a file, pens and paper, the communion stone, some postage, an apple she hadn't eaten, the communion stone—

Hulda paused, turning the selenite rock over in her hands. Reached into the bag and pulled out another selenite stone.

She had . . . *two* communion stones?

The one in her left hand was Merritt's—she'd used it enough to recognize it easily. It was about the size of her fist and had a strong blue tint. The other was notably smaller, shaped more like, oh, a large piece of gnocchi, mostly gray slashed with white. The spell rune on it was smaller as well.

However did this end up in her bag? Was this from Mr. Baillie? Was he ready to speak with her?

Eyeing the ward at her door, Hulda dared to activate the spell.

"Hello?" she asked.

A few heartbeats passed before a woman's voice responded, "Hulda, are you alone?"

She nearly dropped the stone. Sliding off the bed to her knees, she scrambled, "M-Myra?"

"Keep your voice down," the stone murmured back.

Hulda's mouth worked. Chills rushed up and down her arms. When had Myra accessed her bag? Surely she wouldn't have snuck into the hotel in the middle of the night! Hulda hadn't left it unsupervised anywhere . . . That woman in the street, who'd run into her so violently . . . had it been Myra? Had she been *right there* and Hulda hadn't noticed?

"Are you alone?" the voice pressed.

"Y-Yes. I'm in my room at the hotel. It's warded."

A sigh of relief trickled through the selenite.

"Myra, meet me. Anywhere. I'll leave right now—"

"No, it's too dangerous." Myra spoke just above a whisper. "If my involvement with Mr. Hogwood is discovered, I'll be arrested. If you're tied to me, you'll be arrested, too."

Hulda squeezed the stone and watched her fingers turn white. "But—"

"I got your message."

Her heart flipped. "You did? Which one? I sent out so many—"

"Stop looking for me, Hulda." The words were harsh, but her tone softened with each one. Hulda could see the expression on Myra's face in her mind's eye—creases in her forehead; brows drawn; wide, downcast eyes; her only tell the way her mouth twisted toward one dimple. "You're putting yourself in danger."

"Then answer my questions—"

"No." A pause. "I need to go."

Panic pulsed through Hulda's veins. She rushed, "Who threatened you?"

The stone didn't reply, and for a tense moment, Hulda worried she'd lost the connection. But she thought she heard an exhale on the other side.

"I'd like to think you left it for me to find," Hulda pressed. "So tell me."

"I don't know." Myra's voice was airy.

"What does he want?" She brought the stone closer to her mouth and lowered her voice even further. "Myra, you've already wrung me out and left me sun bleached on the line. Tell me what I need to know. Tell me why Mr. Walker is hunting down expenses." She hesitated. "Tell me what happened to Mr. Hogwood."

Another long pause. Finally, "BIKER has control of more than you realize. The man who threatened me—I'm sure it's a man—somehow figured it out."

Control of more? What did that mean? But Hulda didn't know how much time she had, so she kept her line of questioning direct. "Is that where the missing funds are going?"

Silence.

"Myra. I need to know."

"It will work out," the stone replied. "I'll destroy it if I need to, but it will be years of work ruined. You need to stay with BIKER, Hulda.

Promise me. Take care of it so it doesn't fall into the wrong hands. For now, the less you know, the better."

"I want to!" She couldn't keep her frustration from sharpening her words. "One of the reasons LIKER is here is to assign a new director. But it may not go to me. Alastair Baillie is also a contender. Mr. Baillie is a lawyer for BIKER. He's tall, pale, wears glasses—"

"I've seen him."

You have? Was Myra watching BIKER? She didn't seem at all surprised by the mention of LIKER. How much did she know? Which passersby had had their mind delved into by a lurking woman in disguise?

Merritt's voice rang so clearly in the back of her thoughts she glanced to the other communion stone to ensure it hadn't come from that. *It's just . . . why would Alastair Baillie want to be the director of BIKER so badly?*

Hulda swallowed. "Mr. Baillie is, or was, Mr. Hogwood's estate and trial lawyer. And I went back to Marshfield." She rushed her words, fearful Myra would disconnect them. "I found a communion stone there that I'm positive connects back to Mr. Stanley Lidgett, who was the steward at Gorse End. He and Mr. Hogwood were in touch after Mr. Hogwood sailed to the States. I don't know if Mr. Baillie was also in communication with them . . . Explain this to me, Myra. I'm . . . I'm floundering."

A beat passed. "Whoever has BIKER has the facility," Myra murmured.

"What facility?" If there was a secret facility Myra had kept hidden and the person who was threatening her knew about it . . .

Then it stood to reason Mr. Baillie, who was angling so hard for the director position, was the one who sent the threatening telegram. It had to be him! Or was it Mr. Walker using Mr. Baillie as a scapegoat?

Her heart pounded as though Thor himself were striking it.

Trying to wet her drying mouth, Hulda whispered, "If Mr. Hogwood recorded anything about this facility and sent it back to Gorse End, Mr. Lidgett might have seen it. He could in turn have relayed it to Mr. Baillie. And when Mr. Hogwood disappeared, Mr. Baillie sent that telegram! Merritt and I have a theory about the will. We think they might need to produce a body to be paid out—"

"No," Myra interrupted before Hulda could relate news of her visit with Mr. Adey. "No, Silas didn't know."

"Are you sure?" Hulda countered. "Do either of us know how much magic he stole? Did he have psychometry powers? If he didn't pull it from a file, could he have pulled it from *you*?" She paused, then pressed, "Myra?"

"I don't know." Her response was barely audible.

Hulda eyed the ward over her door once more. "What facility?"

Three seconds passed. "I need to go."

"You will tell me. Now." The edge in Hulda's voice surprised her, but she didn't regret it.

"Are you sure you're not being overheard?"

Hulda pulled her blanket around her for extra muffling. "Yes."

Myra took a moment to collect herself. "There's a secret facility in Ohio that banks blood from wizard cadavers and placentas."

Hulda's lips parted. She hadn't expected *that*.

"My associates and I are trying to find a way to amplify, or possibly re-create, magic outside of genetics. It will be completely lost otherwise. Some say by the year 2000. We'll lose all of it."

Hulda didn't know what to say. Fortunately, her former employer continued on without her.

"We don't have the answer yet. But Silas Hogwood is the only person who ever successfully transferred magic."

"*With* magic," Hulda croaked.

"Yes, but he did it, and his body might be a clue to determining how to replicate it without hurting anyone."

Hulda's free hand came up to her mouth. She forced it away so she could speak. "You took his body. It wasn't cremated."

A pause. "No, it wasn't. It's being preserved at the facility."

"Dear Lord." Hulda took a second to compose herself. "How many . . . others?"

"Only him." A whistle passed through the connection—it sounded like Myra was outdoors and fighting a gust of wind. "I tried to get others, long ago, but the cadaver laws wouldn't allow it. BIKER is not a medical facility, and even then, only criminals can be used."

Dryness in Hulda's mouth leached down her throat. "M-Mr. Hogwood *is* a criminal."

"He's also a British citizen."

All the more reason for Myra to go to such lengths to keep the Marshfield incident secret. Hulda shook her head, sick and cold and light-headed. The missing funds, then . . . they were all going to Ohio, to this . . . place. "Myra, where is the facility?"

"You take BIKER, and you'll find it. I made sure you could find it. If *he* takes BIKER—" She sighed. "I don't know. I might have to destroy it. I'll have no other choice."

"Myra . . . is it too late to stop all this? To let it go, to come back? Surely we can work around this—"

"I have to go. Do not tell anyone. Not even Merritt Fernsby."

"Myra, wait. I have to tell you about Mr. Walker! I'm not sure if—"

The sound of breaking fizzled through their connection, and the stone went dead. Turning it over in her hands, Hulda noted that the communion rune was no longer on its surface. Myra had shattered her half of the spell.

Wrapping a fist around the stone, Hulda pressed the blanket to her face and screamed into it. Finally, *finally*, she'd connected with Myra, only to lose her again!

She released the stone and drew three deep breaths through her nose and let them out through her mouth. She hadn't come away empty-handed, at least. Leaning back against her bed, she attempted to sort through the information.

The facility. The facility was important. Illegal, and important. Surely a means to re-create, synthesize, *grow* magic was highly valuable to society . . . but she suspected the cadaver restrictions weren't the only laws being broken. She'd have to see it, learn about it, before making her call. Its value must have been extreme if it was indeed the motivating factor behind the actions of Mr. Baillie and Mr. Walker. That, or her theory about the Hogwood estate payout was correct and Mr. Hogwood had bequeathed an alarming sum to his associates.

Don't fall down the well, she chided herself, thinking of Merritt's earlier metaphor.

So. *If* Hulda became director, how would she find the facility? Myra had indicated she'd be able to find it if she secured the job, but Hulda had combed through all of headquarters for this audit. She'd found no evidence of the kind, except for the financial statements that had alerted LIKER. Yet surely Myra wouldn't leave information about something so critical, so protected, out for *anyone* to find.

Perhaps one of these "associates" would contact her, once it was official. *If* it became official. And what on earth would she do with it?

The idea of being able to create wizardry in a laboratory instead of a womb had appeal, yet to do it so furtively, against the law . . . It was too much to contemplate.

"I have so many more questions," she whispered to the darkness. Twilight begirded the world outside her window. She hadn't lit a candle, and the sun set so early now. Her mind skated to Myra's directive that she keep the information from Merritt. Why? What on earth would he even do about it?

How much more did Hulda not know?

She formed a fist around the stone. She could get it re-enchanted, but there was no way to connect it back to Myra. Yet, Myra *had* confirmed that one of Hulda's missives had reached her. Hulda didn't know which method had worked, but if she were to repeat them all, surely she could reach Myra again. But would the insufferable woman respond? Was it all truly as dangerous as she claimed?

Hulda pinched her lips together until it hurt. Released them. Waited as the blood flowed back in.

Then she reached for the other communion stone and activated it.

"Merritt? Merritt, I need to speak with—"

"I'm here. Just jotting down ideas for a book. What's wrong?"

The sound of his voice coursed through her like a soothing oil. She took a deep breath. "I spoke with Myra." And then, in hushed tones, she explained everything. The time had passed for Hulda to protect Myra's confidence, and she trusted Merritt.

After a moment of silence, he said, "We have to play this carefully, H. Not let Baillie—or Walker—know what we know. If Myra is scared, we should be, too."

Chapter 17

Hulda rose early the next morning to check on the azurite. It wasn't difficult to do so, given the utter lack of sleep she'd had the night before. She'd spent several hours pacing the length of her room. Sometimes muttering to herself, sometimes lying down and staring at the ceiling, occasionally reading the same passage in a receipt book dozens of times because she couldn't absorb a word of it. And at the first hint of dawn, she went upstairs, passed the empty reception desk, and went to the filing room to check on the azurite there.

This time she brought it over to the window, studied it. Was that spot a change? Not wanting to bias herself, she recorded the look, feel, and weight of the stone before reviewing her past logs. Had she mentioned a spot on her first entry? She flipped back a page—

"Miss Larkin."

The deep voice made her jump. She fumbled with the ledger, but it toppled from her hands, landing open, pages down, on the floor. Whirling around, she saw Mr. Walker standing squarely in the door-frame, and Mr. Baillie just inside it, his long arms folded across his thin chest, his pale lips curved into a subtle smirk.

Hulda moved her tongue around her mouth to moisten it. Her gaze darted between Mr. Walker and Mr. Baillie. "I-I'm surprised you're here so early." She picked up the ledger.

"Azurite," Mr. Baillie said, calm as a winter lake.

Indeed, the azurite piece Hulda had been studying was still sitting on the windowsill.

"I see that." Mr. Walker's tone was about as alive as a market fish. He stepped aside, waving his hand, and two watchmen stepped into the room, one tugging a length of rope between his hands.

Hulda's stomach flopped onto the floor, right where the ledger had been. "What is the meaning of this?"

"Do you think me a fool, Miss Larkin?" Mr. Walker asked, stepping into the room as the watchmen seized her arms. One jerked the ledger from her hands; then the other jerked them behind her back.

"A fool? No." Hulda struggled to keep her voice even, but it betrayed her with a heavy waver. "But after this man"—she angled her head toward Mr. Baillie as the watchmen jerked her arms in their sockets and bound her wrists with the rope—"trespassed Mr. Fernsby's home and claimed he was under the control of your psychometry, I thought I'd do a little research."

Mr. Walker let out a weak, mirthless chuckle. "Just as you said, Baillie."

That smirk on Mr. Baillie's mouth deepened.

Blood drained from Hulda's face and onto the floor beside her stomach. "Wh-What?"

Reaching into his pocket, Mr. Walker pulled out a handful of azurite—*her* azurite. He must have collected it last night, save the one here. "I don't know if you've lied about Myra Haigh," he said, "but to be clear, I'm having you arrested for fraud and the misuse of magic."

Hulda shook her head. "What? No, this is a misunderstanding! You can't—Mr. Baillie is—"

"The bespelling of houses to force American citizens to require BIKER's services," Mr. Walker continued.

Hulda's body went limp. That *was* something Myra had done. She'd used Silas Hogwood for it.

"The siphoning of funds from LIKER and its subsidiaries," Mr. Walker continued.

She gaped. "I never—"

"The use of a psychometrist to overtake BIKER," he spoke over her.

"No!" she shrieked as the watchmen tugged her away from the window. "I haven't seen Myra since she resigned!"

Mr. Walker snorted. "There is more than one psychometrist in the world, Miss Larkin." He held up the stones. "I do believe Mr. Fernsby recently came into magic. These stones you've placed around the office would certainly help him bewitch us."

Her knees weakened. It was all wrong—all twisted and splintered and wrong. "Mr. Fernsby is a communionist, a wardist—"

"And a psychometrist," Mr. Baillie finished for her. "We have his lineage, Miss Larkin. There's no point in hiding it."

His genealogy? *She* had it as well, and there wasn't a lick of psychometry in it. Her eyes locked onto Mr. Baillie's. "You doctored it, you conniving—"

"Not to mention the funds that were going to Whimbrel House," Mr. Walker interrupted.

She didn't know whom to plead to—Mr. Walker, Mr. Baillie, or the watchmen around her. "No, never . . ." Had Mr. Baillie doctored that, too? She settled on the lawyer. "What did you do?" Her voice was rough with unshed tears.

Mr. Baillie did not answer. The watchmen dragged her to the doorway. Mr. Walker stepped back. As she passed, he said, "I'll ask you one more time. Do you know where Myra Haigh is?"

"No!" she practically screamed the word.

"Have you spoken to her since this investigation began?"

Denial spiraled up her throat, then died on her tongue. It was only a moment's hesitation, but apparently that was all Mr. Walker needed.

"Take her." He massaged his temples. "Make it quick. I don't need a scene."

The men shoved Hulda down the hallway, never giving her a chance to look back.

⁓

Merritt threw the stitched leather ball again, watching it sail through the air and land in a pile of orange and scarlet leaves. Owein bolted after it, the leaves bursting away from him as he dove for the ball, as though they and he were magnets with opposite poles. If there was one good thing about the chaocracy Merritt had been unable—and somewhat unwilling, given the potential for destruction—to repeat, it had made a nice, smooth playing field off the side of his house, one perfect for a very long game of catch.

Speaking of very long, his shoulder was beginning to ache.

Owein darted back toward him, ball clutched in his jaws, but slowed down halfway back, eyes darting toward the sea. Ears lifting, he dropped the ball. Curious, Merritt turned to see what had caught his eye. Shielding his face from the sun, he watched three men step out of a white boat. They all wore dark uniforms. Watchmen?

It's all right, Merritt said, though he hadn't meant to use communion. He held out a hand to Owein before walking toward the approaching men. This was probably an update on his claim of trespassing against Baillie; he'd gone to the watchmen at Portsmouth for that, same ones he'd alerted after Silas Hogwood attacked Hulda.

"You've news for me?" he asked when he was a few paces away. He didn't recognize any faces, but that could just have been the sun in his eyes.

"Merritt Fernsby?" one of them asked. Apparently they didn't recognize him, either. What was the point of this eccentric hair style if no one was going to bother recognizing him?

"Yes?" A peculiar feeling unwound in his gut.

Two of the three stepped forward, surrounding him. He didn't notice the cord one of them held until the man slipped behind him, yanking his arms back.

Owein started to bark.

"You're under arrest," the first said very matter-of-factly.

Merritt strapped his mask on tightly and tried to maintain calm. Didn't fight the knots forming over his wrists. "A man trespasses on my property, and *I'm* the one in trouble? Do I need to review the laws in Portsmouth?"

"We're from Boston," one of the watchmen clarified, and that peculiar feeling rendered into dread.

Grinding his teeth, Merritt asked, "And what, pray tell, am I being arrested for?"

"Illegal use of magic, fraud, and conspiracy."

One of the watchmen behind him pushed him toward the boat, but Merritt dug in his heels. "Come again? Conspiracy for *what*?"

"You can ask your jailer. Come." The man motioned to his comrades.

Merritt shoved back against them. "I have the right to know! Conspiracy for *what*? Fraud for *what*?"

Owein continued yapping. Heavy footsteps sounded behind them.

The watchman frowned. "I'm just carrying out orders."

Merritt growled. "Surely you know who sent them."

"The constable?" the watchman asked incredulously. Then he shrugged. "Filed by the London Institute for the Keeping of Enchanted Rooms."

Merritt's muscles went slack, and the other watchmen successfully pushed him forward. *Hulda's in trouble.*

"Whoa!" The first watchman shouted, holding up a hand and reaching for a pistol at his side. "Whoa! Stop right there!"

Merritt managed to wrench around enough to see Baptiste barreling toward them like a bull. Jerking from the hold of one of the Bostonians, Merritt turned to face Baptiste head on.

"Stop!" he shouted. "Baptiste, *no*. It's not worth it."

The chef slowed and growled like a bear. Trudged forward until he was five paces away, four—

"I'll shoot!" the first watchman threatened.

"Where will you go?" Merritt pressed as Owein yipped at Baptiste's heels. "Where will you go next if they arrest you, too?"

The Frenchman paused.

"It's all right," Merritt added as the wary watchmen dragged him toward the boat. "It's a misunderstanding. It'll be sorted out, you'll see. Just wait for me. I'll be back before sunset."

Owein whined a little louder with each foot of distance put between them. The watchmen shoved Merritt onto the boat and activated a kinetic rune to send them back to the mainland. Owein barked after them, a loud, high-pitched sound that mimicked a howling winter wind.

Merritt must have lost his touch if Owein had detected his lie so easily.

⁓

It was not yet noon when Merritt—who had been manhandled enough to earn several bruises—was shoved into the Suffolk County Penitentiary—a smaller prison north of Boston that had a cell especially built to hold criminals with spells in their blood. It was about the size of Whimbrel House and as charming as the place had been when Owein was still darkly brooding inside its walls. The entire prison was made of cold stone overly mortared. Merritt didn't get to see much of it on his tour, especially since the guards escorting him kept a hand on the back of his head, forcing him to focus on his feet.

His eyes fell immediately to the woman sitting across the room, and his heart squelched like a soggy boot in mud.

"Oh, Merritt!" Hulda cried as he lost his balance and came down on his knees—they'd unbound his hands, but hadn't given him any time to let the blood wash back into his fingers. Hulda grasped his elbows and hauled him back up; he managed an awkward side embrace as the gate slammed shut behind him.

There were tears in Hulda's eyes as she looked him over and rambled over what had happened on her end of things—a story that made him want to sink his fist into Walker's stomach and rip free the testicles from between Baillie's legs.

The guards had no qualms against conversation, at least, allowing them to exchange stories as the blood worked back into Merritt's hands. The cell they were in was about the size of his sitting room. There was no furniture, only a stone outcropping that ran along the far wall, just wide enough for an average man to lie down and long enough for four of them to fit head to toe. No windows, mayhap to dissuade any elementists with air spells from enacting their magic. Or, just as likely, simply to be cruel.

As for the gate, it was wrought iron and heavy, activated by a kinetic spell via a special rod one of the guards wore on his belt. Merritt hadn't noticed which of them had activated it, but the shimmer of a wardship shield—the same spell he possessed—coated the bars, ensuring no escape. Merritt wasn't sure if he could deactivate other wardship shields or just his own, but even if he could, it wouldn't get him any closer to freedom—not even a child would fit between those bars, and not even Baptiste could bend them. Besides, he and Hulda were innocent . . . Surely there'd be a way to prove that. At the very minimum, they could attest that he hadn't a lick of psychometry in him.

Why go to the risk of trying to escape?

As for their trial, the watchmen and guards had both failed to mention when that might be. Soon, he prayed.

Turning from the door, Merritt noticed one other prisoner in the space, sitting in the far south corner—an older man who had seen better days, blatantly ignoring the newcomers. He wondered, briefly, what sort of magic he had. Perhaps he was a necromancer who'd killed a beloved tree in a park with a sneeze or, like Miss Richards, an augurist who found it all too easy to cheat at cards. Hulda, meanwhile, walked to the stone bench, hugging herself, her spine about as straight as an overcooked spaghetti noodle.

He clasped Hulda's elbow. "Are you all right? Did they hurt you?"

She shook her head, expression tight, tears brimming but not falling. "Not physically, no. But." She worked her hands. "This is terrible." She took off her glasses and wiped her hand across her eyes. "All of it. We've been completely stultified. I don't even know where to start."

Letting out a long breath, Merritt dropped beside her. "I'm afraid you're correct."

"I should have listened to you."

"About what?"

"Baillie." She played with the arms of her glasses, folding them in and out. "He doesn't even deserve that *mister*. He played us."

"We weren't sure," Merritt tried. "We were trying to be sure."

"The vision!" She huffed, getting a little life back into her. "I saw him, like he was scared. Like he was running. Like his story was *true*."

Merritt placed his hand on her knee. "Maybe it was something else. Maybe Walker orchestrated it." Doubt laced his every word.

Hulda shook her head. "He said, 'Just as you said, Baillie.' Baillie was caught, and he concocted his story about Walker so we would hesitate. He accomplished this to get us out of the way. Now"—she leaned close, her next words all air and no voice—"he'll locate this facility, find Silas Hogwood's body, if that's what he's after, and he'll run BIKER into the ground, one way or another." She pushed the glasses back onto her face. Frowned and removed them, then cleaned the lenses with her skirt. "But that vision of Baillie, Merritt! What could it mean? Why did I see it? It felt . . . It felt like I was *there*. He seemed terrified."

He didn't answer for a moment, trying to think of something reassuring. The best he could come up with was "Time will tell."

She returned her glasses to her nose and shook her head. "The director position is utterly ruined now. I've no chance at it, if I ever did." She blinked rapidly. "I failed her."

Squeezing her knee, Merritt asked, "Who? Myra?"

Hulda nodded.

"Didn't she fail you first?"

Hulda sucked in a deep breath and never really let it out. "I've gone over it time and time again. What would I have done, were I in Myra's position? Sick, failing, desperate . . . she didn't know what would come of her decision, hiring . . . *him* . . . but she knew she was playing with fire! She *knew* about my history with Mr. Hogwood, though not my involvement with you." She shrugged. "Or your abilities, obviously. And this"—she eyed the guards and the other prisoner, ensuring she wasn't overheard—"*facility*. But she was—*is*—my closest friend. I still love and respect her, but it's all been shaken, and I can't contact her and get any closure."

Merritt moved his hand from her knee to her back, rubbing her shoulder blades. She leaned into him and rested her head on his shoulder.

"I know," he murmured. "I'm sorry." He looked around the cell; the other fellow appeared to be dozing. "We'll get a trial and lay everything straight."

"But how do we prove we weren't involved without her testimony?" she asked. "She can disprove at least two of the accusations. We had nothing to do with the siphoned funds, nor with the bespelling of houses to keep BIKER afloat." Her body grew heavy against him. "Heaven help me, what if they disassemble BIKER completely?"

"Ask for testimonials without Alastair Baillie in the room, for one," Merritt tried. "And we'll need to come clean about everything and anything, including our necromantic friend. Myra can take the fall for our secrecy—if anyone's willing to believe the man was alive and came to America in the first place." They'd need to use that card to bring in Mr. Adey as a witness, God let him be willing. "If nothing else, both Gifford and I have copies of my family tree, and living witnesses to it. The psychometry accusation will be refuted quickly."

"Mr. Baillie has to know it will be. His argument lacks integrity. Oh, I wish I knew what he was thinking!" She sighed. "I'll have to completely besmirch Myra's character, besides. And . . . she told me not to tell anyone about . . . about *Ohio*, not even you—"

"You don't owe her any favors." Arm around her shoulders, Merritt hugged her. "I don't know. Hopefully it will be enough. Who knows how many pies Baillie—or Myra—have their fingers in."

They sat there for a long while, leaning against each other, staring at rock and bars. Merritt unpicked his thoughts, trying to sort out the best means of getting them out of this mess . . . but through it all kept his focus on Hulda. On keeping her chipper, reassuring her, but also on being present with her, because she was a balm to his anger and confusion, and while he knew incarceration likely hit her harder than it did him, he was grateful they were together.

Maybe, if he played his cards right, he'd never have to be alone again.

His fingers traced circles on her far shoulder. One of her hairpins was jabbing him, but he didn't move to accommodate it. He'd thought she'd fallen asleep, but then she started examining her cuticles. "You know," he spoke slowly, quietly, his heartbeat picking up, "once we get out of here . . . if BIKER is off the table . . . you could come back to Whimbrel House."

She snorted softly, like she couldn't bear to put effort into it. "I'm not sure you could afford me."

"Not as a housekeeper."

She paused for a moment, then lifted her head to meet his eyes.

He pulled his arm from her and dropped his hands in his lap. "I know we've only known each other a short while . . . a couple months and some change . . . but." He paused. Perhaps he should have thought through the wording beforehand. That was a nice thing about writing—when someone read it, they had no idea how long the author had taken to compose it, or how many times he'd discarded something terrible and replaced it with the right phrase. They only saw the finished, polished product. "Well, I'm very fond of you, as you know. And we're both already in our thirties . . . past time to settle down, really. I'll have another work published next year, get the rest of my advance, and Mr. McFarland wants a series, which is a good outlook, career-wise. I'd like to have you around . . . I want to be close—"

Hulda was staring at him, blanched and wide eyed. He lost track of what he was about to say. His heart squelched a little, trying to read her expression—

She swallowed. "A-Are you proposing to me?"

He studied her for a second longer, determining to push forward. "I think this is a poor location for a proposal, don't you think?" He chuckled, but Hulda didn't follow suit. Sobering, he added, "I'm certainly putting it on the table, that is—"

Hulda pulled back, blinking, tears forming in her eyes.

Merritt's stomach flopped into his pelvis. Pulse racing, he reached forward and grabbed her hand. "I'm sorry, Hulda. I shouldn't have brought it up, here of all places. Not with this thing with Walker hanging over our heads—"

"No, no." She shook her head, blinking and straightening. Laughed softly. "No, it's not that at all . . . I just . . ." She lifted her glasses and dabbed the corners of her eyes with her knuckles. "I just . . . I never thought this would be an option for me. I never thought anyone would ever . . ." She dabbed and laughed, sniffed, and Merritt's stomach climbed back to its space below his diaphragm.

"Oh." He tried not to smile but did a terrible job of it. "Well. I apologize that the men in your life have been muttonheads, but then again, I suppose I should thank them—"

This time he wasn't able to finish the sentence because Hulda was kissing him. Not that it mattered—the subject at hand was quickly forgotten beneath the pressure of her lips, which Merritt quickly matched. Her hands worked into his hair, fingernails leaving shivering trails, and he nearly fell off the bench, trying to get a better angle, to explore her more thoroughly—

Banging on the bars startled them apart. One of the guards was running a cudgel over the iron bars. "No sparking, or I'll see you whipped!"

Hulda, red as cooked lobster, retreated as much as she could without actually standing and walking away. Merritt laughed. It felt good to laugh, given their situation.

Once the guard was satisfied and stepped away, Merritt said, "I certainly hope that was because you like me, and not because I'm the first to ask."

Hulda folded her arms tightly across her chest. "You are a rogue, Mr. Fernsby."

Smiling, he stretched, wondering what time it was. Wondering when they were going to eat, and what sort of food wizardfolk prisoners received.

They didn't get lunch, but they did get dinner, eventually. Crusty bread and a slop that could almost be called soup. It sobered both of them, and brought up the question neither wanted to voice aloud.

What if they couldn't prove their innocence?

Then there would be no books, no Whimbrel House, and no Hulda in his future, period.

Chapter 18

Owein was tired. He'd barked until his throat was raw, then run laps around the island until his legs and ribs hurt. Merritt hadn't come back. Hulda hadn't come back. Beth hadn't come back. They were all being taken away, one by one. Soon he'd be alone again. He'd rot away in these walls until his dog body died; then he'd haunt the house again . . . or maybe just move on. Maybe he'd leave, too. See if his family still remembered him, on the other side.

He'd taken up residence at the bottom of the stairs, in sight of the front door, which remained closed. He dozed on and off, his exhausted body at war with his racing mind. *Still have Baptiste,* he reminded himself. Baptiste, who had spouted obscenities in all volumes and punched the woodpile and now read a paper in the living room. At least he still had Baptiste.

But for how long?

Darkness inched around his vision. A nightmare trying to lure him into slumber.

A sound tickled his ear, and he tilted his head. It came from upstairs, faint, a man's voice—but not Baptiste's. Had the stranger come back?

Owein barked twice, earning a faint *"C'est quoi?"* from the living room. Owein didn't wait for Baptiste, though; he bolted up the stairs.

Paused and listened again, until he heard a new sound—a fumbling sound that came from Merritt's room. He bolted that way as the chef's heavy steps sounded below.

New smells enticed him, but Owein forced himself to focus. To follow the sounds to the communion stone on top of the dresser, which he couldn't reach. If he stood on his hind legs, pressing his front against the third drawer up, he could get close.

"—dence in here," a man with an accent similar to the stranger's was saying. More fumbling noises came, one loud enough that Owein winced. Like the man had activated Hulda's communion stone without realizing it.

Owein whined. Even if he could reach the stone, he couldn't talk back.

"What is wrong?" Baptiste asked, entering the room. When he saw Owein, he paused.

A sigh emitted from the stone. "Let's turn over the entire thing."

"No, let's sort through it first, just to be sure."

Owein didn't recognize the voices.

Baptiste, stepping softly now, crossed the room and put his ear to the stone, his dark brows low as he listened.

The first man spoke, but a shuffling sound cut him off. "How long we keeping them?"

"Not long," replied the second. "They get the wizards through quickly, before they cause too much trouble. Maybe a breeding program."

"That's medieval."

"Not sure the lady is strong, so she'll *probably* get indentured labor. The other one is supposedly dangerous."

"Noose?"

"Maybe. I wouldn't think so, but someone's really browbeating for it. For the both of them."

Owein whined. Baptiste's fingers pushed so hard into the dresser they looked ready to pierce the wood.

"What's that?" asked the first. "Give it to me. It looks like it's activated."

"More spy work," grumbled the second.

A few taps and rubs followed, and the stone went quiet.

Owein dropped down to all fours. Baptiste picked up the stone, his thumb hovering over the rune there, but he didn't press it.

"This is connected to Miss Larkin's stone," he explained, accent a little lighter, like he thought Owein wouldn't be able to understand him if he didn't push for an American inflection. "Someone else has it. I think . . ." He exhaled through his nose. "She's been arrested, too."

Owein barked. He spun around the room, not sure what to do with himself. Not sure what to think.

"They'd be in a prison with special . . . *défense*, for magic. In or near Boston." He set the stone down.

Owein's tail beat nervously against the floor. He barked again. *Noose!* If they were hanged, they'd never come home again.

And then what would be the point? What was the point of living and spelling and doing magic if he was just going to be alone again?

Baptiste rubbed the thick stubble on his chin.

Owein bolted into the hallway, down the stairs, and to the back door, still cracked for his use. He clawed it open and raced out into the cold air, winding around the house and the flattened yard, charging down the path toward the boat. He heard Baptiste call him. He kept running until he reached the shore.

Merritt's boat was still there—the watchmen had taken him on theirs. Owein pranced by it nervously, staring at the lapping waves, the mainland in the distance. His heart thudded and flipped and thudded. Cold nipped at the pads of his paws.

Baptiste approached. Owein barked at him. *We have to help!* He dragged his paw across the ground, forming a lopsided *H*. Then an *E—*

"I want to help, too," Baptiste said, and Owein's heart flipped again. The chef approached the boat, then paused. "We can get there in this, but we can't bring them back. Is not big enough."

Whimpers clawed up Owein's throat. He turned toward Baptiste, waiting for a solution.

None came.

Owein ran down the shoreline, as if he could find another boat in doing so. He didn't. A whine turned into a howl, which startled a sleeping whimbrel. Owein darted back to Baptiste's side.

The chef sighed. "I can try fire, alert those close by with smoke. Ask for help." He turned, glancing at nearby trees. "Then . . . what is the word? *Confisqué* their boat."

Owein looked out across the bay. Remembered standing beneath the strange purple snow with Merritt and his letter paper. He still remembered how to spell it. *F-A-M-I-L-Y.*

If Owein wanted them to be safe, he had to leave safety. He could do it. He knew he could. But it was scary out there. People had hurt him out there.

But Silas Hogwood was gone, wasn't he? And Baptiste would protect him.

Turning to the chef, Owein barked. But the chef couldn't understand him, and his letters were in the house. Spinning around, Owein took in his surroundings. He couldn't magic Merritt's boat—he might unintentionally break the spell on it. He spied a piece of bark hanging off a young birch.

Hurrying to it, he tried to get a good hold of it in his mouth, to pull it free, but he kept hitting his sensitive nose. The angle was weird. Still, he kept trying, until Baptiste's hand touched his neck. He backed away, and Baptiste took his place, grabbed the bark, and pulled it free. It was about the length of his ring finger and three times as wide.

"You want this?" he asked.

Owein took the bark in his mouth and trounced back to the path, where he dropped it. Steeling himself, he focused on it and thought, *Big*.

The bark shuttered as the alteration spell seized it, widening and lengthening it. Owein could resize and recolor anything, to a certain extent, and he pushed the first into that bark, even as he felt his spine pop from the side effects. His knees started to bend the other way, and he whined from discomfort. Still, he focused on the bark, growing it to the size of a melon, a wheelbarrow, a *boat*. The edges were curled just enough. When he was done, he panted hard and held still, waiting and praying for his legs to straighten out. Sometimes it happened quickly, sometimes slowly, depending on what he did.

"Wow." Baptiste touched the oversized piece of bark. "With some binds and grease . . . it might sail. We could tie it to the boat."

Owein shook his head as much as his contorted neck would allow. He could make it go. He could animate things. Only . . . he might get confused on the way. He might get scared.

Baptiste crouched beside him, petting his disfigured back. Owein whined, not because the touch hurt, but because he was scared. So scared.

"I will have to find the prison they're in," Baptiste murmured. "But I will do it."

The chef stayed with him until his skeleton rearranged itself.

Then they both went inside to get the rest of what they'd need to make the trip.

⁓

Hulda could not think of a worse way to spend the Sabbath than in jail.

It became real the first night sleeping in this terrible place. She was given a threadbare blanket with a few holes in it. While it was stained, it did appear to have been recently washed. Apparently there was no sense of propriety for criminals, because she had to, technically, share a room with *two* men. There was no cot or pillow brought in—only that long, hard stone bench or the floor. Given she had not been proven guilty of anything, it seemed extreme. And she had to sleep in her corset! Not that she would have changed into a nightgown if given one. Privacy was only for the free. The only time she got an iota of it was once in the morning and once at night, when she was pulled from the cell to use the privy, and that was still done under heavy guard, with little more than a thin wooden door between them and herself. It was humiliating.

If not for Merritt, she might have devolved on Saturday. Sleep deprived, cold, unsure of her future. She didn't know what she'd expected—someone to walk in and say it was all a misunderstanding and let her go, or perhaps she'd wake up from this nightmare, realizing it had all been a bad dream. But a cold morning with a cold, meager breakfast drilled the severity of the situation into her bones. Merritt tried to make light of it, and if nothing else, talking to him helped her focus on other things—as much as one can refocus their thoughts when surrounded on all sides by a human cage. Hulda couldn't tell if Merritt was relaxed about their situation or merely very good at masking his own trepidation. She feared the latter, but again, his mask offered a strange sort of comfort.

She couldn't even relish the idea that he'd more or less proposed to her. Not now, not here. Not like this.

Their cellmate was taken away Saturday afternoon and not brought back. When Merritt asked one of the guards what had happened to him, he shrugged. When Merritt asked what would happen to *them*, the man shrugged again.

Hulda didn't sleep much better the second night. Sunday morning, a different guard announced their trial date was set for Monday, December 7—fifteen days away. Fifteen days in this cold, awful place.

Before lunch was served, Hulda propped herself in the far corner of the cell, where the cold bench met the cold wall, and worried her hands. Wrongly incarcerated, and she couldn't say a thing about it for fifteen more days. Fifteen days without sunlight, without a change of clothing or a proper meal, without contact with anyone else . . . she was going to go mad. She was going to retrogress. And what then? What if no one saw through Mr. Baillie's ruse and he riled jury and judge alike? What if she was found guilty? How many years of prison would be ahead of her? Years of hard labor, no doubt. She'd never find another job. And what of Merritt? He'd likely be sent elsewhere, maybe even deemed dangerous because of his breadth of magic. They might get different sentences, different prison times. That would break her. She'd lose her life's work, her love, any chance of having a family—

"Hulda."

She'd worked her hands to redness. Merritt crouched down in front of her and took them in his own, preventing her from causing further damage. He offered her a soft, lopsided smile. "It will be a funny story to tell someday."

Pinching her lips together, Hulda shook her head. This would never be comedic, however it may end. She couldn't even say so, however, for fear panic would choke out her voice. If she started crying, she might never stop.

"Let's play a game," he offered. "I'll think of something, and you have to guess what it is."

Hulda took a deep breath to steel herself. "That seems rather pointless."

"Give it a try."

She frowned. "Is it a bonnet?"

"A bonnet?" He laughed. "That's the first thing you thought of?"

Flustered, she pulled her hands free. "It could be literally anything. Why *not* a bonnet?"

He stood and took a seat beside her. "You have to ask questions. It's a mystery."

Hulda was not in the mood for games, but it wasn't like she could do anything else, except pace, which she didn't have the energy to do. It was better than worrying, so she asked, "Is it a piece of headwear?"

Merritt's eyes glimmered despite the poor light. "No."

"Is it an animal?"

"No."

"A rock?"

He smirked. "No."

"A person?"

"I said some*thing*, Miss Larkin," he pressed. "A person is not a thing."

She rolled her eyes. Asked a few more questions, none of which got her any closer. Finally, she said, "You'll have to pick something simpler, else we'll not be on good terms by the end of it."

He chuckled. "All right, I picked something different."

She eyed him.

"What?" he asked.

She huffed. "You have to tell me what the first thing was. My sanity is already slipping." She glanced around the stony prison, any flicker of mirth quickly dying.

Merritt sobered. "It was a piano key. The F sharp above middle C, specifically."

She glared at him. "*That's* what you started with?"

He shrugged. "I'm very good at this game."

"How about I go next," she said, "and I'll pick the second flower from the left on the embroidery of my sister's yellow handbag!"

"Hulda"—Merritt opened his hands as if explaining to a child—"it defeats the purpose of the game if you just *tell* me what you're thinking."

She couldn't help it. She kicked his shoe.

He smiled.

The bolt on the door lifted, startling the both of them. Mealtime already?

"Larkin," the guard's low voice called into the room. Hulda stiffened. No food tray. Now she was sure she'd gotten into some sort of trouble, or they were going to lock her alone in a room and interrogate her—

"Fernsby," the guard added, reading off a list—not like there was anyone else here. "You're free to go."

Relief and fear warred with one another inside her. "Wh-What?"

Merritt stood. "Just like that?"

The guard nodded without looking either of them in the eye. "Bail posted. You are not to leave the limits of Suffolk County. Failure to arrive to your trial will result in immediate arrest and additional charges, including evasion of arrest. Understand?"

Hulda worked her mouth. Merritt said, "I wasn't aware we could pay out—"

"I could also just lock this door," the impatient guard retorted.

Hulda grabbed Merritt's hand, confused but determined. "Let's go." But who had paid for them? Surely Myra hadn't come out of the woodwork. Had Mr. Walker changed his mind? Had her sister or parents learned of her arrest and come out to help? Despite the utter humiliation of such a thing, Hulda was incredibly relieved to step foot outside that cell—

And lock eyes with a man she had never seen before in her life. He wasn't in uniform, so she could only assume he was the one who'd paid the sum . . . And how much of a sum had it been?

"Excuse me, I don't—" she began, but Merritt spoke over her.

"Sutcliffe." He sounded surprised.

A shock zinged up Hulda's spine. *Sutcliffe.* Nelson Sutcliffe. This was Merritt's father.

She could see a little of the resemblance.

Then a woman stepped around the corner, dressed simply in blue, her black hair pulled back tightly—

"Miss Taylor!" Hulda cried, and despite herself, she rushed for the maid and threw her arms around her. "What are you doing here? What's going on?"

Miss Taylor smiled and grasped Hulda's hands. "Here, come this way." She pulled her away from the cell, toward the front of the penitentiary—but seeing how blustery it was outside, they stayed inside the door. But at least Hulda could *see outside*. She soaked it in, poor weather and all.

"I felt very uneasy about the transfer," Miss Taylor said as Merritt and Sutcliffe spoke in low tones nearby. "I tried looking into it, but most of my inquiries were evaded, and the people in Winnipeg didn't seem to know anything. Then Myra reached out to me—"

Hulda gasped. "M-Myra?"

Miss Taylor nodded. "She contacted me through a letter—I never saw her face."

"Then she's well?" Given the distance to Canada, however, Hulda's interaction with Myra was likely more recent.

A shrug. "I'm not sure. Well enough to write." She squeezed Hulda's hands. "She must have heard about the audit. She wrote as though she knew."

"I mentioned it in nearly every message I sent to her." Hulda shook her head. "Of course. I'm interrupting. Please, go on." *Unless Myra has been nearby this whole time, keeping tabs on us . . . but how close does she have to be to read minds?* Hulda wasn't sure Myra would take the risk . . .

"She gave me tips on how to get transferred back—language to use, bylaws, forms. And I did! I got back Friday afternoon, only to learn you and Mr. Fernsby had been incarcerated!"

Now Hulda squeezed. "I'm nearly positive Mr. Baillie sent you away because you're a clairvoyant. He's been manipulating all of us—Mr. Walker especially—and someone with your skills would be able to see through his ruse."

Miss Taylor's eyes widened. "I . . . see."

"You may be able to help our trial," Hulda pressed.

"I can certainly try. The skill is so weak—"

"Anything will help at this point."

Miss Taylor clasped her hands together. "So, I learned the charges, and that bail was possible—but I don't have the means, and I don't know how to contact Myra. I thought to look up your sister's residence, but I work solely on contract, so Mr. Baillie barred me from the office." She offered a sympathetic half smile. "Then I remembered Mr. Sutcliffe." She dipped her head toward Merritt's father. "I remembered where he lived because I posted Mr. Fernsby's letter. So I took the coach out to him and explained what had happened. He came immediately."

A burst of warmth in her chest drove back some of the prison's chill. "Thank the Lord," she whispered. Not only that she and Merritt were free, but because this meant Mr. Sutcliffe *cared about his son*. Merritt needed that. He desperately needed that.

The men must have finished their conversation, because they joined Hulda and Miss Taylor—Mr. Sutcliffe looking resigned, Merritt thoughtful. Merritt's attention went to Miss Taylor. "You are an angel."

Miss Taylor smiled. "It's the least I could do. Mr. Sutcliffe is the one who made the contribution."

"Yes, yes." Merritt turned to his father, and for all his nonchalance and masks, he seemed awkward. "Thank you again. I'll pay you back."

"It'll be tight for a bit, but it needed to happen," Mr. Sutcliffe said.

To Miss Taylor, Merritt added, "I am never letting you go anywhere ever again. Even if I must write a thousand books and purchase a new magicked house to keep you on staff."

Miss Taylor chuckled. "That will not be necessary, Mr. Fernsby."

He let out a long sigh. Met Hulda's eyes and smiled. "Well, we're not done with this mess yet. I suppose we'll need to find a hotel, if we can't leave the county. And sort out the rest of it."

Hulda nodded. "If I can just speak to Mr. Walker alone—"

"*Stop!*"

All four of them jolted as one of the prison guards ran down the stony passageway, holding an open letter in his hand. Two more guards, including the one who had released them, tailed behind.

"Stop this instant!" he bellowed. "You may not leave this building!"

Hulda's heart thrust up into her throat, nearly suffocating her. She retreated by instinct, backing into Merritt, who felt stiff as the walls around them. He put a hand on her shoulder.

Mr. Sutcliffe asked, "What's the meaning of this?"

The shouting guard stopped a few paces in front of them and motioned with his hands, sending the other to seize Hulda and Merritt—and none too kindly. Hulda felt stitches tear in the shoulder of her dress as the man wrenched her forward and pinned her wrists behind her back.

"Merritt!" she cried.

"Let us go!" Merritt shouted as his father repeated, "What's the meaning of this?"

A cold wind rushed over Hulda as the prison doors opened, but her captor had her pinned and turned so she could not see if a gale had burst them or if Miss Taylor had run for help.

The guard held up the paper, which had an inked seal at the base of it. "There is *no bail for murderers.*"

"What?" Hulda gasped. "Are you mad?"

The guard merely scowled at them and turned the paper around, reading from it, "Merritt Jacob Fernsby and Hulda Larkin are hereby under arrest for the murder of Myra Haigh."

Hulda's blood pooled in her feet. She went limp in the guard's hold, making him falter.

Myra . . . dead?

"Myra Haigh is well and alive!" Miss Taylor said.

The guard looked over her to the doors. "We'll deal with you later! Stand back—this is official business!"

But just under his sharp comment, Hulda heard Merritt say, "Baptiste?"

Thanks to her captor's misstep, Hulda was able to swing around just enough to see the rain-soaked chef standing in the doorway, breathing heavily. "He is no killer." His voice was cold as the November sky.

The guard ignored them. To the others, he said, "Take them back to the cell."

"No," Hulda pleaded, but it sounded more like a dying breath. There would be no way out of this. Myra couldn't be dead . . . Hulda couldn't accept that. And if she was . . . there was no way to prove they hadn't killed her. The situation was ineluctable—no bail, no escape, no life after imprisonment. No mercy.

How . . . How was this happening? Did Mr. Baillie hate them so much? Who had he manipulated to sign off on that warrant?

Her guard shoved her back down the hallway, back to her cage—

And a dog barked.

She barely noticed it at first, but it barked again, then again, until the head guard bellowed, "Get that mutt out of here!"

Hulda looked back over her shoulder. *Owein.* Stepping out of Baptiste's shadow.

The entire penitentiary began to quake.

Stone tremored around her, raining little pieces of mortar into her hair. A large section of the wall to her right burst free in a cloud of dust and rammed forward, smashing hard enough into her captor to make the both of them fall. The man lost his grip on her, and she tumbled free.

Hulda *knew* this spell. She'd seen it several times when it possessed Whimbrel House. Blood racing, she picked herself up off the trembling cobbles and nearly fell again as pieces of cobblestone jerked from the floor and flew like snowballs at the guards—no killing blows, but hunks of stone hit stomachs and thighs hard enough to leave deep bruises.

The doorway was collapsing. The left wall came loose and inched inward.

A hand grasped her forearm—not Merritt's, but Baptiste's. He said nothing—one glance into his glimmering eyes told Hulda all she needed to know.

If she returned to that prison cell, they would never let her back out. So when the Frenchman pulled her toward the door and out into a growing storm, she didn't hesitate to follow.

Something in the prison creaked loudly, like the entire structure was about to collapse in on itself.

Her wits came to her. "Don't kill them!" she cried, and almost immediately the quaking stopped as Miss Taylor—followed by Merritt carrying a limp terrier—and Mr. Sutcliffe rushed for the doorway.

"Go!" Merritt shouted, and Hulda pulled free of Baptiste and ran, grabbing fistfuls of her skirt and lifting it out of her way. Baptiste sprinted beside her. Merritt quickly caught up, and . . . and . . .

She had *seen* this. In the living room of Whimbrel House, after Merritt returned from Cattlecorn. She'd seen them running through Boston, just like this.

There was no comfort in the thought, and no time to dwell on it. They had to flee before the guards caught up with them. Before they signaled for help.

So Hulda ran, and ran, and ran.

And never looked back.

Chapter 19

Merritt would think he was used to living on the water, but this little hovel of Baptiste's was . . . not exactly quaint.

The Frenchman had taken over their escape and led them to one of many docks in Boston, a smaller one used by hobbyist fishermen and the like. The hovel's entrance was tucked away on the north side, underneath a set of stone stairs leading down to the water, the space dug out of the earth—a forgotten storage area, perhaps, used by early settlers or the natives before them. It was a tight fit for the five of them, yet Merritt couldn't complain. It was certainly more comfortable than the prison cell had been. Apparently Baptiste had discovered this hideout along with a few others after first arriving in America, about two months before Merritt met him. It was cold and poorly lit, but, as Baptiste had shrugged and said, "Worst case, take boat and sail."

Merritt wasn't exactly in love with the idea of adding theft to his growing list of criminal acts, but his chef had a point. Although Owein had made a little raft Baptiste had tied to the little kinetic boat Merritt had inherited with Whimbrel House, both conveyances were docked in Rhode Island.

Readjusting, Merritt leaned back against an empty, split barrel lying on its side and stretched his legs out in front of him, letting the blood flow back to his feet. Of all the things his imagination could conjure up, he never expected his life to take this sort of turn. He thought, if he ever managed to clear his name, it would make an interesting climax in a novel.

He caught a faint *Swim? Food?* from a fish in the nearby water, but managed to tune it out. Hulda sat across from him on an intact barrel, the only other one in the vicinity, trying to clean her glasses on a skirt made filthy from prison, running, and dock gallivanting. She'd managed to rearrange her hair without a brush or mirror, and still sat like she was a woman in power, ready to dismiss anyone who came into her office with the wrong attitude or skewed cravat knot. Merritt knew she was simmering with worry beneath the surface, both for their current situation and for Owein, who, after a sleepy recovery from his chaocracy spells, had been sent out earlier that morning to sniff out supplies for writing missives. Hopefully he hadn't gone too far.

Beth, the only one of them not technically wanted by the judiciary, was near the entrance of the place, putting together breakfast for the lot of them, having purchased a loaf of bread and a fried fish just after the break of dawn. Baptiste loomed nearby, his thick arms folded over his thick chest, standing sentry by their little fire, though he appeared to doze while on his feet, an accomplishment Merritt found rather impressive.

Nelson Sutcliffe had not come with them. If he had, Merritt would have sent him right back. No—he had run from the collapsing building as any sane man would, and no farther. He had done nothing wrong, and he needn't take the blame for this mess. Especially not after the wildly generous sum he'd given over to get Merritt and Hulda out of jail, even if only for a few minutes. If their sudden ineligibility for bail didn't result in the money returned, Merritt would be taking out a portion of his own earnings for the next ten years to pay Sutcliffe back . . . if there was even a shred of normalcy in his future. He was still waiting for Hulda's augury to tell him whether or not he'd be a convict the rest of his days.

He shook his head and stared at the low, moldy ceiling above him. *Murder.* Of all things for them to be accused of! Had he fallen into a novel unawares?

His mind wandered back to the prison. When that guard had seized them and read the absurd charge, he'd considered using magic. But those men were innocent. Fooled, and perhaps foolhardy, but innocent. He didn't want to hurt them, nor indict himself by doing so. He might not have manipulated the workings of BIKER or killed Myra Haigh, but he certainly would be guilty of assault if he fought his way out. And he had such little control over his abilities, besides . . . Who knows what horrors he might have unleashed.

A small smile touched his lips. *Can't arrest a dog.* The good Lord must have been looking out for him there. *Focus on the positive things.* Otherwise he'd start thinking about how cold it was . . . and the unlikelihood they'd find their way out of this mess.

He shoved his hands into his armpits to warm them.

Soft padding outside announced the arrival of a dog, and Owein popped in moments later, shaking sea spray from his coat.

"Not by the fire!" Beth hissed.

He trotted over to Hulda and dropped a gnarled roll of paper at her feet. "Good boy." She rubbed his ears with one hand as she picked up the paper. "That will do. I don't suppose you have a pen and ink vial stashed somewhere?"

Owein whined.

"Here." Baptiste pulled a stick from the edge of the tiny fire, blowing on it and testing its temperature before walking it over. Good ol' charcoal.

"That will do." Hulda accepted it, unrolled the unevenly torn, stained sheet of paper, and began writing. "We know one of my methods to reach Myra worked, else she wouldn't have known to contact Beth and me."

Merritt nodded, though Hulda was so focused she didn't see it. Still, it was better for her to focus on this and not *What if Myra is really dead?* like she'd fretted about last night. To which Beth had promptly declared, *If she's dead, she died in the last two days, and I find that highly unlikely.*

"So," Hulda went on, her nose crinkling in a way that made Merritt want to touch it, "I will have to resend a message to every one of them, to ensure she sees it. Assuming she hasn't moved on." Her writing slowed, then sped up. "She knew of Mr. Baillie. I'm hoping she's been keeping tabs on things best she can from the outside . . . and hasn't given up on us yet." She blinked. "God let that be the case."

"Miss Taylor should send it," Merritt said. "Just to be safe."

Hulda nodded with a frown. "I suppose being a fugitive might make a trip to the post office unpleasant."

"Is not so bad," Baptiste said, which earned a confused look from Hulda and a chuckle from Merritt.

His duties fulfilled, Owein plopped at Beth's side, resting his head on her lap. It was good to see him happy, even if their circumstances were dire. The maid fed him a piece of fish.

"Telegrams wherever possible," Hulda added. She paused, thinking, and wrote another word. She'd smeared charcoal on her jaw, but Merritt wouldn't tell her until she'd finished. "For speed."

"I suppose," Merritt added, "we won't be showing up for our court date." Not with the bogus murder charge added to the list of their supposed wrongdoings.

Hulda deflated into a slouch. "There is that. One thing at a time . . . Oh yes, I wrote to her cousin." She scribbled it down. "The address . . . I think I remember it, but . . ." She bit her lip, turning the short stick over to get at more charcoal.

She finished her list, which was more substantive than Merritt had realized. When she showed it to him, he subtly gestured to his jaw, and Hulda quickly removed the smudge with her dress sleeve, as the prison guards hadn't let her keep so much as a handkerchief. She then took the paper to Beth, who read over it carefully.

"We need to determine a safe place and time to meet, and include it discreetly in each message," she said.

"Not here," Merritt added, "in case there's interception."

Hulda nodded, then folded her arms against the chill. "It won't take long for them to bring in a wizard to hunt us out."

"I doubt they'll assume we're still in Suffolk County," Merritt tried, but it didn't seem to alleviate her stress.

"Might be best to wait until evening," Hulda said.

Beth shrugged. "I'm not worried about it. If I'm stopped and identified, they can't detain me. Besides"—she smiled—"most white men can't tell me apart from any other Black woman."

Merritt sat up. "That's preposterous."

Beth smiled knowingly at him, which told Merritt he was quite wrong and should probably say nothing more on the subject.

Standing, Beth folded the list and pocketed it. Owein whined softly, and she rubbed under his chin. "I'll be back, little one." She kissed the top of his head, distributed their meager breakfast, and went out into the weather-choked sunlight.

Merritt envied her.

In the meantime, came a familiar, youthful voice into his head. *Let's have a lesson.*

He sighed. "If you want to practice your letters, fetch me another piece of charcoal."

Hulda looked around, confused, then nodded her understanding. "I don't mind playing teacher. It will give me something to do."

Not letters. The dog huffed. *Time to practice your magic.*

Merritt frowned. "Considering that we're trying to lie low, I don't think now is the best time to do it, nor here the best place."

There's never a good time. I'll tell you everything I know.

"I may not even have the same spells—" His throat itched.

Owein ignored him. *First, if you want to make something move that doesn't move, you have to see it in your head. Imagine that rock is growing legs and getting up to walk . . .*

The meeting place they set was an overly large intersection about three-quarters of a mile from Baptiste's dock hovel, a place where it would be easy to scan for passersby. One-quarter of it cut through a patch of forest, which loomed dark and foreboding in the night, though the light of a nearby streetlamp glimmered off frost forming on the branches of the closest trees, which Merritt had to admit was eerily beautiful. A money-changer's shop, shadowed and closed until morning, was just past the intersection to the west. A lot for parking carts and wagons stretched to the east, and a wide, diverging street looped southward. The cobblestones were slick but not icy, and Merritt lingered across from the streetlight, just off the road, his hands in his pockets to keep himself warm, his breath clouding on the air. A fisherman's jacket he'd nabbed on his way here yesterday—he was going to return it eventually—stretched over his shoulders, and his hair was tucked up under its accompanying cap.

This was his second night of lingering at the intersection at the designated time—a quarter after eleven. He didn't want Beth doing so—cold or not, it wasn't so late that any drunkards had turned in for the night, which was also the excuse he'd used with Hulda. An unnecessary one, possibly, because Hulda, ever practical, had pointed out that both she and Baptiste had more distinguishing features, leaving Merritt the obvious choice for watching for Myra.

He didn't know how to feel about the lack-of-distinguishing-features bit. Minus the hair, he supposed it was true. But at least he hadn't noticed any Wanted signs posted around with his or Hulda's faces plastered on them.

Owein sniffed at a dead weed. He'd brought him along, just in case, but had forbidden any unnecessary instruction along the way. *If* Myra showed, Merritt needed to be able to speak with her. That, and he wasn't making any progress, besides. But it was eleven thirty already, which meant this was another cold and fruitless night. Time to head back.

Closing his eyes, Merritt listened. Not to the sleeping sounds of the city, but to the creatures hidden within it. There weren't many—he imagined that would change come spring—but there was an owl not far off, mice speckled throughout the area, a smattering of . . . he shuddered. *Cockroaches.* He'd rather not know about those. Still, he pressed, *Do you see her? A woman?*

Search. Search. Listen. The owl.

Hide. Hide. Mate. Hide. Mice.

Food, hissed the roaches.

His sigh coalesced in the cold air. A couple more nights. He could do this a couple more nights. Then they'd have to figure out something better. *Anything* better. Their situation wasn't sustainable.

"Fortunately," came a soft, feminine voice from the shadows of the money-changer's shop, "you won't need to wait much longer."

Merritt whirled around; beside him, Owein perked, ears up. He searched the intersection but didn't see anyone until a silhouette, carefully checking the street, crossed, shoes tapping softly on the stone.

Relief practically bludgeoned him over the head. "Miss Haigh," he spoke quietly. "Lovely meeting you again."

She stopped about a pace from him, close enough to keep their volume down, not close enough to appear intimate.

"Glad you're alive," he added.

Her head tilted. "As am I."

Keep an eye out, he told Owein, who turned and scanned the intersection. To Myra, he said, "Which message reached you?"

Her lips twisted, like she didn't want to answer. "Telegram to Agatha. She's a friend of mine who agreed to forward any messages I might receive." She pulled her coat tighter. "I left an unassuming letter from her on my nightside table in case an ally came looking for me. Or an enemy."

Hulda had mentioned finding letters at Myra's house. She'd be relieved to learn it had paid off.

Reaching inside her coat, the ex–BIKER director pulled out a newspaper. "You've been busy."

Merritt took the paper and tilted it toward the oil lamp, though he could make out only the headline: *Two Wizardly Fugitives Escape Suffolk County Penitentiary.* Merritt grumbled low in his throat.

"Are you dangerous, Mr. Fernsby?" Her voice carried a hint of mirth, yet sounded wholly serious at the same time.

Merritt shifted his weight to one leg. "I think we can agree that I'm the least dangerous person here." He didn't want to say anything about the facility in Ohio. He wasn't supposed to know. Casting the thought from his mind, he focused on the uneven lines of the street's cobblestones in case Myra decided to skim his brain.

She paused, looking toward Owein. "Indeed."

The dog looked back.

Before Merritt could ask, Myra said, "I can hear his thoughts, and I've not a lick of communion in me. There's a human soul in there. Is he the same from Mr. Hogwood's . . . ?"

Merritt nodded. "That dog used to be my house."

"Fascinating." She crouched down, and Owein quickly came to her, tail wagging, likely excited that someone else could understand him.

"And while we could have a very long conversation about it," Merritt pressed. "There is the issue of the *murder charges.*"

Sighing, Myra stood. "Utter nonsense. That man will do anything to get what he wants." Her face wrinkled like an obscenity had risen into her mouth and she didn't like the taste of it.

"Baillie, or Walker?"

"Alastair Baillie." Myra sneered. "I've known Mr. Walker a long time. He's being played like a fiddle."

Merritt nodded. "So Walker isn't a psychometrist?"

Half a laugh escaped Myra's mouth before she clamped down on it. "Absolutely not. That man is the unluckiest wizard in the world. All he can do is turn—"

"—small things into gold," Merritt finished. And Myra would know, with a gift like hers. But any iota of relief he felt at having correctly interpreted the situation was short lived. "You'll have to show yourself to get the charges dropped."

She folded her arms. "Let me think on it."

His gut twisted. "Think on it? Hulda and I will be imprisoned—"

"I didn't mean let me think on whether or not I'll do it," she interjected, "but on *how*. Relax, Mr. Fernsby. I'm fully aware of the mess I made, and I'm prepared to clean it up." She worried the newspaper. "I'm sorry, for all of this. It's not worth anything, but I am." A pause. "You might not realize it, but I *need* Hulda in BIKER."

He knew very well that she did. A stiff breath wound out of his windpipe, fogging the air between them. "Thank you." He hesitated. "Come back with me. We're staying in a little hovel nearby. It'll be warmer than this—"

"No." She lifted a hand, as though to catch the offer midair. "It's too risky. But if you need to reach me, send me a message." She indicated the oil lamp across the way. "I'll check it as close to dawn and dusk as I can. If you send him"—she gestured to Owein—"I can glean the information from him without making contact." She reached into her pocket and retrieved a few coins, which she pressed into Merritt's hand. "I doubt you've been able to stop home or withdraw from a bank."

He closed his hands around the money. "It's appreciated. As is your swiftness."

"Of course." She sounded dejected, but Hulda had so much faith in the woman, Merritt strived to have the same. Unfortunately, she was the only basket in which they could put their proverbial eggs. "Be careful," she added. "The more time I have, the better."

"Our trial date for the initial crimes is December 7. Fraud, conspiracy, misuse of magic."

A quiet chuckle issued from her throat. "Preposterous."

He hesitated to argue but felt compelled to do so. "Some of the charges have merit, Miss Haigh. Such as the enchanting of houses to give BIKER work."

The woman remained silent for several heartbeats. *She* had done that.

"Stay safe. Take care of Hulda," she whispered. Then, with a glance around, she crossed back to the money-changer's storefront and then slipped into the wooded area. Its shadows summarily swallowed her.

Merritt watched her go. Two sailors stumbled down the road from the opposite direction, laughing at something. *Let's go,* he told Owein, and the two took a roundabout way back to the docks, staying out of sight, watching for any witnesses. Seeing none, Merritt climbed down the stairs and into the fire-lit hovel. Baptiste was asleep near the entrance, a hat over his eyes. Hulda sat nearby, picking bark off a stick with her thumbnails.

She looked up and offered a smile. "I have to poke him every now and then, when he starts snoring."

"I saw Myra," Merritt said.

Hulda was instantly on her feet. "She's alive!" She placed a hand on her chest, like she'd been holding her breath a few seconds too long. "She came? Where? What did she say? She's well?" She grasped his elbows.

He took hers as well and explained the meeting in as much detail as he could while Owein sniffed around the area and licked one of their makeshift plates clean. At their insistence, Beth had arranged to stay with a local friend, so she wasn't there to chastise him. Hulda squeezed him a little tighter with each sentence, and when he finished, she took several seconds to process the information before turning away and pacing, hunching over so her head wouldn't strike the low ceiling.

"This is good. This is good. She'll follow through." She pressed a knuckle to her chin.

"Are you sure?"

"Unless that was a spirit wearing Myra's body, she'll follow through." She rubbed her hands together. "Hopefully our fleeing will be forgiven . . . or paid off." She shook her head. "She can set this right." Hulda pinched her lips together and made a sound of approval. "We'll have to speak with a lawyer. See what advice he has. I do *not* want Mr. Baillie in the room for testimonies. I still think, if I could only talk to Mr. Walker alone—"

Sighing, Merritt pulled off his hat, his hair spilling onto his shoulders, and sat on one of the barrels. "Even if you can," he said with care, "negative feelings have barbs. They . . . last, whether or not an enchantment helped them along."

Hulda paused, and her silence told him she wasn't convinced. "I just . . . I don't understand how Mr. Walker can't feel that he's being manipulated! I understand a hysterian might operate with finesse, but if one looks at it with reason, they can tell. *I* could tell."

"Perhaps Mr. Baillie has been working on him a long time."

"Perhaps." She perched on the other barrel. "If they have that much history, it might be hard to break it. I wonder if Miss Richards or Miss Steverus have experienced anything."

"If they aren't connected to Mr. Baillie's desperation for power, perhaps not."

"They'll be called as witnesses, regardless," Hulda said. "I'd be shocked otherwise. And Mr. Baillie will know this, too. He'll be working on them." She threw her hands in the air. "I just . . . I don't understand it. He would have to manipulate so many people. How does he keep it all straight? It sounds exhausting."

Merritt deliberated over the conundrum a moment before something sparked in his brain—something like an excellent story idea, but this was very much rooted in reality. "That's it."

"What?"

"How talented could the man possibly be?" Merritt asked, a smile forming on his mouth. "I think we have to test it. But we're going to need as much help as we can get . . . and Myra's assistance."

She studied his face for a few seconds. "I'm listening."

Chapter 20

The city was still scary, especially during the day. There were so many *people*, and so many ways to go. Owein couldn't keep track of it all. But it was less scary when someone went with him, like Baptiste or Merritt. Today, though, he was with the new lady, who had been introduced to him as Miss Haigh but whom everyone seemed to call Myra. Owein went with the latter, since it was shorter.

He'd waited at the lamppost, as instructed, for almost an hour—or what felt like an hour—before she came along at the cusp of dawn and summoned him with a snap. He didn't need to be summoned with a snap, but the dog part of him liked it. He fell in step with her, and they walked far enough that Owein's paws were starting to hurt by the time they reached a two-story building that Owein might have thought was big before he'd wandered so much of Rhode Island and Massachusetts with Baptiste. Myra slipped through a side door, telling Owein, "Light on your feet," as they went.

Owein glanced at his paws to check, then realized she hadn't meant his feet were glowing.

They passed an office that appeared to still be closed. Owein stared at the sign, making out *R-E-G-I-S-T-E-R O-F* before having to quicken his step to keep up. His nails tapped lightly on the floor, so he tried walking a little funny to keep them quiet. He didn't know how to trim his nails as a dog. Maybe not even as a human, not anymore, though he'd seen Merritt do it enough times that, should he grow thumbs, he could copy it.

Maybe one of these days an alteration spell side effect would give him thumbs. To think of all the things he could do then!

They went up a narrow flight of stairs that smelled like wood, mold, and something clean Owein didn't recognize, then down a hall to a room with a few short rows of chairs and a high desk on the far end. Myra pulled her hat down and sat as far away from that desk as she could, then gestured for Owein to lie down next to her, leaving him nearly out of sight.

Owein grumbled and obeyed. He'd already lain down a lot. He wanted to run and chase whimbrels. But he also understood this mission was very important, so he tried to focus.

They waited a *very* long time.

A couple more people trickled in, only one looking Myra's way, though they sat in the front. Then two more, a man and a woman, and finally a guy in a wig and dark robes came and sat at the too-high desk. They all started talking, using words Owein wasn't entirely familiar with, like *infidelity* and *divorcement*, sounding angry sometimes, and he quickly lost interest. He dozed off for a while, jerking awake at a loud sound, like two pieces of wood smacking together. No one else in the room looked startled. Must have been a normal sound, then. A few people walked out with papers. The room grew quiet. When the guy in the wig started to stand, Myra did the same.

"If I might have a moment of your time, Judge Maddock."

The man glanced over. "There are no animals allowed in the building."

Owein paused. Should he leave?

Myra held out a staying hand to him and approached the desk. She pulled a newspaper from her coat. "I will be brief." She set the paper down. "Have you heard of this scandal?"

Judge looked over it. "I have."

"These two persons have been accused of the murder of Myra Haigh."

He frowned. "Madam, are you trying to sell me a newspaper?"

"I am Myra Haigh."

Judge paused, his eyebrows—which did not match his wig—crawling up the ridges of his forehead like caterpillars.

"I . . . see." He picked up the paper.

"It's all a misunderstanding," she explained, calm and smooth. She hesitated a moment before saying, "You know how the wizarding system works. A lot of hullaballoo about nothing. Trying to make a case for themselves for relevancy."

Owein tilted his head. He remembered Myra could read minds— she could hear what he said, anyway. He wondered if she was doing that now.

It'd be pretty nifty to read minds. What was the side effect for that? He'd have to ask Hulda.

None of them liked this new "house" on the dock, but at least they were together again.

Judge nodded. "Indeed. I apologize for this . . . though I will need to see identification and make an official record. I'll have to call in the gentleman overseeing this case as well. Do you mind waiting here?"

She nodded. "Of course not."

He returned the nod and stepped down from the desk, disappearing through a side door Owein hadn't noticed.

Now Myra pulled out another stack of papers from her coat and set them on the desk.

What's that? Owein asked.

"Everything they'll need," she said so quietly even Owein's dog ears had a hard time hearing it. "Affidavit that I'm alive, a copy of my identification, information on Alastair Baillie." She turned from the desk and started for the door.

We're not waiting?

She shook her head. Opened the door, checked the hallway, then slipped out, Owein at her heels. "I left a means of contacting me if absolutely necessary," she murmured.

Owein frowned as well as he could with his muzzle as they approached the stairs. *But I didn't get to magic anyone.*

That was the reason anyone took him anywhere in the city. *Just in case,* they said, over and over and over. Owein was just better at magic than everyone else.

"That's a good thing, Mr. Mansel." They took the stairs quickly.

Owein didn't think he'd ever been called Mr. Mansel in his life, but it triggered a memory. His dad had been called that. His dad . . . he couldn't really remember what he looked like. Taller than him. Mustache.

Cherries. His dad had always smelled like cherries. Dried cherries. A jar of dried cherries on the table—

The harder Owein tried to grasp at the memory, the more it faded, until it was little more than a strange taste in the back of his throat. A taste that made him sad. A taste that fed that buried darkness in his mind, just a little.

They stepped outside, the morning sun blinding. Myra's pace quickened, and Owein jogged to keep up. She didn't say anything more, even though she kept her head downcast. Led him as far as that one wide road that led down to the docks.

Then she turned toward the trees and vanished, leaving Owein to trot the rest of the way to the hideout on his own.

∽

Hulda stoked the tiny fire with the sticks Baptiste had collected during the night. *God help us,* she prayed. Not with the fire, but everything else. Could Silas not have made his move in the summer? It would have shifted up the timeline for all this nonsense, and she'd be hiding out when it wasn't so wet outside. Boston usually wasn't *too* chilly this time of year. By midday it was really quite pleasant. But the nights got cold, and the sea didn't make it any better.

She'd nearly finished breaking sticks over a bruising knee, ignoring the state of her dress, wondering how long she'd need to endure this lifestyle, when Miss Taylor slipped into the space. "Oh!" Hulda said, then chided herself for her volume. Dropping the stick and wiping her hands on a skirt that may never again be clean, she amended, "Please tell me you got it."

Miss Taylor smiled and held up a folded piece of paper. Relief washed over Hulda like the tide.

They gathered around one of the barrels as Miss Taylor opened the note.

Bless you, Miss Steverus!

Miss Taylor had contacted the secretary yesterday, and Miss Steverus had obliged them by leaving a copy of Mr. Walker's and Mr. Baillie's schedules in a tree nook. Heads pressed together, Hulda and Miss Taylor read over it. There was a note that Miss Richards would be departing for England that weekend. Hulda's stomach dropped. Did that mean Mr. Baillie had officially secured the director's position?

Worry about one thing at a time. She pointed at the notations under Monday. "This might be the best time to do it. It means suffering here a little longer, but the office will be emptier, and it looks like they might have some overlap here. This will be easiest if we can get them into a room together."

They'd enacted a plan devised by Merritt, one that seemed sensible one moment and incredibly absurd the next. He'd been bouncing back and forth between the two all day. Yet no better ideas had struck the others, and the date of their trial was quickly approaching. If Myra did her part, that would help immensely. The rest was up to them.

"Three o'clock?" Miss Taylor asked, bringing the paper a little closer. "Or el—"

The wrinkles in the note stood out like they'd lifted themselves from the page, detailed like a geometric spiderweb. Hulda's augury took hold, and she saw the two men as clearly as if they stood right in front of her, Mr. Walker at his desk, Mr. Baillie leaning over it. A clock ticked on the wall. The curtains were drawn on the window, hitting the bookshelves with yellow sunrays. A wisp of Merritt was in her peripheral vision. She was there, walking into the office.

She blinked, and the vision ended. Tiny bumps riddled her skin, and not from the cold.

"Miss Larkin?"

Hulda shook herself and smiled. "Finally."

"Finally?" Miss Taylor repeated.

Taking a breath, Hulda said, "*Finally* my augury gives me something I can use! I saw them, Beth. Just now." She wondered if one of the men had handled the paper, or if their names and information written on it was enough. "I saw the confrontation. Or, what I believe is the beginning of it."

Beth brightened. "You did? Did it go well?"

Hulda shook her head. "I don't know. But I did see Mr. Walker's *clock*." Or rather, Myra's clock. It was a black-and-white piece that hung on the wall to the left of the desk, and from the angle Hulda had come in, she could just make out its hands.

"Two seventeen." She scanned the schedule and put down her finger where Mr. Walker's and Mr. Baillie's tasks aligned at that time. "Friday, not Monday."

"Tomorrow." Hulda sucked in a deep breath. "I'll have to let Merritt know as soon as possible."

Beth looked around. "Where *is* Mr. Fernsby?"

"Getting help, or so we hope." She pocketed the schedule and stood, brushing off her skirt. "If you're up for the task, I need you to send a telegram for me."

Miss Taylor rose. "Of course."

"To Judge Maddock at Johnson Hall." She pressed her palms into her middle to still the butterflies there. "He'll need to meet us there."

 ҉

One advantage of being an unimportant bachelor with "no distinguishing features" who lives on an island in the middle of nowhere is that not many people know what you look like, and few people are likely to recognize you even if given a description. At least, that's what Merritt was banking on when he approached the young sailor on the dock in the light of day, having just watched the man interact with a colleague. The man looked to be in his early twenties and knelt by a pylon, wrapping rope around his hand and elbow.

Merritt pushed his hat up, hoping to show more of his face. Face equaled friendly. "Hello there."

The sailor started, looked up, and smiled. "Hi! You lost?"

"Not really." Merritt crouched down and pasted on a smile. "I have a proposition for you, if you're in town for a bit."

"Until Saturday," he said, looking curious but not suspicious, which meant Merritt had picked the right man.

"It's going to sound strange."

The sailor laughed. "Once you've been on those waters"—he tilted his head toward the ocean—"nothing seems strange anymore."

Merritt nodded. "It's just, I've noticed you're a rather chipper fellow."

The sailor paused winding the rope. "Well, I try to be. Life's better sweet than sour, my mother would say."

"That's a good attitude to have. Would you say you're chipper even under stressful circumstances?"

The man studied Merritt's face. Which was not what Merritt wanted, in case any officers of the law came around asking questions, but with luck, this would be resolved before that happened. "I'd like to think so."

"Great. I have a meeting this week—I can get you the exact time by the end of the day—that I'd like you to be present for. All you have to do is stay chipper."

Now suspicion drew the man's eyebrows together. "What sort of meeting?"

Merritt shifted, his legs cramping from his crouch. "One where you don't need to do anything but stand by and stay as happy as you possibly can. You don't even have to pay attention. Half an hour, tops. I'll pay eight dollars." He reached into his pocket. "Half now, half after."

The sailor put his elbow on the pylon and leaned onto it. "Just stick around and be happy? And this place is in town?"

"Indeed. I know it sounds strange, but I need to prove a point to a . . . coworker of sorts."

He rolled his lips together. "Nothing illegal?"

Merritt drew his finger over his chest. "Cross my heart."

The man took his money. "All right. I'll be at the pub tonight." He gestured to a building down the way. "Let me know the time."

Merritt tipped his hat. "Many thanks, my good fellow. Many thanks."

❧

Merritt continued walking around, although he didn't wish to venture too far from the hovel. On his rounds, he spied a distraught woman on a bench at the end of the fish market. Even if she didn't help his master plan, it seemed wrong to merely pass her by.

He sat on the bench beside her, as far as the wooden planks would allow, so as to give her space. "My dear woman," he said, "whatever is troubling you?"

The woman looked up from her handkerchief—she appeared to be in her fifties, but red and puffy eyes gave her a few extra years. Her bonnet and coat were both worn—he guessed her to be a fisherman's wife, with that and the rough hands clutching an even rougher handkerchief.

He reached into his pocket to offer her his, only to remember the guards had taken it away. Which reminded him that he needed to procure a new pocket watch. Nothing fancy, so long as it kept time. That was another important part of the plan.

The woman drew in a shuddering breath and wiped her nose. "M-My husband's gone."

Merritt's body sank a little more into the bench. Softer, he asked, "To sea? Or . . ."

"Gone," she repeated, dabbing her eyes. "To heaven. Or hell." She chuckled, then pressed her lips together to stifle a sob. "Only God knows."

She pressed her face into the cloth and cried.

"I'm terribly sorry," Merritt offered. "Will you be all right?"

"Who knows." She wiped her nose again. That handkerchief wouldn't last much longer. "Son should be coming up for the funeral. Maybe I'll go home with him, if he'll have me." She blinked rapidly. "Won't s-survive . . . on my own."

"Then you need a job?"

She met his eyes for the first time. Shuddered. Shrugged. "Can't do much work anymore."

"I have a meeting I need . . . witnesses for," Merritt offered. "Hopefully before the weekend—I can get the exact time tonight. Nothing illegal or untoward. Just standing in a room for half an hour."

She sniffed. Eyed him. "You work for the court o-or something?"

"Or something," he offered. "I'll pay you ten dollars for your time. It's local—in Boston."

She blinked again. "Ten dollars to stand around for h-half an hour?"

He nodded. "I know it sounds funny, but it's important."

She considered. "I live right down there." She pointed down a road that ended in small apartments. "Number two. Let me know when." Her eyes teared up. "N-Not like anyone else needs me anymore."

Merritt frowned and sat with her a little longer, patting her shoulder while she cried. When he left, he bought a clean handkerchief from a woman sweeping outside a shop, using a little of Myra's money. He passed it to the mourning widow before heading back to the hovel.

Once he got the date and time from Hulda, he made sure to inform his new employees.

And with luck, Misses Steverus and Richards would play a part as well.

༄

Merritt's ragtag group waited outside the Bright Bay Hotel; he, Hulda, and Beth lingered close to its back door—BIKER's front entrance— while Owein, Baptiste, Matthew (the sailor), and Nettie (the widow) lingered in the shade of an old oak tree. The sun was nearly halfway between its peak and set. The weather was relatively agreeable.

Merritt held a newly purchased but rusted pocket watch in his hand. He hoped Hulda didn't notice how tightly he clutched it, or that he had to adjust his grip every now and then because his skin was so clammy. His heartbeat was off rhythm with the ticking second hand, and no matter how hard he tried not to focus on that, he couldn't help it. Someone might as well be hitting him in the chest with a mallet for how hard his heart pounded.

If they screwed this up, it was over for them. Possibly *literally* over. Owein had said it'd gone well with Myra, but would the documents she'd left the judge be enough? If not, their necks could be in nooses before Christmas. Even still, they needed this part of the plan to work so they could be free.

He glanced up at Hulda's face. Her lips were pressed in a thin line, her glasses pushed up as high on her nose as they could go, her eyes glued to the pocket watch's scratched face. If they failed, this might be the last time he could be this close to her. To kiss her, though he knew she detested public displays of affection. Should he tell her he loved her? That he'd meant what he said in that cell?

Her eyes lit up, and he wondered if she'd somehow heard his thoughts.

"Now," she said.

One thought pushed to the front of his mind, scattering the rest: the plan. He pocketed the watch and waved to the others. Opened the door and let Hulda step through first. If only her foresight lasted more than a few seconds. Then they would *know*.

Because truthfully, Merritt would sail for anywhere—India, Africa, Sweden—before he willingly let that bastard of a hysterian put him or Hulda in prison. They were risking everything on the slender hope that they might clear their names.

Merritt had trained himself for years not to hope. This was a steep gamble.

He found himself envying Miss Richards as they ascended the first set of stairs, stepping quietly. What he wouldn't give for even a lick of her luck.

He walked beside Hulda, Beth immediately behind, followed by the somewhat confused Matthew and Nettie, with Owein and Baptiste taking up the rear. As they rounded for the second stairwell, however, they ran into a hiccup in their plan.

Her name was Megan Richards.

She was walking down the hall of women's apartments, toward them, drinking something—and immediately choked when she saw them, dropping her beverage. Miss Richards would be an excellent witness for what they were about to do, but not if she raised the alarm first.

"You—" she began.

And Merritt whipped up a wardship shield in the hallway, blocking the woman from progressing any farther. If he weren't so on edge, he might have been proud at the finesse with which he enacted the spell. To his relief, he managed to put up a second, which stifled the shout the secretary let out an instant later.

"Go," he murmured, and Hulda hurried up the next flight, Merritt at her elbow. One more, and they reached the office floor of BIKER. Sadie Steverus sat at the desk—while she had provided Beth with the schedule, she hadn't been informed of their plan. Her eyes widened as they approached. She stood but seemed at a loss for words.

Hulda hesitated only a second before pushing forward to Mr. Walker's office. Merritt and the rest followed behind.

The scene was just as Hulda had described her vision. Walker sat at his desk, afternoon sun pouring through the window, edging his hair and suit jacket in gold. Baillie lingered over his desk to one side, going over some paperwork. The black-and-white clock on the right wall read two seventeen.

"What in—" Walker rose from his seat, bristling. "What is going on here? M-Miss Taylor?"

Baillie immediately stiffened. "What is the meaning of this? A coup?" He retreated—good—and turned to Walker—bad. "They're here to finish the job."

"Spread out," Merritt said before either man could eke out another syllable. The group did as requested, forming a semicircle around the desk. His pulse hammered.

Baillie cringed from Owein, who barked.

"Believe me, Mr. Walker," Merritt tried, "this is not a coup. At least, not against you. You've been manipulated by Alastair Baillie for far too long."

Mr. Walker opened his mouth, looking confused, and a little frightened—and then his thick brows drew together. Baillie's gaze was locked on to the side of the man's head. He was manipulating him.

Good.

"Call the police immediately," Baillie said, cool and calm.

Mr. Walker shouted, "Call the—"

"Um," Matthew began, rubbing the back of his head. He glanced at Merritt, who nodded and pulled out his pocket watch, tilting it so Beth—who'd armed herself with a pencil and paper—could see it. "This is . . . not what I expected. But I'm supposed to tell a joke or a fond childhood memory. That is, why is a willow tree called a willow tree?"

"Good heavens, man," Merritt said to Walker, gesturing to Nettie. "Her husband just died and left her destitute. Say something!"

The brash reminder sent Nettie, who'd been staring wide eyed, into tears.

Hulda looked away, focusing on her part. She was doing a good job, if the worrying of her hands was any indicator.

Because that was the plan—they were all to focus on one emotion, as hard as they could. Merritt was angry; it didn't take much for him to focus on that. This very situation filled him with rage, and when nerves started getting the better of him, he just thought of his father or of Ebba, and his blood flowed hot.

Hulda was supposed to worry. Worry about herself, about them, about Myra and the future of BIKER.

Beth was to remain calm and play record keeper.

Baptiste was to be intimidating. Confident. Not hard for a man his size.

Owein got into character quickly, chasing his tail, barking over Nettie's sobs, even howling. He was annoying.

And of course, Matthew was chipper and Nettie was utterly miserable.

"Will oi don't know!" Matthew said with a chuckle.

"What's going on?" asked a feminine voice from the door. Miss Steverus had arrived right on time. She was unknowingly playing confused.

Miss Taylor, without looking up from her paper, said, "Mr. Baillie has been manipulating you, sir. He sent me to Canada because my abilities would betray him."

"Lies!" Baillie shouted.

Hulda straightened. "It's true. He's played all of us for fools. If anyone wants BIKER for himself, it's Mr. Baillie."

Mr. Walker's expression contorted one way, then another. "I don't . . . that is . . ."

"He drowned!" Nettie sobbed, pulling out the new, plain handkerchief Merritt had purchased for her. "A fisherman all his life, and he drowned. And for what? We've no savings, no prospects—"

"I can't hear what you said!" cried Miss Steverus.

"And you *dared* to accuse *me*!" Merritt shouted, pointing a finger right at Baillie. The lawyer's attention flashed to Merritt, then to Hulda. Beth wrote furiously on the paper.

"You think you can imprison me?" Baptiste asked, his accent thicker than usual. He cracked his knuckles. "I'd like to see you try."

Matthew swayed on his feet. "That is, whenever *I* start feeling blue, I think of this silly song my sister used to sing when we were little—"

Merritt caught Miss Richards's voice in the background, but it was drowned out by Owein's barking and Nettie's sobbing. Either his wardship spells hadn't held or she'd found an alternative exit.

Merritt feinted a lurch forward. "If they don't take care of you, Alastair, I certainly will! You'll point the blame anywhere so long as it's not on you!" Then, a little quieter, "Not sure you'll get your payout now."

He knew he'd hit the mark when Baillie recoiled.

"You're ruining BIKER!" Hulda wailed, and the genuine sound of it nearly threw Merritt off his game. But a glance at Beth's writing told him to keep pushing. She was writing down Hulda's name—either she was worried to the point of tears or Baillie was getting her emotions confused with Nettie's.

"Listen to reason," Beth said as she glanced at the pocket watch. "Mr. Walker, we are unarmed. We are not dangerous. We're merely trying to state the facts. My record is clear—"

"And now I'm here," Nettie cried, "and I don't even know why. And my daughter-in-law hates me, so who knows if they'll take me in—"

"—little mouse, round and fat—" Matthew sang.

"I went to prison once," Baptiste growled. "Want me to tell you what happened to the man who put me there?"

Bark! Bark! Bark! Owein jumped in place.

Mr. Walker started laughing. *Laughing.* Yet his expression was bewildered.

And Baillie . . . Baillie looked utterly mortified. He grabbed his hair with one hand, mussing it. A shiny film began to coat his face as his attention flew from one person to the next. He took a step back.

"What's going on?" Miss Steverus bellowed.

"How dare you!" Nettie screamed, and shoved Matthew, who had just finished his sister's song.

Merritt readied another threat, taking a step forward, and suddenly feared it wasn't enough, none of this was enough, he was going to fail—

No, he reminded himself, and thought about Ebba outside that concert hall, ready to jump into the carriage and leave him behind without a word. *No, those are Hulda's emotions.* The sudden influx of his own concern wasn't his doing.

Movement in his peripheral vision caught his eye—a quick glance toward the door revealed a newcomer, a stout older fellow in fine clothes and well-fitted cap. Judge Maddock, Merritt was guessing. But he didn't have time to focus on that.

He thought about his father throwing him out of the house instead, and his fingers twitched at his side. He used it as fuel and leveled his glare at Walker. "He's using you! Can't you see that?"

Walker blinked and touched his head. "What's going on?" he asked, sounding utterly baffled.

Beth wrote down his name.

"No," he went on. "Get out! All of you! This is trespassing!"

"We're BIKER employees, sir," Beth offered.

"It's just—" Walker clutched his heart, and his eyes misted. "Why am I . . . I don't understand why . . ."

Merritt folded his arms and glared at Baillie, whose attention shifted from Walker to Nettie, then to him. He had one hand in his hair. Merritt smirked. "Can't keep your story straight anymore, can you, Baillie?"

The lawyer's narrow shoulders lifted and sagged with his deep breaths. He wiped sweat from his lip.

Merritt held up a hand. "Silence!"

Everyone quieted, except for Nettie, who continued to sob quietly. Hulda grabbed Merritt's arm tightly. She looked ill. Whatever Baillie had tried on her hadn't been good.

Merritt nodded to Beth and pocketed the watch.

Steadying herself, Beth approached the desk, eyeing Baillie warily as she did. She handed the piece of paper to Walker. "You might remember I'm a clairvoyant, Mr. Walker. I apologize for this demonstration, but on that paper you'll see the name of every person Baillie manipulated in the last few minutes, along with a time stamp of when it happened."

Baillie lost all color in his face.

Mr. Walker took the paper with an unsteady hand. Read over it. Pointed. "I'm on here several times."

Beth nodded. "Did you feel any surges of emotion? Especially irrational ones?"

Baillie's head whipped toward Merritt and Hulda. "You—"

"Good gracious," Mr. Walker muttered, touching his head like it hurt. "I . . . I *felt* it." He crumpled the paper in his hand, sending alarm through Merritt, but then wheeled on his colleague. "All this time?" he asked, perplexed, but his voice grew in strength. "For how long? *How long, Baillie?*"

Baillie shook his head. Backed into the window. Apathy or not, real fear shined in his eyes. "They're lying, sir—"

"I-I felt it," Nettie said. "I felt it . . . Do it again. I felt . . . better."

"He'll manipulate you again, Mr. Walker," Hulda pressed, voice firm, recovered from whatever swell of emotion had last been thrown at her.

Merritt nodded. "Listen to the clairvoyant if you won't listen to us—"

His words cut short at the sight of the gun suddenly in Baillie's hands, pointed at Hulda, then at him. "Back up. All of you."

Baptiste's hands went into the air. "No need for violence."

"No need?" Baillie's voice was deadpan, but then again, apathy was a side effect of hysteria, and he'd used a lot of it. Was it strong enough to affect his judgment? Yet often a man didn't carry a gun unless he intended to—or feared he might have to—use it. "You're cornering me like wolves and telling me there's *no need.*" He pointed the muzzle at Baptiste, then Beth, who quickly dropped the pencil in her hands and backed away.

Nettie started sobbing.

He's going to hurt us, Owein said.

Wait. Stay low, Merritt warned, keeping his focus on the lawyer. The gun pointed his way again. He stepped back, pushing Hulda behind him.

"Put it down," he pressed.

"No. Get out. All of you!" A spark of his own emotion broke through his words. He pointed the gun at Walker, who tripped over his chair, trying to retreat.

"This is insanity," Walker said. "Put it away, Alastair!"

"This isn't worth eight dollars," Matthew whispered.

"Merritt," Hulda murmured, but Merritt shook his head, watching Baillie.

"Let's talk," Merritt said. "I'm reasonable."

"Shut up," Baillie snapped. His gaze darted from face to face, his mind likely trying to work out what to do. He was outnumbered. Too many witnesses. Too many people to control. "Miss Richards, you will—"

"Leave the women out of—" Merritt started, but his words were interrupted with a shrill, *"Look out!"* from Beth.

Warning enough.

Baillie fired. Merritt winced and stumbled back into Hulda, not identifying the loud *pop!* as the bullet hitting his newly erected shield, then the soft patter as it fell to the carpet. His legs wobbled a little, but from fear or a side effect of wardship, he didn't know. It took him a few seconds to realize what had happened—to smell the smoke coming off that pistol, to feel Hulda's nails digging into his jacket.

He blinked, forcing himself back to the present. Reassessing. Looked at Baillie.

Ah—there was one thing Merritt *was* certain of.

Baillie had just fired an E.-Allen-style rifled single-shot percussion pistol at him. Fletcher had one just like it.

And it was *single shot*, so Baillie was no longer a physical threat.

"Out of ammo," Merritt said.

Baptiste charged, crossing the room in three strides. He collided with the lawyer, knocking him to the ground. Walker followed next, jumping into the fray and wrestling the pistol away, regardless of its current lack of utility. Dropping his shield, Merritt bounded for them as well, helping get Baillie on his stomach with his hands behind his back.

Miss Steverus called the constable. No one left as they apprehended Mr. Baillie, not even the newcomers Merritt had acquired. They would all be questioned, which Hulda didn't mind in the slightest. The more testimonies, the better.

Truth was on their side.

She noticed the gruff-looking man still lingering by the door and crossed to him quickly, so as not to block the watchmen hauling a ruffled but stoic-looking Alastair Baillie out of the office. Clearing her throat, she introduced herself. "Hulda Larkin, sir. I'm a housekeeper with BIKER."

Judge Maddock looked her up and down. "I know the name. From the papers."

Blushing, Hulda nodded. "Unfortunately, yes. I—" She watched for a moment as the lawyer was led away. "I do hope this clears up a few things. I believe my former supervisor has already spoken to you."

"Huh." He snorted. "Something of the like." He looked around the room, at Merritt sitting wearily on the desk, Owein at his heels, at Baptiste staring out the window, at Miss Taylor speaking with Misses Richards and Steverus, at the sailor comforting the widow. Finally, his dark eyes drew back to her. "It certainly is not by the book, but I do think you've made your case."

Hulda smiled, a sigh escaping her. "You know, if you like books, I have an excellent recommendation . . ."

Chapter 21

After being questioned and writing down her testimony of the previous week's events, Hulda stood outside BIKER, watching the sun set over the mottling of city and arboreal stretches, including mostly bare trees and the distant steeple of a church. She'd collected a shawl from her room but hadn't yet changed from the dress that had seen her through false imprisonment, dock camping, and one of the most terrifying situations of her life. It felt wrong to, when it wasn't over yet. When Merritt and the others were still being interrogated.

It struck her that Mr. Baillie would go to the same penitentiary he'd gotten her and Merritt thrown into. There was something ironic about that. It didn't make her feel *good*, but it did make her feel safe.

She sighed, the air not quite cold enough to reveal her breath. There were so many questions ahead of her, so many unknowns to sort through. Another irony, for a woman who could see the future. How strange that the vision of Baillie that had made her believe his story had actually proven to be a peek at his unwinding. She wondered if there was any sort of augury training she could undergo, like what Merritt did with Mr. Gifford . . . mayhap with a trained augurist instead of a scholar. Something to help her hone her abilities. Then again, sometimes knowing the future ruined the present, and now that this hysterian nonsense was taken care of, her present was beginning to look just fine.

A soft whistle touched her ears, not that of a bird, but of a person. Stepping back from the hotel, Hulda scanned her surroundings, until she saw a woman standing beneath the old oak tree, pressing against its trunk like she might become one with it. Her heart flipped painfully in her chest. Pulling her shawl tight, she crossed the way, not bothering to check for passersby. If there were any, Myra wouldn't have called her.

She stepped into the cool shade. "Is it wise for you to be here, with the constable still inside?"

Myra glanced to the hotel. "I'm not too worried, but I can't linger."

"Where will you go?" So many questions, but Hulda knew her time was short. She had to prioritize.

Myra glanced behind her. "I'm not sure. North, I think."

"You won't give me specifics?" Hulda pressed. "I haven't said a word about any of it to the law."

Hulda had never had any issues with the law—she'd been an upright citizen her whole life, until Silas Hogwood had reentered it. And now the looming possibility of being in charge of this unknown facility . . . She wouldn't know *what* to do until she saw it with her own eyes.

"I know." The older woman smiled. "Keep writing to Agatha. If means of contacting me changes, I'll let you know. For the rest . . ." She glanced down the street, not really focusing on any one thing. "*They* will contact you. Take care of it, Hulda. And try to understand it."

Hulda pressed her lips together. Not everything had been resolved. She feared what this "facility" might have in store for her, and what she ought to do with it. But she knew Myra enough to recognize the woman had said her piece and would say no more. Not now. And they had so little time left together. "And might I go to Agatha for responses as well?"

A small smile spread on her lips. "Thank you, Hulda, for caring about me. I wasn't sure you would, after all that's happened."

Hulda folded her arms, cinching her shawl tighter. "That is not an answer."

Myra nodded. "I'll have her forward messages to BIKER."

Hulda's shoulders slumped. "I might not be with BIKER anymore."

The smile faded. "You will be. They would be fools not to keep you." She paused. "If not there, Whimbrel House."

"It's not magicked anymore. You know that. It has no need of BIKER."

She raised a delicate eyebrow. "That is not what I meant."

Hulda warmed.

Pushing off the tree, Myra said, "Have faith. You're invaluable to the institution."

"So are you."

"So I *was*," Myra amended. "I've laid the stones of a new path and do not have the means to uproot them." She sighed. "I'm sorry, Hulda. For everything."

She nodded. "It turned out well enough, in the end."

"But is it the end?" Myra asked. "I won't read your mind for the answer. I'd rather not know."

Dropping one end of her shawl, Hulda reached out and touched her friend's shoulder. "I forgive you, Myra. Truly, I do. And if BIKER needs an agent in the field, well, I expect you to step up."

The woman paused. Put her cold hand over Hulda's. "Thank you." Her attention returned to the hotel. "I need to go."

Hulda pulled back. "I understand. Be careful. Stay in touch."

She nodded. "I will try."

And Myra Haigh vanished into the shadows, as though she'd always been part of them.

∽

267

It was colder in Cattlecorn than it was in Boston. Merritt tried not to let that get to him.

Because after being imprisoned, running from the law, and confronting Baillie . . . after having all that pent up *something* burst out of him on the island, before he could have a future with Hulda . . . he knew what he had to do. What he *needed* to do. So he was going to do it.

He was still scared. He wouldn't lie to himself and pretend otherwise. But it was time to either turn the page or close the book for good.

He didn't want to be angry anymore.

Merritt hadn't told Fletcher he was coming. This felt like something he needed to do on his own, though Hulda had again offered to come. Besides, with BIKER and LIKER in somewhat dire straits, it was better for her to stay behind and sort through everything with Walker. Start the audit anew, without Baillie's influence or the need for secrecy. Piece together that fundamental part of her life, while he pieced together the ruins of his past.

Though, in the end, Merritt hadn't come alone.

He knocked on the entrance to the constabulary before letting himself in; it was late enough in the morning for Sutcliffe to be around. And he was, at the same table where Merritt had found him on his last trip back. Only this time the man wasn't expecting him.

"Merritt!" he exclaimed, standing up. He glanced to the door leading into the house, as though worried his wife might walk in and suddenly figure out their connection. "What brings you here?"

"Him." Merritt gestured to the terrier at his side, and Owein's tail started wagging. "He's your great-great-great-great-great-great-great-uncle. Give or take."

Hi! Owein said.

"He says hi," Merritt related.

Sutcliffe glanced between Merritt and Owein. Froze. "That's the dog from the penitentiary."

"Yes, and no. Physically, he's a dog, yes, but one of your progenitors lives inside that body. He's getting rather good at spelling." Reaching into his bag, Merritt pulled out Owein's letterboard and set it on the ground. "I'll be back shortly."

"W-Wait!" Sutcliffe looked at Owein nervously. "What do you mean? Where are you going?"

Merritt paused at the door. "Home," he said.

∽

He hesitated at the intersection again. The one where he'd turn to get to his house. Winter had dulled everything about it. Clouds snuffed sunlight, the trees reached barren fingers skyward, horse droppings spotted the road, mushy from a recent rain. He held his breath when he turned and walked with a measured pace, scanning the way for familiar faces. But no one was out and about this morning, almost like he was a storm they knew was coming, and they'd hidden, doors and windows bolted.

He slowed as he approached his house. Fourth from the end of the lane, with a hip-high fence made from twisted tree branches, constructed before he was born. The plum tree in the front yard held on to a few leaves, like a poker player gripping his hand, desperate to win one last game before he was ruined.

He had the thought to turn back. Instead, he slipped through the gate and approached the front door. It was nostalgic, in a strange way—he *knew* this place but felt detached from it, almost like he'd read about it in a story rather than actually lived there. More dreamlike than nostalgia, perhaps.

There was a brass knocker on the door. That hadn't been there when he'd left. Reaching for it, Merritt paused again. Contemplated. Lowered his hand and took the knob instead.

Unlocked. His ribs seemed to squeeze in as he depressed the lever with his thumb and opened the door.

Homesickness slapped him in the face. *That smell.* Like sweet potatoes and lemon tarts. His throat closed, smelling it. It smelled like his childhood.

Forcing a breath in, he slipped inside and shut the door behind him. Noted the furniture—some of it was new, some old, some reupholstered. Taking a few steps, he ran his hand along the couch. He'd broken its back leg jumping on it when he was . . . ten? Eleven? And the grandmother clock hung in the same spot on the wall, its pendulum swinging gently. It would need winding soon.

A soft hum came from the kitchen. Stepping softly, Merritt passed through the corner of the dining room, which had new wallpaper, and peered through the open door of the kitchen.

His heart stopped. *Mother.*

She was there, wearing a maroon dress, an apron tied around her neck and waist. Her hair was pulled up in a familiar bun, but it was half-gray—it'd been a rich auburn, when he'd last seen her. She was a little plumper, too. Her back was to him, one arm around a mixing bowl, the other pumping as she whisked batter, her head tilted so she could read a recipe set out on the counter. She was humming "Scarborough Fair." She used to sing that one, too, especially when she gardened.

Merritt pressed a hand to the doorjamb if only to keep himself upright as he took her in. *Thirteen years.* He hadn't seen her for thirteen years. Suddenly he regressed more than that, and he was that ten-year-old boy who'd broken the couch, sobbing apologies into her breast, afraid his father would switch him. And his mother had held him tight, smelling just as the house did, assuring him it would be all right, they would fix it, and what was done was done.

He was so lost in memory he barely noticed the moment his mother turned around and gasped in fright, dropping the bowl—and then her eyes went wide and both her hands slapped over her mouth, and her whole body shook as she eked out, *"M-Merritt?"*

The sound of her voice nearly broke him.

Merritt smiled, so relieved he wouldn't have to explain who he was. So happy that she still recognized him, after all this time. "Hi, Mom."

She wailed and ran to him, throwing her arms around his waist, burying her face into his chest. "Oh, Merritt! My boy! *My boy!*"

Tears stung his eyes as he hugged her back. As concrete chipped and shattered inside him, statuesque pieces became flesh once more. Sorrow sharp as whiskey burned through him. *How he'd missed her!* The shock of it muted him. He'd never let himself miss her. He'd forced himself not to. Played pretend for over a decade. A drowning man who insisted he didn't need to come up for air.

Tears ran down his cheeks. He pressed his face into her hair and slowly aged under her sobs, turning from ten to eleven, to twelve, to seventeen, twenty, twenty-five, thirty-one. All in an instant and yet it took an eternity, standing in that doorway, neither of them really standing on their own.

His mother pulled back first, and Merritt wiped wetness from his face. She put her hands on either side of his jaw. "Look how you've grown! You've filled out!" She patted him down like she had to assure herself he wasn't a specter. Her hands came back to his face. "You can grow a beard now!"

Merritt laughed. Tried to swallow the sore lump in his throat.

"And this!" She grabbed fistfuls of his hair. "What is this mess? You always liked it short."

He shrugged. "Got lazy, I guess."

She released it. Smoothed it back. "I think I like it."

He laughed again, and it felt so good, like taking off a heavy jacket midsummer. "You would be the first."

She grabbed his hands, pulled him into the dining room, and made him sit, ignoring the batter on the kitchen floor. "I can't believe you're here . . . oh, you're here!" She wiped her eyes and let out a shuddering breath. "Let me get you something to eat—"

"I'm fine, really." He grasped her hand. "I just . . . I wanted to talk to you." He sobered. "Where's . . ." *Father?* "Peter?"

Her face fell a fraction. "Not here. Not now." She smiled and sat beside him, pulling her chair close. Her eyes lit up. "The house! Did you get Whimbrel House?"

He nodded. "I got the house. Living there now."

"Oh good. Good." She took his hands and squeezed them. "And work? You're working?"

"As a writer."

"That doesn't surprise me at all!" She released him long enough to dry her eyes on her apron, then squeezed his fingers again. "You always had an imagination."

He told her about *A Pauper in the Making* and *The Path of Rubies*, as well as the articles he'd written. Where he'd stayed in New York, and how surprised he'd been to hear from his grandmother's lawyer. He told her the house was enchanted, which shocked her, and related stories about it, though he didn't disclose the Silas Hogwood business—that could be a tale for another day.

Another day. He could have *another day* with her.

"And you?" He squeezed back. "What have you been doing?"

"Oh, not much. Just keeping the house. We had a bake sale last week to raise funds for the church—it went well."

"You made poppyseed bread."

She laughed. "Yes! Yes, I did!"

He grinned. "That was always my favorite."

She nodded, eyes tearing. "I know. I know it was." She turned and wiped her eyes on her shoulders so she wouldn't have to let go of Merritt. "Knee's been acting up the last few years, especially with the cold weather—"

"Have you seen a doctor?"

"Oh yes, but it's just fine." She chuckled.

"And Scarlet? Beatrice?"

Her face fell, and for a moment, Merritt panicked. But then she said, "They're good. Both good. Oh, Merritt, I tried to write to you, back then"—she ran a knuckle under her eye—"but Peter wouldn't have any of it. He forbade all of us. When I pushed . . . he never left me, even when I made . . . mistakes." She glanced away in shame—it was the most acknowledgment of her affair with Sutcliffe he'd probably get from her. "He threatened he would go through with it if I persisted in trying to write you. And how was I to choose between the love for my husband and the love for my son?" Her eyes glimmered with unshed tears; Merritt squeezed her hands. "In the end, a woman can't survive around here without a man's support. Oh, Merritt." She closed her eyes, letting a few tears fall. "I'm so sorry."

Throat tight, Merritt rubbed the back of her hand. "I waited thirteen years to come back. I could have tried sooner."

His mother merely shook her head. "I didn't know where you'd gone, after you left the Portendorfers'. Ruth gave me an address—I did get one letter out—but I never heard a thing. I thought it would blow over, but it never did . . ."

Clearing his throat, Merritt tried again. "My sisters?"

"Oh, yes." She lifted her head. Wiped her eyes and steadied herself. "Married. S-Scarlet is in Albany with her three littles—all boys. And Beatrice got married, oh, almost seven years ago." She squeezed his hands tighter, almost to the point of hurting, and he realized why her expression had turned so sad. Because he'd missed it. He'd missed all of it. "They moved to Concord. She has two little girls, Bethany and Maggie." She paused. "You haven't seen them at all, have you?"

He shook his head. "No. I . . . I didn't know."

"They'll want to see you," she assured him, and the words were a bandage around his heart. "Of course they'll want to see you."

Her grip loosened, and she turned his left hand around. Clucked her tongue. "Not married yet?"

Merritt smiled. "No. But there is someone."

His mother bounced in her seat, eliciting another laugh from him. "Tell me! Tell me who she is!"

"Her name is Hulda Larkin," he said. "She's the housekeeper I mentioned, who helped me with Whimbrel House."

Her mouth parted into an O. She released him and swatted his arm. "Your housekeeper!"

"I promise I've been perfectly decent!" he protested with a grin. "I think you would like her. She's very . . . polite."

"Very polite and interested in you? You're spinning stories again." She grinned. "I want to meet her. What does she look like? I want to imagine her—"

The front door opened, letting in a burst of cold air. Both Merritt and his mother froze, speech cut through.

The chill from the draft seeped into Merritt's every pore.

His father's footsteps sounded heavier than he remembered them as he trudged into the front room, kicking the door shut behind him. Merritt's back was to that room.

The sound of his voice zipped over Merritt's skin like rotary cutters. "Rose, what are the Gorringes . . . Oh, who's this?"

Merritt gripped the sides of his chair.

His mother stood. "Now, Peter, it's been a long time. It's time to let it go—"

"What are you talking about?" Peter Fernsby's voice grew an edge. "Who is—"

Slamming his palms onto the armrests, Merritt stood up and turned around. His father's hairline had receded a few finger widths and grayed over the temples. He'd lost weight. It took a second, like it did with everyone, but recognition quickly dawned on Peter Fernsby's face.

And just like that, Merritt understood where all his own anger had come from.

"You!" Veins in Peter's head rose and pulsed; he'd been holding a leather satchel, which he threw on the floor. "How dare you step

foot into this house!" His gaze whipped to his wife. "How dare *you* let him!"

Tears filled Rose's eyes. She held up her hands as if staying a wild animal. "Peter, listen to me! It's been thirteen years!"

"I threw you out once," his father snapped, barreling into the dining room. "I'll throw you out agai—"

His words cut off as he slammed into an invisible wall. He reeled back as though shocked, his hand coming up to his bloody mouth. He'd bitten his tongue.

"Don't speak to her that way," Merritt said, and despite his own anger rising, his words were steady. "And don't speak to me that way, either." He met his father's eyes. "I'm not a little boy anymore."

Wide eyed, Peter reached out and touched the shield. Prodded it. Punched it.

"What is that?" his mother asked, grasping Merritt's elbow.

Merritt's eyes narrowed at Peter. "Consider it a gift from my father."

His mother's grip loosened. The veins in Peter's forehead pulsed all the harder. "How dare you—"

"I ran into Ebba in Pennsylvania." Merritt refused to break eye contact. "I know everything. I know you bribed her to make a pregnancy claim. I know you paid for her schooling."

"Wait, what?" His mother came around, nearly pressing against the wardship spell, to face Merritt, who still refused to look away from the man who'd raised him. "Ebba Mullan? Bribe?" She whirled around. "Peter?" She touched the shield in wonder. "Merritt . . . this is magic, isn't it?"

"You shut your dirty mouth," Peter warned.

"Or what?" Merritt asked. He stepped forward, and the shield moved with him, shoving Peter back. He nearly lost his footing. "You'll switch me?"

"Merritt, don't." His mother grabbed his arm. "This won't help anything."

Although he was trying to relax, Merritt didn't trust himself to let down that spell. He finally broke his gaze from Peter and looked at his mother. "I figured it out from the Genealogical Society for the Advancement of Magic. Or, Hulda did."

His mother covered her mouth and shook her head, eyes glimmering with unshed tears. "I'm so sorry."

"Don't apologize." He managed a smile, which quickly vanished when Peter reasserted himself.

"Get out of my house. Off my property," he spat. "Or I'll—"

"What?" Merritt whirled on him. "Call the *constable*?"

Peter sputtered.

Merritt let out a long breath. "But I'll go." To his mother, he said, "If you think you'll be safe."

Rose nodded without hesitation. "Of course, Merritt. Your father"—she gestured to Peter—"has never lifted a hand to me. I promise you that."

Peter Fernsby simmered on the other side of that shield. Exhaustion began to bite at Merritt's limbs from holding the spell so long.

He nodded, comforted by that fact. But such was not true for Merritt. "Back off," he warned.

"In my own house," Peter growled, but he retreated, not wanting to be slammed by the wardship spell again. Merritt followed, keeping the shield between them, until he could access the door.

Still, to be safe, he added, "You lay a finger on her, and I'll beat you into a bloody mass, do you understand?" Red-faced, Peter stepped right up to the shield, but before he could speak, Merritt added, "Do you think I couldn't do it?"

The man hesitated, which was all the answer Merritt needed.

But he paused as he reached for the doorknob. Turned toward his mother—his beautiful mother. Emotion thickened his words. "Where are my sisters?" He knew the cities, but they were big cities, and he didn't have addresses—

"Don't you dare tell him." Peter fumed. Hard eyes locked on Merritt, he added, "Do *not* return to my house. Do *not* write. I will push every legal right I have. You are *no longer part of this family.*"

Merritt pressed his lips together, then felt himself, strangely, relax. His shield came down, but Peter Fernsby did not approach him.

"Then why are you so afraid of me?" he asked, and to that, his father had no answer.

Opening the door, Merritt stepped out into the cold afternoon.

And it was enough.

Chapter 22

December 9, 1846, Blaugdone Island, Rhode Island

"This is about as far as I can take you," Gifford said as he collected his papers from Merritt's desk. The walls were freshly painted as of two days ago and still bore the faintest scent of it. Owein dozed in the corner. Although he'd insisted on participating, he'd lost interest rather quickly for a boy who was supposed to be twelve and some odd centuries. Merritt stood from his chair, surprised—he'd expected their discussion to last another hour.

"That's it? That's the end?" he asked. While, admittedly, Gifford was a droll fellow, Merritt had begun to grow fond of him. While his lessons hadn't directly solved his issues, his theory of magic being connected to his personality—wardship to his protective instincts, communion to communication, and chaocracy to anger—had helped him understand himself a little better. That, and Merritt was a sociable person, and there weren't a lot of people in the Narragansett Bay.

He checked the time on his pocket watch—his *nice* one, which had been returned from the Suffolk County Penitentiary, along with his other belongings, earlier that week. Hulda had nearly sobbed over the sight of her trusted and beloved black bag. Were it large enough to step into, she'd live in it.

Gifford smiled. "The end of *my* tutelage, yes. I am no wizard, if you remember. Only an appreciator of magic." He opened his briefcase, carefully placed the papers inside, then pulled out one more. "Though I *do* think you might find this of interest. I hope you don't mind the, uh, personal accounting of your genealogy."

He handed over the paper, written up with straight lines and his flawless handwriting. The lines branched together and ended in numbers.

"What's this?" Easier to ask than to decipher it himself.

"My estimation as to your active spell percentages," he explained, then stepped around to view the paper as well, pointing as he explained. "In total, I believe you are sixteen percent wizard."

Merritt lowered the paper. "Sixteen, eh?" Hulda was eight, and Beth only four. Still, for such a small number, it was phenomenal he could do so much.

"A very good percentage for this day and age! And my guesswork at your spells," he went on.

Merritt brought the paper back to his face and scanned it until he found a short list in the bottom left corner. It read,

Wardship: Shield
Communion: Talk with animals
Communion: Talk with plants
Chaocracy: Restore order
Chaocracy: Random subterfuge
Chaocracy: Discordant movement (weak)
Chaocracy: Animate object (weak)

Merritt blinked at it. "This is what I can do?"

Gifford waved a flat hand back and forth. "It's an estimation, based on what I've seen you do and your account of the island mishap." Merritt had seen Gifford shortly after Baillie's arrest, and explained as best as he could remember—Hulda had filled in the gaps—what had happened when his deeply buried chaocracy had . . . well, exploded. Gifford went on, "You definitely do have chaocracy in your family line, though I would have, admittedly, dubbed it lost on you if not for this occurrence. I so regret not having witnessed it myself."

Merritt was rather glad Gifford hadn't witnessed it.

"And so that's from where I pull *restore order* and *random subterfuge*."

Nodding slowly, Merritt asked, "And what is 'random subterfuge'?"

"Ah." Gifford looked pained. "It's hard to say. Chaocracy is . . . messy. The messiest of magic, unless you count necromancy." He chuckled, but it took Merritt a second to understand the joke. The morbidity of it surprised him. "Honestly, it's sort of a messy area that everything that can't be categorized gets shoved into."

Owein lifted his head, suddenly awake and apparently interested.

"I see. And these other ones," he pointed to the last two on the list.

"Those," Gifford said apologetically, "are ones I believe are lost on you. Though you may have experienced them—or something similar— in that one instance, I can't find any other reason why you, especially so far down the line, would possess such capabilities. However"—he leaned in close, as though to share a secret, despite no one else being in the room—"*I* think the Nichols line is incorrect." Nichols was Merritt's mother's maiden name. "I believe there may have been another sexual partner or two in there somewhere, which, for obvious reasons, was never reported in any of the hospital records or our surveys." He shrugged. "We may never know. But take it for what it's worth."

"I understand. Thank you for this." He lifted the paper.

What about me? Owein asked.

"Say, Gifford," Merritt went on, "what percentage do you think my, oh, eight-times-great-uncle might be? Presuming he was in a magical line?"

"Eight times?" Gifford reeled back, then began counting on his fingers. "That would be what, the fifteen hundreds?"

Merritt shrugged.

"Well . . . and this is just a rough guess, mind you," he said, as though having a bad estimate be publicized was his worst possible fate, "given the statistics and finnicky nature of magic, in your line specifically . . . I'd say anywhere from twenty-four to thirty-six percent, in order for you to have accumulated, especially by *chance*, as much as you have presently."

"Interesting." Merritt glanced to Owein, putting on his "impressed eyebrows."

Owein barked, startling Gifford.

"Thank you for your efforts." Merritt extended his hand, and Gifford shook it happily before picking up his briefcase. "I'll see you out."

"I would love to hear about any other phenomena you experience," Gifford said as they went down the stairs. "It might help us winnow down precisely what's going on in there." He made a rough gesture toward Merritt's person.

Merritt supposed knowing the specifics couldn't hurt, even if life as a *wizard* still seemed like someone else's life. He certainly didn't have any desire to be employed for the use of his unexpected abilities, though anyone who would hire someone as green as he was would have to be desperate indeed.

Merritt stopped short. "What is that smell?"

Gifford paused and sniffed. "Something gone bad in your house?"

"Is cheese," Baptiste's voice sounded distantly, likely from the kitchen. "Smells perfect."

I want to see! Owein took off through the reception hall and into the dining room, nails clacking on the floor.

"Terribly sorry about that," Merritt offered, nose wrinkling. The fresh burst of air as he opened the door was much appreciated. "Plenty of light left for the trip back."

"And Miss Larkin in time for dinner," he replied.

Merritt squinted. Sure enough, Hulda was taking the path up to the house, the white boat she'd hired already sailing back for the mainland. Merritt smiled. "Indeed. Do stop by again."

"You as well." Gifford donned his hat and stepped off the porch, taking a more east-leading path to where his vessel awaited him. Merritt strolled down the well-worn one to his own tiny, enchanted boat, meeting Hulda halfway. Her hair was meticulously pinned, as always, though the wind from the journey had persuaded a few locks loose, making her look like she was part fey, softening her features. When he reached her, Merritt swept the loose hair behind her ear, and she smiled at him.

"Just two weeks ago that would have made you blush," he commented.

Hulda shrugged. "Perhaps I'm getting used to you, Merritt Fernsby." She glanced toward Gifford, who was stepping into his boat. "What did he say?"

"Done with lessons, for now. But I have a chart you might find rather interesting inside." He paused, studying her stance, her shoulders, the line between her brows. "What's wrong? Something happen in Boston?"

Hulda licked her lips. "Yes. Something I wanted to talk to you about."

"And what's that?"

She pulled her shawl tighter. "I've been offered the director position."

Merritt's lip parted. "What, really? Hulda, that's excellent!" He grasped her upper arms and searched her face. "Aren't you excited for it?"

"I am." She took a deep breath. "I am. I want it, and I really *am* the best person for it." She smirked, but the expression fell. "But the position will require me to spend a lot of time in Boston, especially in the beginning, as we get everything running again."

It took Merritt a beat to understand. "And I am not in Boston."

She nodded.

He smiled, warmed by her concern, and ran his hands up and down her arms, banishing the chill. "We've made it work so far, haven't we? And once the Brits are out of the way, it'll be fine."

She rolled her eyes. "The rest will leave next week. But it *is* a concern."

"It's what you love." Merritt remembered being in a pit in the middle of his kitchen while Hulda, whom he'd then known as Mrs. Larkin, hovered above him, unsure how to get him out. She'd encouraged him to give the house a chance, told him why taming Whimbrel House was important to her. He knew that had not changed. "I won't get in the way of it. I'd be cross if I had to stop writing." Speaking of which, he had an article he needed to finish, and a third book to start while his editor sat with the second. "Perhaps I'll be wildly successful and rent an apartment down the street."

She chuckled. "Thank you. Really, truly. Thank you." Glancing away, she rolled her lips together. "I do want you to understand that . . . it's not only BIKER. That is"—she fidgeted—"that's not the only thing I love."

Warmth bloomed in his stomach and spread out to his limbs. "Miss Larkin, I am not a *thing*."

She swatted at him. "Do not make this difficult."

"Am I difficult to love?"

She met his eyes. "No."

Those strands came loose, so he tucked them behind her ear again. "I love you, too."

He leaned down to kiss her, but the reeds sang, *Sssshhhhhheeeeeee.* Glancing up, he saw a new vessel docking and a familiar figure stepping out of it.

He waved a hand. "Miss Taylor!" He hadn't seen her since the confrontation with Baillie. He took Hulda's hand, and they walked out to meet her. "Wonderful to see you. Do say you have good news for me?"

Beth smiled. "I do! I'll be stationed here, until otherwise assigned." She glanced knowingly at Hulda. "Though I do have a very good case for staying. That is, is an enchanted house still an enchanted house if its enchantments move bodies? Surely it requires more study. Wouldn't you agree, Miss Larkin?"

Hulda smiled. "Owein will be very happy to see you."

Beth beamed. Reached into her satchel and pulled out a few letters. "I took the opportunity to check your mail for you, Mr. Fernsby." She handed them over. "Is Mr. Babineaux inside?"

"He is, but with a terrible concoction he calls cheese. You've been warned."

"Oh dear." She chuckled before stepping around them and heading to the house.

Curious, Merritt thumbed through the mail. "Oh, a letter from my editor. Hopefully not too many revisions." Another letter about property taxes, an advertisement, and one that had no return address on it. The writing was feminine.

Hulda turned back to the house. When he didn't follow, she paused. "What is it?"

"Not sure." He broke the seal on the letter and pulled out a single paper, only the size of his hand. It read,

> *My Dearest Merritt,*
> *I am so, so happy to have seen you. It will not be the last time, but don't write back here, just to be safe. Your sisters will want to hear from you.*
> *Scarlet Moore*
> *57 Adelaide Ave.*
> *Albany, New York*
>
> *Beatrice Blakewell*
> *14 Fisher St.*
> *Concord, New Hampshire*
> *We love you. We always have.*

And I expect to meet this young woman of yours.

Love,
Rose Fernsby

The words blurred in Merritt's vision as he read them. Hulda touched his shoulder, and he blinked the tears away. "What's wrong?"

"From my mother," he whispered, unable to find his voice. "My sisters." He showed her the letter.

Hulda scanned it. "Oh, Merritt, this is wonderful. You'll be able to meet them again!"

He reached up to touch his scarf, but he'd been too focused on Gifford when he came out—he hadn't grabbed it. Still, he nodded. Carefully folded the note and stuck it in the inside pocket of his vest. Grinned so wide it hurt.

Grabbing Hulda's waist, he spun her around, eliciting a shriek. "Marry me, Hulda Larkin. Here or in Boston. Now or next year. Just say you'll marry me."

Her response was a delighted laugh and a kiss, which was good enough for him.

∽

Meanwhile, in London, someone was reporting news of an enchanted canine defiling an American prison to a very prominent woman by the name of Victoria . . .

ACKNOWLEDGMENTS

Another adventure done! I'm so grateful to the team of people who helped make this book happen (and it takes a TEAM, I tell you).

Thank you so much to my beloved bed warmer, Jordan, for being an idea board, a beta reader, and a huge support in all things writing and otherwise. You are a wonderful human being, and I couldn't do it without you.

Many thanks to Marlene Stringer, Adrienne Procaccini, and Angela Polidoro, who got the stone rolling and made this book and series happen. Thank you for believing in me and my work. And, Laura, you are a wizard at repeated and anachronistic words.

Huge congrats to the critique partners who managed to stick it out to a second book! Rachel Maltby and Leah O'Neill, you are angels.

Of course, thank you to all the editors, formatters, designers, and unsung heroes behind the scenes. I appreciate every one of you. Your efforts do not go unnoticed.

As always, my utmost appreciation to the Big Man Upstairs. Thank you for helping me get my spark back.

ABOUT THE AUTHOR

Charlie N. Holmberg is a *Wall Street Journal* and Amazon Charts bestselling author of fantasy and romance fiction, including the Paper Magician series, the Spellbreaker series, and the Whimbrel House series, as well as contemporary romance under C. N. Holmberg. She is published in more than twenty languages, has been a finalist for a RITA Award and multiple Whitney Awards, and won the 2020 Whitney Award for Novel of the Year: Adult Fiction. Born in Salt Lake City, Charlie was raised a Trekkie alongside three sisters who also have boy names. She is a BYU alumna, plays the ukulele, and owns too many pairs of glasses. She currently lives with her family in Utah. Visit her at www.charlienholmberg.com.